I0822877

OF MEMORIES AND ENDINGS

BEGINNINGS AND ENDINGS SERIES
BOOK TWO

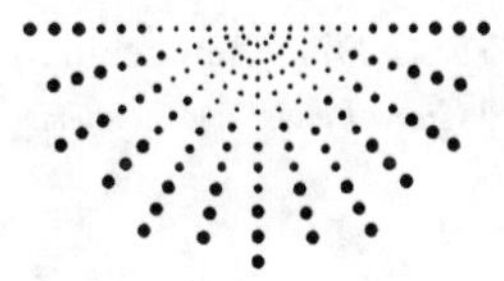

ASHLYN B. RUDD

COPYRIGHT

Cover Design by Rebecca Frank/BewitchingBookCovers.com
Edited by Ciara Lewis/ www.clewisedits.com

Of Memories and Endings is a work of fiction, however, it does deal in topics including, but not limited to: death, loss of a loved one, war, blood/gore, mentions of rape, torture, kidnapping, familial loss, sense of failure, sense of guilt, illness/disease, and dismemberment.

This is not a comprehensive list as triggers/triggering events are specific to every person. If anything in this work puts your mental health at risk, please do not risk your safety. I appreciate your support, but you and your health are more important. Stay safe lovelies.

DEDICATION

To all the goddesses who have forgotten their own power...
Shine bright enough that no one ever forgets again.

Irropia
Cliffs of Barae
Wayfa
Crian Mountains
Eskira
Straight of Laos
Elona
Lasaego
The
Divinian
Sea
Atallia's Village
The Outskirts
Basige
Cothir Forest
Feardin Forest
Southern Hills
Western
Reaches
RHA

Moors
Ophiñeas
Pyre Forest
Serpent's Bay
Eastern Vale
Gravelands
Malise
The Sea Smoke
The Eye Stones
Vallenia
Island of Corosa
Kingswood
Saitian
Sallin Marshes

CHAPTER ONE

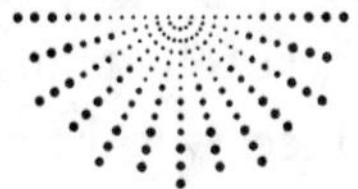

Silence rang true across the burning battlefield. No one dared to break it, knowing exactly what my question entailed. What it meant.

There was a crackling of fire. Ash and ground bone fell down around the amassed army, a death snow that had begun to cover the blood stained ground once again.

Everyone stared at me, waiting with bated breath for what I would do next. I was their goddess after all, my word law. They needed help and guidance, a warm face and the strong light of their queen. But nothing, not even the Cosmos himself, could have torn my gaze from the devilish one in front of me.

His mouth was set in a tight line, guilt eating away at his perfect features like acid on stone, pinching the corners of his eyes. He stared, saying nothing to assuage the lies breaking my heart.

No words broke past his full lips, but his eyes were blazing in a way I had never seen before, saying more than any useless speech could. Need and relief warred for the strongest emotion, combining to create something raw and savage. A jagged, cutting emotion that was doing its best to tear away at my defenses.

Holding on with what little strength I had left, exhaustion

weighing me down in more ways than one, I stepped closer. By sheer force of will I kept my expression neutral as I raised my chin. "I believe I asked you a question, Warlord." I rolled the name around once again, narrowing my eyes at him. "What is the name of the God of Death? Or does he prefer God of Endings? I admit my memories are not what they once were, and I no longer know his preference."

The words came out simply, with all the ease one would feel when relaxing in a warm bath, but on the inside a tumultuous storm raged within the confines of my chest. The pain and anger and lies twisting my emotions until all I could feel was the cutting bite of betrayal.

I would make him admit it out loud even if he choked on it.

The wind picked up suddenly, answering my unspoken call. The loose golden strands of my hair floated in the breeze. The fires that were consuming the dry, dead trees that peppered the dying land, flared higher. The wood creaked before snapping in half. I could have sworn the ground rumbled beneath my feet, a giant yawning, deciding whether or not to wake. The gray gloom opened up above us and rain began to drizzle down. Black and red blood ran down armor in rivulets.

The Descendents had not moved, barely feeling the elements' presence, as they watched a new battle be laid out before them.

Kanan closed his eyes, and I ignored the small pang that went through me at being denied his gaze. He swallowed harshly before opening them, reading what must have been clear in my eyes. I could see him almost begging me to not make him say it, wishing beyond anything that the answer wasn't right there at the tip of his tongue. My resolve must have been clear for his scarlet gaze hardened.

"Kanan," his voice of the deepest darkness, soft as it was, didn't need to be raised for everyone to hear. The word sounding in every direction like an explosion. "My name is Kanan. It has been since I took in my first breath of air on this world."

The few Descendents who hadn't kneeled, too stunned to do anything but stare, fell to their knees. They looked on with awe, a hope filling their eyes that spoke volumes to how important this moment was to all of them.

Whereas I just wanted the ground to split open and swallow him whole.

A buzz of noise overtook the silence, thousands of voices raising in question. They deserved answers, just like I did, but for some reason my voice refused to work. I couldn't find it in me to bust through the numb cold that worked its way through me, different from the bone-chilling emptiness behind me.

Now it was my turn to close my eyes, everything too much for me to handle. Knowing it in my heart was one thing, the opportunity to be wrong was still there, but to hear him say it. There was no denying it any longer. Who he was.

Who I was.

"Atallia," his tone was soft, but it still broke through the hum of noise.

Snapping my eyes open, I saw he had moved closer, attempting to reach me. Stepping back, I shook my head, whispering, "You had every chance. Every chance to tell me."

Pain radiated from him with every breath, but I couldn't bring myself to care, because if I did it would erase every feeling of anger. The fact that my trust was destroyed would be kicked under the rug, like it didn't matter that everyone thought they knew how to run my life better than me.

Forcing myself, I looked away from him, unable to bear his piercing gaze anymore. There was always a first for everything.

Glancing behind him I saw the Council members clustered together, Bron standing not far off to the side. I swept over all of them, an array of emotions on each of their faces. Even Lars stood in disbelief, eyes wide, the massive warhammer he carried hanging loose in his hand. The typical bullshit he spewed seemed to be frozen in his throat.

It was the ones who didn't appear shocked that held my attention. Calmly, peering up into the sky in contemplation, rain hit my skin as I ordered, "Raise your hand if you were aware of the God of Endings's true identity, and thus my own."

The army quieted, anticipation sparking through the air like lightning. I looked back at the group, waiting for a response. I had a feeling of who had been complicit, but I needed the confirmation. I needed to know who had lied to my face. My heart, the small bud of trust I had been growing but that was now a shriveled, wilted flower, deserved nothing less.

No one complied, which only served to fuel my anger. They had done this. Lied and kept secrets that weren't even theirs to keep, and now they didn't want to confess to it. Like hell.

"RAISE THEM," I roared, lightning snapping across the sky, the force of two thousand years of pent up magic and pure rage behind the words. The ground shook and the rain turned ice cold. The fires that were devouring the sickly trees refused to yield to the frozen bullets. My point was made: answer me or face the consequences.

Slowly, as if wading through their guilt, four hands lifted into the air. A gasp came from my right, Zanaya's face set in shock. Cashim looked near tears at his niece's betrayed expression even as his hand was held high. Maris and Geoff walked through the gathered crowd to stand at the front, an apology in their eyes, even as they kept their arms raised.

Bron, the least surprising of them all, shook his head in annoyance. Appearing extremely put out, he sighed heavily, "I told him there had to be a way to tell you."

Those words, while seemingly in good faith, did little to waver the overwhelming feeling of losing control. How had I let it happen again? After Maris and Geoff, I did everything in my power to take control of my life—my destiny—and yet here I was, standing on the edge of the world surrounded by people who had caged me and thrown away the key. I never had a chance. These lies were woven together long before I would have ever guessed. I never had a chance to be the ruler of my own fate.

Maybe he saw the rising panic in my eyes, or perhaps he felt it through that tether that had now become all too real, but Kanan took a step toward me. "Atallia, give me a chance to explain."

I didn't let him near, instead turning away and giving him one last conflicted glance. I let him see what he had done, what his lies had caused. I showed him my heart, scarred from the abuse it had suffered, and let him watch as it broke all over again.

His broad shoulders deflated, the aura of strength and confidence and power dimming under my look. His agony seared itself into my brain, making my chest constrict and the air leave my lungs.

I still turned from him.

"Zanaya," I called out, looking back towards the towering mountain I had burst free of. The whole front side was blown to pieces, the wreckage of my escape still lying in shattered crumbles at the bottom.

"My queen," she replied formally, the title making me jump in my skin. I guess that's what I was…or had been…or will be. Fuck, this was going to get confusing.

The clink of a chain being undone had my attention returning to her, watching as she pulled her blood red cape from her shoulders. She handed it to me in offering, making me glaringly aware that I was still naked as the day I had been…created? I wasn't sure. Maybe I had never been born to begin with.

All I knew was that I was butt ass naked. The Descendents would never forget the day they met their reincarnated queen in her skin suit.

Taking it from her, I threw the thick material around my shoulders and knotted the black chain at my throat. It covered most of me, though I still bordered on indecent. Nodding my head in appreciation, I inquired, "What's the report?"

I ignored the shuffling of feet behind me, no doubt Kanan and the Council moving closer to hear. Right now the most important thing was checking on our people and getting home to Eskira. The big conversations I'm sure everyone was chomping at the bit to have, could come later.

"The battle went on for approximately forty minutes before the horde's reinforcements arrived and we were boxed in," she supplied. "Up to that point we had mostly sustained injuries, our forces worked together to keep the wraiths from feeding. However, once we were flanked, we took some heavy losses to our ranks. You showed up just in time, any longer and the horde would have swarmed us."

She surveyed the gathered soldiers, eyes calculating, taking in every detail she could with the efficiency of a warrior. "It could have been worse, but we'll need the time to allow those who need it to recover, we won't be able to make it to one of the cities before some of them succumb to injuries."

Orion appeared over her shoulder, his gray skin covered with dirt and ash, holding twin axes that dripped with dark blood. He dipped his head towards me, "My queen, we were able to assemble our forces and arrive quickly because we came through the Strait of Blood by air, but with the injured we won't be able to sustain any path of travel for long. Our healers and supplies are stationed right outside the strait, but even still, it is too far away for us to walk and this is no place for our people to recover."

He was right, the Gravelands was no place to save anyone. The sickly landscape was a remnant from a long past war, bones and blood making up its very air, and its yard of death had now been added to.

Staring up at the craggy peak, an ice cold draft coming from its depths, my soul shivered in dread. An intrinsic wariness crept through me, the hum of power buzzing in my ear in response. I knew what I needed to do.

Taking a steadying breath, I looked over my shoulder to where Kanan stood only a few feet back. "I can get us out of here."

He stared at me for a single second, finding something in my gaze that seemed to satisfy any question he might have asked right then. He gave me a nod, his eyes never leaving mine even as he spoke to the others, "Commander, get the warriors ready. Send an airborne to alert the healers to relocate south of the strait. Anyone that is able to must carry the injured or dead."

Zanaya listened carefully before shifting her attention to me, one look making it clear whose side she was on. "My queen?"

"Go," I ordered, glancing around at the sad, pathetic stretch of land. "Our people's bones do not need to be added to this grave. I will take care of the rest. The faster we leave this hell and reach the healers, the quicker I can assist them with our wounded."

With that she took off at a run, Orion and the rest of my friends going through the ranks to spread the word. The dazed army came together, abuzz with new energy as commands were shouted over the commotion.

Ensuring everything was going as planned, I strode forward. At least, I tried to, but a heavy hand encircled my arm, stopping me in my tracks. I didn't need to glance over my shoulder to know who it was, the energy pinging between us making my entire body feel like a live wire. My pathetic heart stumbled to catch up.

"What are you planning, love?" His voice caressed my bare skin, brushing against it, and making it hard for me to think.

"I'm getting our people out of here, or was there something more pressing that needed to occur?" I bit out in reply. It felt weird, to both love and loathe his touch, his every word.

I felt him move closer, the heat of his body breaking through the thick barrier of the cape and soaking into my own. His other hand came down to rest on the sensitive spot where my shoulder met my neck, and I tensed. I wasn't sure if my anger was capable of withstanding him like this. Touching me with those strong hands, the agony of his choices riding every word that came from his sinful lips.

"You don't have to do this alone, little goddess," his warm breath whispered against the top of my head.

A new wave of anger raged through me, stoking the fire that had fallen low from fatigue. With gritted teeth, I barely restrained myself from yelling, "You're right, I don't." I could feel the relief that left him and almost felt bad as I continued, "But I certainly don't have to do it with you."

His hands clenched around me faintly, as if he couldn't find it in him to let me go. I wasn't giving him that choice though, just as he hadn't given me one.

Breaking his grip I walked away, heading in the direction of the mountain stronghold, pretending that my heart and soul weren't shrieking in pain.

When I was half way between the mountain and my people, I halted. Sending out a wave of energy that went out in every direction, I made sure no one was left inside the mountain. Thousands of sparks popped up in my mind's eye behind me, the army gathering together, and none rose from the mountain. A cold nothingness brushed against my mental shields, an unsettling emptiness on my radar.

Shivers worked their way down my skin, my entire body reacting to the void within the mountain. Like life, death, everything had been sucked away, leaving not a single thing behind.

Whatever Kasis had done to cause such nothingness to seep into the walls of the mountain stronghold, needed to be crushed.

Later I would ask myself how I knew what to do, how any of this was possible, but right now all I cared about was wiping this stain from the world.

Raising my open hand high, the glowing power around me flared brighter, reacting to my every move. Two thousand years. My hand began to shake, streaks of gold crawling up my arm. Two thousand years I had been locked away, doing the bare minimum to keep the planet alive. Two thousand years before I was reincarnated, and now with the cosmic force used to build the universe, it was time to crush mountains.

My fist clenched and I did just that.

A concussive boom echoed across the world as the mountain shattered. Rock and stone and a millennia of standing strong against any force came crumbling down.

My power exploded out of me like an invisible hammer, smashing against the cracks in the stone, splitting it apart with ease. Boulders rained down, some crashing to the ground only to break into a thousand pieces. The entire structure collapsed, falling into itself with an ease that shouldn't have been possible.

It was almost sad how quickly it fell, dust shooting up into the clouds as the last rock settled, but as it cleared the only thing remaining was an enormous pile of stone. Useless and broken it still stood nearly as tall as the mountain had been.

Off to the side, however, a path lay before us. And on past it, I could see the barest hint of a rainbow-filled sky.

The army was silent behind me, no one making a sound.

Taking one last look at the rocks that had been my prison—both times—a new sense of purpose filled me. Twice Kasis had done this to me, one I barely remembered, but never again was I going to be trapped. Confined to a prison.

This power was mine and mine alone, and if he wanted it, wanted *me*, he would have to find a way to kill me and claw it from my cold, dead body. He better hope he did it before I found him, because I was going to hunt that bastard down and rain a hell down upon him like he couldn't imagine.

With the fire in my soul beating in time to those words, I walked forward, the army at my back and my blood red cape billowing behind me in the wind.

CHAPTER TWO

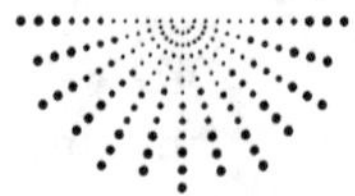

Exhaustion threatened to take us all as the army made its way carefully through the path I had carved. What had once been a mountain fortress had now been reduced to chunks of stone. Cleaved and crushed, Kasis's stronghold of torture was all but gone.

Jagged slabs of rock, that may have once been walls with their smoothed out faces, lay in our path. The ground dipped and had cracked from the weight of a crumbling mountain.

Thousands of footsteps echoed off the unbroken peak to our left, the shifting pile of rocks to our right a mockery of the standing summit.

Thrums of conversation reached my ears from the front, all of them focused on one thing. Kanan and I. Or rather who and what we were.

I wished I had the answers for them. I knew what it was like to stare into the unknown of the future and see no clear path; instead of a wise and knowledgeable goddess, they had me. I don't think there had ever been a time in which I had felt so incompetent and it was pissing me off.

We trudged on regardless. Answers would be found when our

wounded weren't on the brink of death. So many straddled the line. Too many.

The Cynthonians with larger animal forms had shifted, carrying the wounded across their backs. Others were lifted over shoulders or rode along invisible winds created by the Aetherians who weren't completely wiped from the battle. Kanan alone carried dozens with his shadows, the darkness spreading throughout the ranks to lift the downed warriors.

We were a bruised and battered group, fatigue weighing heavily on us all like a thick fog. The majority continued on by sheer force of will.

A shuffle of rocks had me looking over my shoulder, Zanaya jogging up to where I was walking ahead of the group. Slowing so that she could match my gait, I navigated around a crack in the ground, kicking at the loose pebbles that skittered across the stone.

"You know, you might be the only woman I know who can walk around in nothing but a cape and give zero shits about it," she said in greeting.

I let out a pitiful chuckle, looking out towards the far away glint of color in the distance, "Oh I don't know, you could probably pull it off."

Truth be told, I had forgotten about my lack of clothes, all my attention turned inward to the jumbled mess of emotion that was sharp enough to cut me to ribbons every time I tried to untangle it. That and the seemingly endless storm of power that swirled inside me, beating against the cage that was my physical body.

It was no surprise that my skin kept cracking apart at random, revealing the golden core beneath. It would close back up in seconds, disappearing without a trace, but it was there nonetheless.

I was more concerned, however, with the sensation that accompanied those splits. A slipping of some sort. Like I could simply fade away, discard my body like a shell and become something else entirely.

Because that was normal.

"Doubtful, I'd be too worried about getting boob-punched or something."

My eyebrows furrowed as I tilted my head, "Can't you get boob-punched with clothes on?"

"I mean, probably," she shrugged, raising her eyebrows in speculation, "but I think the risk increases when they're out and about like yours."

I tossed her a questioning glance, "Do I need to be concerned about you boob-punching me?"

She pursed her lips before glancing at me with a serious expression on her face. "Do you need to be boob-punched?"

I thought about it. "I don't think so, but I'll let you know. With all this shit going on, I might need it to bring me back to reality."

Her face fell, that reality crashing back around us without any need of help. Reaching out instinctively I grabbed onto her hand, giving it a squeeze before dropping it, too afraid of the unstable power that continued to stretch inside me.

"I'm sorry about Cashim, for what it's worth. If anyone knows what it's like to be lied to by a parental figure, it's me."

"Gods, Atallia, what are you apologizing for?" she exclaimed with a shake of her head, "I can't even imagine what you must be feeling. Your parents. My uncle. Bron. The warl—king."

I flinched as she stumbled over the words, *his* betrayal shoved to the forefront for the millionth time.

"If anyone should be apologizing it's me, I should have paid more attention. I should have seen all the secrets my uncle was hiding, I could have helped you figure it out without needing to be kidnapped by a deranged psychopath."

"Kasis," I supplied.

"Who?" she asked, confusion thick in her voice.

"It's Kasis, the God of Chaos," I said with finality. "He's back."

She looked taken aback, stuttering out a few sounds but her words failed her. The haze that I now recognized as some sort of memory block crossed her ice blue eyes before fading out strangely, like it was trying to scramble the information but it wasn't sure how to do it.

"Don't think about our history too much," I recommended. "Not until Kanan fixes whatever the fuck he's done to make everyone forget it in the first place."

She rubbed at her temple, face scrunched in pain. "It's giving me a headache just thinking about it."

"Yeah," I sighed heavily at the cursed manipulation. "Just chuck it up to god-fuckery and move on, I'll figure out how to get it removed."

I played with the edges of my cloak, running a finger along its seam. The dark red was a stark contrast to the pale ivory of my skin, the fleeting flashes of gold through my veins and across my skin only adding to the effect. There was no denying the strengthening power beneath the fragile layers, nor the erratic wildness teaming throughout.

"And to your last point," I added, looking over at her, "Yes, I've been through a lot. There's no denying the absolute shit show I'm going to have to unravel to figure this all out, but that in no way makes your uncle's secrets from you any less maddening. You don't need to apologize for anything, and I'm the last person who's going to judge or tell you how to feel about what he's hidden."

"It's just," she paused, her beautiful face drawn tight with pain and confusion, "he told me stories. So many stories. About you and the king, him and his mother. Our histories were my bedtime tales, and now I don't know if any of it was real or not. I'm not sure how to deal with that."

"I wish I could give you some kind of advice, words of wisdom maybe, but so far every step I've taken to find peace with my life—with myself—has ended in disappointment."

We walked on in silence, comforted by each other's presence even as the harshness of what we faced burned us to the bone. "Well aren't we a pitiful bunch," she voiced bluntly.

A surprised laugh escaped me, the heaviness that had been building inside calming for the time being. "How are the troops?"

Taking the escape, she pulled a heartsglass dagger from its sheath, playing the dark blade through her hands. "Tired beyond reason, but strong in their resolve. After seeing what this battle has gained them," she glanced at me before peeking over her shoulder to where I knew a god watched on with a patience that resembled a stalking predator. "Well, it makes the losses easier to bear."

I hummed noncommittally, not at all sure if they had gained anything of worth. Truly, what could I offer them? I may have been their reincarnated goddess, but I had none of the wisdom and memories that went with it. Nothing to give and everything to take.

"They could do with a break though. We've been pushing hard, but with the wounded and dead, I don't think they can take much more without resting."

"How are the wounded?"

"There are a few I'm not sure will even make it to the healers without your help now," she answered, voice trembling.

Pausing, I turned to look at the following mass of soldiers. Their sweat and blood covered faces stared ahead, fatigue slowing their steps. It felt strange, giving orders, having people look to me. Especially my friend, but even Kanan was starting to look drained. Someone needed to make the call.

I wasn't used to this, to any of it, the expectations I could see in everyone's eyes were already beginning to weigh on me. But they had come for me, had marched to free me from Kasis's grip; now it was my turn to step up. I just hoped it wouldn't blow up in my face.

"Spread the word," I said with a jerk of my head. "We'll rest here, it's as good a place as any in this hellhole. I'll be right behind you to help with the wounded."

She took off with a nod and soon after the command for a halt spread through the ranks. Relief poured out in waves from the battle-worn warriors. The injured were gently lifted from the backs of Cynths and set against the rocks, those with any medicinal ability doing their best to help. The dead were respectfully laid down against the stone floor, their bearers' faces streaked with tears.

Clusters of warriors broke off and relaxed as much as possible, some dropping where they stood. Far into the distance, there were echoes of the same being done down the lines.

Satisfied that they would take the time to rest, I whirled back around before my eyes could be inevitably drawn to Kanan's. I knew I wouldn't get away with avoiding him for long, but a girl could dream.

I should've known better though, this was the God of Endings after all. The dragon king of Irropia. A man I thought I was beginning to know.

And I couldn't have been more wrong.

Though I found I wasn't the least bit surprised when I felt him come up behind me, his presence as dark and cool as the shadows that trailed him. The aura of violence and power that always surrounded him was back to full strength, brushing against my skin until it pebbled under the feeling of it. It said a lot more about me than I cared to admit that it was a heady, intoxicating sensation.

Sometimes I wanted to slap myself over the head.

I stood with my back to him, both of us stewing in the silence that stretched between us. It was filled with the unsaid, lies and betrayals mixing into a toxic, vexing concoction that threatened to seep into my very being.

"Tell me what to do," he whispered. "Do you want me to apologize? To beg? Because I will."

His voice carried grief and hurt beyond what I could understand, his words twisting those dagger-like emotions in deeper. It was a wonder that I hadn't bled out since it felt like I carried a million brutal cuts, my peace of mind spilling from the wounds.

"Just tell me what to do, love, and I will."

"The only thing I want," I said, finally turning to look at him, "is to know why? What reason could you possibly have to keep this from me?"

His scarlet eyes darkened as they met mine, an insatiable inferno lighting their depths. "It's…" he sighed, dropping his head with a shake. "It's complicated. I would tell you in a heartbeat if I could."

I felt my jaw clench, power pushing against me harder. My skin broke apart in several spots, my spark flaring brighter than a star. A golden tinge began to cloud my vision, igniting like wildfire as my anger rose yet again.

"I have no use for bullshit excuses, Kanan," I spit venomously. "You could uncomplicate it if you wanted to."

I made to brush past him but he gripped my arm, pulling me back. My skin hummed at his touch, a cool breeze pushing past the heavy cape draped over me to sweep against my naked flesh. A near painful heat built low in my stomach, my traitorous body not caring about the reservations of my mind, more than happy to be touched once again by tall, dark, and sinful. I was suddenly, painfully, aware of just how bare I was.

He leaned in, his lips brushing my ear, "Two thousand years, little goddess. Two thousand years I have waited."

For you. That was what he didn't say—the words he had no need to speak. The warmth of his body soaked into mine, the heat of his breath running down my neck, drawing me in. He ran his calloused thumb across the skin of my arm, and like all inevitable things, I found myself gazing up into his eyes.

His lips curved into a sad facsimile of his wicked grin. "I am a patient man, so be mad, my love. Be as angry as you need to be. Yell, scream, curse my name to the Cosmos. I'll weather it all without complaint, because even if you spend the rest of eternity hating me for a decision I already hate myself for, you're *here*. Breathing life back into this world. Into me. I'll survive off of the small scraps of your attention with a smile if it means your light shines bright once again."

And with one last look, taking me in as if he was memorizing every last inch, he walked away. The warmth left with him, leaving me cold and even more broken than ever.

CHAPTER THREE

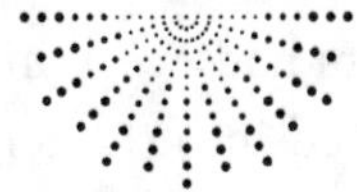

It took us the remainder of the day to meet up with the healers. As soon as we ran into them the army all but collapsed. Everyone was bruised, beaten, and bleeding. An audible sound of relief had spread through the ranks as Kanan ordered camp to be set up.

The dark gray mountains of the Gravelands loomed in the background. The ominous giants weren't the most comforting, nowhere close to the security the Crians brought to Eskira, but they would have to do.

Thankfully, Kanan had sent airborne ahead with supplies for the army when they were making their way towards the stronghold. He had pushed them, making what I'd been told was at least a four day trip in three.

Unfortunately, that same time couldn't be made again. There were too many wounded needing care, and those lucky enough to be uninjured were on their last leg. After the punishing journey and then a battle immediately afterwards, everyone was on the verge of falling unconscious. Even Descendents, powerful as they may be, needed to rest.

That hadn't stopped them from trying to set up my tent first, despite my protests that the makeshift infirmary be constructed. After reminding them that I needed the least amount of help out of anyone, they finally relented, doing so reluctantly until I explained that I could kick their ass with or without being their queen. That got them moving.

Even wounded and tired, the camp had been set up in minutes. Magic really had a way of speeding things up. There was now a sea of red where a field of green once stood.

After ensuring the healers had everything they needed, promising to return and help, I retreated into the tent that had been set up for me. The black fabric was stark in the midst of all the red.

Truth be told, I was hiding. It was one thing to know who I was. To understand why when I took even a single step outside I was met with bows and reverence. I was a queen. A goddess. Or at least I had been. I sure as hell didn't feel like one now.

I had no memory of it, no idea what it truly meant to be those things. Now that the adrenaline had worn off, the haze of battle fading in the wake of everything that had happened, I wasn't even sure I knew how to do half of the things I had done at the Gravelands.

A part of me knew that with the power at my fingertips I could turn a flame into a wildfire, a drizzle into a downpour. The breeze could easily become a tornado, and if the ground let loose a rumble, with a bare thought from me it could become an earthquake. I felt it in my bones.

But whatever instinctual side of me that knew how to do that had disappeared as soon as the mountain had fallen. If possession had been a possibility I would have called it that, but whatever it was had left me feeling empty and confused.

The things I could do. Feel. Irropia's heartbeat thrummed all around me. I felt it, knew it felt mine, but that knowledge came from somewhere. Where though, I couldn't say. Every time I tried to follow the thought, find the memory, it was like staring into an abyss. I would get to the end of the line, stand at the edge, and look into nothing but pure darkness. My memories were somewhere in there, hidden deep where I couldn't find them.

All the power and no understanding of how to use it. If I had been a breath away from exploding before, unsure when or how that power would erupt, I was a godsdamn weapon now, like one of Nala's shattershells, but far, far worse.

It was frustrating on a whole new level. I finally figured out who I was, why I am the way I am, and yet I was still left missing something.

"My queen, the Council and the king have assembled, and they're requesting your presence." Zanaya's voice broke through my thoughts, the sounds of the camp coming in through the open flap.

Turning, I saw her standing in the opening still covered in dust and blood. I walked over to her, brow wrinkled. "I need to go help the healers with the wounded. The talking can wait."

"I spoke with the Mender on my way to get you, she has reassured me that until they've assessed the damage done they'll manage. The ones you helped along the way are still stable."

Not stable enough though. When I had reached the ones Zanaya was concerned about, they had been on the verge of death. I had no clue how to use my magic to heal them, so I figured I would do what I could with the knowledge I did possess. I had been a healer before anything else.

The power had all but burst out of me as soon as I laid my hands on them, ripping through me and into them. From the weak cries of pain, I was lucky I hadn't been the one to kill them. By some grace of the Cosmos their wounds had healed enough for them to make it the rest of the journey.

I bit my lip, maybe it was best that I didn't help the healers. The last thing I needed was to hurt these people—my people—any more than I already had with my stupid decisions.

"Alright," I said in resignation, a strained smile pulling at my lips. "We'll have to get this over with at some point, I guess."

Her brows furrowed in concern as she asked, "Are you okay, my queen?"

I grimaced. "You know you don't have to call me that."

She tilted her head, shrugging her shoulders. "It's what you are."

I sighed heavily through my nose, watching the chaos outside through the opening. "But it's not." I smiled wanly. "I have no memories or even an idea of who I apparently was two thousand years ago. I'm exactly who I was before I was taken, just with more power. And even then I have no idea how to use it properly. I am no *queen*."

The corners of her lips lifted sympathetically. "I hate to break it to you," she said, stepping out into the open and holding the flap for me. "But try explaining that to them."

She tipped her head toward the dozens of soldiers rushing around, busy with whatever duties they needed to complete, all of whom had stopped to stare at me. Almost as one, they bowed their heads in respect.

It was overwhelming to say the least. Having people bow to me was an abrupt change from where I was only weeks ago. Hated and treated as less by the village. Even at Eskira, where I was treated well, regardless of the power I did or did not hold, no one had really paid me any mind.

Not wanting to insult them, I tipped my chin in thanks. Regardless of how I felt about it, I was their reincarnated goddess. I guess I was going to have to get used to the reactions and the spotlight that came with that revelation.

Leading me through the parted crowd, bows and awe-filled looks following in our wake, we made our way to the opposite side of camp where the only other black tent had been constructed. The anger that had reduced to a simmer in my chest roared back to life, wanting to lash out at the liars.

Zanaya must have been able to read my mind—that or I was doing an absolute shit job of keeping my emotions off my face—because she seemed to guess exactly how I was feeling. "Saanvi was the one that figured you might want some space."

So they had decided to put a whole damn war camp in between the two of us. I couldn't help but snort, "Good guess."

She stopped us at the entrance to Kanan's tent, placing a hand on my arm. "You didn't answer me before. Are you going to be okay?"

It was a question I had been asking myself for the past couple of hours, since this whole thing started, really. Secrets had turned to lies, and it felt like I was drowning beneath the weight of them. I was wading through the darkness, completely alone, no memories, no idea of who to trust, and I wasn't sure if I was going to make it out the other side. I was going to try my damndest to do so, though.

"I will be. Eventually."

"You've got this," she stated, squeezing my arm. She made to leave, but an emotion I couldn't explain burst in my chest. It was an odd feeling, a mixture of anxiety and loneliness, as if I desperately needed to cling on to something, anything, so that I didn't have to face this alone.

It was that feeling that had me calling out, "Where do you think you're going?"

She stopped in her tracks, confused. "What do you mean?"

I pointed behind me. "I don't really trust anyone in there at the moment. I don't have the memories to validate what they're saying, and to be honest, I'm not sure I could believe anything that comes out of their mouths even if I did. I have quickly been promoted from dangerous new girl to queen," I remarked dryly. "And I'm completely ignorant to the happenings of my own people."

I looked at her with all the seriousness I could muster. "I'm going to need someone to advise me." I swallowed, my chest constricting as I put myself out on a limb, adding, "I'm going to need a friend."

Her eyes widened, mouth parting, before she swept it all away as if she wasn't shocked by my openness. I could have kissed her for not making a big deal out of it, even though the little girl inside me, who never got to play with the others, was beaming.

I ignored the burn in my eyes as she walked back to me, her gaze warm and fierce. She nodded her head in support, standing at my shoulder, as she declared, "Let's do this. I'll be there to boob-punch you if you need a dose of reality."

I snorted, "I appreciate that."

And together, side by side, we walked into the dragon's den.

CHAPTER FOUR

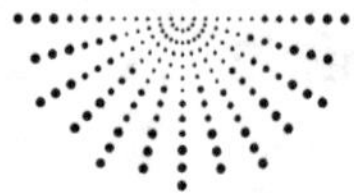

It was just as warm and masculine as the last time I had seen it, Kanan's smoke and amber scent enveloping me the second I stepped inside. The tent was less furnished than it had been, which made sense for an army traversing the entire width of the continent in only three days. However, a long table had made the trip, enough to seat the entire Council and more.

The tent vibrated with tension, and with the Council, Maris, Geoff, and Bron all in attendance, we were pushing the personality capacity.

The occupants stood and bowed upon my entry, all except for the brooding lizard at the far end, who saw fit to do nothing but sweep his gaze across me. A mask was set firmly in place over his face, the impenetrable steel of it flickering just barely as he looked over me.

Refusing to give him an inch, I resisted saying anything snarky, instead moving to the last remaining chair on the end of the table. Zanaya came up behind me, situating herself at my side, barely sparing her uncle a glance.

With a pinched expression, lips pressed tight, he no doubt caught the snub. He appeared genuinely saddened by his niece's anger towards him, and for a moment I felt bad that it was coming between them. At the end of the day though, Cashim had made his decisions and now it was his time to live with the consequences.

"Unfortunately, this is a closed meeting Commander," Kanan's smooth voice broke the silence.

I straightened in my seat, narrowing my eyes at him. Our eyes locked, a stalemate. I wasn't going to back down though, not now. "She's here on my request, and as far as I'm concerned she has more right to be here than some of you."

My meaning wasn't missed, several heads dropping in shame. A muscle in Kanan's jaw twitched, some kind of emotion breaking through his thick walls and flickering behind his eyes. Aside from that he appeared completely at ease, bored even.

"Very well," he retorted. "She may stay."

"I don't believe I was asking for your permission," I expressed, irritated beyond belief. I could be a bitch on a good day, and this was definitely not one of those. He'd be lucky if he survived unscathed.

He tensed at my tone, the muscles beneath his black leathers bulging as if preparing for battle. I could see it in his eyes, the way they steeled with determination. He had the advantage over me having probably been through hundreds of arguments with my former self, but no one had ever accused me of being a pushover and I wasn't about to let them start now.

Closing his eyes, he breathed out through his nose, a curl of smoke the only indication of what he was feeling. "You know that's not what I meant."

"No I don't," I say with a snort, raising an eyebrow. "What, in the past couple of hours, has given me any indication that I know you at all? For a man of few words, you sure know how to waste the ones you do say."

His hands clenched the arms of his chair, a low groan giving way as his fingers dug in. The tent darkened, shadows crawling on the fabric, circling the table.

Cashim cleared his throat, eyes darting between the two of us, probably hoping to stop the explosion before it began. "Your

Majesties, please, we asked this meeting to discuss…everything that has happened."

"Yes, like how the fuck we didn't know about any of this," Lars exclaimed, sneering in Cashim's direction. "Or at least how some of us didn't know."

"For once, I agree with Braxix," Lady Oakina voiced, her razor sharp expression easily cutting through Cashim's innate charisma. She looked between Kanan and I. "This Council, generations before us, advised you in almost all matters. Why would you not wish for us to know of your rebirth? We could have put aside centuries of petty squabbling."

"Well, if it makes you feel any better, Lady Vyn, I did not know myself, that I'm apparently the fucking queen." I quirked an eyebrow at Kanan, a sardonic grin lifting my lips. "So I would just love to hear how we've ended up here."

Kanan licked his lips, my eyes falling to watch his tongue dart out, which inevitably led me to remember just how masterful that tongue was. I sighed internally, really wishing he wasn't a lying bastard.

"You'll all be made aware of what you need to be soon. I understand you're confused, but that conversation first needs to happen between your queen and I."

Lars scoffed in derision, the first wave of shock unfortunately seeming to have already worn off. "You expect us to just sit here and wait for you to fill us in when you feel like it? You've fucked with our heads long enough, don't you think?"

The entire tent went silent, everyone glancing at Kanan for his reaction. I knew they were expecting his anger, but what they got instead was somehow so much worse. He was smiling.

A terrifying, calm smile. One that would be best described as those seen on the truly insane, those who were locked up to protect the world from their madness.

It was the kind of smile that sent chills down your spine, made your blood run cold. The one I saw him wear as he tortured Jasco, blood speckling his chest as he watched him writhe in pain.

Lars froze, like a deer locked in a hunter's crosshairs, stupidly assuming if it didn't move the predator wouldn't still kill it. The deranged curl of Kanan's lips lifted higher, sensing the fear in the air.

A satisfied dragon.

"Yes." He spoke quietly, having no need to yell or shout. "You will wait. You ignorantly assume that you're someone of great importance. You are not. Instead of doing your duty, living up to the title that was *gifted* to your ancestor—a man who would be greatly disappointed in his bloodline today—and shepherding the Descendents in our absence, you've done nothing but cause problems and dissension for decades."

The words hit like cracks of a whip, striking true and deep. No one dared interrupt; even Lars's closest ally Elaric kept his eyes turned down.

"You want nothing but the power to hold yourself above everyone else. You'll do anything that serves your self gain, when as a member of this Council you should be one of the most selfless. Let us not pretend we don't all see it, with you being as subtle as a newborn fawn stumbling through the grasses. I never had any intention of taking the position of warlord. I was perfectly willing to bide my time and wait, but you forced my hand. Throwing your weight around like some stuck boar and instilling fear into the men and women who served under you. You're a sniveling worm that I would crush if only I didn't have more pressing matters at hand. I suggest you remember that."

Turning towards the rest of us without giving a now red-faced Lars a second thought, he continued. "You all want answers, that is understandable, but do not assume you will like my choices. I did not make them selflessly or without emotion, quite the opposite in fact. I do not have a nice and neat explanation that will make you understand my motives, I don't need you to. That is not why you are here, and it is not why your families have been helping rule Allasea for the past two thousand years. We have more important things to deal with at the moment other than your bruised pride."

It was surprisingly Lady Yeva who interjected, "The king is right. We have close to two thousand souls who need guidance at the moment, not infighting. Our wants and needs come last."

"Has the block been removed?" I interjected without care, picking at the skin around my nail. Glancing up, I shot Kanan a hard look. Doing right by our people started with giving them the truth. What a shocking concept.

"What block?" Oakina asked suspiciously, her sharp gaze bouncing between the two of us.

Sparing her a look I answered, "The mind wipe that keeps the truth of our history hidden. It keeps any information that might betray our true identities from ever being remembered. Isn't that right?"

I glanced at Kanan, catching the brief—and satisfying—flicker of surprise at my question.

That's right asshole, I know what you did.

It could have been my imagination at work, but I could have sworn the corner of his mouth crept up. A hint of proud amusement unfurling across his lips. Cheeky bastard.

"How did you figure it out?" His genuine curiosity irritated me, but I didn't know why. I had wanted answers, and one way or another I had found them.

I decided to be truthful, because that was the right thing to do… and maybe I was gloating a little bit. "No one knew what I was talking about when I started putting things together. The War of Three. Kasis. Any of it. And then Wrynn confirmed it during our escape."

My forehead wrinkled, swiveling around I looked up at Zanaya. "Where is Wrynn? I didn't see him at all during the trek here."

Knowing the little sprite, he was hiding. He probably assumed I was mad at him. I wasn't angry per se, but I did want to know his side of this story.

Zanaya shook her head. "I have reports from some of the soldiers saying they saw him fly south immediately after your escape. I knew you'd want to know if he made it out, but the last anyone saw of him he was headed away from the Gravelands."

Where the hell was he going? I knew better than anyone that my tiny friend could take care of himself, but he was also prone to getting into trouble. Trouble of his own making, which was even worse.

"Keep me updated?" I asked, completely confused. "If anyone hears of or sees him I want to know about it."

The last thing I wanted was him running away from me because he thought he had done something wrong. I couldn't say I wasn't a little hurt that he had kept some things from me, but at the very least he had tried to steer me in the right direction. It was more than most had done.

A feminine chuckle of disbelief had me whipping around. Surprised, Maris's soft laughter caused my eyes to narrow.

"Something funny?" I raised a questioning eyebrow, both loving and hating how still she went. Geoff winced out of the corner of my eye. He knew us well enough to know when a fight was coming.

She swallowed, lowering her eyes. These were the first words we had spoken since her near death, and my anger towards them both no longer had to contend with worry. "It's just, every sprite I've ever met is a notorious trouble maker. They're not exactly—reliable."

Oh she'd done it now. "Well considering that sprite is the reason we all escaped, and is the reason I finally found out about *my* own history, you might want to change your perception of sprites; they seem to be a hell of a lot more reliable than you've ever been."

I knew my words had hit, pain flashing over her face as she went silent. Guilt ate at me, an instinctual response, but I forced it down. I wasn't trying to purposefully hurt her, but I also wouldn't pull my punches to save her feelings. Not when every lie I had been told had stemmed from her and Geoff.

A deep sadness settled in my heart, one that originated from the long dead wish to live a simple life in the countryside. Before everything changed, my life had been that cottage. The three of us against the world.

Now I couldn't imagine going back to that, living naively in a cage I hadn't realized had always been there. But I could mourn the peace I had once thought existed on those rolling hills. Mourn the life I would have lived with Maris and Geoff.

"Can we please get back on track?" Lars uttered in a commanding tone that had everyone stiffening in their seats.

"My Lord, it might be best to explain. At least about this," Cashim implored Kanan, ever the diplomat.

Kanan eyed him, seeming to think it over. Sighing, he ran a hand over his face, a weight settling on his shoulders.

"When I learned that you had reincarnated, I immediately planned to follow you, but I needed to be assured that we'd be safe upon our return. I knew we'd come back as children, young and impressionable, so with the help of our closest friends," he inclined his head towards Cashim, Bron, and Maris, "we hatched a plan to ensure we wouldn't be taken advantage of."

"How did you know you would be kids?" Lady Yeva chimed in with the same question on my mind.

Kanan opened his mouth and then closed it with a snap. Tilting his head with an irritated grimace, he pinched the bridge of his nose. "It's complicated."

I rolled my eyes, turning to stare at the flames burning away in their sconces, so close to the tent wall I worried they'd burn a hole through it. I could feel the cryptic asshole staring, his own blazing gaze burning a hole into the side of my head.

"All you need to know is that the block I placed has already begun to fade. Once I reincarnated, I needed it to stay put, so I disconnected it from myself in a way, tying it to Atallia finding out who she was. I figured by the point she knew, we'd be old enough and reunited by then, if not soon after. It's a little more complicated than that, but that's all I can say for now."

"Then that will have to satisfy our curiosity," Lady Yeva spoke up, her sweet voice somehow coming out on top of all the rumblings. "So long as the memory compulsion is wearing off, then we will have to accept your reasons for holding the rest back. We have no other choice."

"Lady Yeva is right, there are far greater priorities than questioning your judgment on something that has already been done," Cashim said, taking over the conversation. "We need to know the plan —if there even is a plan. I think we can all agree that coming to the

Gravelands in order to rescue the queen was ultimately necessary, but now we have dozens—maybe even hundreds—injured or dead."

I forced the wince away, knowing he hadn't meant it that way, but I couldn't help feeling responsible for all of this. The dead and wounded were only here because of me. Something began to fester in my stomach, clawing away at my insides like a rot.

"The closest city is Hassere, they'll be the quickest to reach and equipped to handle the encampment. It'll give us an excuse to allow those that joined us from there to return home, as well as an opportunity to rest before making our way back to Eskira," Oakina added, quick to move on to more effective means of action.

"Will they have the infirmary to care for all the wounded?" I questioned.

"Hassere is run by Lady Yeva and Lady Jai," Zanaya spoke up next to me. "It's second only to Eskira in having the most established network of healers, and only because Eskira is the capital."

Lady Jai gave a small nod of appreciation to Zanaya, before turning her impossibly dark eyes to me. "We'll be more than prepared, and it'll give us a chance to see what our forces look like. Our weaknesses and push points."

"With Kasis back it'll be critical that we know every hole in our security. He'll use any advantage he can to tear us down piece by piece," Kanan said, stroking his long fingers over his lips, his unfocused gaze letting me know he was deep in thought. "It's also imperative that we figure out his next move. Where he is, what he wants—all of it."

"He wants what he always does," I muttered mostly to myself, picking at the soft material of the leather trousers I wore.

"And what is that?" Elaric inquired. The red-headed lord appeared appropriately concerned about the answer. Normally I wrote him off as Lars's lackey, but something in the way he paid attention to everything going on, silently taking in the conversations, made me question why I had dismissed him so casually.

"Atallia and I dead. Or at the very least me," Kanan answered, red irises glowing like hot coals. They pulsed as he looked over at me, memories of death playing out across them.

"What happens if he succeeds?" It was Lars who dared to ask the question on all of our minds.

I still hadn't come to terms with everything, but the personifications of Life and Death not existing was almost incomprehensible. Could anyone—anything—subsist if the very aspect that made it possible didn't?

I knew Kanan could see the panic rising inside me, his sad smile confirming all I needed to know. "Everything would cease to exist."

CHAPTER FIVE

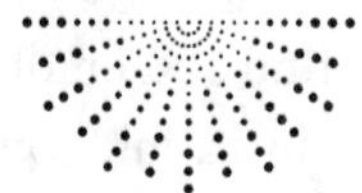

The meeting went on for far longer than anyone was prepared for, Kanan's declaration enough to set off a chain of questions that lasted into the night. Questions that he avoided answering in full with vague statements and sometimes just outright refusal. It was finally Cashim who had called for an end to it, reminding us all that we needed to rest just as much as the army.

Even still, I wasn't surprised when I heard fabric shuffle and a light breeze blow in from the dark plains outside. The firelight dimmed before growing stronger and shadows bounced off the sides of the tent, throwing shapes all across the space. The darkness trembled and swayed as if to a silent song, reaching out to dance along the floor.

I didn't need to turn to know who had come, his mere presence was enough to set off every one of my senses, threading through me with an unmistakable caress. With a quiet serration the flap fell closed, cutting us off from the outside world. The room seemed infinitely smaller than I remembered it being just seconds ago.

I couldn't make myself turn and look at him, knowing that I would find myself sucked in. With what I knew now, I at least didn't feel crazy. Memories or no, I had a connection to this man. Beast. God.

Whatever the hell he was. An undeniable one at that, otherwise I wouldn't feel the need to rip my heart from my chest just to see if it was still beating every time we were around each other.

But who was here to help me figure out all the rest of it? Who could explain how I was supposed to process all the shit that had happened? It felt a little selfish, what with so many people who had been lost. Who were hurting and in need of help, but godsdammit, didn't I deserve a little help too? I was alone and drowning in a sea of chaos, nothing but my own mind and emotions ready to crush me.

They had already been doing a fabulous job of that on their own before, they didn't need the extra push that would send me spiraling.

"Are you not going to look at me?" he asked curiously.

"No," I sighed, moving over to the small table that had been set up with a pitcher of water and several goblets. "Looking at you makes my chest feel funny and my head spin. I'm not so sure it's good for my health."

"Mmmm," he hummed, moving about the room. "Sounds like something you should get checked out. Could be dangerous."

I poured myself a glass, hoping the cool water would calm my frayed nerves. I took a long sip before answering. "Probably, although I've never been very good at keeping myself out of danger."

And despite my words, I did turn, goblet held loosely in hand. He stood with his side facing me, rubbing his calloused fingers over the blood red cape I had thrown onto the soft pallet of furs that had been hastily set up.

All shadows and darkness, the light appeared to bend away from him. The ebony tendrils, that I'd come to acknowledge as simply a piece of him, ran along his arms. Curling against his skin, they licked at the air as if tasting the tension that stood between us. Several slid along the floor, headed in my direction before being jerked back against his taunt body. No doubt their master reprimanding them for their boldness.

If shadows could hiss, Kanan's almost certainly did, displeased by the situation. Had I felt capable of it, I might have laughed at the sight. It was unsurprising in the least that no part of the dragon god in front of me appreciated being restrained. Tame didn't seem to be a word he knew or understood.

Finally dragging his gaze from the bright material, dropping it to the bed as our eyes clashed in a battle that I was now realizing had been going on for millennia. I wondered how many times we had fallen into this trap, how long and hard we fought to break free of its effects? How often had we been sucked into each other's orbit?

There was a tug in the back of my mind, an insistent beat that wouldn't leave me alone, like a word I couldn't remember balancing on the tip of my tongue. My chest tightened, but all too soon the feeling faded, taking the answers and any memory I may have teased out with it.

"What do you want, Kanan?" I asked wearily as the emotional fatigue of the past day began to take root, threatening to stamp out the burning anger inside me. I shuffled over to sit in front of the unlit hearth, a set of low-cushioned benches stationed around it.

He stalked to the empty seat across from me, his eyes glancing down but for a split second before grabbing hold of mine once again. The bench looked like a child's seat with him in it, his long legs stretching out on either side to accommodate his height.

Shifting his gaze to the hearth in front of us, he lifted the top grate. Leaning forward he blew a small breath towards the split logs and like dry grass in the heat of summer a fire blazed to life, crackling and popping without restraint.

Show off.

The sting of bitterness slapped me in the face. Had I known how, I could have easily done that with the power I had at my fingertips.

"We need to talk," he stated roughly, staring at me from across the flames. The light from the fire swayed in his eyes, moving in time with the ones that already lived inside him.

"Unless you're here to tell me the truth, I don't think I can deal with anymore tonight."

"I know, love, and I wish I could give you your peace, but you need to hear this. It's not what you want, but it's what I can give you right now." His voice was sad and tired, and for the first time I felt like the mask was slipping.

The shield he showed everyone, even sometimes to me, that kept him protected and hidden from view. Always strong, always ready to fight if needed. When was the last time he had been able to confide in someone? When was the last time he let down those walls and showed someone how he truly felt beneath it all?

Maybe it was for that reason I couldn't find it in me to be angry at that moment. It didn't take away from what he had done, was still doing, but for a second I could see how his choices weighed on him. They had left him beaten and battered, and maybe, for a moment, it would be better to put my own feelings aside and realize that I wasn't the only one going through hell.

"Okay," I relented, my heart pounding as relief filled his eyes. "I'm listening."

He let out a breath, wide shoulders dropping like he had shed some of that weight. "It's a long, messy story," he warned, eyes never leaving mine.

I shot him a narrowed look, setting my cup next to my foot. "Then start at the beginning, I'm sure you'll figure it out. After all, you've had all this time to prepare."

The fire brightened in response and it took me a second to realize a fissure had opened on the back of my hand, gold light sizzling through.

A shimmer began to tinge the edges of my vision. The tiniest wisps of energy floated out from between the cracked skin, and almost in a trance I rubbed my thumb over it, feeling the heat and power that burned beneath. It made me feel like I was on the edge of a cliff overlooking a great chasm, one wrong move and I would slip right off.

"Easy love," a dark voice filled with heady promises whispered. The words bounced all around in my mind. A cool sensation wrapped me up within it, dragging my attention away from the ledge and back to the present.

Blinking rapidly, I shook my head to clear it only to see a single shadow had reached up from beneath my seat to curl over my hand. It pulled away once I noticed, running down my skin until the last second. I didn't reprimand it. *Him.* Instead, focusing on Kanan's gaze, the tether—undeniably connecting me to him—kept me centered. "Sorry, it's been doing that off and on since the block was broken."

He was staring at where the crack had formed, a tense and stormy look on his face. I went to ask him why, but just like always, his walls fell right back into place. "Don't waste your apologies on me, love," he said roughly, leaning over his knees, arms bracing his upper body as he stared into the fire. "I'm certainly not owed them."

My eyebrows dipped, immediate denial popping to the front of my mind. I don't get the chance to push him on it as he changes the subject, a hand scrubbing down his face. "When we learned of Kasis's betrayal, of his plans and his experiments on our people," his mouth twisted in disgust, "we were sent straight into war. By the time we figured out what was happening, he'd already built an army that rivaled our own. What his people lacked in magic, they made up for in numbers and greed."

I froze, leaning forward in my seat as flashes of my nightmares—memories—played out in my head. What I once thought were the dreams that hunted me in the night, were real. Somehow, in the dregs of sleep, my memories had peeked out of the darkness to haunt me.

"We were in the middle of the battle on his stronghold—a damn near replica of the one we found you in this time—when Kasis was able to incapacitate you somehow. I was right above you, about to burn him alive, but one second you were both there and the next you were gone. It didn't matter how far back I could trace your scent, or how hard I searched, you were just gone. I've had years to think it over and I still don't know how he was able to get away with you."

The words were forced out between clenched teeth, his head bowed as his bestial anger heated the tent far quicker than any flame. The air quivered around his figure, waves of it coming off him.

"I think I know how," I interrupted, remembering how Kasis's minions had dragged me through the rift. The mirage-like ripple in the air as the landscape changed completely. Kanan's head snapped up, but I waved him off. "I'll explain later."

He looked like he was going to argue, but seemed to think better of it. "After that I spent an entire year searching for you, but..." his voice shook with unrestrained emotion, the words choking him. "I didn't find you in time."

My hands shook as they gripped the edge of the bench, my mouth drying up as things began to come together. I didn't need to remember it to know what had happened next.

"You were somehow able to get away, and you lit up the world, taking energy from the Gravelands and making it your own. In your escape you destroyed the majority of Kasis's forces, and the explosion alerted us to your location."

There was pain in his eyes as he closed them, one leg bouncing with barely contained power, the next words a bare whisper. "Before I could get to you, you reached out to me, told me you loved me...and then you scattered your energy across the world."

I couldn't move, breathing had become an afterthought. In the midst of all this, I had somehow forgotten that I used to be his pair. His wife, queen, mate. I loved him—*had loved him,* I reminded myself. And as much anger coursed through me, I couldn't help but share in his pain. He had lost everything, and even after reincarnating, starting fresh, he still remembered.

Every interaction we'd ever had took on a new meaning. To me, I had only just met him, but to him...

To him I was something else entirely. The being he was irrevocably tied to, the one he had entered into existence with.

I swallowed harshly, my breath catching in my chest, the overwhelming feelings from before threatening to consume me. I had an entire life before this one. I had been a queen loved by her people, and loved by her king. How could I reconcile that life and the one I now lived? How was I ever going to bridge that gap?

"I was already close to madness at that point." His gaze pierced through me, like it was trying to break the shields around my heart, imprint itself onto my soul. "Losing you was the last straw. I spiraled, and in a fit of rage I finished off what you started. I burned the rest of Kasis's forces alive, but not before I had ripped through their minds and filled them with their worst fears. Not before I tore a few apart with my bare hands and made them line up to face their death. I made them scream and beg, and I didn't stop until the ground was drenched in blood and the air smelled of nothing but melted flesh."

His voice was almost mechanical as he spoke, going through the motions as he relived the moments that had brought him here. Most would have found the recounted scene horrifying, but all I could feel was a deep sadness for the man that had been brought to that point.

He was lost in thought, back on that field two thousand years ago. He was stuck reliving the loss of his mate and the horrors he enacted afterwards. He kept on even as every part of him seemed to scream in pain, "I did the same to Kasis, spending quite some time carrying out all the things I wished to do to him while he had you."

"Sometimes that was all that kept me going during that year," he muttered. "Imagining all the ways I could hurt him, make him feel all that I had when you were gone. I thought I killed him, but I should have known it wouldn't be that easy to get rid of him—he always had a way of getting out of sticky situations. I used to joke it was part of his power, that he might be the one person who could cheat death. Cheat me." He let out a contemptuous chuckle, "Funny how right I was."

"Then what happened? I mean, if I scattered my energy, how are we both here?"

He shook himself out of the memories that bound him, running a hand through his thick curls. "Well after taking my pound of flesh, I was able to regain some clarity." He shifted back, placing his forearms, corded with muscle, on the bench behind him. "I mentioned earlier that we can't truly die, at least not fully," he explained. "With who we are, it's essentially impossible. Any universe where we don't exist would be *nothing*. It's not vanity or self-importance, it's a fact. Give us as many titles as you want, but at our core…" He spoke directly to me, peering into my eyes as if he could see my soul, "At our core we are Life and Death, and together we make up Existence. It's what we were meant to be in the first place, and without us there would be no beginnings or endings."

"How does that work though?" I ask, confused as to how something as seemingly insignificant as a person could be so vital to the universe.

"This," he indicated his body, "is nothing but a shell. One that I created because a long time ago I had the inclination to make one, just like you created yours. At the end of the day though, we are essentially sentient cosmic energy. What makes us who we are is intrinsic to the wellbeing and function of the universe. To kill us or destroy our seat of power would cause the collapse of totality. We can't be killed, and if, by some act of the Cosmos, Kasis is able to find a way…" He shook his head. "The only reason the Cosmos was able to fall into the Endless Sleep was because he shed his power; otherwise it would have been impossible for him."

The reality of our situation hit me. The weight of not just a kingdom and its people, but the universe was now thrust upon my shoulders. Wasn't that just swell.

"Why would Kasis want that?" I asked, more confused than ever. "His whole thing is about power. He'll rule over nothing if he kills us."

"I'm not sure if he even knows what he wants. He didn't always used to be like this, at least I don't think he did," he said, running a hand once again through his hair in agitation. "It had to have been over time or else I would have seen it. At least I like to think I would have. It's something that keeps me up at night, whether I could have stopped all of this had I been paying more attention."

"You couldn't have known," I said with a certainty I felt in my bones. "It's unfair to put that on yourself."

He shot me a look over the fire, one that said he appreciated the sentiment but didn't believe me.

We sat in silence for a moment listening to the soft cracks and pops of the fire logs as both of us were left wondering what could have been, had Kasis's betrayal been found out sooner.

"Why did you follow me?" I finally asked, looking down at where my boot had dug a small divot in the ground. I couldn't bring myself to look at him as I asked, too scared of what I'd find.

He gave a low chuckle, one that sounded as broken as I felt.

Glancing up I saw his smile, far gentler than any I'd ever seen. "Because that's our nature, love. Life and Death, forever intertwined. We began our story together, and I'll be damned if we don't end it that way. It's you and me."

The world fell away, leaving just the two of us as he finished his declaration, "Always."

CHAPTER SIX

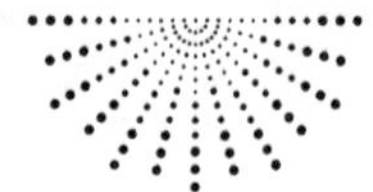

I stared at him as a choking panic began to build within me. I couldn't take it, I was suffocating. The tent walls started closing in, surrounding me on all sides until I felt like a cornered animal. Standing abruptly, I bolted out through the flap in the tent and into the night air. I didn't care which direction I went, I took off.

I was running from him and also the crushing heartache that threatened to break me. Ignoring the stares and whispers that followed from the warriors on watch, I ran through the lines of tents. As far away as I could from the bond that tied me to him, that made me feel all too much for someone I both barely knew and felt like I had known forever.

I ran and ran until I couldn't anymore, breaking past the last line of tents and out onto the open plains. The sibling moons hung high and bright in the open sky, the entire field glinting in the light of the stars. The colorful wind had turned luminescent, purples and blues and silvers undulating above the flat landscape like a river of light and magic.

Stopping, I folded over gasping for breath as emotions wracked me. My chest constricted in pain, and tears that were part mine, part someone else's, fell freely from my eyes. I couldn't stop them, little metallic drops of grief that were tangled together with feelings I couldn't place or understand. Unraveling it seemed pointless, all of it simultaneously a piece of me and yet not.

I straightened and put my hand to my chest as harsh, heaving breaths left me. I swallowed, trying to calm down, but a sob escaped my throat, throwing me back into the drowning sea of anxiety. It felt like I was sharing my body with someone else, everything crashing together inside of me until I couldn't tell what was real and what wasn't.

I pressed my lips together, trying to smother the scream that wanted to escape. Hands shaking as I clasped them over my mouth, I tried to capture the broken sounds that tore free. Golden tears dripped over my fingers, falling to the ground uselessly, dotting the long grasses with their shine.

I let out another shaky breath, the air wobbling between my lips as I tried to slow my heart. Taking in a deep breath of the night air, so sweet and fresh, I wiped the tears off my face with the back of my hand. My chest tightened, the pain almost crushing in its intensity.

In. Out. In. Out.

I repeated the words over and over in my head as I stared out across the horizon, my mind spinning in a thousand different directions. My heart was simultaneously breaking and healing, anger and love warred, and stories of who I used to be collided with who I was now. Nothing made sense and now everything was riding on me getting my shit together.

A breeze tugged at the grass and played through my hair, sweeping it across my back. Closing my eyes I lifted my head into it, letting it dry the salt lines that stained my cheeks. My fingers clenched and released as I tried to find some semblance of balance, anything that would keep me from falling into that unknown abyss.

I had been teetering on its edge since I had broken the block on my magic, feeling like anything could send me over, but at this moment I would give anything to be back there. At least balancing on the ledge wasn't as bad as grasping onto it for dear life.

In. Out. In. Out.

I was nearly there when I felt a wave of heat hit my back, the smell of smoke and amber hitting my nose. My head dropped and I shook it as more tears began to drip down my face. I was unable to ignore the feeling of rightness that came as large, callused hands gripped my forearms.

"Please don't cry, little goddess," his dark voice pleaded with me. He leaned the front of his head against the back of mine, breathing in deeply, as he whispered, "Your tears are blades to my heart, and I can tolerate them no more than I could two thousand years ago."

My shoulders sank, a forlorn sigh escaping my tear stained lips. "I don't know who I am anymore," I whispered, the words nearly stolen by the wind. "Everyone is looking at me like I'll have all the answers to their problems, and I don't have the heart to tell them that I have no idea how to fix this."

"You don't have to have all the answers, love. No one is expecting you to know how to handle this. Just be you, I promise that's more than enough." Dragging his hands down my arms, his body heat sinking into me, I felt my heart slow. My breaths began to even out despite the tears that continued to fall.

"They're all expecting a queen. I have no idea how to be that." Wiping the tears from my face, I leaned back into him. I was already regretting letting my barriers drop even for this, but nothing had felt better than being in his arms. I was on the cusp of no return and right now I needed someone to hold me up, even for just a second.

He didn't disappoint. Wrapping his massive arms around me, he pulled me in tight. I let my head fall back to rest on his chest, closing my eyes as he held me close. I tried not to let the fact that the world seemed to fall into place as we stood there, soaking in the rays of the four moons, affect me more than it already was. The wind caressed our skin in adoration as colorful light fell upon us, and for a moment in time, everything was okay.

It was beautiful, the different hues hitting the grass blades of baby pink and magenta. Yellow and navy leaves—from the trees that dotted the edge of the plains—drifted in the wind, swirling around to a silent song. Soft chirps of crickets and the quiet sway of the long stems serenaded us as the energy stream above undulated along the night sky.

The stars were twinkling gemstones in the sky, and right then and there the crushing emotions simply receded, the crackling power beneath my skin calmed, and the world righted itself for but a second.

Kanan leaned his head down, unfairly soft lips brushing my ear as he spoke, "You listen to me, Atallia. You do not have to be anything but exactly who you are. It's far more than we deserve."

I shook my head, pushing against his arms for him to let me go. The muscles beneath my hands tensed, tightening around me slightly, like releasing me was the last thing they wanted to do. Slowly, almost painfully so, he pulled back until I was able to turn and face him. Giving in to the desire, I selfishly stared.

He was gorgeous in the daylight, that was no question. I could appreciate the advantages the light of the sun could bring, but under the cover of darkness…

He was indisputably perfect.

So much so it was almost alarming the response I could have towards him. The moonlight illuminated his giant form. His raven curls were so stark they appeared to be shadows in the night, unrelenting to any light. His sun-kissed, bronze skin was warm even in the cool darkness. His red gaze had turned downright bejeweled, two cut rubies alight with an inner fire, and his perfect face stared at me with a mixture of soul deep desire and agony. He was, simply put, beautiful.

It was hard not to stare at him for too long, his gaze pulling me into their depths, begging—pleading—me for something. I licked my lips, my mouth suddenly dry, as I tried to catch my breath.

"What is it, love? You can talk to me," he spoke so calmly, yet I could tell underneath everything he was anything but. I couldn't help but think who exactly he was trying to convince, me or himself.

"Can I though?" I asked, my brow wrinkling in disbelief. "You've done nothing but lie to me, kept"—I threw my hands in the air—"everything from me."

He winced, running a hand over the back of his neck as he briefly glanced down. "I know. I know I hurt you, and if you believe anything that I tell you ever again, believe me when I say I would endure all the pain in the world rather than see you hurt."

He closed his eyes, swallowing hard as he clenched his fists tight. "And knowing—" he let out a pained sound, "knowing I was the one to do it anyway, is a worse torture."

I looked at him with a furrowed brow, my mind failing to understand why he had done it then. "You had every opportunity to tell me," I insisted. "Every chance to come clean and help me. I was drowning Kanan."

My voice rose, the anger I had set aside deciding to replace the panic and sadness. Regret was written on every inch of his face. I would have felt bad had a steely resolve not also been there. I didn't have to ask him if he would have done it differently, the guilt ridden evidence was right there for me to see.

"I had nothing," I shouted, uncaring of how loud I was. Our only audience were the celestial moons, and I very much doubted they cared about the petty squabbles of deities. "I was completely alone, confused, and lost in a world I had no clue how to navigate. The people who raised me were either dead or captured, and all of sudden I have magical abilities. But oh, wait, they're not going to work because past me decided that future me didn't need to know about them, but I don't get to know that until I'm kidnapped because of my own stupidity and tortured by some deranged, psychopathic god."

Every word looked like it was a slap to the face, but he stood there and took it all with clenched hands. Blood dripped out between his white knuckles, and I knew at some point his claws must have come out.

"I even told you about how Maris and Geoff's betrayal made me feel, and you still said nothing. I told you about my dreams, my nightmares, the sleepwalking, how I felt like I was going crazy for my entire life. You said nothing," I exclaimed, pacing back and forth in front of him. "You knew *everything*!"

"I know," he agreed solemnly, bearing the brunt of my rage without complaint.

"Just tell me why," I implored, "At least give me a reason as to why I was the last to know about my own godsdamn life."

He looked miserable, shame a heavy cowl around him. He stepped closer to me, only to pull up short as I backed away, eyeing him sharply. My message was received and his eyes pinched at the corners. Dark shadows curled out of his bloodied palms, slipping in between his fingers and wrapping around his wrists.

"I wish I could," he spoke quietly, a darkness clouding his eyes. "You don't know how much I want to, but I can't; and you won't want to hear my excuses. I'm begging you, Atallia, just trust me. I have a good reason for it."

My jaw clenched at the response, and my blood boiled. Good reason or not, it was my life he was playing with, and I'd had more than enough of this bullshit. I could feel the power simmering and writhing, my vision turning gold as I stared at him.

The telltale hum began to build in my ears until all I could hear was the sound of the cosmic power rippling beneath my skin. So fragile in comparison it could rip free without restraint if it wished. It was a tempting thought to see what would happen if it was set loose. If the chains, that even now kept it at bay, were removed.

Regardless of my own feelings, and no matter how much I wished I could disappear off into the woods far, far away from this mess, I wouldn't abandon my people. Because they were mine now, and that meant I had to find a way to deal with all of this. If he wouldn't tell me what I needed to know then fine, but I sure as hell wasn't going to sit around waiting for answers either. I was done waiting for anything to be handed to me.

A war was on the horizon. Hell it might have been here already, and I needed to be ready to face whatever it brought. With or without Kanan's help.

The man in question appeared just as resolved as I was, and I knew we weren't going to get anywhere this night. Both of us were too stubborn and too sure that we were right. If we allowed it, we'd be butting heads all night.

"If I could I would have done everything differently." He declared, his voice carrying the words across the distance, their meaning not lost on me.

My lips twitched, something like a sad smile taking shape. "I want to believe that. Really, I do, but I don't know if I can let myself trust you. I don't think my heart can take another betrayal like that again."

With that I walked past him, knowing that if I stopped I might fall apart and break. Lifting my chin high, I kept my eyes forward, refusing to let my golden tears fall again. They were all in the wrong to keep who I was from me, and I knew that giving into what I wanted wouldn't fix anything. That I had to stay strong and remember what was right. But then, why did every step I took away from Kanan feel like my heart was shattering?

CHAPTER SEVEN

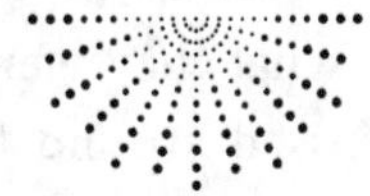

I was too restless to go back to the tent. I knew if I laid down to sleep I'd find myself staring up at the ceiling for hours on end. And if I didn't do that then I would wander around camp, and I couldn't handle how exposed that would make me, all the expectant looks on everyone's faces bearing down on my peace of mind.

They thought I was the answer to their prayers, the solution to their problems. In actuality I was as blind in all of this as them.

I found myself moving towards the white tents that had been set up to act as the infirmary, the healers and wounded somewhere inside. I moved toward the smell of familiar herbs, the scent reminding me that I had never been just one thing. I was a warrior *and* a healer.

I may not know how to save the Descendents, spare them from Kasis's horrific plans, but I could help those who had come to help me.

Even before they knew who I was, thousands had marched to attack the stronghold. I wasn't arrogant enough to believe it was all for me. Several of them had lost their loved ones to the attacks or kidnappings, nonetheless they had come. The least I could do was return the favor.

Stepping inside I was met with the certain kind of chaos healers where known for. It was something that I had come to adore. Completely different from the tense calm outside, the uninjured either sleeping or keeping watch, a quiet holding over the entire camp.

In here everything seemed like it was in shambles, people running about like they had no clue what they were doing. Bundles of herbs and bandages were being tossed around like balls in some twisted game, and yet it was seamless. A well-oiled machine that had gone through countless trials until it was perfect.

The main tent was the hub of the operation. An opening in the middle of each of the four walls connected to additional tents. An endless string of healers and aids ran in and out, reporting back on their patients and gathering supplies.

Low-lying cots held the wounded, lining every space along the walls. From the peek I saw into the connecting tents, even more were packed into each of the spaces. It left the middle open for scrambled together workbenches and surgical tables, all made from the crates and boxes that had held the camp's supplies.

Nearly all the beds were full, the tortured groans of those being tended to filling the space until it became nightmarish background noise. The silence from the sheet-covered cots, however, was deafening.

It was a testament to how hard the healers were working that it took someone crashing into me for anyone to notice I was standing in the entry. The poor trainee, the half filled insignia of a lotus blossom on her breast pocket giving away her position, was so focused on making sure her count of barberries was correct that she ran straight into me.

Nearly taking us both down, she dropped her supplies, letting out a surprised gasp. Reaching out, I steadied us both before asking, "Are you alright?"

The novice didn't even look up as she replied, dropping to her knees to pick up the berries one at a time, tossing them into her apron skirt. "Oh my Cosmos, I'm so sorry. I wasn't looking and now these will need to be washed again. How many was I at? Oh my gods, I'm so clumsy."

The young girl was so frantic she was mumbling to herself at the end, barely paying attention as I began to help her gather the long, red buds. "It's alright," I chuckled, hoping to calm her down. "No harm done."

With the last berry picked up off the ground, the petite trainee finally looked at me. She was young, no more than sixteen, and with her big brown eyes that shot wide with recognition and her curly, light brown hair she reminded me of a doll.

She let out a squeak, nearly dropping the berries again until I reached out with a cautionary hand. "Careful."

That seemed to shake her out of it as she looked down and carefully gathered the edges of her apron, making sure not a single berry fell. Shooting her eyes back up, settling on my nose, she dropped into a wobbly bow, "My queen, I am so sorry."

The title grabbed everyone's attention as heads whipped around to look at us. The young girl looked mortified, a red blush slowly creeping up her neck as she shifted her eyes downward. I felt for her, not much liking being the center of attention myself.

"It's okay, truly," I said with a sincere smile, tipping my chin towards her apron, "You best get those to your mentor, I'm sure someone will greatly appreciate the pain relief."

She gave me a relieved smile, dipping her head in a little bow, before heading off. "Oh," I said suddenly, reaching out to stop her, "You have thirty-seven by the way, grab three more before you go back."

She peered into her makeshift sack before looking back up at me with a grin, running towards where I'm guessing the stores were being held. "Thank you so much."

A woman, who couldn't have looked any older than me but somehow carried herself with the no-nonsense command of a war general, took her place. She was dressed in the Zuberi dark blue, the family's crest marking her tunic, and her black hair was pulled up into a tight bun. Her dark brown skin was a pleasant contrast to the stark environment, and her dark mahogany eyes held an intelligent, sharp spark.

Similarly to almost every healer in the tent, she had a visible sheen to her skin. Nothing that would make someone glance twice at, or even pick up on unless close by, but when the light hit her skin just right it shimmered. It wasn't as flashy as Nala's embers or some of the other Aetherian traits I had seen, but there was a subtle beauty to it that could not be beat.

For some reason she seemed—felt—familiar. It was just on the tip of my tongue as to why, an itch building at the back of my mind.

Stopping before me the woman bowed, bending her knees slightly and dipping her head with a hand across her chest. "Your Majesty, you honor us."

"Oh no, please, you are dealing with too much to be concerned with formality," I asserted, motioning for her to stand. Straightening the woman didn't hesitate to meet my gaze, lasting longer than I would have thought, before shifting her eyes up to settle between my brows.

"My name is Moian," she said politely, "The Mender of Eskira."

Despite not understanding, her tone implied its importance. "It's my pleasure to meet you, Mender Moian," I greeted respectfully. Queen or not, this woman and her team deserved the respect owed to them for treating and caring for our wounded.

"Forgive me if my assumptions are misplaced, but you strike me as a woman I may have met in my past life. I apologize if that is true, my memories have yet to return to me."

"Ah," she replied, a flash of understanding entering her dark gaze. "Yes, we did meet long ago. I was born around the same time as Lord Cashim, we grew up together as childhood friends, and if I remember correctly we were mostly under your feet causing trouble. You were always so kind to us, even joining in on the fun every once in a while."

I smiled at her warm tone, the memories seeming to be fond ones.

I may have had conflicted feelings about who I was, but knowing that maybe my past life hadn't been so different brought me some peace.

"I don't mean to be rude, Your Majesty," she said, her brows drawing together, "but how can we help you?"

"I've actually come to help you, if you'll have me. I have magic to burn, although I'm not sure how much help I can be with that, but I know how to heal the natural way as well."

"We would be happy to have you," she expressed, relief in every word. "Truth be told, we're all running on fumes and we're burning through our magic quickly."

She motioned for me to follow, walking over to a group of four healers in the center. All of them were bent over a patient on one of the surgical tables, their hushed whispers and frantic movements making me uneasy.

Clicking her tongue against the roof of her mouth, Moian waved the healers aside so that we could stand next to the man resting on the wooden crates.

"His name?" I asked the healers, peering down at the badly wounded soldier. He was lying unconscious with deep bloody scratches marking his bare chest. The veins of black and green that snaked out from the cuts had only just begun to crawl along his sternum, but his unresponsive state was concerning.

"Wylan, my queen."

I looked around the main tent, at the other cots filled with people, although it didn't appear anyone else had been affected yet. "How many others?"

Moian pointed towards the back tent, the cots inside barely visible through the connected opening. " Forty-two so far."

I whipped my head towards her, my disbelief clear as I clarified, "Forty-two?"

She inclined her head, despair pinching the corners of her eyes. "Yes, unfortunately nothing we do seems to help much. By the time we even know they've been infected it's too late. It seems that only some of the wraiths carry the disease on their claws or teeth, so unless we find a way to test for it before they fall unconscious, we're playing a guessing game with all of them."

"Has the warlo—" I paused, forgetting how much had changed in such a short amount of time. "Has the king been informed of the number of infected?"

"I'll send a novice to bring him our report," a young woman at the end of table offered.

I shook my head, interrupting, "Go yourself, I don't want one of the trainees being stopped."

She dipped her head in a bow before rushing out of the tent and into the stream of activity outside.

"How many do we have showing signs with each hour?" I asked, glancing between the remaining healers.

"We haven't been able to deduce if there's a pattern. We've gotten as many as six in one hour and then sometimes we go three with nothing. The other infirmary tents set up around the camp are bringing us anyone who is showing signs of warping as soon as they can," another healer added.

"Warping?" I questioned.

Moian cleared her throat, shooting the man a pointed look. "The Warp. It is what the novices have taken to calling the disease, it seems to have stuck."

"It's a sufficient name," I replied, nodding in agreement. It did exactly that, warped who you were until there was nothing left to recognize. It ate away at your soul, the very thing that made you who you were, and turned you into a mindless beast that committed horrors at the whim of a demented god.

"What has been tried to slow it?"

The group grew dim, a dark cloud hanging over all of them. "We have tried nearly everything we can think of," Moian replied. "Some of our healers have burnt themselves out trying to support their patient's sparks, only for the warping to barely slow its spread."

"Any medicinal plant we've tried has had little effect, even ones soaked in magic haven't made so much as a dent," the man in green continued.

I could see the failures weighing on them, each one hitting them personally. It was hard work, healing. Not because of the physical tasks—although those could be just as grueling as any combat drills—but because of the emotional and mental toll it took to watch your patients wither away regardless of anything you did to save them.

Healers were warriors in their own right, standing defiantly between their patients and the elements that would seek to take them from this world. When they were unable to do that, it hit them as hard as it would a warrior losing a battle. I had seen Maris experience the same thing time and time again, hopeless to do nothing but try.

Reaching my fingers out, I hovered them over the gaping wounds that covered Wylan's chest. The gashes had been packed with gauze, the thin white material having long turned red. Without even touching the crawling infection I could feel its taint, pulsing steadily beneath his skin. It was slowly creeping its way towards his spark, the heart of his magic.

"What have you found out so far?" I asked, glancing over at Moian. The Mender would have the most knowledge about the disease. If she was anything like Maris, she'd been toiling over it since the very first case in Rhaelyth. They may have been the mortal lands, but this *warping* was very much a magical creation.

"The Warp seems to eat away at the spark, taking it piece by piece until there's not enough left to fight it off. At least that's our leading theory; to be honest, it's a very tricky disease. It doesn't act like an illness normally would to our magic."

Her eyebrows knitted together, lips pinching together in frustration. "There haven't been many diseases in history that have affected Descendents, certainly none like this, but even the few that have been able to spread into our populations don't react like this one."

"What can I do to help? It seems likely that Kanan and I might have some immunity to it. I was attacked during my Awakening and have interacted with them enough that if it was possible for me to be infected, I most likely would be by now. I may be able to combat it more easily."

"We've seen the most progress when we assist and strengthen the spark," a blue cloaked healer answered, her dark skin shimmering faintly in the lamp light.

"How do you do that?" I grimaced at my own question. Some goddess queen I was. "Unfortunately when my power returned, my memories did not come with it."

Instead of the sneers or confused glances I expected, Moian smiled kindly, placing her hand on my shoulder and squeezing gently.

"Healing is much more instinctive than you would think, especially for those who already have an intuition for it. This is more about sharing energy than shaping it into any one thing," she explained. "It can be difficult in many ways, strengthening one's spark with your power is dangerous if you get in too deep. Too much power could overload the spark, doing as much damage as doing nothing."

"Then I don't think I have to tell you how bad this could go," I laughed warily, the self-deprecation thick in my voice.

"Under normal circumstances I wouldn't have anyone do this without proper training, but these are not normal circumstances. You may be the only one strong enough to give any of the infected a fighting chance until we find a way to cure them."

The danger I could place these warriors in didn't sit well with me, but Moian was right. Kasis had set a plague upon the world, a sickness that had somehow been able to render the Descendent's near-immortality useless. Despite the tumultuous feelings I had towards my new reality, if there was any foil to Kasis and his plans, it was Kanan and I.

If that meant I could help the sick fight off the Warp for a little longer, I had to try.

"Okay," I relented. "What do I need to do?"

"You'll make contact with him," she said, gesturing to Wylan. "It'll initiate an easier transfer between your energy and his. If you allow your magic to, traces of it will reach out to him and should become aware of the disease inside. You need to be careful," she warned, her voice grave, "When you find his spark you need to make sure you don't become too wrapped up in his emotions, his thoughts, and memories—that is when you'll be at your most vulnerable, which could give this necrose illness the entry it needs to infect you."

Rolling my shoulders back, I took a deep, steadying breath. Locking eyes with Moian for a split second, her encouraging nod was enough to steel my nerves. "We're right here. If we need to, we'll help break the connection."

Nodding I moved my hand up, gently placing it on Wylan's unblemished shoulder. Closing my eyes, I slowed down my breathing, easing the air in and out of my lungs. I was tense, muscles clenched since camp had been made, fighting against the total wave of magic inside that was just waiting to burst free.

Gently releasing the grip I had on myself, on my magic, I sucked in a breath nearly jumping forward from the force as it unleashed itself. Every instinct in me wanted to fight against the amount of power, but instead I let it pour through me, shifting through my veins.

Building in my hand, it poured into Wylan. Still unconscious he arched up as the ancient magic entered his body without mercy.

My heart raced as the energy forged ahead. I did what little I could to guide it—restrain some of its strength—relying on sheer will rather than control. Wraiths had turned to ash with my power inside them, leaving not even an ember behind, the last thing Wylan needed right now was another creation of the Cosmos fucking him over.

I wasn't completely sure what I was looking for, only that I had a feeling I would know when my magic found it. It was all instinct, Moian had said; I could only hope my instinct would override whatever barrier stood between me and my memories.

Almost immediately I could feel a sense of wrongness inside him, a nauseating twist in my stomach, like when the ground drops out from beneath your feet. It was a sludge, sticking to every inch of him it could reach.

Whatever it was pulled at me, trying to weigh me down until I sank beneath the oily pit. In my mind's eye I could picture it, a contorted green and black amalgamation. Thrashing like some rabid beast.

While Wylan's body didn't show many markers yet, the rot had already started to set in, chipping away at integral parts of him.

Sooner rather than later there wouldn't be much left of his body to recognize. Not if the putrid magic had anything to say about it.

Without much thought my magic forced its way forward, sensing far more than I could comprehend, a golden beam of light in the dark muck.

I tried to feel for Wylan's spark. The warping inside him took notice, moving in on the intruding presence. It seemed to circle around me, like it was looking for weaknesses, sizing up its competition. The sense of being watched washed over me, a foreboding feeling tickling at the back of my neck.

Staying put, needing to see what would happen, more energy bolstered the power I had pushed into Wylan. The gold ray glowed brighter, fizzing and crackling. Finally, an oil black tendril, a sinister green swirling through it, cautiously reached out.

It barely grazed my light, before a full body flinch went through me. A wave of nausea hit me, bile rising in my throat, as the tendril reared back in pain. The Warp's writhing mass seemed to screech in both anger and agony.

"Your Majesty," Moian's voice carved through the haze, almost sounding like I was underwater.

Splitting my attention, keeping it mostly on the god-created disease, I opened my eyes. Everything seemed out of focus, but I could tell Moian had moved to the opposite side of the table from me and looked on with concern.

"Are you alright, Your Majesty?" she asked anxiously, glancing down to where my hand came in contact with Wylan's wounded body.

"It's more intelligent than I thought it would be," I quietly muttered, as I tried to keep my concentration. The waves of sickness kept hitting me long after the disgusting magic had retreated. Breathing through it, refusing to break my hold despite the overwhelming need to vomit.

By the look in Moian's eyes, she understood what I meant. "Have you seen it?" her voice was riddled with questions and urgency, "It always leaves us alone when we try to contain it."

So it had sought me out for a reason, possibly because of who its maker was. I filed that away for later as the hair all along my body stood up, unsettled by the littlest touch from the rot.

"It tried to touch my energy," I added, the revulsion clear in my tone, hoping someone was recording down the whole interaction.

The mass of black and green appeared to get itself back under control, the feeling of being circled, watched, starting up again.

Moian's eyes went wide in shock, and she appeared speechless. Somehow I was able to get the queasiness to abate, a warmth overtaking me. I tried to urge my power on, relieved when it answered in turn, ensuring no spot was open to an attack.

I closed my eyes again, focusing all my attention back on the insidious disease spreading through not only Wylan's body, but his magic as well. Everywhere I looked was covered in green slime, black tar. It was a wonder that Wylan didn't look any worse than he already did.

I had no clue how I was going to find his spark in this mess, for all I knew it could have already been consumed by now. Doing the only thing I could think of I attempted to send out a pulse of energy, similar to how I checked for anyone left in Kasis's stronghold, hoping that even if only a sliver of Wylan was left, I could find it.

Compliant for now, a wave gleaming power shot out, exploding to life in my mind's eye. Seconds felt like hours, but just as I was giving up hope, I felt it. A dull, pathetic ping in the back of my mind. A call for help. It didn't take much to find his spark after that, the pulse leading my aether to where it had hidden itself away.

The spark manifested as a burnt orange orb, cowering deep in the recesses of Wylan's energy. It was dim and weak, but it still glowed with an inner light. He wasn't completely lost to us just yet.

Unfortunately the Warp took notice and started inching its way towards the magical heart. My energy pushed forward instinctively, surrounding the orange globe until the ugly disease couldn't reach it without first hurting itself.

Angered, it swiped out, coming so close to connecting but at the last second it pulled back. If the swirling, oily mass of corruption were a person it would have been glaring at me murderously, its harmful intent clear.

There was no doubt in my mind that the second my magic pulled back, it would swarm the sunset-colored spark and swallow it whole. Wylan would be no more and instead be replaced as a vessel for Kasis to use to inflict pain and sorrow.

An instinct took over, the itch at the back of my mind becoming incessant, and without knowing exactly what I was doing, I began healing the small flame of magic. I connected to him, and in doing so I learned so much.

He was a Cynthonian, a falcon-like creature to be exact, and for some reason I could tell he had no pair. Perhaps it was the slight tint of hopelessness that hovered around the edges of his mind or the lack of a tether connected to his magic. Either way, he was incredibly weak from the sickness and was barely hanging on.

Unsure how I eased my power into his, gently strengthening it, not too much for fear it would overwhelm him; but just enough that the dim orange glow began to brighten. Slowly, making sure to keep it contained within my sphere of power, it grew.

My energy took over, stitching together the splits and breaks—the edges tinged with black and green—that were threatening to pull his magic apart at the seams.

I grunted in surprise at the tug in my chest, more of my magic charging into the fray. The colossal golden nebula inside of me hardly flinched at the task. The knowledge that I could only use so much magic on Wylan, before it began to hurt him, hit me hard. I didn't know how to contain it, but I did what I could, trying with all my might, to slow the indomitable force.

Utilizing every last drop I was able to, I did my best to rally the spark. It was by no means healthy, held together by the last dregs of strength Wylan had left, but it would have to do.

Not giving the Warp any warning, my golden storm released its hold on the orange orb, striking out at the disease first. Energy exploded outwards, snapping at the foul mass. It reacted as if it had been burned, screeching and pushing as far away as it could.

I could feel my physical body begin to shake, breaths turning ragged and heavy, but I held on. Nausea hit me again, burning in the back of my throat. I dug my hand into Wylan's shoulder, refusing to let go. Hands gripped me from somewhere, holding me steady as an invisible battle warred.

My magic was followed by the orange energy, the aura wild and animalistic, as it fought against the intruder. Together my gold and Wylan's orange became a deluge of magic that slashed away at the foul tendrils. It's hold weakening on his physical body.

The near-sentient disease fought back, focusing on Wylan's orange magic rather than my own. Thankfully, backed by my power, it held on, refusing to back down even as it began to tire.

I don't know how long it went on. How much magic spilled out of me and into him, but while Wylan's spark was spent, it was still beating with lively magic. The Warp had retreated, not fully gone, but at bay. For now.

It was eerie how I could feel it pulsing with anger, pure hatred coming off it in waves as it waited, beaten for now.

Releasing my hold on his shoulder, I opened my eyes. The healers had gathered around, torn between looking at me in awe, and staring down at Wylan's body in shock. The trails of infection had receded, the black and green roots of corruption gone. The edges of his wounds still held hints of decay, the muscle tissue beneath sicklier than normal, but otherwise there was no other trace of the Warp.

I wasn't fooled, knew it still hid inside Wylan waiting for the opportunity to strike again. This was no normal sickness. No normal plague. It had been forged from evil, and its creation reflected that. Fueled by an unnatural magic, it was more alive than any real illness, and it was intent on acting in the interests of its master.

"My queen?" Moian questioned, worry etched on her lovely face.

"I'm alright," I reply, taking a few gulping breaths before checking on the still unconscious man, "How is he?"

At that the healers jumped into action, Moian filling me in. "He began to glow right as you tensed, we argued whether to pull you out, but then the rot began to recede. What can you tell us?"

Receiving reassuring nods from the healers checking him over, I begin to replay the entire encounter. Making sure to leave out no detail as someone began writing everything down on a piece of blue-gray parchment.

"It's much smarter than I thought, intelligent even," I mentioned, making sure the gravity of the situation was not lost on them. "It was created by a god stricken by madness, so I shouldn't be surprised. Do not catch yourself unaware in its presence if it focuses on you. We aren't sure of its capabilities within a body or vessel of some kind. If it has the ability, I would not put it past it to attempt to take you over from within a patient."

They all shared a look, the wariness I expected spreading through the group. It was one thing to treat and heal a patient's ailments, it was another thing entirely to go head to head with an adaptive disease created by malicious magic with a goal to consume the very thing that made you who you were.

It was intimidating to say the least.

Moian began ordering those around us, "Spread the word, I want every healer, aid, and novice aware; no one is to attempt a healing of a warped patient alone."

The group of three bowed their heads before running off, two into the connecting tents, and one presumably to alert the other infirmaries around camp, leaving just me and Moian.

"Is it gone?" she whispered, our bleak reality setting in.

"No, just waiting," I muttered back, looking over at her, our gazes crossing as I got my meaning across.

She glanced back down, pursing her lips as dread filled us both. She understood what it meant for a disease to be powered by magic, one that was able to adapt and that knew when to retreat.

It meant that unless we found some way to cure it, there would always be the possibility that it could overrun us, hiding within each and every person until the day it decided to strike.

"We have to figure this out."

"We will," I reassured. She gazed back up at me, doubt having crept in. "We will," I stated again with more resolve, hoping that I at least sounded confident.

It seemed to work because that calculative, intelligent light—that I was sure was the reason she had been made Mender—flickered back to life in her eyes. "You are right," she said with pure determination in her voice, looking as battle ready as any warrior. "What do you want to do next?"

"I want to try again with the other infected, see if we have the same results."

"Do you have enough power for that?"

I grinned, "Moian, I may not know how to do shit with it, but if we have one thing going for us, it's an abundance of power. I'll be just fine."

She smiled back, a righteous fire building between us. Both of us set on making sure this *Warp* was eradicated from our world. She strode off to the back of the tent, where the connecting quarantined area had been set up.

I followed after, preparing myself, leaving everything else behind. I even found some way to ignore that the light in the tent had dimmed significantly, and the shadows on the floor looked to be moving. I thought I saw red eyes flashing in my peripheral, but even that was pushed to the back of my mind as the magic beneath my skin pressed against its mortal cage, ready to fight a completely different kind of war.

CHAPTER EIGHT

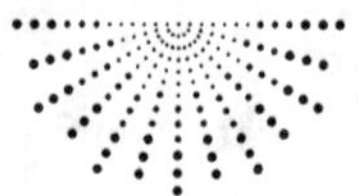

"Are you sure they're all still okay?" I asked, picking at the skin around my nails.

Moian smiled gently, laying her hand on my arm in support. "My queen, they're as stable as they were last night. You did the best thing for them, now it's up to us to figure out how to cure them of this horrid disease. Please do not worry, this is as good a time as any to move them. Waiting any longer won't do anything but delay the inevitable. We are at the mercy of our patients, unfortunately, whether they make it or not is up to them."

It had taken me nearly the entire night, but I had gotten through all of the soldiers that had been touched by the Warp. Boosting their sparks' power had varying degrees of success—for what reason, we couldn't figure out—but all had shown improvement of some kind.

It was a win we were willing to take given we had been prepared to light their funeral pyres had they risen as wraiths or something far worse. We had all come to the same conclusion and agreed that once they reached that point, where their spark had been consumed and twisted into nothing resembling life, there was no coming back from it.

Until then though, we'd give them the best damn shot we could.

Even I heard the worry riding my words, knew they were unfounded and that I'd done what I could to help the infected, but I still needed to be sure. "I can delay the journey. Kanan and the Council can figure something else out for us to get them there."

"All will be fine," she reassured me, "Hassere will have the equipment and medicine we need to heal the rest and keep watch over the infected. It's best that we move them now when they're stable, lest they fall to this Warp without us having what we need to prepare. Even with our attempts last night, we may still lose them."

And we both knew what that meant.

"Okay," I relented, "but promise me if anything happens during the journey, send an aid to come find me and we'll stop."

She bowed her head, "I promise, Your Majesty."

Inclining my head back in respect, I left her to her team, all of them working relentlessly to get everything ready for the long ride to Hassere. The river city happened to be the closest major hub of civilization to us. It would have the supplies needed to make it back to Eskira, as well as give the injured warriors that weren't infected time to get back on their feet.

Making my way through the deconstructed war camp, I passed crates holding the meticulously folded tents and poles, while aids and couriers ran through the crowd attending to the higher commanders within the ranks. Everything was completed with an efficiency that was nearing scary, not one person out of place or where they shouldn't be.

At this pace we would be on our way before the sun even reached its peak. The morning mist was lending us its cool embrace from the high heat of summer, making everything just a touch more bearable.

I eventually made it back to where Zanaya and her squadron of soldiers had been stationed. Most were milling around, placing the last remaining items in crates or loading them onto the large carts that would be pulled along with us. There were some that I even remembered from the many nights Zander had attempted to get me roaring drunk at the Rapscallion.

I smiled at a few, the memories fond ones even though I wasn't big on socializing. It quickly dropped as shocked and embarrassed looks crossed over their faces. They all dropped into bows, careful to avoid my eyes.

Loneliness shot through me, something I hadn't felt in awhile, alienation once again setting into my heart. I had always been on the outside looking in, never fitting in how I should. It was different here, of course, from my time in the village. The soldiers didn't hate me, first off, quite the opposite in fact, but this wasn't how they had treated me before and how they probably never would again.

I couldn't even blame them though, to them I was their long lost queen. Worse, I was their goddess. No matter how little I deserved it, there was no changing how they now saw me.

It didn't stop the isolation from creeping in, or the absolute wave of dread that crashed over me at the thought of my friends treating me as such. I wouldn't hold it against them, knew they had every right, but that tiny crumb of hope and trust they had kept alive inside me was begging them not to.

Nala's giggling laugh freed me from my spiraling thoughts. Looking up, the group that had adopted me into their odd family had gathered around their horses, chatting and joking with one another.

Saanvi was the first to see me, peering through dark lashes with her viper green gaze. Her pupils became slits, similar to Kanan's, but more vertical. She watched me approach, giving nothing away as usual. Her staring didn't go unnoticed and soon the whole group saw me walking slowly towards them.

I braced myself, the walls they had torn down already attempting to rebuild themselves. I took a deep breath, losing their friendship wouldn't break me.

It'll hurt, but you won't break. You will not break.

Unsurprisingly, it was Zander that broke the tension. Racing forward, his face creased in pain and his hands clutched to his heart, he threw himself to the ground on his knees.

"My queen! My glorious queen, you have returned to me," he cried out. "I begged the Cosmos for us to never be separated again, and he has answered. My sweet goddess, my shining star—"His face smoothed out into an expression of exasperation, hands falling to his sides in defeat. "You don't look convinced of my undying love," he whined.

I chuckled, relief hitting me harder than I would care to admit. Zander's antics immediately had me dropping my guard, as I'm sure he planned it to.

"What was it?" he asked in complaint. "Was it the pet names? It was too much wasn't it?"

Nala skipped up to the griping fox, patting him on the head as she said, "Oh Zander, leave the poor girl alone, we both know if she was going to believe anyone's proclamation of undying love, it would be mine." She winked, her yellow eyes flashing as smoldering embers fell around her.

Zander stood, wiping the dirt from his leathers. "Proclamation, Nals? That's a big word for you isn't it?" he teased.

"I don't know," she contemplated, pursing her lips as her eyebrows drew together in thought, "It's smaller than your ego, but bigger than your dick so I think I can handle it."

The gathered soldiers roared with laughter, taking quips at Zander's expense as he squawked outrage.

"Okay, that's enough, you two," Zanaya voiced over the rowdy crowd, forever the responsible one.

The red-headed rebels simply looked at each other and grinned, both grabbing one of my arms and dragging me into their circle.

"Imploding the mountain," she groaned euphorically, leaning into my side, "Downright orgasmic."

I glanced over at her, blinking rapidly. "You concern me sometimes, you know that right?"

The crazy pyro giggled, eyes alight with fire, "Yeah, but it's okay, I do that with everyone. Although I have no idea why." The poor thing looked so confused, I would have felt bad, if that comment hadn't concerned me more. How do you explain crazy to crazy?

"You doing okay, golden girl?" Saanvi asked quietly, not even glancing up from where she was organizing her saddle bag.

"Been better, but I'll get there," I responded. "It might take me a second to get used to everything."

"That's to be expected," Orion voiced, coming around from the side of his big draft. "It's not every day you find out you're a queen and a goddess."

"Definitely not," I huffed.

He smiled softly, reaching out to tilt my head up, his gray skin surprisingly soft despite its rock-like appearance. "Chin up, it'll get better, my queen."

I groaned, "Oh please not you guys too."

The stoic rock of a man only shot me a teasing grin—a rare sight—amusement shining in his black eyes.

Zander snickered, throwing an arm around my shoulders, "Don't worry, we figured you'd need some people to keep you humble. We can't have all that bowing and formality going to your head."

Zanaya walked over and knocked his arm off, shooing him away, "Go finish packing, trickster."

"Mayhem specialist," Zander stressed, mumbling his complaints to Nala as she pushed him towards their horses. Zander dug his heels in, dramatically moaning his plights. Her tiny form was comical as she dragged him behind her, placating words bouncing off the impassioned fox.

Zanaya snorted, "I don't know what I'm going to do about those two."

I shrugged, "They wouldn't be them if they weren't at least a little bit weird."

"Yeah," she drawled, "that's typically the problem. Too bad I love the shitheads or I'd drop them off in the Blackwood somewhere so that their own kind could take them back."

"Oh, come on," I joked, following her over to the horses. "You'd miss them too much."

She grumbled but said nothing, instead pointing to the bay mare next to her own gray. "She's yours. Her name's Neva. I went ahead and put your daggers in her bags if you want to strap them on."

"Thank you," I blurted, the genuine kindness lifting the leaden weight of past hurts, the group's welcome chasing away any sense of loneliness.

Moving towards the mare, I made sure to hold out my hands, allowing her to get a sniff. She blew out a hot breath, lipping at my knuckles. "Hi Neva, nice to meet you beautiful girl."

Her short ears flicked towards me at the sound of her name. I grinned, her sweet face and perky ears reminding me all too much of Gideon. Giving her a pat on the neck, I moved to the saddle bags that had been thrown over her hindquarters. Digging around, I pulled out the two black heartsglass daggers inside, quickly buckling them to my thighs.

"How long until we get going?" I asked.

"Not much longer," Saanvi replied, already seated on her horse. Most of the soldiers who would be riding were already mounted and waiting for orders. Those traveling on foot would follow behind, switching out with the other riders occasionally. "The king and the rest of the Council are already leading at the front, we should be moving on soon."

Stepping into my stirrup, I threw my leg over Neva's back, careful not to kick her rump on my way over. Zanaya followed suit next to me, situating herself atop the big gray mare. "A few airborne were sent ahead to alert the stewards of Hassere."

At my questioning glance, she elaborated, "They were put in place by Lady Yeva and Lady Lilyi. Stewards are instituted when the Aether and Primal of each city are away. They take over the duties of the city leaders and report on anything that needs further attention. Lord Elaric and Lady Oakina have them as well back in Ophineas."

"If Lady Lilyi helps run Hassere, why is she always in Eskira? I know the other Council members were already headed there when I showed up, but I noticed the lotus flowers in the infirmary."

"She splits her time between the two," she explained, "but technically her seat on the Council is as one of the two families representing Hassere and its people. They were close friends when they were younger, and she apparently spent a lot more of her time in Eskira before she took over her family's spot on the Council. If you ask me, she wishes she could stay in Eskira, but that's not always the case."

"Hassere is one of the most beautiful places in Allasea," Zander added, coming up beside me on a palomino stallion. "All of the main cities are. Nothing beats Eskira, not to me at least, but Hassere is something to behold."

"I'm excited to see it." I'm sure past me could remember when Hassere had been built, but I hadn't gotten a chance to see much of Allasea outside of the capital, and I was itching to explore. "How long will it take us to get there?"

Zanaya looked around at the gathering forces, everyone ready and waiting. "We'll be traveling slowly, the path we're taking is uncut and not used often. With the carts and wounded, we will have to guide them through the rough patches, but if we head out soon we might be able to make it by sunset if we're lucky."

On cue, a loud shout from somewhere near the front had everyone filing into line. Moving with the others, we maneuvered the horses along the outside, making our way to the front of Zanaya's squadron. It only took a few minutes of jostling and getting into position before we were off.

...

"But why?" Zander asked for the thousandth time, the conversation having been going in circles for what felt like hours.

"I don't know," Zanaya replied, rolling her eyes. "That's just what they do, or maybe they find you as annoying as I do and decided it was the only way to get rid of you."

The red-head seemed to contemplate this, biting his lip before shaking his head, "No, that can't possibly be it. I'm fantastic."

Nala's girlish laugh had me smiling, her bright yellow eyes darting from one thing to the other; it reminded me of Wrynn in some ways with his easily distracted attention span. I hoped the little sprite was all right.

"Zander, did it ever occur to you that the grellins didn't particularly enjoy having a fox sit at the opening to their burrow?" Saanvi offered sarcastically from the back.

I looked over my shoulder to see the trickster thinking over that answer with a boyish pout. "I just wanted to see if they really shit diamonds. I don't know what's so bad about that." He threw his hands up in exasperation, letting go of the reins and startling the palomino he rode.

I turned back around, silently chuckling. Zanaya was staring up at the sky with her eyes closed, silently counting to ten before answering. "What's bad is that you picked one up and scared the diamonds out of it. And then, for some reason I can't fathom, you tried to cuddle with it, pissing it off enough that its squabble took turns biting you on the ass. *Moian* had to fix you up after that stint, dumbass."

The fox waved her words away like they had no relevance. "I still don't know why they shit diamonds," he mumbled petulantly.

"Because that's what they do," Zanaya stated reluctantly, her expression weary, already knowing where this was going.

It was silent for a second before he chimed again, "But why?"

The group groaned, Nala giggled again, and the whole conversation started over. It had been this way for hours, telling stories—mostly of Zander and Nala's escapades into trouble—and I had never smiled so much in my life.

The ride wasn't exactly easy, the journey long and rough despite the mostly flat path, but the company definitely made it more fun.

If there was one upside to this whole thing, it was that we were traveling through Allasea's plains. The magnificent land was like something out of a dream. Fields of colorful flowers and long grasses for as far as the eye could see.

The open air allowed us to see the four sibling moons in full view, their partially faded faces making their way around the planet, waiting until dark when they could shine bright. The magic that floated in the sky swayed this way and that, and while the hot summer sun beat down upon us, the crosswind breeze immediately cooled us off.

Wrynn would have been ecstatic, darting from colorful flower to colorful flower, not sure which he wanted to pick. I missed my little friend, wanted him here with us. I knew he could handle himself, had zero doubts he'd be just fine, but I still couldn't help but worry if he was okay. I knew he'd find me eventually, the sprite had an uncanny sense of direction that always seemed to point him where he needed to go.

I hoped he would catch up to us at Hassere. I needed him to fill me in on his side of this crazy story. I still hadn't fully processed everything that had happened yet. Right now, the most important things were finding Kasis and stopping this plague, everything else could come after that. I knew in my heart that it wasn't going to be that easy, Kanan's flaming red gaze reminding me of what else I had to deal with.

I knew he was being patient, waiting me out until I was ready to finally confront everything. He knew we'd eventually have to talk, figure out what we were going to do about *us.* In the end he was right, it didn't really matter what we wanted, we were Life and Death. There really wasn't any way to get around that.

And even now, conflicted and pissed off, I found that maybe I really didn't want to get around it.

That's because you're an idiot, Atallia.

At least I acknowledged my shortcomings.

It had taken us nearly all day, but after hours of riding, we eventually reached one of the two southern bridges that crossed the Dalisin River. The expansive waterway originated from Lake Thesian, which in turn received magic-laced water from the Crian Mountains that encircled Eskira. That is to say, I wasn't surprised the river was so beautiful.

The water was crystalline, clear as a gemstone and as blue as the sky. Similarly to the Falla River that bisected the lower and upper city in Eskira, magic ran through it like silk threads. Shades and hues of every kind moved with the current, making the whole river shine like a rainbow. Silver fish darted in and out of rocky crevices, purple frogs jumped around in the tall grasses that grew on the bank, and dragonflies that resembled jewels flew through the air.

The bridge itself was exquisite, made of a white, marble-like stone and carved with depictions of the landscape around us. The sun and four moons hanging above an open field with the wide river cutting across the front, plant and animal life in abundance. A perfect mirror to the real thing right in front of us.

It wasn't a large bridge, barely wide enough for three people to cross side-by-side, but the crossing was quick with Kanan organizing the force into lines.

He rode up and down the ranks on an all black whisper, the magnificent stallion taller than any I had seen, standing hands above the rest of the army. His crushed onyx markings shimmered against his matte black coat, as did his amazingly long horn, the color sparkling like a midnight sky, full of stars and darkness. With Kanan on his back, shadows twining around the both of them, they made for one hell of a sight.

Intimidating. Powerful. Godly.

The clairvoyant horse was one of the few I had seen outside of Eskira's borders. I was equally as surprised to see him being ridden. Wrynn had often mentioned the precognitive horses were just as picky about the people they allowed around them as they were about those who were allowed to hear their premonitions.

It was rare for someone to be allowed a ride, the bond and care of the creature was typically inherited through familial ties and by earning its respect, but most whispers would only have one rider their entire life, if that.

The bond between them was evident, the two of them moving together seamlessly. Kanan's strong legs gripped the stallion's muscled side, sheer strength keeping him seated without a saddle or bit. The bridle was made of only a few straps of polished black leather, just enough for Kanan to grip on to.

No one *controlled* a whisper. If they ever gave you the gift of a ride, you said thank you and respected the wild freedom they all carried in their hearts.

Attempting to saddle one would only end in being impaled by their horn, which looked decorative but was in fact razor sharp and deadly. Their magic, similar to the other unique creatures that roamed Allasea, made them some of the only things that could injure Descendents outside of heartsglass. No one would dare insult the horses to their face, not unless they were stupid.

As we passed them I couldn't bring myself to meet Kanan's gaze, the feeling of being sucked in overwhelming in its intensity. Instead I glanced down, accidentally meeting the dark, intelligent eyes of his steed.

Crashing waves breaking against the shore during a raging tempest; ebbing away only to come back stronger. An ethereal song cutting through the storm. Teeth chattering against the cold lick of a fro—

Yanking my eyes away, I pulled myself from the haze of the chilling visions. The sounds cut off, the black stallion threw his head up in agitation, prancing to the side until Kanan patted his thick neck to calm him.

The creature snorted in stressed irritation. I silently sent out apologies to the beast, hoping he didn't take it as a slight. The noises had haunted me since I had first heard them in the stables so long ago, and I had no desire to add anything new to my nightmares.

Kanan's narrowed eyes bored into the side of my head, but I refused to acknowledge him. I knew he understood what had just happened, knew he would want to know what I'd heard, but I was unsure whether trusting him with the information was possible. I was also mature enough to acknowledge the petty satisfaction I got keeping something from him.

Goddesses had their faults too.

I knew out of anyone in the world, he was who I should trust intrinsically. I was quite literally his other half, but our history showed that maybe that didn't play much into his decisions. But if he was to be believed, he had his reasons for keeping everything from me.

Pinching the bridge of my nose, I tried to take steady breaths. This was my problem, going around and around in circles, playing everything over in my head until I went crazy. Somehow I always ended up right back where I started, more unsure than ever.

We eventually crossed the bridge, the group hanging back with me to make sure the infirmary carts made it safely across without any problems. The passing soldiers all bowed their heads respectfully. I shifted in my seat, the undue respect making me uncomfortable. I didn't want to be rude, so I smiled and beared their attention.

"You look like you're in pain," Saanvi quipped, a grin curling the edges of her mouth.

I flicked my eyes over towards her, rolling them at her amused expression, before dropping the grimace I was trying to pass off as a smile. "I was never good at being social, I don't have practice with it."

"You don't have to be anything but yourself," Orion added, his voice sounding like he had swallowed gravel. "You are compassionate, caring, loyal. Protective of those you consider your own, and powerful on top of that. You'll learn, and until then, you're doing just fine."

The words were almost exactly what Kanan had said the night before, as if the universe thought that if I heard them enough I would eventually believe them to be true.

I peered over my shoulder at him, his calm, supportive nature giving way to a possible future where I could believe such things. "Thanks," I whispered. Even if I was skeptical, it was nice to know I still had people around me who had faith that I wouldn't completely fuck this up.

Turning back around I pretended not to hear Saanvi mutter, "Softy," to him.

By the time the last cart of wounded had crossed and Moian had reassured me all was still well, the burning white sun had already started to fall. The pale forms of the four moons hung behind us, waiting for their time to shine in the dark. The sky began to turn colors as we continued on, trotting to catch up with the squadron, pinks and oranges taking over the blue as bright rays shone upon us.

"Atallia," I was snapped out of my thoughts as Kanan rode up on his majestic stallion. Making sure not to make eye contact with the whisper, I nudged Neva over to him.

"The stewards are going to want an audience as soon as we make it to the city," he stated firmly, although he appeared no happier about it than me. "I'm going to need you with me when we reach the gates. I'm sure the scouts have already spotted us and informed them of our arrival."

"Which means the entire city will also know very soon," I supplied.

He chuckled darkly, "Yes, which means the entire city will be there to greet us."

I glanced over my shoulder to see every soldier within eye sight looking at us. Brushing off the unsettling feeling I got when attention was forced upon me, I gave a nod to Zanaya to let her know where I was going.

Tipping her head up in acknowledgement, she gave me a questioning thumbs up. When I returned it, she nodded in acceptance. Turning back I found Kanan still watching me, his heated gaze never straying.

"Let's go." I gave Neva a squeeze, urging her forward, hoping the distance would stop the ache in my chest that he created within me.

Coming up beside me, he trotted along easily. I peered over, his face set in hard lines as he stared out towards where the city likely stood, readying himself for battle it seemed. I couldn't help but wonder what sort of fight we were heading into this time.

"Are you ready, my queen?" The soft question spooked me, reminding me of all the reasons I was as twisted up inside as I was.

"I'm no queen."

Heading into this city, the title of goddess thrust upon me, I felt like nothing more than a woman far out of her own depth. Without hesitation, however, the dark dragon king beside me decided to crush that thought, determined beyond belief to make me see it his way. His eyes were alight with fire, unyielding, as he said, "You couldn't be more wrong."

CHAPTER NINE

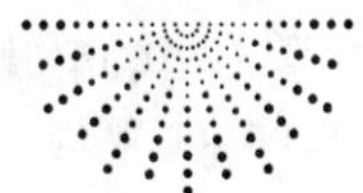

It took us a few miles to reach the front of the caravan, trotting along until the group of Allasea's most powerful congregating together came into view. It seemed they had deigned to ride together during the journey, although I had no doubt snipes and jabs had been thrown.

I almost felt bad about leaving Kanan to deal with it all, but then I quickly shook it off. Sympathy would get me nowhere with these people, Kanan especially. It was either stand my ground or get trampled beneath the weight of a strong, demanding personality. He was a big boy, he could handle it.

The Council members watched with reserved glances as we came upon them. Heads turned as we passed, hundreds of stares boring into us. We received bows as we came to a stop at the front, those nearest to us looking on with expectation and respect.

It felt undeserved.

What had I done to warrant such faith from these people? I stared out across the sea of hopeful faces. It was as if they hadn't been in battle two days before, nightmarish creatures attacking them with a perverse maliciousness, created from the diseased bodies of their fallen. And I knew that I was going to have to ask them to do it again very soon. The thought made me sick to my stomach.

Kanan, seemingly able to read my thoughts, glanced over at me out of the corner of his eye. I knew by that look that all I would have to do was voice my concerns and he would bear every single one of them without complaint.

I turned away, unable to hold the connection. Even just looking at him had the ability to make me feel too much. The jumbled mess of emotions threw me for a loop, swinging from one end to the other. Anger. Sadness. A desperation that was edged with something feral and unstable. Anger again.

I shook my head to myself, but that was all Kanan needed, his face going cold, jaw clenching. The lines of soldiers had stopped, waiting for their warlord turned king. Cutting through the crowd, bored indifference plastered on his godly face, the masses parted before us.

Facing the direction of the city, Kanan lifted a hand wreathed in shadow, and with a flick of a finger, the army was on the move. Unsure of what I was heading into, I followed beside him.

We were quiet for a long time, neither one of us really knowing what to say to fill the silence. Odd bits and pieces from the conversations behind floated to our ears, but neither one of us seemed to feel the need to join in. We were stuck in this strange place where everything needed to be said, but nothing was able to come out.

Last night had been the tip of the iceberg, barely a scratch at all the twisted emotions that lay beneath the anger. I wasn't ignorant enough to think that he didn't also have things he needed to get off his chest, with past or present me, but neither of us seemed ready for the consequences of what that could bring.

"Are you okay?" His voice, soft and quiet, echoed through my mind, brushing against my startled senses. I had forgotten about that little aspect we shared. The mental bridge that connected our minds was as clear and open as the sky before us, unbothered by our turmoil.

I could feel his dark, smokey presence at the back of my mind, his mental presence as recognizable as his physical one. It took me a second to remember how to project my thoughts, but once I did, I quirked an eyebrow at him, *"Is that really what you want to talk about?"*

He snorted, expression hard, *"You won't talk to me about anything else."*

I conceded to that, looking out over the fields of color. The smallest hint of a city in the distance. I could just barely make out the bright gleam of glass far out on the horizon.

"I've been better," I relented, repeating what I told Saanvi and leaving it at that. There wasn't much else to say. What words could sum up what my life had been like for the past few weeks? What about the life I apparently had long before this one?

"Despite what you might think of me right now," he murmured, his timbre glossing over me, *"I do understand what you're going through. I may have my memories now, but I didn't always. I know what it feels like to be split in two. When you're not sure what is real and what is a memory."*

"But that's the difference between you and me," I snarked, all the negative emotions jumping to the surface, *"I didn't get my memories back, and the few that I had haunted me and made me think I was crazy."*

He visibly winced, opening his mouth to respond, but at the last minute his jaw snapped closed. A muscle twitched in his cheek as I continued, *"And on top of all that, the people around me—the people I love—knew exactly who I was, and kept it from me on your orders."*

"On my past self's orders," he retorted.

"You're going to tell me that the moment you regained your memories and remembered everything that happened, that you ordered Maris and Geoff to bring me back?" A pregnant pause as I raised my eyebrows in question. *"But instead of listening they chose to go against their newly reincarnated king and keep me secluded in the Outskirts? You expect me to believe that you would have done nothing about that for years?"*

He didn't say anything, lost for words. I scoffed outwardly in derision. "That's what I thought. You had every opportunity to have them bring me back. Hell," I exclaimed, "you could have had them explain themselves to me. Gotten me to believe in Allasea and the Descendents, so at the very least I didn't feel so alone."

I stared at him, my eyes boring into his side, for once making him look away. I turned back towards the front, straightening in my seat again as Neva began to drift closer to Kanan's stallion.

"But you didn't. Instead you said nothing, even when I first arrived. Even when I was an anxious mess worried about Maris and Geoff," I paused, hesitant to say what I wanted, as if speaking the words out loud made them real. I didn't know if I wanted them to be, afraid of what that might mean for me, him, us.

Shutting down the defensive walls that wanted to shoot up at any sign of vulnerability, I admitted in my mind what I had known for a long time, and yet was still unable to say aloud. *"Even when I started to fall for you."*

His head snapped in my direction, eyes wide and holding far too many emotions for me to understand. What looked like hope shined in those red depths, nearly breaking something integral inside of me.

He swallowed harshly. "I have my reasons, and not a single one of them is or ever was to hurt you."

A thousand words lingered in the space between us as we looked into each other's souls, unable to help recognizing the missing piece of ourselves held within the other.

"And yet you did," I whispered, almost to myself. I didn't want to see the pain on his face or the resignation in his eyes. His small bit of hope slowly dwindling beneath my unrelenting anger. Whatever his reasons were, he was betting everything on them. It was just a shame that it had to be at the expense of what we could have been.

We fell back into a silence, the divide now a glaringly obvious wound that refused to heal. I felt my stomach twist, thinking about spending the rest of our lives with it living between us.

Soon, though, the sight of the city broke through my thoughts, tearing my attention away from the future and back to the present. Coming over the last rise, we were met with high walls of dusty pink stone marbled with veins of burnished orange, the bottom blending in perfectly with the magenta grasses surrounding the city.

Similar to Eskira, with its dark walls protecting an inner city of cream stone cradled tightly by the mountainous woodlands, Hassere was just as much an intrinsic, seamless part of the landscape. It would have been easy to think that it had sprung from the river itself, sitting snug along a bend in the water. I could just make out the edges of Lake Thesian behind the great city.

However, that was where the similarities ended, Hassere every bit its own masterpiece as the capital. The main palace structure could be seen from the rise we stood atop, smaller than Eskira's but notable nonetheless.

It was made of three main cylindrical structures of varying heights. The bodies were the same pale pink stone as the walls mixed with a crystalline glass that looked like gemstones. Instead of the spires I was used to back home, the dome shaped tops had been turned into giant skylights, the dazzling glass appearing as multifaceted as a diamond.

The whole palace appeared to meld with the sky as the sun disappeared over the horizon behind it. The beautifully blended color highlighted by the crawling vines holding large teal blooms that sparkled like jewels.

Accents of cream stone and white-washed wood only enhanced the rich colors. Like the capital, nature flourished in every crevice, terrace, and ledge. Large, drooping willows of color sprouted with abandon, similar to the few we had seen lining the riverbank.

Some of the ancient trees even reached far above the walls, their thin switch-like branches brushing the upper ramparts. A few saplings even grew from cracks in the sides of the walls.

Large birds, possibly Descendents some of them, swooped in and out of the shaded inner city, their wings carrying them on the gentle breeze that brushed the plains on an almost constant basis.

From what I could see, the lower city was just as beautiful. Buildings of clear, crystalline glass and river stone made up the majority. All of them looked like small greenhouses, the lives inside like hothouse flowers ready to flourish in the world.

As the golden rays fell upon the city, it sparkled, the light shattering in a million directions. A city of dawn and dusk, of sunsets and glass, a shining beacon of the sun.

"Are you ready?" Kanan asked, pulling his stallion up beside me.

He looked out to where there was no doubt a crowd of people waiting to catch their first glimpse of us.

I knew the airborne would have reached the city well before us, giving them plenty of time to spread the startling news. I had little hope that the secret hadn't been let out of the bag. It wasn't everyday the reincarnations of your king and queen—your god and goddess—dropped by.

"If I say no?" I joked pathetically.

He glanced over at me with the barest hint of a smile curving over his face, the dregs of our last conversation waiting in the wings. "I would probably tell you too damn bad."

I snorted, the honesty refreshing. "Wow, thanks."

He reached over and grasped onto my forearm, pulling my attention to him. The red of his irises pulsed outward, the pupils slitting into the diamond of his dragon form, before returning to normal again. "Really though," he said, "if you're not ready to deal with this, I would understand. I can make them all go away if that's what you need. You tell me what you want, little goddess, and I'll make it happen."

Despite my anger, I knew with absolute certainty that he meant it, and had no doubt that he would and could do just that. But what would that make me? A coward or someone in desperate need of time, space to heal? I refused to be a coward and I didn't have the ability to give myself the latter, so my decision wasn't really a decision at all.

"Would you run and hide?" I asked him, already knowing the answer. He stayed quiet, nodding his head to the side, his eyes saying all that needed to be said. I gave him a pressed smile, "I'll be fine. Our people are likely about to go through hell, the least I can do is show up."

He dipped his head in acceptance, before peering over his shoulder at the gathered army. Ensuring they were ready again, we began making our way towards the city.

The golden rays of the sunset competed with the first beams of colored moonlight. Day and night fighting for supremacy over the sky. Two undeniably intertwined entities battling over the inevitable.

The universe could be so damn obvious sometimes.

CHAPTER TEN

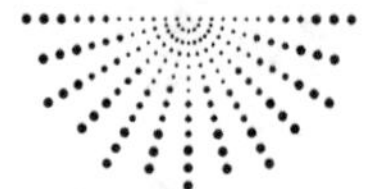

It didn't take us long to close the distance that separated us from the city. The closer we got, the more stunning details I could pick out. Like the large chunks of rose quartz along the wall that caught the light and refracted it back out onto the plains. Or the roots of the large willows, some of which peeked out over the top of the battlements, stretching as far the river bank and as thick as person was wide. All things that added to the city's unique magnificence.

As we neared the front gate, I could see that two large, white doors had been pulled inward, and inside the beginnings of a crowd gathered. We could hear them too. A loud hum of noise and commotion made it seem like the whole city was present, and as we crested the last hill I could see that I was right.

Hundreds were flooding out through the gate, even more waiting their turn to exit the walls of the glass city. Everyone wanted to get a look at us now that they knew who we were. Excited faces were upturned, those in the back standing on their tiptoes. Little kids were thrown up high on shoulders or raced in between the crowd to reach the front.

Some soldiers must have taken pity on those in the back as a new wave of people gathered up on the rampart, waving and cheering as we came to a stop. Banners and flags carrying the Divine sigil—our sigil—were held high as they blew in the wind.

The tree crowned in gold sparkled with each flick of a hand, its black, twisting trunk impervious to the bright light. Dark red blood dripped from its leaves, catching my eye almost as if to remind me of all the blood that had been spilled...and of all that would be shed soon if we didn't get to the bottom of Kasis's plans.

The warm welcome was both overwhelming and amazing. I was almost brought to tears, seeing them all so happy. To them this must have seemed like the beginning of a new era of peace and prosperity, a time of celebration and hope. I wished beyond anything that I could have given them that, would do anything to not have to wipe those dreams away.

At the front of the crowd stood a man and woman. They were both impeccably dressed and although they were surrounded by the crowd they still had an air of aloofness to them. Two well groomed aristocrats who had come down from their castles to visit the village people.

Or at least that's what they looked like. They kind of reminded me of the lords and ladies that sometimes walked the halls of Eskira for no reason other than to simply be seen.

Their clothes would have been acceptable at any high society ball, but here in this moment they looked completely out of place amongst most of the gathered group. The man was short but well built, sophistication surrounding him like a well-worn cape. His purple tunic was tailored and suited him nicely, complementing his sandy blonde hair and strong features. He held himself stoically, showing no outburst of emotion, nothing more than a reserved expression set on his genteel face.

The woman beside him wore a chiffon floor length dress in a lovely pale green. The plunging neckline bordered on indecent, dipping far enough to show off her toned stomach.

Although, the Descendents had never been ones to care overly much about showing skin, so it could have been what she preferred.

Two slits on either leg reached her hips and diagonal cut-outs along her waist completed the revealing look. Lucious brown hair was done up in a style that accentuated her long neck and caramel brown skin. She was beautiful, unarguably so, but the hungry and ambitious look in her eyes set me ill at ease.

I had seen that power-hungry, eager look in the daughters of the Outskirts. The ones with fathers rich enough that the only thing they would ever have to worry about was finding a husband who was richer. One who had the drive to take them far away from their boring, unnamed town.

They often paraded themselves around the square, hoping to catch the eye of a traveling merchant or passing dignitary. They always had sweet smiles and rose-flushed cheeks, all the while they could spew venom better than any snake.

I kept my eye on both of them as we came to a stop, my hackles raised. Just because one predator showed their stripes and the other did not, didn't mean they weren't both deadly.

And if Lars was any proof, simply because you knew someone could kill you didn't necessarily mean you wouldn't try your own luck. Arrogance could make you forget your fears, and fear didn't always erase stupidity.

Dismounting Neva, I reached out to pat the soft hair on her neck. Her coat was sweaty and she breathed hard, no doubt exhausted from the long day despite the many breaks we had taken, but the sweet mare reached back to nuzzle me regardless.

"What a good girl," I cooed, smiling as her ears perked up. Giving her a once over to ensure no sticks or churned up rocks had clipped her hocks, I passed her into the hands of a groom who had emerged from the crowd. He bowed his head, downcast eyes having gone wide at the sight of me, before grasping Neva's reins in two hands and walking her off to the side.

Kanan's stallion, whose name I had yet to learn, looked down at the groom who had approached him with scrutiny. The young man didn't seem to know what to do, but the whisper chose for him, snorting out a sound that sounded a lot like the draconic rumbles of his bonded rider, causing the man to fall back several steps.

It wasn't until Kanan unclasped the leather halter that the stallion relented in his crusade against the offending groomsman. He shook his head, long dark mane flying into the wind. Turning his thick neck my way, his intelligent eyes boring into my soul, he gave me an irked huff before walking off into the surrounding fields, headed who knows where.

"I apologize, my king," the groom stuttered out, face red and eyes turned downward, "I did not mean to offend."

Kanan waved off the apology, looking at me with a question in his gaze, even as he passed the bit-less bridle off. "It is alright, Cadoc is irritable on the best of days."

Cadoc.

It fit the horse who was so well suited to his rider. Dangerous and battle-ready at any moment, a true warhorse. Although as the large beast made his way through the pink grasses and into the sunset, light glistening off his coat, I wondered if he was as layered as Kanan was.

"Off you go," the scantily dressed woman sneered as she and the man—the stewards, if I had to guess—walked up to us. Well...she sauntered more like, turning her honey brown eyes on Kanan. "I'm sure His Majesty has more important people," she purred, eyeing him like a piece of meat, "to attend to."

The groom, a young man who couldn't have been older than twenty-one, grew even more red. His shoulders dropped in shame, the small blue vines that grew from his back and wrapped around his arms shuddered, the delicately shaped leaves drooping.

He looked like he wanted the ground to swallow him whole, a feat he might have been capable of as an earth Aetherian.

He tried to scamper off, no doubt used to the treatment from those who thought being born into a higher station meant they could treat others how they pleased, but with one outstretched arm from me he screeched to a halt.

Holding the nasty woman's gaze, with a piercing one of my own, I waited until she couldn't bear it any longer, quickly glancing down. My judgment of her was spot on and I paused for a second longer, debating if slashing out with a dagger would make the wrong impression to the people of this city, ultimately deciding that yes it would, which was a shame.

Looking back to the groom, his eyes were still cast downward as if expecting an even harsher lashing from me. "Look at me," I insisted softly, not wanting to scare the lad anymore than he already was. "Thank you for your help," I said when he finally raised his eyes.

Tilting my head at him, I attempted a kind smile. It must have come out alright because he relaxed slightly, a smile of his own gracing his lips.

"We've had a long journey, as have our mounts, and we appreciate the assistance. There are actually many more coming in behind us," I continued, looking over my shoulder to where the Council had begun to dismount. "Could you make sure there is enough space for them too? Maybe see if there are others who could help you? I believe it was only Cadoc who accompanied us," I said teasingly, giving the young man a wink, "so you shouldn't have to deal with any more surly whispers."

His smile widened, bright and full, as was the look in his eyes. "Of course, my queen," he replied with a bow. I lifted my chin to indicate he could leave, turning back to Kanan and shifting a glare to the two stewards who watched on.

The woman had a pinched look on her face, twisted in a mix of humiliation and disgust. She was the type to think *the help* was beneath her. I couldn't give a fuck, however, and easily ignored what I assumed was her hidden look of disdain. I had seen it enough times in the village to recognize it for what it was. What she was.

The man beside her had no reaction, silently watching, which in some cases was worse. At least I knew what to expect with the woman.

"Is she important," I mused, my tone serious as I asked, *"or can I kill her?"*

The darkness inside my mind that I associated with Kanan shook with laughter. *"As she was given her position by Lady Jai, it may cause some unrest."*

"Pity," I replied dryly, disappointment clear in my voice.

Kanan caught my eye, an amused glimmer shining in his eyes. I raised an unruly eyebrow in question. He just shook his head before looking away, but not quick enough that I didn't catch the grin he tried to hide, his lips tugging up at the corner of his mouth.

I tried to ignore the funny little flip my stomach did at that smile, wishing all too much to see its full glory. A small, possessive part of me hoped I was the only one that had seen it, his true smile. For it was a thing of breathtaking beauty, often making my chest hurt as I lost all ability to breath, and the idea of someone else getting graced with it, made a not so subtle green-eyed monster rear its ugly head inside me.

"Your Majesties," the silent man finally spoke, bowing his head, "It is a momentous occasion to have you with us again. Although we've already met, my king, allow me to introduce myself to Her Majesty." He turned towards me, bowing once more. "My queen, I am Leto Nix, the steward for House Ikaria. We once met many years ago, but I've been informed that your memories are not yet with you. If there is anything you need, all you have to do is ask."

"Pleasure to meet you. Again, I guess." His pleasant manner put me more at ease, but I didn't allow my guard to drop, knowing first hand how easily hideous intentions could be hidden behind refined words.

He chuckled politely before motioning beside him, "There is much for us to catch you up on, but please allow me to introduce you to my counterpart. This is Nissa Murelo, stewardess to House Jai."

Nissa put on a sickly sweet smile, venomous honey dripping from her petal red lips. Dipping low, she peered up through her eyelashes at Kanan, "Your Majesties, it is an honor. Truly a miracle that you've both returned. I do not mean to be so blunt, but I think I can speak for both of us when I ask why you did not inform us of it yourself, my king, you've visited our fine city many times over the years."

She rolled the title off her tongue, a sensual caress that was meant to entice. The slight possession in her voice set off alarms in the back of my head. She seemed to think herself a master of subtlety, carefully hiding her intent and desires behind thinly veiled intimations. Instead her heavy handed words and heated looks, eyeing Kanan up and down like she knew how he looked beneath his dark leathers, had me contemplating slitting her throat. Again.

It would be fun, watching her gag on her own blood, poisonous words choking off into gasping breaths. Or maybe I could convince the guards watching the wall to let me drag her up there by her hair before tossing her off. I think I would like hearing her scream, but then again, I wouldn't get the same satisfaction of having my blade coated in her blood.

So many choices.

I knew I was being irrational, but the knowing glimpses in her eyes had a black, roiling anger burning my veins.

One small, measly murder wouldn't cause too many problems. Right?

It didn't matter that I didn't have a personal claim to Kanan…

I sighed internally, that didn't sound convincing even to myself. Things were complicated beyond reason, which made her blatant disrespect all the more enraging.

So imagining her dying in a pool of her own blood to cool the raging fire that wanted me to scald her alive it was. It didn't help that the wave of anger that rushed over me at her forwardness was quickly followed by self-doubt.

What if she felt she could act this way because they had been in a relationship before? There had clearly been something there, at least on her part. I hated that the thought was even on my mind, but it couldn't be helped. Not with how rocky everything felt right now. With so much between us it was hard not to feel entangled with him regardless of the betrayal I felt.

Insecurities fucking sucked.

A part of me, like a faint voice echoing through my mind, whispered that he was a part of me—belonged to me—whether I liked it or not. We were something to each other that no other person in the universe could ever be.

The other part, however, didn't know how to feel, or think, or act. Everything was moving around me like a tumultuous storm, close to knocking me over in the chaos of it.

The irony wasn't lost on me. We had defeated Kasis for now, the corrupted God of Chaos on the run, and still he found his way into my life. Doing what he did best and causing problems that the rest of us were left to clean up.

Truthfully, despite what Wrynn had said about my eventually figuring it out on my own, I didn't know if I would have. Kasis's torture, his abduction, forced all the players on the board to move their plans forward, which in turn allowed me to find out who and what I was.

It was fucking with my head to say the least, no doubt to his satisfaction.

Kanan glanced down at Nissa like a cat did a bug, a bored sort of fascination that made me wonder whether he would simply watch in perplexity or crush her without a thought. "Because you did not need to know. If your patrons had no knowledge I don't see why you would think I would disclose that information to you."

I pressed my lips together to keep from laughing at his confusion. Nissa's embarrassed expression said she expected exactly that, and was shocked he hadn't informed her. Left gaping, she squawked out a flustered apology in order to save face.

"Of course, my king, my apologies for my forwardness. I meant no offense." She gathered herself quickly, her gaze turning calculative, before peering back over at me. No doubt looking for an in, a way to reach the top echelons of Descendent society. Too bad I was just as uncomfortable being up there as I was new to them.

"My queen, if I ma—"

"We have many wounded and our soldiers have traveled quite far after a hard battle," I interrupted, having no intention to deal with her for longer than necessary. "We will need to see to it that our injured are transported to your infirmaries. Mender Moian will oversee the transfer and organize the proper arrangements for the infected."

Moian would ensure the quarantined warriors stayed near her and under supervision. The last thing we needed was for my treatment to backfire and the Warp to overtake forty plus soldiers with us none the wiser.

"Of course, Hassere would be honored to host the Mender of

Eskira within our walls, along with all those who accompanied you," Leto replied instantly, picking up where Nissa's clenched jaw didn't.

"We might have to shuffle things around, Hassere isn't quite the size of Eskira, but we can make do." He bowed before moving to greet the Council, leaving us with Nissa.

What joy.

"Perhaps, My Lady," she began, stepping closer to my side, "once you get settled, I could join you for a cup of tea. I'm sure after all you've endured and the journey here, you could use a relaxing drink."

I just stared at her in disbelief. Was the woman blind to our situation, or was she just an idiot? "I think we have much more important things to deal with than tea," I bit out, voice hard and unrelenting. "Excuse me."

Pushing past her I started walking, no real destination in mind. A warm hand settled along my waist, startling me. Looking up, a devilish pair of red eyes glanced down at me with amusement. Rolling my eyes I shook my head before grumbling, "I hate tea."

His chest shook with silent laughter as he simply responded with, "I know."

"Who has time for tea right now? Oh, yes, let me just forget about the thousands of people currently exhausted and beaten up from a battle that included several warriors having their chests ripped open, and go have a cup of fucking tea. Because that seems like just the right thing to do at a time like this."

He just nodded his head along, shoulders still shaking as I continued. "She's annoying. And rude. Did you see how she treated that poor groom?"

"I did," he agreed simply.

"He wasn't harming anyone, and she dismissed him as if he didn't even exist. Who does that?"

"A lot more people than you would think," he replied with grit. "For too long the greedy have been left to their own devices. Two thousand years without a strong oversight and they've all but implemented a caste system."

He shook his head in disgust. "Those who are born into families with power or strong enough to gain it for themselves have taken to using that as a means to all but subjugate those with less. It's better in Eskira where our presence has always been felt the most, but you can still see the traces of it even there."

"That's awful, how could it have come to that?"

He shrugged his shoulders. "Time, complacency, opportunity, take your pick. Either way it has led to some rather foul personalities."

Pulling us to a stop I tipped my head up at him, his towering height making it difficult. "How do you deal with them all then?" I asked, the reality of my new situation falling over me like a wet blanket.

"Well," he chuckled evilly, "I typically kill them, or break them into so many pieces they see the error in their ways. Then again, no one expects me to be wholly good or merciful. Not as the warlord, and certainly not as Death."

I scowled up at him, quipping dryly, "That's charming. I'm sure they really appreciate your attention to detail, but what about me? What do they expect from the Goddess of Beginnings, hmm?"

He hummed in response, a ghost of a smile unfurling across his mouth. With him gazing down at me, with so many memories and emotions floating through his eyes unguarded, it was hard to keep looking. And yet I couldn't bring myself to pull away, intoxicated by the feelings he created within me. Addicted to the way he looked at me like I was his world. It made me feel overwhelmed and wanted and guilty all the same. Knowing that I couldn't give him the same back, not when I was just me.

If I was her. If I became Life, became the true Goddess of Beginnings, I could tell things would be different. Feel different. Because while this Atallia had begun to fall for him, starting history over, the trust had been lost, the deception and lies burning like acid in my veins.

But past me…

Atallia two thousand years ago was so in love with this man she gave up peace and calm for a never ending lifetime of heartache and happiness. That's why I had stayed away, even now without my memories I understood why I had chosen to observe Irropia instead of taking a form like Kanan had at the beginning of everything.

Life is messy, it's full of so many emotions and thoughts. Sorrow and joy can come within the same breath, loving something can be the same as smothering it, and pain can bring something wondrous.

Who knew those things better than Life, open and unguarded to all that she—I—had created?

I came to this world of beauty and color so long ago to help Kanan. Refusing to let him suffer his fate alone.

So I knew without a shadow of a doubt that the love we must have shared could have kept the universe alive. Remorse chewed away at my sanity knowing he still felt that, still remembered the things we must have gone through to be together.

To finally be reconnected with his lost love again, only to find that she has no memory of him. I couldn't imagine a worse fate.

He brushed a calloused finger over my cheek, his eyes searching for something that wasn't there. It affected him, that much was clear from the wince he tried to hide, but that didn't stop him from comforting me. "You're asking the wrong question, little goddess. You should be asking—What do you expect from yourself?"

What kind of question was that? "I barely know myself," I say, trying my best not to close my eyes and fall into the feeling of his skin touching mine. "How the hell am I supposed to figure that out?"

"Only you can decide that, love. The good thing about being a goddess though, is no one can tell you what you can and can't do." His smile was almost boyish, and I found myself laughing along. "Although if I can give some friendly advice. As much fun as killing her might be," he said with a knowing look on his face, "it will probably cause you more problems in the long run…at least for right now."

I narrowed my eyes up at him, "Did you read my mind?"

He huffed out a chuckle, his smile turning sad, as he leaned in, "No, I just know you. Inside and out."

"But do you though?" I asked, leaning in to him, genuine curiosity forcing me to face one of the nagging thoughts that had lingered since learning about my origins. "Or do you think you know me because a long time ago, you knew a different version of me?"

He tilted his head, seemingly thinking it over. If nothing else, I could appreciate the fact that he listened to my concerns. He didn't brush aside how his decisions made me feel or how unsettled I felt by everything.

"I understand your worries, more than you'll ever know, but a hundred lifetimes, a million, and I feel I would still know you to your core in every single one. The parts that truly matter don't ever change."

He tugged on a stray curl, the glittering strand throwing splashes of light around as the last rays of sun fell beyond the horizon. "Even if I'm wrong, and you somehow turn out to be completely different, I'll learn all the ways to love this you instead."

My heart pounded away in my chest, the air catching in my lungs making it hard to breathe. My mind raced as he bared himself to me. I had never felt lost until him. He was never content with the surface level that I showed to most of the world, he wanted it all. Dug deeper until I was forced to give it. "What if I'm not someone you can love anymore? What if every bit of the woman you knew is gone?"

He smiled then. His true, breathtaking smile. The one that made the sun look dim in comparison. It was magnificent, wild and free in a way that was contagious. Making you want to join in on whatever trouble brought it out of him. He was a stunning man, would always be, but when he smiled, when he let go of his walls and showed the world who he was on the inside, he was fucking glorious.

"She's not," he argued with not even a hint of doubt. "*You're* not. And even if you were…you could ask me in a hundred different lives, a million different versions of us, and I would love you in every single one. You make it easy enough. You simply exist and my world keeps spinning."

I let out a heavy sigh through my nose, giving him a look. "You know you're not making it very easy to be mad at you."

His sneaky dimples flashed, "Good, then it's working."

CHAPTER ELEVEN

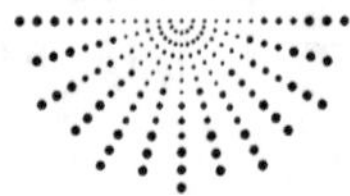

I wish the day had gotten easier from there, but in some cruel twist of fate Kanan and I were tasked with dealing with the tiring, and never ending, rotation of Hassere aristocrats. Lords and ladies of fair houses that sought us out for a variety of reasons. Unfortunately, I was told by an incredibly amused Zanaya that stabbing myself to get out of it was in fact *un-queenly* of me.

Some, like House Forona, who I learned were loosely related to Lady Yeva and House Ikaria, appeared to have genuinely good intentions, going so far as to offer their own home to any of the displaced soldiers.

Others, however, completely dismissed the problem of impending war in exchange for vapid, useless city politics. Because obviously there was no higher priority than jockeying for house position, enabling their abilities to push their agendas, and garnering the favor of the king and queen would accomplish that goal.

We were accompanied by Nissa, whose sycophantic flattery and feigned interest only served to make the entire thing unbearable. Throughout the endless cycle of the same conversations, she continued pushing her luck with Kanan. The familiarity with which she spoke to him, inserting herself in any way, wrecked my patience.

Threats of blood and violence occurred very often throughout the day. In my head of course, and fortunately for the stewardess they stayed there.

It only took me snapping at two catty, poison spewing ladies and for Kanan to nearly behead a snotty nosed lordling for us to call it quits.

It regrettably came just in time to save Nissa's life after the she-demon put her hands on Kanan again, all but offering her bed for the night. It was frustrating, feeling so insecure. I'd had my fair share of moments that caused me to second guess myself, but I'd never felt so unbalanced as I did right now. I knew it stemmed from my uncertainty of where Kanan and I stood, as much as I liked to ignore it.

There wasn't much to be done about the fact that we were literally made to complement each other, but I also couldn't let go of everything he had done. I had so many emotions tied up in one man, twisted in ways I thought they sometimes bordered on hatred. For him. Myself. The position he had put me in again. This place of helplessness to control my own destiny. It was a slap in the face to realize that maybe it was never controllable in the first place.

It was war, raging inside me. An internal battle of both desperately wanting someone while also wishing to stab them just a little. He wouldn't die from it, and knowing him it would probably just turn him on. That or make him laugh. Both of which were seriously dangerous for my health and will power.

Stepping into the suit that the palace servants made up for me, I wondered if he ever felt the same. It might make me a bitch, but some part of me would feel the teensiest better knowing I threw him off axel just as much. With that unreadable face of his, shutting down at any turn in the conversations he wasn't comfortable with, it was damn near impossible to pick up on anything he was feeling.

The room was wide and open. Large windows, made up of that amazing crystalline glass, took up the wall to my right. The open archway was draped with gauzy white curtains that led out onto a balcony overlooking the rainbow plains. Rays of multicolored light shined into the room from the moons that hung high above the flatlands.

Walnut furniture mixed with lovely sage accents gave the impression of some kind of forest or garden. Gold hardware was shaped in the forms of vines and leaves. Simple and yet stunning all the same. Nissa had scoffed in disgust at the poor maid who had stayed behind to ensure I had what I needed.

Apparently this was not a room fit for a goddess. I strongly disagreed and instead thanked the shy woman with the lovely blue hair that shimmered like the surface of a lake. The woman's timid smile had been worth it, but watching Nissa's face twist, embarrassment tingeing her cheeks, was almost as satisfying.

Rolling my eyes, I stepped over to the four-poster bed, unsheathing my blades and dropping them onto the coverlet. After the almost near constant chaos of the past couple of days all I wanted was to be clean. Maybe my brain would give me a couple of hours off to sleep instead of keeping me up all night.

Walking into the connecting chamber, a warmth skated over my skin. Someone had filled the claw-foot tub halfway, making sure I wouldn't have to wait long for a perfectly tempered bath. I could have kissed that maid for her kindness.

Turning the knobs that controlled the water pipes—I was still fascinated by how it all worked—steaming water began to pour out. Leaving it to fill, I stripped off of my clothes.

I kept finding myself looking for changes, skimming my fingers over the spots I knew had ripped open with each crack of the whip. After everything it felt strange to not somehow be different on the outside. It was like I carried a thousand new cuts on my heart and soul, but not a single one on my skin. Even the burns from the heartsglass shackles had faded when my power erupted, tearing through the last shards of that glass wall

Bending over the tub to test the water, my eyes stared back at me, the liquid gold irises holding far more than any twenty-one-year-old should. But that was the point I guess—I wasn't just any twenty-one-year-old. I was the reincarnation of a goddess that had lived for fifteen thousand years. That was bound to leave a mark on anyone. Not even the two millennia that separated my lives could heal the scars of those memories.

Dipping one foot into the large copper basin, my reflection broke apart, rippling away with the movement of the water. I moaned low in my throat as the warmth rushed over my skin. Stepping all the way in, I sat with my back against the far side so I could watch the door. Just because I didn't think anyone was suicidal enough to try and attack me here with a full army encamped throughout the city, didn't mean I would have my back turned when I was so exposed.

I'm sure old me hadn't gotten through thousands of years of ruling without being at least a little paranoid either. Leaning my head back I closed my eyes, enjoying the heat of the water, my tired muscles finally relaxing.

It was the first time I had gotten to actually process everything. To sit and inspect all the information that was thrown at me. I knew moments like these would be more and more rare until we stopped Kasis. This was simply the calm before the storm. A storm I had no doubt would decide the fate of Irropia for millennia to come.

Kasis had two thousand years on us, preparing for this moment since he escaped Death's grip. We had Kanan on our side, which was a blessing. I may be a goddess, but I was a goddess with no memories. Of her life or her powers. I could feel the bottomless well, a warhammer of power rather than a precise dagger. I could direct it, knew how to move it through my hands and release the concussive wave that would come, but that was about it. Sometimes you needed to crush mountains and other times you needed to lift a single pebble. I could do one, barely, but I didn't know how to do the other.

I was always considered dangerous, the villagers never knowing what to do with me, but now...now I was downright deadly. I risked hurting my own people as much as our enemies if I opened the hatch and set that cosmic power loose.

I needed to learn control and fast. I could be one of our biggest weapons, but at this moment I might as well have been a dull sword.

Fully capable of *some* damage, but in no way competent enough to be of any use.

Thinking of it brought the power to life. Light broke through the darkness of my mind, burning bright as the sun. A tug pulled me forward, and dammit if I didn't move closer.

In a daze, I was unable to look away from the primordial power. It felt like someone else was in control, commanding my body as they pleased. A part of me shouted, yelled and screamed for me not too, but I was helpless to do anything but watch as my hand was placed against the wooden cover in the floor. Beams of gold blasted out from between my fingers, shattering the blackness in a blaze of power.

That voice, a faint cry in the distance, screamed again, begging not to do it.

I pulled the hatch open.

Why are there bubbles?

My head whipped up as I was thrown out of my thoughts. I glanced around the bathing chamber for the source. The water had heated well past a comfortable temperature, and glancing down I saw the water had begun to boil. Gleaming light pulsed around me, illuminating the inside of the tub.

Jumping out as the temperature continued to rise, I ignored the rivulets rolling down my body, dripping onto the floor. The water immediately began to settle, the light nowhere to be seen.

A glow caught my eye. My skin was breaking apart, cracks covering my body, cutting across my thighs and moving up my stomach. The edges blurred where the smoking gold core shone through, as if it wasn't entirely a physical thing anymore.

It skated across my abdomen like branches of lightning, and as the rush of power hit me, a hum building in my ears, I felt my stomach drop and I was in free fall.

The air seemed to sail around me as the ground felt like it gave way under my feet and I dropped through…something. It was beautiful in a dangerous, hypnotic sort of way. The fiery light breaking through my ivory skin, wisps of aether floating free. More fissures split open, painless and otherworldly. Soon my entire body was covered and the bathing chamber was alight from the power within me.

The cosmic, nebulous tempest ran like a river inside the cracks, swirled through with flashes of vibrant colors. My vision turned hazy as a fog of glinting energy began to slip free, whirling around me in a miniature tornado.

It all began to seep out, leaving me breathless. My ribs tightened, compressing as if a boulder rested on my chest. I couldn't put two thoughts together, everything spinning around me as the room continued to fill. My legs began to shake, muscles quivering as an all encompassing weakness hit me. I fought against the plummet, trying to find the foothold of my power, clawing at anything that would stop the drop.

The onslaught wouldn't stop, my body becoming near transparent as I crashed onto my hands and knees. I gasped for air, but it was like I had forgotten how to breathe, my lungs refusing to expand. I wrapped an arm around my waist, grasping at my chest. I collapsed to the floor in a heap. My eyes burned as the power blazed, a wildfire of color, until it was the only thing I could see.

My mouth opened on a scream, not of pain, but fear, as it consumed me. Rising higher it broke my body apart until there was nothing left. Until I was pure energy.

I did the one thing I could think of and screamed down the tether that remained untouched, impervious to whatever was happening.

"Kanan!" I screamed, any other words dying as energy flooded my mind.

The thick braid of unrivaled black and sparkling gold shook with force at my call. The indestructible bond quivered, hammering in tune next to my heart. The link jerked, tightening in my chest like it was being pulled taunt on the other side.

On cue, my energy flared with a finality that had a silent cry tearing through me, a single tear dripping down my cheek. More intense than the sun, I was blinded as something deep in my soul tugged, trying to wrench free.

I screamed for help, the noise scratching at my throat, though no sound came.

A wave of black fell across the room, encircling the golden magic and me within its dark caress. Pushing the power together, moving it towards me, the smokey barrier refused to budge as the resplendent power tried to intertwine with it.

Slowly, so slowly, it began to filter its way back through the fissures. As the last few wisps were sucked back in and my vision cleared, I felt grounded again, no longer slipping down the slope into pure power.

I saw nothing but darkness as I lay cocooned in shadows. They wrapped protectively around me, not letting a single curl of power loose as the rips in my body closed. My breaths were shallow, body weak in a way I had only ever felt after my Awakening.

A cool, pleasant sensation swept over me just as two blood red orbs, a fire burning away mercilessly inside them, moved into sight. I wanted to let out a sigh of relief, but I couldn't seem to do anything but breathe. I blinked tiredly as each rasping breath eased the fire in my lungs.

A calloused hand cupped my cheek turning my head until I stared up at him. Worry was etched into every line of his too perfect face, a completely different darkness consuming him, his pupils taking over the pure red of his irises. His mouth moved but I couldn't make out the words.

Slipping his arms underneath, he cradled me to his chest as he lifted. Standing up his shadows peeled away, choosing instead to wrap around me in comfort, covering my naked body. I relaxed into him, soaking in the warmth of the fire blazing in his chest. I would think about my actions later, but at this moment I trusted him implicitly.

Leaning into the crook of his neck, I closed my eyes as he led us out of the bathing chamber.

"Don't worry, love. I've got you." The smooth rumble of his voice finally broke through the roaring of energy inside me. His words circled around me in promise. They were the last things I heard, playing over and over in my head, as my eyes closed and I fell into sleep.

CHAPTER TWELVE

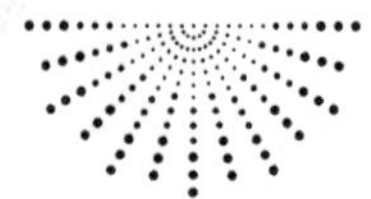

I woke to gentle darkness, a soft light playing against the walls. It was quiet except for the occasional pop of a fire somewhere around me. Sitting up slowly, I quickly realized I was no longer in my room.

The pastels and soft furnishings had been replaced with dark wood and velvet blacks. The large four-poster bed I was in could have held at least four people. The sheets were soft as silk and a black fur blanket had been laid over me. The fireplace I heard was situated exactly opposite the bed on the far wall, a sitting area set up around it. And sitting casually in a high back chair, a glass of amber liquid held loosely in his hand, was Kanan.

He was staring into the fire, oblivious to the fact that he looked like sin incarnate. With his long legs stretched out, dark leather encasing his muscles, and the thin linen tunic he wore that stretched across his shoulders. It was the same color as the shadows that climbed around the back of his pseudo-throne, curling over his ear as if whispering all the secrets that happened in the dark.

He dragged his fingers over his lips in thought, only drawing my attention to them even more. When it was like this, just him and I shielded away from all the world's problems, I found myself forgetting about all the things between us. During these brief moments of peace, when neither of us were battling for our lives or sniping at each other, I wanted to sit and listen. Listen to his stories, figure out what made him tick, and learn all the little things he'd never told anyone.

It was wishful thinking.

Eventually we would have to face the music, acknowledge all the problems that stopped us from having what we wanted. Sometimes I envied the naive and ignorant, but then I remembered a cage was a cage no matter how it was dressed up.

Throwing the covers off, I slid from the bed, the distance between it and the floor much higher than my own. I was dressed in an obscenely large shirt, the thin fabric hanging to my knees. I felt his eyes on me as I steadied myself, making sure my feet wouldn't fly out from under me, but whatever weakness had turned my muscles into mush seemed to have passed.

Gently padding over, crossing the plush carpets and smooth wooden floors, I took a seat in the chair across from him. I finally looked up and our eyes clashed. His were living flames, even more so than the embers that seemed to burn in them constantly. I curled my legs beneath me, turning to the fire, letting the waves of heat warm my bones.

"How are you feeling?" he finally asked, breaking the silence that hung over us.

"Better than I expected," I replied honestly. I would have been lying if I said the whole thing hadn't scared me shitless. "For a second there it felt like I was dying."

He hummed noncommittally, lifting his glass to his mouth to take a sip. His throat bobbed as he swallowed before he reached over and set the crystal glass onto the side table. Standing, he walked to the cart that stood against the wall, decanters of different liquids covering it entirely.

He was quiet as he grabbed a rounded glass and poured a blue drink over a block of ice, the easy movements seeming almost like muscle memory as he performed them so casually. Picking it up he strode over to me, gently setting the glass down on the table next to me.

Our eyes caught as he stood over me, the flames making his features sharper. He was shadow and fire merged into one. His raw power stroked along my skin, every hair on my body standing up at the proximity. The violence and strength that he carried always found a way to set me on edge, fanning my own power into a wild blaze that couldn't be stopped. It was intoxicating in the best and worst of ways.

He was the one that broke the contact, rocking back on his heels as he leaned away. Running his hand through his hair, I saw him close his eyes, a half-hidden grimace etching hard lines across his perfect features. Falling back into the high-back chair he lifted his glass and drained the liquid inside.

Picking up my own, the clear blue liquid was iridescent in the fire light, I took a sip. A surprising sweetness hit my tongue, a pleasant burn trickling down my throat as I swallowed.

"This is delicious," I said in appreciation. "What is it?"

His lips quirked slightly, a satisfied expression on his face as he stared into the fire. "Lunai, it's an alcoholic drink made from a fruit grown in Ophineas. It was always your favorite."

His last words were a loaded statement, a touch of something in his tone that had me narrowing my eyes. I knew what he was trying to prove, that me and my old self weren't all that different. Or at least similar enough that I should stop worrying about it. Either way I didn't know whether I wanted to be grateful he cared enough to help me find myself again, or slap him for his arrogance. Maybe both.

"What happened to me?" I finally asked. I had a feeling I wasn't going to like the answer, but if there was one thing I had learned through all of this, it was that hiding from your problems sure as hell wasn't going to solve anything.

"We call it *drifting.* You've always struggled to hold onto a physical body," he shrugged. "We couldn't ever really figure out why, but regardless, because of it you tend to *drift* out of your form when you're not careful."

I set my glass down, fully invested in hearing what he had to say. "And just what is drifting?"

"It happens when you don't have full control over your powers, and so it breaks free of your body. It tries to slip through the cracks I guess is the best way to put it," he surmised with a dark look. "You told me it feels like falling through the air, unable to stop as you plummet into your power. It begins with the cracks, they're your warning, and then your power starts to slip out of its physical restraint. We've had close moments, but you've never gone past that point."

That didn't sound good at all. "What will happen if I do?"

He glanced over at me, dragging his gaze down my body, taking in all of me. From my sleep mussed hair, to the triangle of skin visible at the neckline, and down to my bare legs that were curled up against the side of the cushioned chair. My skin heated under his gaze, turning into an almost physical touch that grazed my every nerve.

"I don't know for sure, but I am guessing it will revert you back to your original form. Pure cosmic energy. Whether you're sentient or not, I couldn't tell you, but my main worry has always been whether or not I could bring you back from that should it happen."

"How do we stop it from happening?" Because turning into pure energy, and only maybe retaining my mind, sounded *so* fun.

"You gain control," he stated, the hint of an order hidden in his cadence. He stood up from his chair, tall and commanding, and walked over to the fireplace. Placing his hands upon the dark wooden mantel, he let the warmth seep in. The light threw his shadow wide throughout the room, and I swore the darkness came together in the shape of wings.

"In case you haven't noticed," I said with my arms spread, "I don't exactly have the whole goddess thing down yet. I have about as much control of it as pointing in a direction and hoping it works."

He hummed in reply, the sound eerily similar to the rumbling growl of the dragon that lived beneath his skin. Taking that as an end to the conversation, I leaned my head back against the chair, blowing out a sigh through my nose. Glancing over, I jumped in shock as he weaved his hand in and out of the fire, the flames roaring as they licked at his skin.

"What are you doing?" I shouted, rushing to my feet. Racing to his side I yanked his hand back, clutching it gently in my own. I ran my fingers over the unharmed skin. Flipping it over to inspect the other side, I was left gaping. Nothing. Not a mark on him.

Peering up at him, my words of admonishment froze in my throat at his expression. His eyes were closed, hidden from my view, and his face was set in the closest expression of peace I had seen on him.

The tumultuous storm that always seemed to hang over him was gone, the smallest smile curling on lips. Finally opening his eyes, the pupils changing quickly from diamond slits back to normal, he gave me a wicked grin.

"You weren't worried a dragon would burn, were you love?" There was a devious note to his voice. I shivered, in defiance of the heat of the flames, my body tingling in all the right—wrong—places. Somehow he always made me feel like I had committed every dirty sin in the book.

Sometimes I wanted to hate him for the simple fact that he could pull emotions from me that no one else could. That he could break past my walls as easily as if they were not there to begin with. I had spent years keeping everything to myself, sharing very little even with Maris and Geoff, but no matter what I did, no matter if I said the words or not, he always seemed to know. It put me at a disadvantage, one that had me feeling vulnerable on a whole new level.

That was our problem. I was always the one left exposed, never given the choices, never given the chance to understand or explain how I felt. He carried all the power, whether on purpose or accidentally it didn't matter, and until that power was shared between us I didn't know if I would ever be able to get over any of what he had done. We needed balance and I wasn't sure if we would ever find it. Not like this.

His brow furrowed as he reached up to cup my cheek. "What happened there, love? I lost you."

Now it was my turn to close my eyes, leaning into the feeling of his rough, callused hand sending electricity through my veins. My entire body ached at the feeling, coming alive under his touch in a way that it never had before.

"I never know where I'm at with you," I muttered, the words like sand in my mouth. I hated them, but that didn't make them any less true. It was on that admission that everything came spilling out. "One moment I feel like you know me better than anyone else in the world. Like I can trust you. The next I remember exactly why you know me better than sometimes even myself, and I get angry all over again," I explained, a shaky breath leaving me. "One second I want to scream and yell at you for everything you've done and in the same breath I question why I'm fighting whatever the hell is between us. It hurts, hurts so damn bad sometimes, resisting this bond but I don't see any path around what's happened."

"I know I've hurt you, love, and there are no words for how that will haunt me into eternity. My words mean nothing, not after what I've done. I know that." He leaned down from his towering height, pressing his forehead to mine. He breathed me in, stealing the breath from lungs as he cupped my cheeks. "But why fight it? Why fight us?"

"Because," I say, ripping myself away from him, "what would that make me? Huh? What piece of me would that destroy if I gave in knowing that you still willingly keep secrets from me? You say you didn't mean to hurt me, and yet you continue to do so by refusing to help me understand any of this."

"I never said it was willingly," he whispered, eyes aflame.

That had me pausing, staring at him intently. "What?"

He took a step towards me, closing the space between us. "I said I *couldn't* tell you, not that I wouldn't."

My brows furrowed, the distinction was there in his tone. The difference being one was a choice and one wasn't. "What does that mean?"

The room darkened as he pushed into my space, his shadows crawling along the wall. "It means," he said softly, our noses brushing against one another, "that you're going to have to trust me."

"What if I can't do that?" I say impertinently, lifting my chin up at him. "You're the one who always says words can lie, how do I know yours aren't just that? A lie."

"I never lied to you," he bit out roughly.

I scoff, "Oh, I'm sorry, you're right, you never lied, you just never told me the truth either." I threw my hands out, my face twisting into something both mocking and hurt. "How fucking convenient for you then that you get to sit there on your high horse telling me I should trust you because you didn't outright lie to me, just by omission."

He just stared, jaw clenched so hard I was afraid it might break, but he didn't interrupt save for the small flinch as my words hit their mark. I almost felt bad, nearly stopped, but I was so fucking done with all of this shit, the half-truths and misdirects about ready to rip me to shreds from the inside out.

"Did that hurt?" I asked him, titling my head. "Did it hurt to hear that *you're* the one causing me pain? Because for some godsdamn reason it hurts me to hurt you, but I can't tell you why, Kanan. I can't tell you why because I don't know who the fuck I am anymore. I'm not her!" I finally shouted, breathing heavier than I ever had as the last bit of fight drained out of me. Shaking my head as tears filled my eyes, I stared up at him as I whispered, "I'm not her, Kanan. I never had a chance to be her because I wasn't given that choice. Even my own past self didn't give me a choice in remembering. No one told me any of this, and now I'm drowning here."

A flash of understanding crossed his face, and for the first time I think he actually heard me. All this time I had been trying to make him see that maybe I wasn't the woman he fell in love with all those years ago, maybe I was someone new and, more than anything I needed to figure out who that person was. Even more so than the need to understand the bond between us. If there was ever a chance for us, it rested on my ability to find myself again, there was no other option.

"Can you honestly tell me that you want me for me?" I asked gently. "Or is it because I might be similar to the woman you used to know?"

He was silent, a hopeless look sucking all the light from his eyes like cooling coals. I looked up at him, emotionally exhausted. "You can't, can you?"

Pain pinched his features as he struggled to put his thoughts into words. I could see the disagreement in his eyes, see that he wanted to argue that I was wrong; but perhaps it was the way defeat curved my shoulders or the weariness that was undoubtedly plain in my gaze, because he didn't say a word.

"It's okay, Kanan. It's okay not to know." A tired smile lifted the corners of my mouth, relief hitting me in waves as a truth was finally exposed. "Maybe you want me for me, or maybe you want me because of who I represent, but that's something that you're going to need to figure out. I've lived my entire second life surrounded by lies and half truths. It was all fake and I didn't see that until it was too late."

Making my move before I chickened out, I placed my hand on his hard chest, admiring the way it flexed under my fingertips, and went up on my toes. Cupping the back of his neck, I brought him down until our lips met.

Sparks lit up where we touched, the soft press of his mouth readying me faster than any foreplay. Moving my mouth over his I reveled in the way my body ignited, as if it knew just exactly who we had in our grasp. A single second had passed before he understood what was happening.

His large hands took hold of my waist, clenching around me like I was his lifeline. Such a small touch, yet it made the world feel right. He pulled me closer until our bodies were flush and I couldn't tell where one person began and the other ended. Immediately taking over, he swept into my mouth with a groan. He licked and sucked, pulling out all the unholy tricks that made me whimper and moan.

Dragging my hand through his hair, tugging on it to pull him closer, heat coursed through my veins as a delicious pressure built between my thighs. This is what he did to me, turned me into a mewling mess with an ease that would have spooked me if I wasn't drowning in his taste, his scent.

He made me want to forget what I was even fighting for to begin with, so I bit his lip in reprimand. The cheeky bastard just bit me back, his four canines digging into my bottom lip before he laved away the sting. Plunging back in, my mind was becoming dizzy on the hedonistic pleasure of it all.

Pulling away before it could get out of hand, satisfaction zipping through me as he tried to follow. I put a hand on his chest to stop him. We were both breathing hard, his eyes dilated with a crazed passion. A look that I knew was reflected in my own. I could feel the flush in my cheeks as well as the ache at my core, the need to fall back into him was almost overwhelming but my point was more important.

"The next time that happens," I said with conviction despite breathing hard, "I don't want to have to wonder whether it was real or not."

And without giving him a chance to answer, I broke free of his grip and strode towards the door. I reached for the handle but his voice stopped me.

"Atallia."

I looked over my shoulder at him. I knew if I moved any closer my restraint wouldn't last much longer.

"I don't want you," he said, taking a step closer to me, the light of the flames throwing a halo of fire around him. His words were a punch to the gut. A flash of pain struck me, rooted deeply into every insecurity I had, and a part of me panicked at the thought of losing something that hadn't even begun. A note of desperation, one that I wasn't even sure was my own, began to weave its way through me.

I would have shut down, closed off all the pathways to my heart, if it weren't for the look he pierced me with. It was filled with an intensity that rivaled the sun, a savagery of emotions that were jagged, anguished. There was so much of the dragon—the beast—in it I would have been concerned had his pupils not been round.

It said way too much about me that I was torn between running into his arms or running away from him. Something told me he wouldn't be remiss about either.

"I want you to hear me, and make no mistake in understanding, when I say that I don't want you, Atallia. I *need* you. I need you like I need the fire in my veins, the darkness in my soul. I need your mind and your heart, the feel of your skin on mine. The whimpers you make when I kiss you, the way you respond to my every touch."

He slowly, so slowly, stalked towards me. A predator on the hunt, and never had there been a moment when I had felt so very much like prey. The level of excitement that drew in me was bordering on unhealthy.

"I need that smile you make when you see something beautiful and think no one is looking, the way you shine with an inner light that could burn away any shadow. The kindness you hide away from the world, except to those who truly deserve it. That stubborn tilt to your chin when you think you're right and Cosmos be damned what anyone else thinks."

Closer and closer he came until he had me backed up into the door, arms braced around me like a cage until I was swallowed by him. His smokey amber scent surrounded me, that hint of darkness lulling me into submission.

He leaned down until his face was barely an inch from my own, our breath mingling between us. The tether that connected us tightened, my chest constricting from the near pain of it.

"I *need* you," he stressed. "And if I have to spend every waking minute of eternity proving it to you, I will. If I have to relearn every inch of who you are in this life, I will do so happily, knowing that I get more time to indulge in my ever growing obsession with you. I'll do all this and more, and do you know why?" he asked wickedly, a draconian grin curling his lips. His fangs flashed as he picked up a golden curl that had fallen over my shoulder. He rubbed his fingers over it gently, a look of fascination in his eyes, like a cat with a ball of yarn. Except this cat was a fire-breathing dragon god who didn't know what the word 'relent' meant.

He continued as if my silence was answer enough, "Because, little goddess, a dragon's treasure—his gold—is the most important thing in the world to him. Isn't that what all the fairytales say? Nothing, not even the Cosmos himself, could tear a dragon away from it. Seems fitting, don't you think?"

His words were almost mocking as he talked to himself, still playing with my lock of hair. "So run, hide, push me away all you want, love, just remember that I'm no man. I believe in a fair fight so you should know what you're up against."

His eyes flicked up to mine at that point, and it wasn't the Kanan I knew staring back at me. It was the dragon, an ancient creature of death, destruction, and darkness. Death came in many forms but his first was that of wings and fire. Feral power rolled off him in waves. Tame and controlled were not words that could so much as be spoken in his presence, let alone describe him.

I knew he wouldn't give up, it wasn't in his nature, and I'd just drawn a line in the sand, waved a red flag that he couldn't ignore. What he'd do about it, however, was less clear. I only hoped I'd make it out the other side with my heart intact.

CHAPTER THIRTEEN

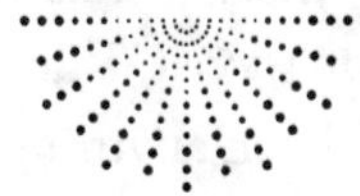

"There's been no change, My Lady." Looking over my shoulder, Moian stood in the doorway to the isolated room where the warped were quarantined. The Hassere medica was almost as impressive as the Eskiran infirmary, fully capable of handling the sudden rush of wounded patients.

I was in awe when I first saw it. The entire structure was made of interconnected circular buildings. The outside was cream stone covered in carvings of the plains outside the walls. Domes topped each of the sections, the crystalline glass fracturing the sunlight into a million beams of color that lit up the room.

"Nothing at all?" I asked in concern. I had hoped that whatever I'd done would fix all of this. It shouldn't be surprising that it wasn't that easy. Nothing had been easy so far, why should this? With Kasis's involvement it was likely more complex than we had even figured

The Mender wandered over to the two semi-circular benches in the center of the room. The stations had been quickly set up for the healers to monitor the warped from. She set the bundles of herbs that she'd brought down on the table, dropping her head as her knuckles turned white from gripping the edge so hard.

"Unfortunately not. They've all entered into the same stasis.

They're not dead, and they're better off than the warped I've treated before, thanks to you, but I don't know…there's something about this disease," she paused, a foreboding look crossing her face. "I can't put my finger on it. Whatever it may be, I don't like how sentient it is. It adapts to everything we try no matter what we throw at it. I almost feel like it's mocking us."

Moving to join her, I began separating the bundles into groups. "I felt it, the vileness. It's not wholly of this world. It's more of a feeling than anything, but it shouldn't exist. I don't know what Kasis did to create it, but it couldn't have been anything good."

Moian nodded thoughtfully, worry swimming in her gaze. "I'm concerned about what this could mean for our people, our way of life. We have always lived knowing that while we can die, it would never be from such mortal means as a disease. If we suddenly have a plague spreading through our ranks, tearing that belief away, I fear we will be unprepared for the consequences of our own hubris. We worship and respect Death, of course, but there's a part of us all that must feel we would only meet him after millennia well spent. I hope that our arrogant assumption doesn't come back to bite us all in retaliation."

"Well," I drawled, reaching for the ball of twine on the shelf underneath the table, "if all else fails, I happen to know Death personally, so…"

Letting out a hearty chuckle, she took the twine, cutting it into even strings. "Be that as it may, My Lady, I don't know if even the king can save us from this."

I felt she was right, the rising dread that seemed to be sinking into us all was telling enough. We settled into a comfortable silence, wrapping the herbs for the healers to use later. The repetitive motions, ones I had been doing since I was a little girl, had a way of stilling my mind. It was why I'd always been drawn to it. The same as Maris, and Moian, and probably all healers.

I loved to fight, appreciated the discipline and security it gave me. The adrenaline rush was always something to look forward to, but at the end of the day, when the fighting was done and it was just me and my thoughts, working with my hands brought me a clarity I couldn't find anywhere else.

Amidst the chaos of the past few days, I felt normal for the first time in a long while. Even as the medica's healers came and went, bowing or curtsying every damn time, it didn't bother me as much. A needed calm had settled over me, and I finally had time to think clearly. Moian must have sensed my need for silent contemplation, because other than an odd comment here or there, we worked together seamlessly without words.

It reminded me of how it used to be with Maris. Years of working together had made it an almost faultless dance between us.

As if my thoughts had summoned her, my foster-mother walked into the room. Her steps faltered as she noticed me, our eyes locking for a split second before her gaze dropped to the floor.

I looked back down at my work, refusing to watch as she continued on to one of the patients. Moian had implemented hourly checks in order to monitor any changes. I was surprised to see Maris though. I knew she must have been a healer in Eskira before she was saddled with me, it only made sense, but it was still shocking to see her fall back into her old life so easily.

I didn't know whether it was jealousy or anger that came to life inside me, but either way I didn't like how it made me feel. There was no helping it though. Here I was, thrown into an entirely new world, wishing I could go back to those busy mornings and quiet nights in the cottage, and yet she knew exactly where she fit into this world without having to fumble around aimlessly.

Resentment. I realized with a jolt, that what I was feeling was resentment. An ugly emotion, one I wish would disappear, but alas I didn't think it would be that easy.

"She loves you, don't ever doubt that," Moian said, her eyes shifting from where Maris was stationed to me. Following her gaze, I caught Maris peeking at us. She averted her eyes as soon as she saw us looking.

Shaking my head, I tied off another bundle, moving it off to the side. "That remains to be seen. The lies...you don't do that to the people you love, not about something as serious as this."

Her lips pursed, a sad look on her face as she watched me. "I don't condone what they've done My Lady, and I don't know why they made the decisions they did; but what I do know is that she gave up everything to raise you."

"What do you mean?" There was so much that I still didn't know about my own family. The early days with them both were clouded, the fog of childhood cloaking most memories of that time.

"She met Geoff only twenty years before she decided to retire from the infirmary. It was a decision no one understood." She placed her hand on mine, stilling my movements. "She was going to be named Mender of Eskira, everyone knew it. Then one day, out of the blue, she decided to take a temporary leave for some time in the countryside. No one ever knew why, but we wrote it off as wanting to spend personal time with her pair after all the time without one. We would get correspondence every now and again, but it wasn't much, just enough to know she and Geoff were alive and happy."

Moian's mouth twisted, her hands pulling and winding through a strip of cloth to remove the residue from the herbs. "She gave up her life, everything she knew, to raise you. So be mad at her, but don't ever question that she loves you."

I let out a sigh, eyes closed, the war raging inside me at her, Geoff, Kanan, everyone...it was driving me mad. I didn't know how to forgive them, how to move past the life I had already lived. It could have been so different, filled with acceptance instead of torment and prejudice.

"I feel guilty," I murmured, "holding on to this anger when I have such happiness within reach. Even with the threat Kasis poses, I know what I could have if only I let them back in."

Fists clenched against the table as the room dimmed, I let out a choked laugh. "It probably wouldn't be surprising to know I have a bit of a self-sabotaging streak. I'm jaded and cynical, and I don't trust easily, but I was made to be that way. They didn't physically hurt me—the villagers—at least not always," I muttered mostly to myself, "but they made me feel disgusting. Small and weak like some rabid animal. All for existing. There are others who have had it worse, but it doesn't make what I went through invalid."

I looked down at my palms, stained brown from the herbs, and clenched them as the tell-tale burn in my eyes began.

"I-I," I stuttered, swallowing harshly. I blinked tears of frustration from my eyes before finishing. "I was so lonely, Moian."

Looking up I saw tears of her own welling as I spoke. "I had no one that truly understood, not Maris, not Geoff, no one. I felt crazy. I woke up screaming most nights and the others I'd end up in the Blackwood with no idea how I got there."

Unclenching my hands when I felt blood begin to bead, I ran one through my hair. "The amount of times the villagers saw me walk out of the forest, bloodied, covered in dirt and leaves—I mean who could blame them for what they thought of me? Who wouldn't? For the longest time *I* believed it."

Glancing to the side, I glimpsed Maris as she moved to another patient with an aura of peace that frayed my already raw nerves. I turned away before my volatile power turned the medica into a war zone. "And then to know I could have had all of this," I said, waving my hands around, indicating far more than just the medica. "It's just hard. Hard to move on."

An understanding became clear between Moian and I as she nodded, although sympathy clung to her. I was grateful, however, when she dropped the subject.

Turning back to our work, hoping to find some inner peace again, I was startled as that tell-tale tug yanked hard in my chest. I jerked my head up just as Moian dropped into a bow and greeted him, but I heard none of it. Time slipped away from me as Kanan entered the room.

Like always I was sucked into his irresistible orbit. I was only mollified that he appeared to be just as stuck as I. Two undeniable forces circling around each other forever, never alone.

Snap out of it you fucking idiot, he's a liar.

Coming to my senses, I began unstacking and re-stacking the piles of herbs as I tried to ignore his presence. If only it were that easy. Trying to ignore him was like trying to ignore the sun.

He cleared his throat, the rough grumble echoing throughout the chamber. "Moian, would you give us a moment?"

There was a long pause, where she no doubt was looking between the two of us. Him piercing a hole into my soul, and me trying to act completely oblivious to that fact. "Of course, My Lord."

"Traitor," I muttered, glaring in betrayal as she rolled her eyes at me, gathered the bushels of herbs, and left with one last bow.

Kanan and I watched as she disappeared through the doorway. The tension was palpable, bouncing around the circular room without an escape.

"If I didn't know any better, love, I'd say you were avoiding me." He turned back to me, walking up to the other side of the bench.

"Well good thing you know better then," I replied impertinently as I placed instruments back into the drawers of the workbench.

He hummed in response. With a sigh I finally glanced up, catching the slight curl to his lips. Dressed in all black leathers, his favorite color, he looked ready for a fight. I wondered if it was me he was preparing to battle.

"What do you want, Kanan?"

He came in closer, placing his hands against the tabletop in order to lean into my space like he had every right to. "Are you still mad at me for last night?" he asked with a predatory excitement in his eyes.

"Being mad would imply I care," I replied without thought, lifting my chin with a boldness I didn't feel.

He stared down at me with that infuriatingly arrogant grin. His massive shoulders shook with quiet laughter. "Oh come now, little goddess, we both know that's not true. Even if it was, how long do you think you could hold on to that apathy?"

His grin grew larger, having fun at my expense as I ground my teeth. "Come with me," he said with a sudden seriousness, finally backing out of my personal space.

Confused, I was momentarily knocked off guard with the quick change. "What? Where?"

Looking over his shoulder as he made his way out of the room, his eyes hardened in a way that surprised me. "You can hate me all you want, but you still have the power of the Cosmos at your fingertips and you don't know how to use it. I won't have a repeat of last night."

I knew he was referring to finding me in the bathroom, nearly consumed by my own power. "What are we going to do to stop it from happening again?"

He turned at the doorway, staring at me with a determination that looked to be backed by fear. Because I wasn't already terrified enough.

"We're going to train, love."

CHAPTER FOURTEEN

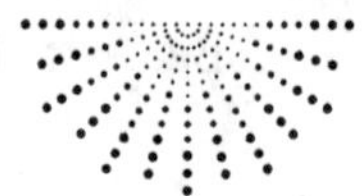

"Where are we going?" I asked. We'd left the medica behind, the sparkling building of crystal and stone growing smaller as we walked through the city streets. Kanan led us through the bustling crowds without so much as a hesitant step, ignoring the shell-shocked faces and reverent touches that seemed to come whether we liked it or not.

"You'll see," he replied, peeking over at me with a glint in his eye. Striding down the cobblestone path, the busy crowds slowly died down, the buildings became smaller, less frequent, as we approached the city wall.

The rose pink stone was even more mesmerizing up close, chucks of quartz embedded into the solid structure, allowing rays of sunlight to scatter across the city. A massive willow clung to the side, ancient and twisted by centuries of wind, it was as much a part of the wall as it was the earth below. Delicate yellow leaves covered the thin drooping branches, glowing in the day's light like crafted metal.

It stood sentry beside a dozen guards on the battlement, watching over one of the city's gates. The watchman bowed their heads, but otherwise kept their position as we walked under the archway and out onto the open plains.

The shimmering waters of Lake Thesian stretched out before us as far as the eye could see. The Dalisin river was birthed from this very lake, yet it paled in comparison. So full of color and swirling magic, the lake no longer looked like water at all. Lilac, teal, and magenta. Silver, copper, and bronze. Shades and hues, that I would never be able to describe, took shape as we closed the distance, the shallow bank with its tall grasses bringing us within touching distance of the enchanting water.

I had the strangest urge to dive in, to submerge myself under the lake of rainbows and add my own magic to its rippling surface. Stopping near the edge, under the shade of another willow with leaves of dazzling white, I took in the view as a breeze blew through, carrying with it the song of the tiny jeweled birds that had made Hassere their home.

"I thought you might want to see it before we leave," Kanan breathed. Coming up beside me he seemed to soak in the moment as much as me, looking far out towards where the sky and water touched.

"Leave?"

He nodded, squatting down at the base of the willow to brush his fingers across the lone flower growing through the twisted roots. "We need to get back to Eskira. It's our seat of power, and the most likely place Kasis will attack while we are stuck in this stalemate. He's not subtle, my brother, despite what he may think."

He wasn't wrong. Kasis was highly intelligent—crazy as fuck, but intelligent; yet every single one of his motives were driven by his singular need to possess things that weren't his. Most of which revolved around Kanan. Like a little kid who threw a tantrum because he couldn't have the toy his big brother was playing with.

More power. Respect. Me.

He could have had all of those things—except maybe the last one—had he just earned them. The only reason he was stuck in Kanan's shadow was because he put himself there all those years ago, tying his worth to anything that made him feel more powerful, more like the victor in any given situation. I didn't need my memories to see that.

So much unnecessary death, two thousand years of stewing in hate, all because of jealousy. Of greed. It was sad really, how far this had all gone.

"When was this decided?" Honestly the idea of going home to Eskira brought me far more comfort than I was prepared for. Freezing, I felt the air rush out of me as the realization hit me. *Home.* Eskira was my home.

The smallest of smiles curled across my face as a piece of my cracked heart put itself back together, healing over like an old injury. A memory of the wound that had caused it, but hurting no more.

"When you fell unconscious last night, I was actually coming to get you when—" As he stood he caught the expression on my face, going so still I don't think he was breathing. "What's that smile for?" he whispered reverently.

Smile growing wider, I let out an awe filled laugh. "We're going home."

The corner of his mouth lifted as he stared at me, but his eyes grew dull, the red fire that seemed to be perpetually burning growing dim. "Did you mean what you said to Moian?"

Turning away from him, I ran my hand through my hair, the strands of gold blowing freely in the wind. Avoiding this conversation for as long as possible, I bent down to pick up a flat pebble along the bank, flipping it over in my hand. The smooth stone was cool against my skin, mimicking the iciness that was trying to infiltrate its way back into my heart. "Which part?"

"All of it." He stepped closer, almost instinctively knowing those bad thoughts and feelings were attempting to get a foothold inside me. The heat radiating from his body sunk into my skin, searching me out inside the chilly storm, until the numbness began to fall away.

Playing the rock over my fingers, I glanced over at him, peeking up through my lashes. He waited patiently, his gaze searching, always looking for something. Nodding, I turned back to the lake, swinging my arm back to throw the pebble.

"Yeah, I meant it," I replied, watching as the stone skipped across the surface of the water. One, two, three, four times before it finally sank beneath.

I startled when his calloused fingers gripped my chin, turning it up until we locked eyes. His thumb rubbed gently against my skin, my heart rate picking up as a hundred emotions went through me at once.

"You know I'm not big on words, but I hope you know that I am truly sorry for the part I played in making you feel that way." His words were filled with regret so deep it bordered on self-disgust, and despite the betrayal I felt, I believed him.

"I know," I whispered.

Clearing his throat, he dipped his head in acceptance. Dropping his hand he stepped away moving back to the small flower, except this time when he brushed his fingers over its pale blue petals they slowly withered. Turning brown and brittle it drooped sadly, a wretched thing mourning its premature death.

"Heal it," he said, stepping back.

"What?"

Crossing his arms across his massive chest, he lifted his chin at the pitiful flower, "Go on. Heal it. Last night only happened because you have no control over your powers. What we are, what we hold contained in these physical forms could consume us if we're not careful."

"I have some control," I say defensively, "I brought down that mountain."

He scoffed, "That's not control. That's pointing a deadly weapon in a direction and hoping it doesn't kill someone in the process."

I narrowed my eyes at him, "What about the warped I helped Moian with?"

He lifted an eyebrow. "Strengthening their sparks with your own isn't control, it's healing, which is something you can do in your sleep. And I can tell you without any doubt in my mind that had you attempted that on anyone who wasn't a Descendent, they would have burned up from the amount of power you poured into them. I've seen you reattach a butterfly's wing without so much as a thought or hesitation."

I crossed my arms in indignation. I knew I was being a brat, but I had never felt as inadequate as I did now.

Kanan chuckled, knocking my shoulder with his as we looked down at the miserable flower. "Swallow your pride, love, I had to go through the same thing when I got my powers back, except I was sixteen and only had Bron to help. Imagine how that went."

I couldn't help but giggle, the image of a young Kanan staring down Bron as destruction rained around them played through my mind.

Sighing, I let my arms drop. "Okay so what will happen if I can't get this?"

"Like I told you last night, if you can't figure out how to gain control over yourself again, you'll start drifting more and more. We never figured out what happens after because I was always there to contain it if you couldn't get it under control. I was barely in time last night, which is far too close for comfort."

A burning question popped into mind. "How were you able to get to me so quickly? One second I was alone and the next you were there."

"I shadow jumped," he explained, moving to sit against the roots of the tree. "We may be the God of Endings and Goddess of Beginnings, but we're also the dark and light of the world."

Leaning back on his elbows he spread his legs out, looking far too perfect for what had to be an uncomfortable position. "I can travel by somewhat turning myself into a shadow, and you can morph through the light, even if it's only a single candle flame."

My mouth dropped because damn if that wasn't cool, and handy too. "How do I do that?"

"By learning control," he snarked, waggling his brows at me. Flipping him the finger, ignoring his rumbling laugh, I knelt next to the shriveled flower.

"Right now you're a hammer. A blunt instrument with power behind it, a useful tool in many situations, but now you need to learn how to be a blade. Sharp and precise, only as dangerous as you decide to make it."

Cupping my hands around the sad flower, out of place amongst the vibrant nature around it, I tried to keep a blade in mind. Capable of a thin slice or complete evisceration given the right circumstances, that's what I needed to be.

Diving deep into the gilded storm that could consume me at any moment, I let the burn rise, gave myself over to it. My nerves quivered as the electricity struck them and my blood vessels turned into golden rivers. The pressure built and built until my skin felt too tight. The power pushing against its cage. Prickles erupted over my body as the hairs on my arms stood on end. The breeze and the bird's song fell away, leaving only a thundering hum.

Doing my best to grab hold of it, nudging it outwards through my hands, I gasped as the energy leapt forward. The air took on a metallic hue, shining like the stars in the sky. Streams of power rushed from my hands, diving into the flower with abandon.

Streaks of gold ran down the stem, color and life soaking into the wilted plant. Vibrant green leaves and sky blue petals returned to life, vivacious and glowing.

If only it had stopped there.

Sprouts, small and budding, popped through the ground. Unraveling as if awakening from a long winter's nap, they grew and spread until the base of the willow was covered in them.

"Well," Kanan quipped, his amusement undeniable, "you sure are a pretty hammer."

Narrowing my eyes at his teasing, I couldn't stop myself as I threw my hand out, gold power erupting in a stream of light that singed the top of the grass and burned my eyes.

Throwing his head back with laughter, Kanan's shadows darted out from every direction enveloping him completely from head to toe. As the ray of energy hit with a boom, they dispersed in every direction, and once the smoke and darkness cleared, all I saw was the smoldering roots and grass where he had been sitting.

"Temper, temper, love." Spinning around at his amused voice

behind me, I shot out blindly just for the hell of it. This time the blast met its mark, hitting him square in the chest and sending him flying onto his back.

Slapping the outside of my legs with a chuckle, I dashed over to him, standing triumphant above him like a wolf above its prey. My heart was beating wildly and I could only guess how I must have looked, eyes wide, sparkling with an excitement that felt more right than anything had in a long time.

And Kanan, well Kanan looked happy. An emotion that I had rarely seen from him, but as he lay there laughing with an openness that made my heart clench and hurt in the best ways, I found myself joining in.

Despite everything, the anger and mistrust that still lingered between us, there was something pure in the moment, like for this drop in time everything was right and whole. There wasn't a war brewing on the horizon, a deranged god wasn't chasing after us, our people weren't being hunted for their magic, and we weren't a king and queen whose history dated back seventeen thousand years, all of which one of us doesn't remember.

We were just us. Kanan and Atallia. Two people connected by the tethers of the universe, bound together in a way that even we didn't fully understand, but were happy to accept because it meant we weren't alone on this floating rock in space.

And as I looked down at his wide smile, fangs and dimples out in full, I found that maybe that wasn't such a horrible thing.

"I liked this tunic," he chuckled, staring down at the hole I had burned through it. The leather was singed and charred, but his skin was perfectly intact, not a scratch to be seen. I guess lighting a dragon on fire wasn't very effective.

My shoulders shook as he looked back up at me, seeming content to stay where he was on the ground. Letting out a shriek as something yanked my legs out from underneath me, I fell against his shaking chest. Rolling onto my back, leaning my head back against his outstretched arm, two thin shadows cheekily curled back around Kanan's arms. I let out a huffed laugh, "Cheater."

We laid there on the bank for what seemed like hours, staring up through the willow's canopy at the brightly colored sky, listening to the soft movements of the lake. Kanan's hand played against the skin of my arm, the warmth from his body soaking into my side as the breeze brushed against our entangled bodies.

Closing my eyes, breaths evening out, I couldn't help but think...

Not so horrible indeed.

CHAPTER FIFTEEN

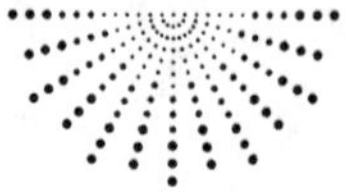

Despite numerous attempts, healing the flower continued to elude me. I could use my magic, which was an improvement from when I had been blocked, but Kanan was right. If I didn't get a hold of myself soon I had no doubt I would go off and who knows what I'd take out with me.

By the time we left Hassere two days later, I wasn't any closer to figuring it out, which pissed me off to a whole new level. This inevitably led to Nala and Zander cracking jokes at my expense.

"How can you not find this cool?" Nala asked in disbelief as we trotted along the main road that would eventually bring us to Elona, the river town that ferried travelers upstream to Eskira. It was the only way to access the mountain capital from the land, unless you wanted to traverse over the Crian Mountains, which was no one's first choice.

"Maybe because I don't want to blow someone up by accident," I said with a shrug of my shoulders. "Seems like something you'd want to do on purpose or not at all."

"Boring." She stresses the word and rolls her eyes all while looking at me with a wicked smile. "Blowing someone up by accident can be quite exciting. No one expects it." She giggles, the crazy pyro looking way too excited at the prospect.

"Right, Zan?" she asks, looking down at the pony-sized fox padding along between us. "Why did you have to go and get into trouble again?" She frowned, her pout way too cute for how insane she was, realizing her back up couldn't speak.

Zander snorted in annoyance, not appreciating Zanaya putting him into time out for the third time of the trip. It was hard to stay mad at him for long, but he could annoy a priestess, so he often found himself in the same predicament.

He did, however, love the attention he received from it. Covetous glances were shot his way, all in awe of his beautiful bright coat, the red so vibrant it could have been made from rose petals. The streaks of black only served to show off the flawless color. With his striking hazel eyes, greens and browns mixing throughout, he made quite the sight to behold. He was upset for about three seconds before he threw his fluffy head back and pranced along to show off his best angles.

That's how it had been since we had moved out early in the morning: Zander and Nala providing entertainment, Zander ultimately frustrating Zanaya—or, in one case, Saanvi—and being forced to follow along in his fox-form. His *silent* fox-form.

I had been content to enjoy the company, relishing in the distractions from...everything. I hadn't seen much of Kanan in the past days, him having been busy commanding and preparing the force that would be following us back to the capital.

Those that had joined Kanan from Hassere on his way to the Gravelands had stayed behind. Eskira, as of right now, had no need of the extra forces and I wouldn't put it past Kasis to use the soldiers' absence from the glass city as a means to kidnap more Descendents for his army of wraiths.

After the battle we had no idea how many of the reanimated corpses had been Descendents, animals, or possibly even humans. I had destroyed most of the corpses in my anger, leaving very little for us to gather information on.

To be fair, I hadn't been thinking too clearly, flooded by a temperamental cosmic power, so I was trying not to be too hard on myself. It didn't mean I was succeeding though.

If only I could figure out how to control it, how to do more than just point it in a direction and shoot. The defeat I felt, failing again and again at healing a simple flower, whether it disintegrated or grew into a field of petals, was disheartening.

Each time I came back I saw hopeful faces looking at me, their supposed queen, and I felt like even more of a fake. Atallia, the goddess with no memories and who was a useless one at that.

I was hopeful that Eskira would bring me some answers, show me the right path to take to get through all of this. It was my *birth* place after all, no matter how long ago that had been, and it's where I inevitably ended up the second time around. A beacon amongst the unknown, something drawing me to it over and over again.

It was why, despite the long day of riding across the bright sunlit fields of Allasea, anticipation coursed through me. If it wasn't for the war party, it almost felt like I could have run there. However, I was stuck following along like everyone else, which gave me time to enjoy the countryside.

To make new memories.

As we made our way to the campsite that had been scouted ahead by the airborne, I was given the opportunity to do just that.

"What are those?" I asked Orion, who had made his way up to the spot on my left. Saanvi was only a few lengths behind him, and both turned their heads in the direction I was pointing. Dozens of large rock formations appeared to be moving, large and commanding out on the horizon.

"Ratheons by the looks of them," Orion replied. Lifting a hand to block out the setting sun's glare, he froze for a split second as whispers of slate gray magic played through his fingers. "Yeah, they're ratheons alright, I can feel the rock that makes up their outer shells."

"A hunting party if I had to guess," Saanvi chimed in, unbothered by the bright glare. "This far away from the Crians, they must be out looking for prey. They're really far south for this time of year."

"Where are they normally?" With the sun hitting the horizon right behind them I could only make out their silhouettes. Four large, thick legs carried rounded bodies of jagged stone, thin spikes covering their entire backs like armor. Massive oblong heads carrying three curved horns, that even from this distance I could tell were razor sharp, swung heavily back and forth as they moved in three single file lines in the opposite direction.

"They stay close to the mountainside near the northern coast," Saanvi replied offhandedly, her eyebrows drawn in confusion. "The Cliffs of Barae, Wayfare Isles, sometimes even the Northern Moors, but the only time they move further south is during the winter when food is scarcer; and even then I've never seen any south of the lake. They're built for colder weather than this."

I hummed in reply, all of us—even Nala stopped chatting—watching the creatures as we passed, until eventually they were nothing but small specks in the distance. We stayed quiet for the rest of the ride, all of us concerned by the animals' weird migration patterns.

At this point anything out of the norm made us wary. Kasis had a head start on us, at least by twenty years if not more, so weird wasn't always just *weird* anymore. If there was one thing I had learned since this all began it was that chaos's trail often manifested first as common, but out of place things. An illness appearing out of nowhere for example. Not unheard of, but strange nonetheless.

Ratheons, known for living in the cold mountainous north, traveling in the southern plains seemed to fit that description pretty well.

As we finally came to a stop near the farthest edge of Lake Thesian, we set up camp in silence. A chill had permeated the air throughout the encampment, even as the last of the sun warmed us. The slow creeping freeze infiltrated into my bones and immediately put me on edge.

Turning my head in all directions as I built up the fire stack, the hair on the back of my neck prickled as if someone was watching. Everyone else seemed to feel it too. Hurried movements and cautious glances were shot all around, everyone waiting for something to pop out of the tall yellow grass.

As the first shift of guards took stance around the tents, I couldn't help but notice the increase in the number watching out into the fields and even across the lake. Kanan had to be feeling it too.

It was like a weight had settled upon the camp, everyone seeming to know something was coming, but not from where or when. All I knew was that we would all be sleeping with one eye open tonight.

CHAPTER SIXTEEN

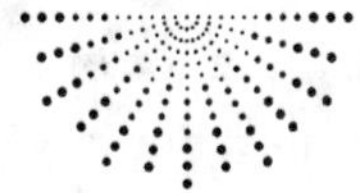

"Fuck," I growled down at the stupid flower I found wilted near the bank of the lake. "Grow, godsdamn you!"

After hours of twisting and turning inside my tent I finally admitted defeat on ever getting to sleep. The jumpy feeling hadn't passed in the hours since the sun had set and the moons had taken front stage in the sky making it damn near impossible for anyone to get comfortable.

That's how I found myself kneeling next to the moonlit lake, shimmering in the starlight. The swirling colors had started glowing as soon as the last rays had fallen to the horizon. It was a true wonder. A beacon to light your way in the dark.

Sighing, my hands fell uselessly to the side as ten more flowers sprouted from nowhere. My shoulders dropped as they continued to spread, the lilac petals mottling with the moon's colorful light and their pink stems streaked with a pulsing gold magic.

I gritted my teeth, trying to contain the scream of frustration that was working its way up my throat. Forcing it back down took a strength I wasn't really feeling in the moment, but if I let it fly free the guards who stood watch over the short bank would come running and I really didn't feel like explaining myself tonight.

That didn't stop me from glowering at the bane of my existence. A goddess beaten by a flower. What a joke.

How was I not getting it at this point? I felt like a fawn learning to walk, wobbly at best and falling flat on my face at worst.

I ran a hand into my hair, another long suffering sigh escaping as I watched the small flowers gently wave in the wind. They were so delicate and pretty it was a wonder they weren't plucked up and carried off into the night.

Would it be petty to crush the lot of them and go find something else to occupy my time? Probably, but it was still a nice thought.

"What are you doing out here all alone, love?" a rough voice called from behind me. Shivers skittered down my back as the feeling of fingers running down my skin hit me. My breath was shaky, remembering just how those calloused hands felt against me.

Twisting on the spot, my heart wrenched, nearly knocking the breath out of me, as he stepped out of the surrounding shadows like some apparition. My dark god come to introduce me to all number of sins, and I found myself a willing victim.

He was in loose black pants, the silk rippling like water, and a matching linen shirt that was so thin there wasn't much left to the imagination. His bronze skin was warm even in the cool silver night, colorful moonbeams and shadows moving across his skin in caress.

His own threads of darkness curled around him, chasing after his long strides like loyal pups. Wisps of the shade magic ran through his midnight curls, rumpled and messy in a way that had no right to look so good. His blood red eyes were alight with that inner fire that never seemed to dim, twin flames burning strong in the night.

But it was the look within those flames that had my heart racing, breaths coming up short until I felt like there was nothing left. Unadulterated need, a desire that could have rivaled the sun's ability to shine. I would have been lying if I said it wasn't affecting me, if that same desire wasn't pulsing away inside my soul like another heartbeat —and I hated liars. A problematic moral to have in this moment. One that was getting harder and harder to hold on to.

Ignoring his question, I cleared my throat and turned back around, trying my hardest to stay focused on the patch of flowers I had created. "Couldn't sleep?"

Wincing as the husky words left my mouth, I prayed he couldn't hear the difference.

"You could say that," he answered quietly.

I felt his eyes moving over my figure, fire tracing a path up and down my body leaving me wanting more. Whatever tethered us together outside of the pair bond was at a constant ache, unfulfilled and needing more, and it sure had a way of making that known.

His near silent steps drew closer. Closing my eyes I pressed my lips together, drawing for any strength I had left against him. Stretching my neck to the side as my skin tightened, I could feel my resolve slipping.

My center throbbed. Traitorous bitch.

"The flowers still giving you trouble?" His shadows finally came over me, encasing me in his darkness. I had always felt safe in the dark, never fearing what could be lurking in its depths. I had to wonder if it was because of him. Because his world of twilight—death and darkness—would always welcome my glowing light with open arms.

"Yes." The sadness in that one word made me flinch inside, hating the vulnerability. Glancing up at him, with his halo of moonlight and ruby gaze, I waited for the pity or the disappointment.

Instead his brows pinched and a stormy look settled across his features. Kneeling down behind me, close enough that his thighs encased my own and the fire in his chest warmed my back, he swept a few loose curls behind my ear. "Why are you sad, little goddess?"

"Because I'm failing at this. At all of this," I whispered back.

A pained expression crossed his face, one filled with understanding and loss. My heart wrenched, skipping a beat as a wave coursed through our tether, like someone had hit it on one side and it was reverberating back towards me; and in that split second before our hearts regained control, it was as if his emotions were mine and mine his.

There was loss and pain and understanding, but amidst it all—

shining brighter and more clearly than anything else—was belief. Hope. Desire. Love.

I looked away as the feelings that weren't mine faded back across that bridge connecting us. If I had felt his then there was no doubt he had felt mine. Cosmos only knew how messed up they were, twisted and knotted together until nothing made sense.

"Oh love," he whispered in understanding. I swallowed harshly looking out over the lake, hoping that he wouldn't bring up what a fucking disaster I was on the inside.

He breathed out heavily, his chest brushing against my back as he watched me with the intensity I had come to know him for. "Look at me," he demanded. When I didn't immediately respond he grasped my chin, turning my attention towards him anyway.

"Let's get one thing straight—you are not a failure. Far from it. After everything that you've been through, losing your parents, having your world turned upside down, Kasis, you're far from a failure. You handled everything with grace and a strength of will no one would have expected from you given the circumstances."

"Grace?" I lifted an eyebrow, my self-deprecation coming out strong. "Smacking a dragon in the nose because I was having a bad day? I think you and I have different definitions of grace."

His rough chuckle filled my ears, chest shaking against me. "Maybe so, but what I mean is that you never fell apart. Not fully. You took punch after punch and when most people would have broken down and given up, you didn't."

I broke out of his grip, unable to keep looking at him as I picked at my nail beds. The constant vulnerability was too much for me to handle. I was emotionally stunted in that way, but maybe he was right.

When your life gets thrown into the deep end you either sink or you swim. I had never been one to lie there and take it, so I swam as best as I could. That didn't mean I wanted to be in the water in the first place.

"Give yourself some credit, love. All that power, it was locked away for two thousand years," he said, running his knuckle down my cheek. "*You* were locked away. Fifteen thousand years. That's how long you had to get a handle on your powers before, you can't expect yourself to figure it all out in just a few days. No one is that perfect, not even you."

"I'm supposedly a goddess, Kanan, I shouldn't be struggling to heal a single flower," I bit out, my voice ringing with the frustration that was eating away at me bit by bit, stealing any patience I had for myself or for anyone else.

Laying his hand on top of mine until they stopped picking at each other, he waited. Peering up at him through lowered lashes, I met his expectant gaze. I let out a harsh breath, the fight leaving my body as the savage emotions fled as quickly as they had come. "Sorry, I know I have a short fuse sometimes."

He smiled gently, "Even goddesses have faults, although I find yours ridiculously adorable."

We stared at each other, everything and nothing passing between us. A thousand words waiting to be said and yet at the same time we both seemed content to let them stay that way in order to have this moment.

"Here," he said, nodding down at the dainty flowers. Reaching out, near invisible wisps of his shadows curling around his hand, he picked one unfortunate bud. The petals browned in a blink of an eye. "Try again, except this time I'm going to walk you through it."

Looking at him over my shoulder I lifted an eyebrow. The cheeky bastard lifted one right back. We were both too stubborn for our own good, it was a wonder we hadn't killed each other in our last life.

"Okay," I sighed, shaking my head, "but it's not going to work."

"Just try," he replied. Moving my hands so that they cupped the flower, he held on gently until we were both sitting there kneeling before the moons and flowers.

"Close your eyes." His lips brushed my ear sending shivers down my spine and electricity through my body. Complying, I shut them, blocking out the light until there was only darkness.

"Now find your spark. The center of your power," he murmured, placing one hand over my chest, eerily close to where the heart of my magic anchored itself inside me.

Falling deep into myself, I followed the building light that seemed to pulse in waves the closer I got to it. The energy unfolded before me like a nebula, wild and uncontrolled. It was ablaze with fiery light, shooting out in every direction like a golden sun.

The radiant spark reached into every corner of my being, so far and wide I couldn't see an end to the seemingly limitless power. Standing before it was unlike anything I had ever experienced.

"I want you to embrace it. That power was used to create planets and galaxies. To create life and beauty. I know it can be intimidating, but it's not just magic. It is *you*. Before the Descendents. Before Irropia," he paused, his warm breath running over my skin, "Before me. That's who you were. To fear it is to fear yourself and that is beneath you. You have survived too much to accept fear as your reality. In that way you would be failing, but not everyone else. You would be failing yourself."

I couldn't bring myself to argue because he was right. This whole time I had been hyper-focused on meeting everyone else's expectations, so concerned that I wouldn't be able to give them what they needed. To be the queen they had waited so long for.

In doing so I hadn't been fair to myself.

Steeling my nerves I dove into the swirling storm of power with my head held high. I braced for the cosmic power to rush through me, reshape me like it had before, but instead it felt like being given a hug. Warm and inviting, relishing in the contact, and rejoicing in my newfound acceptance of it.

A luminous glow broke through my lids, shimmering carelessly. Sounds fell away, the rush of power filling my ears.

"Control it, Atallia," he instructed gently, "It's yours to command. You decide what it can do and when, not the other way around. Giving life back to a flower doesn't require the strength to break mountains. It needs the soft caress of rain drops. The invisible rays of light from the sun. The grounding force of the earth, keeping it from blowing away in a raging wind."

Listening to his words, holding them close, I gathered the power to me. I collected it tightly inside, taking as much in as I could until my mental figure blurred and turned into a silhouette of light.

Near bursting I slowly turned my attention outwards, finding the small flame that lived inside the flower. Dim and practically empty, I directed a strand of energy—no bigger than a thread—through my hands and into the flower.

"Look," Kanan muttered, a smile clear in his voice.

Keeping the power contained inside, ready and waiting for me to use at will, I opened my eyes and was met by dusky purple petals.

"I did it," I breathed in disbelief. Coming to life, I turned in Kanan's embrace, a smile breaking out across my face. "I did it!"

He laughed, deep and without restraint. "You did, just like I knew you would."

"Thank you. For helping me," I breathed.

He had a look in his eye, one that sucked the air from my lungs and made my thoughts stumble to a halt. "Always. I will always help you," he said while cupping my cheek, memories that were millennia old staring back at me. "Until the stars are dust in our hands."

My heart stuttered and I froze as something came to life deep within my soul. It unfurled, as if waking from a long nap. My head pounded, not in pain, but with pressure. A deep resounding pressure that pushed against my skull, beating without care until I could almost hear it.

My breath came out in a rush, knocked out by the tether in my chest that was yanked tight, but not from the other side. No, it was coming from me, demanding to be answered.

Kanan seemed to be feeling the same, staring at me with a befuddled look that told me he was just as shocked. Steam billowed from his mouth as he panted, breathing hard and fast as if he were exhausted, not kneeling on the bank beside me.

Shadows twisted around us, climbing over his lap and around my wrists. I couldn't look away from him, every part of me entranced. My skin was on fire from every delicate touch, sensitive to his every move. Kanan's eyebrows drew together, mouth parted in what could only be described as shock.

Another jerk on the bond, this time from his end, drew a gasp from me. The cord was so taunt I wondered how it hadn't snapped, splitting apart from the tension much like I was. Longing ran rampant between us, coursing through the strange bond like life-blood.

We were locked together yet again, sharing in this endless cycle of life and death. Forever entwined we were. Across time. Across space. We couldn't escape it. I guess the real question was if we wanted to.

Maybe Kanan had come to the same realization, or maybe he had always known. His red eyes brighter than I had ever seen them, scarlet mirrors that matched my own gilded ones. Older than they should be, far older, and yet here we were. Memories, pain, desire, we shared them all.

For once I didn't fight against the pull, let them drag me in willingly. I was tired of it, for the moment at least, of fighting. Fighting him and whatever kept pulling us together like the galaxies depended on it.

I would deal with the consequences later, but right now—fuck the consequences. I was well beyond giving a damn.

We came together in a clash of heat and untamed passion, unable to help ourselves as the desperation, the longing, reached its peak. A whimpering moan left me as our lips met, a savage need racing through me wherever we touched.

Gripping me by the hips, he flipped me around so that I straddled his kneeling form. Even in that position I was still shorter than him, but I used it to my advantage. Burying my hand in his hair, I clutched on to the black silk strands. Pulling him down to me, so far I was arched over his arm, I devoured him with an intensity that ate away at my control.

He didn't seem to mind, quite content to allow me my fun. I wasn't an idiot, I knew who I was dealing with. He was only being patient, in a way unique to this dragon, enjoying the predatory thrill of letting his prey think it had won.

His large hand stroked up my thigh, slowly sliding under the long night-shirt I had thrown on carelessly. I bit his bottom lip, licking away the wound before going back in, starved for his taste. He growled in satisfaction, fingers digging in as his chest rumbled. The sound was nowhere near human and maybe there was something wrong with me because it sent shivers of excitement down my spine.

A ravenous hunger burned between us, setting off a dangerous wildfire. I was wanton, unable to stop myself as I ground against his cock that was pressing painfully against his thin pants. It seemed that was all that was needed to shear through Kanan's control. It seemed he was done letting me play, it was his turn now.

He palmed my ass, rocking me back and forth against him. Wrapping a fistful of hair around his hand, he held on tightly, directing my head where he wanted it. Taking my mouth, he slid his tongue in like it was his right. Kissing me harder, deeper, he swallowed the small sounds I made like they were his favorite thing in the world. He tasted like fire and smoke, something deliciously spicy.

Fuck. I was going to get addicted to that taste.

We broke away, both of us breathing hard. Tugging my head back, he moved his lips down to my neck, I groaned as he started sucking. Each hard draw only served to work me up higher, soft cries leaving my mouth without warning. I trembled as he scraped his fangs against my skin, the high of danger was a drug I had no antidote to.

Hands gripped the neckline of my dress, and with one resounding jerk tore it apart further, exposing my breasts to the cool breeze and to him. He nipped at my neck one last time before taking a hard nipple between his sharp teeth and drawing it into his mouth.

My brain damn near short-circuited as pleasure rained down upon me, sweeping through with every strong pull, until he'd worked me into a frenzy. Kanan snarled in ecstasy, lost to his own rapture. Pulling back he moved to the other, laving it with his tongue before blowing on it until it was puckered and ready for him.

The hand on my thigh moved between us, reaching down to find that sensitive bud that never failed to set me off. My jaw dropped as he gave it a pinch, air rushing out of me as my eyes rolled to the back of my head. He rolled it under his finger, continuing to lather my nipples with attention, until I was a sobbing mess.

My moans grew louder, my entire body like a raw nerve, and then he plunged a finger inside without warning. My pussy clenched, hard and tight around the thick digit, my eyes fluttering as I fought against my orgasm.

I didn't want this to end. Didn't want to go back to reality where I would most likely regret my decisions, go back to being mad at him. Because damn if he wasn't trying to change my mind.

My release hit me like an explosion, rocketing through me as my core shuttered around his finger.

Pulling me in, our lips coming together, he swallowed everyone of my gasps. He continued to thrust in and out as I came down, stroking my inner walls with a precision that was near artistry. I always forgot he was a pianist until he took the time to remind me in his own sweet, tortuous way.

I fell against him, balancing my hands on his shoulders as aftershocks hit me one after the other. I closed my eyes, our chests brushing together as ragged heaving breaths left the both of us. He pulled his finger out causing shivers to rack my body and another round of spasms that sent spikes of pleasure through my weak muscles.

"What are the chances we don't talk about this just yet?" I breathed, slowly catching my breath.

I felt his body tense beneath me, and I immediately regretted my words. It wasn't fair of me to play with him like this, knowing the position we were in. I said as much to him.

He hummed, "You're still not getting it, love."

"Getting what?" I asked, pulling back to look at him.

He smiled gently, a heartbreaking smile full of sorrow that poorly hid the pain he was trying to conceal. "I'll do whatever I have to, do whatever it takes, to make it up to you. *I* hurt you," he swallowed harshly, like the words wounded him. "*I* did that. I knew what I was doing, and I still chose to do it. I had my reasons. I still do, but it in no way makes up for what you're going through now. If that means I only get you in bits and pieces, stolen moments when I convince you I'm worth something more than your anger, I'll take it."

Tears welled up in my eyes, the damn things. What a position we were in. Stuck together, but unable to move on from our past, forever lost in the mistakes we had made along the way. Kanan with his choices in this life, justified reason or not, and me in my past one.

Even angry I had never meant to make him feel that way, all too familiar with the trap that self-loathing could be. "Kan—"

We both jerked as a scream echoed over the plains, carried to us by the wind that had turned far too cold for the middle of summer. Then someone far off into the distance shouted, the urgency heard even from here.

Kanan lifted me off of him, both of us getting to our feet as we listened. There was silence, and then the signature screech of a shattershell flying through the air before a great boom rent through the air. The night became ablaze in yellow light, flickering wildly like a candle flame.

Then we heard the wraiths.

CHAPTER SEVENTEEN

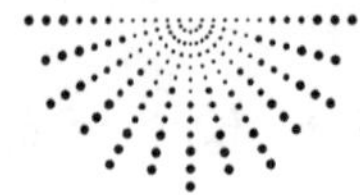

We took off running. The clicking of bones hitting against each other and their ungodly screeches tore through the air with a chilling clarity.

We were blurs in the wind, speeding across the distance between us and the camp so fast I barely felt my feet touching the ground. More explosions shook the earth, lighting up the sky in a myriad of destruction.

"Atallia," Kanan shouted, pulling my attention. I flicked my gaze over to him, keeping the brutal pace. He matched me stride for stride even as his great broadsword, ruby-eyed dragon hilt and all, appeared from the shadows that pooled at his feet. Grabbing hold of it without a thought, he tossed me a dagger he had pulled from seemingly nowhere, and I watched as shadows began to cloak him. Catching it with a practiced grip, I shot him one last look before he faded into the darkness.

"Be safe," he commanded, leaving no room for argument, before the shadows took him.

Refocusing on the scene in front of me, wrapping the dangling leather strips attached to the hilt of the dagger around my wrist to keep it on me, I shoved my worry for him back into the box it came from. I couldn't get distracted, not when we were facing a head-on attack from Kasis's abominations.

Cresting the hill unhindered, the sentries having already entered the fight, I caught sight of groups taking on the wraiths together. Standing with their backs to each other, they ensured nothing could sneak up from behind as they slashed out with claws and heartsglass. Magic and fangs.

Aetherians and Cynthonians worked together seamlessly to fill the weaknesses of the other. When one fell short, feeling the fatigue of battle, the others were there to pick up the slack. Had complete chaos not been raging around the encampment, I would have stopped and stared, awe-inspired by the harmonious teamwork.

Ducking into a mostly undamaged tent, I rummaged around until I found what I was looking for. Shoes.

Why was it that I never had my godsdamn shoes when I needed them?

Slipping into the too tight leather boots that were standard amongst the ranks, I stopped for nothing else. I had already wasted enough time.

A maniacal laughter preceded the consecutive wails of multiple shatter shells being lobbed, concussive booms following seconds later.

Found Nala.

Taking off in the direction of the explosions, I darted in between the tents, some burning from the fires they had held within, others torn and ripped to pieces.

Two boars, one decayed and rotting, the other perfectly healthy, both twice the size of any I had ever seen, had locked tusks in a deadly battle of strength.

Narrowing the focus of my power like Kanan had showed me, I sent the pulse straight into the earth, praying my intentions got across. As I ran, a root from the neighboring willow shot out in an instant, grabbing hold of the wraith and pulling it to the ground giving the Cynth just enough time to eviscerate the struggling corrupted with his foot-long tusks.

I let out a harsh breath, sending up a thank you to the Cosmos.

Whether he listened from his eternal sleep or not, it felt right at the time. Maybe if we garnered enough attention he would wake and save us all from this evil. One could hope.

Sprinting through the fighting, I kept pushing towards the pained sounds that followed Nala's blasts.

A scream of exertion, of someone fighting to the very end, however, had me moving off my path. A tall silver-haired woman, whose teal skin rippled like water even amongst all the flames, stood over man's fallen body as three wraiths circled in for the kill.

Soot smeared her fear-stricken face. Even still, she fought with a ferocity that would have made war maidens proud—teeth bared in a vicious snarl as she slashed out with a sword far too big for her and blades of water that tore through the wraith's skin like wet parchment.

Flinging my hand out without thought, only partially paying attention to how much power I poured into the strike, a blast of golden fire shot free. Having seen me only a second before, the woman pulled water from the barrels behind her until they crested over her and the man, protecting them from the brunt of the inferno.

Damn it. Too much.

Flakes of ash rained down where the wraiths had once been, and I wished the souls they had once been a peaceful rest.

The wall of water fell and the beautiful river woman stared, exhaustion etched into every part of her. "My queen," she panted, distracted. She was going through the motions, her eyes glassy as she took in everything going to hell around her.

"Is he alright?" I asked bluntly. I was already backing up, looking over my shoulder for where to go next. There would be time to console the shocked, but right now a death I didn't think even Kanan could prevent loomed over us all.

Thankfully my words snapped her out of it as she ripped her head down to the man unconscious beneath her. Dropping to her knees she checked his pulse, a split second's pause, before nodding up at me. "Yes, My Lady, I think he's okay."

That was all I needed to hear before I turned and—

The air rushed out of me as I hit the ground, a heavy weight rolling with me. Pushing up with my hips, I forced the blood-covered wraith under me until I straddled it. Without hesitation, or even a pause to glimpse what it was, I thrust Kanan's dagger down into its heart with all my might.

The beast didn't put up a fight, falling limp against the hard ground. Whipping my head back, my dirt and blood-crusted hair flipping behind me, I pulled the dagger free with a strained snarl.

Finally coming loose, a gust of air burst from the wraith's mouth and I froze. A thin strand of pink, edged in violet, floated upwards. Following it as it rose higher and higher, I watched as it joined the river of color above in a small flash of light.

Getting to my feet, I glanced down at the wraith, a mere skeleton draped in skin, tilting my head at its sagging form. I needed to move on—staring down at a dead corpse wasn't going to help anything. Picking up my pace, I took one last glimpse over my shoulder at the limp body and the magic that swayed above it, unbothered by the destruction below.

Shaking it off, I followed the charred craters in the ground and the scent of smoke. It didn't take long until I caught up with Nala's reign of fire. The pyro was at the center of a ring of flames, her yellow eyes glowing in the light.

Whips of burning power snapped out in all directions, warning off wraiths or grabbing hold of them and pulling them into their fiery deaths. Her giggles were even more terrifying to hear, as she watched on with an eerie glee.

Not to my surprise, Zander was taking down those who fled, his red coat matted with black sludge. I entered the fray, rushing over to Zander's side just in time to catch a wraith lunging at him from behind.

Jumping in front, I grabbed it by its throat, yanking it from the air with a strength that shocked me. I didn't dwell on it though, pulling it down to the ground and burying my dagger into the side of its neck. Black, bubbling ooze spurted out, covering the blade and my hand completely.

Pulling free, I wasted no time finding my second target. Darting in and out of Zander's path, the three of us worked together to take out those that gathered.

I looked up as a broken screech filled the air. A hawk, or what looked to be one, dove at Nala who was too engrossed in her own fight to catch sight of it. I had never seen an airborne wraith, and now I knew why. Even as it flew for Nala, sickly green feathers trailed behind it, wing bones shining through as it all but plummeted out of the sky.

Sweat drenched my spine as I unwrapped the dagger's leather straps from my wrist. I flipped it in the air, caught it by the blood soaked blade, and threw it, holding my breath as it spun towards its target.

Landing with a wet squelch in the bird's side, I let out the breath as the wraith fell far off its mark. Seconds later the rest were dispatched, the two redheads working together flawlessly, moving as one as they navigated around one another.

Nala jogged over to us, hands on her hips as she tried to catch her breath. She handed over my blade, having yanked it free from the bird's side. "Well that was fun."

I wrapped the straps back around my wrist, staring at her incredulously, but she only laughed, the embers from her hair raining down endlessly.

The sharp cracks of bone and the sound of shearing muscle came from behind, a hazy red mist rolling away to leave Zander standing in his human form. Shirtless, with a sheen of sweat across his impeccable chest, he grinned down at me. His two fangs and the wild gleam in his eyes made it all the more canine, but it was one I was happy to see.

"Tali," he laughed in astonishment, "did you take your boobs out for me, because they are quite a sight to behold."

Nala clicked her tongue at him. "Don't point it out, stupid. It's rude."

My brows creased and I glanced down. *Well shit.*

The two flaps of my nightdress from where Kanan had ripped it, were stuck to my body from the mud and sweat, leaving my skin—all of my skin—bared. The blood and dirt didn't hide much, leaving my top half completely exposed.

They both watched me with amused, expectant looks. "I don't want to talk about it," I muttered with a sigh, pulling the material back over my chest, barely covering anything.

Nala giggled, but it was Zander who shouted, "On the left."

We both jerked around, just in time to see a wraith dash from the shadows towards us. It lunged, claws flashing. Throwing my arm up without thought, I let out some of my power. A torrent of wind shattered the air, pulling from every corner of the plains as it hit its target with a thunderous crack.

Hitting the wraith like a stone wall, it crushed the creature against its invisible strength. The wraith's bones were pulverized, what was left of its skin sagging uselessly as it sailed through the air. The gust hit several standing tents, ripping through the canvas and grinding the wooden beams to a powder.

"Whoops," I said in apology to no one. "A little too much?"

Dozens of other tents in the vicinity that had somehow survived the battle thus far crumbled as the wind died down, dust and ash puffing up around them.

I nod my head, lips pursed, "Definitely too much."

Zander threw his head back and laughed until tears streamed down his handsome face. He fell over onto his hands and knees, unable to breathe through his laughter.

Okay, so I clearly still needed some practice.

"Where are Zanaya, Saanvi, and Orion?" I asked, turning to Nala while Zander got a hold of himself.

"Probably where the healers set up," she replied with a shrug. "Zander and I were on our shift when shit went down, but they were all back at the fire with Moian when we left. Orion had convinced her to sit down and eat something."

I took off, not even taking the time to explain why, trusting that they would follow without question. Only one thing was on my mind as I sprinted towards the makeshift infirmary.

The warped.

CHAPTER EIGHTEEN

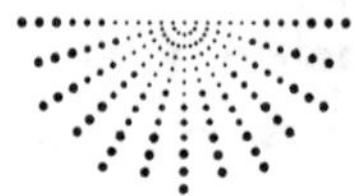

We moved together through the ruined camp, dodging burning canvas and wooden poles as they collapsed under the weight of the heat. Descendents were fighting all over, pushing back against the wraiths. Thankfully most were winning, taking the rabid corpses down one by one.

"Zander!" I yelled in command, watching as a huge wolf took down an Aetherian from behind. Before I could I point it out, Zander was already on the move, picking up on my intentions before I could voice them.

Nala and I kept going as he tackled the mammoth beast to the ground and away from the stunned man. We didn't look back, trusting that he could handle himself, although I could feel Nala's tension hitting me in waves as we moved farther away.

"He'll be fine, Nala. We need to get to the infirmary," I shouted back to her. Knowing the sly fox, he would catch up with us any second, laughing and covered in blood. Nala knew that better than anyone, so we pushed forward. My legs barely hit the ground as we raced through the smoke and fire, across the burning embers to the sound of screaming. Whether from the wraiths or our people, I couldn't tell; they all mixed together into one horrible noise that could have frightened the dead.

After what seemed like forever, we made it to the tents that had been set up to quarantine the warped from the rest of the injured. Guards and warriors encircled the tents, the healers only one step behind them.

Light wreathed their hands and sharp-edged tools were gripped tight as they stared down the instrument used to cause their patients' slow demise. There was an intensity in their eyes only seen in those who chose to look death in the face and fight tooth and nail for every second outside of his grasp.

It was why, despite being creatures of Life, they still worshiped Death. For there was no greater respect than that for an opponent well fought. Healers, in a different way, were warriors in their own right.

Zander ran up behind us, a smile on his blood-spattered face. He shot a wink towards Nala and I heard her sigh of relief, feeling it like my own.

I glanced at them both, hoping it wouldn't be the last time I saw either of them. "Find the others, help where you can, and keep these fucking things from getting to the warped. Put them out of their misery if you can, but stay safe."

They nodded and took off, heading to the left and coming up behind some of the advancing wraiths.

A metallic taste coated my tongue, the air rich with blood. The scent of it filled my nose, tinged with something that made my stomach roll. It felt like I was covered in slime, so much that my skin itched with the need to be rid of it.

Shoving the feeling away—the task more difficult than I imagined —I made for the soldiers on my right. Circling around the large beasts without them noticing wasn't too hard, they were completely absorbed by the Descendents in front of them.

I focused inward, searching for that golden storm. Finding it was becoming easier, like a guiding light pulling me in from the endless sea of nothingness. Centering myself within its depths, I welcomed it with open arms. The surge of power flowing through my veins intensified, cementing its place inside of my soul.

Jumping into action, an aura of light surrounding me, I gave reign to my instincts, keeping my grip loose on the dagger.

I targeted a wraith whose lower jaw was no longer attached, and yet was still determined to fight. The creature's bones were exposed in more spots than not, slime covered and so brittle I could tell one well placed kick would shatter them.

I did just that. Striking out, I heard the crack of bone, felt it beneath my foot. I moved quickly as the strength of my blow knocked it to the ground. With little thought I stabbed hard into its exposed upper mouth, ignoring the crunch of the hard palate as I drove through to its brain.

I was on the move again before it could give its last heaving breath. Tucking into a somersault as another wraith flew overhead, I came to a crouch and released a bolt of energy that sent it barreling into a willow. It was already disintegrating as its back snapped against the unwavering trunk.

Snarls drew my attention towards the entrance to the infirmary tents. Three healers stood facing off against four snapping beasts, all waiting for the right chance to rip into the magic-filled bodies. A singular warrior stood in front of them, slashing with his sword as the beasts drew closer, swiping out with red-stained claws.

I could see the exhaustion on his face, in the tremble of his sword, and by the sweat on his brow. The determination in his eyes, however, was just as strong. A true warrior, battling to the last blow, and there would be one. Eventually his steps would falter too many times and his luck would run dry.

My feet pounded against the dirt, closing the distance. I evaded attacks, catching an unidentifiable creature in the foot as it went for my legs.

Cynths attacked head on, shifting from human to animal and back again within seconds as they worked around each other. Aethers switched between close combat and long ranged attacks, utilizing their more versatile magic to their advantage.

It felt like a dance as I moved between them to reach my goal, everyone following the steps they needed to take to survive.

I gathered my power, concentrating as I reached the entrance. Commanding it to do my bidding, I pushed against the unforgiving earth. I dove through the air, throwing my blade with all my strength into one of the skeletal creature's chests, hoping to gods that my plan would work.

And then I released it.

A blinding light erupted from the center of my chest in a burst of pure power. I hit the ground hard, my shoulder taking the brunt of the fall, as it washed over the wraiths in a wall of golden starlight, leaving not a speck of their rotting corpses behind. The black hearts-glass blade fell to the ground unharmed.

The surge kept going, catching a few others in its grip. Erasing them just as easily from this world before fizzling out into tiny specks of light.

I lay stunned, my face pressed against the cold, hard ground. Shivers racked my body at the quick release of power, dark spots floating across my vision through the glow.

There was a feather's touch against the bond in my chest. An unknown question? One that I couldn't read if it was. Reaching out on instinct, I sent one back, somehow knowing Kanan would feel it on the other side.

As if that was the start I needed, I came to with a sharp breath. Shaking myself free from the self-induced shock, I pushed up from the ground. I brushed the dirt from my mouth, no doubt smearing it across my cheek.

"Are you alright?" I asked the group offhandedly, reaching down to pick up my dagger once again. I took stock of the surrounding battle that seemed never ending, feeling like there were more wraiths now then there had been to begin with.

They all nodded, checking each other for wounds. The male warrior answered, "Yes, my queen."

I nodded at his sword, "Can you still wield that?"

"Yes, ma'am."

"Good g—"

Movement inside the tent caught my eye. "Keep guarding the entrance, don't leave this post, no matter what."

Plowing through the opening in the tent, I came to a halt. The wraith and I froze, locking eyes. The muted black and electrifying green had already taken over the whites of the animal's eyes. Whether it had previously been a Cynth or just some poor unfortunate creature who happened to be in the wrong place at the wrong time, all I knew now was that it would do anything to feast on the magic that made up my very being.

Springing into action, I vaulted over the table between us. The feline-like beast jumped out of the way with an agility that surprised me. Twisting in the air, it had barely landed before it came at me again, its exposed boney claws making for my exposed skin.

Coming together in a crash, we rolled across the floor. My skin broke as its claws found purchase, digging in until a scream loosened from my throat. Gritting my teeth, I pressed my forearm into its throat, stopping it from gouging out mine. I felt around blindly for my dagger, the blade having slipped from my grasp as we hit the ground.

Blood-tinged drool dripped onto my neck as the big cat snapped and snarled, bearing down on me with all of its weight. I cried out as it began tearing at me with its back paws, catching my exposed thigh and ripping the nightdress further. Damned thing was thin as parchment, I might as well have been fighting naked.

Rage and self-preservation exploded through me, mixing together into a dangerous concoction. With a mighty yell I punched upwards with my fist…and straight through the beast's chest cavity.

It yelped, freezing over me as I gripped its heart in my hand. Blood drenched my arm, coating it in that thick, sticky tar.

Staring the wraith in the eyes, wanting nothing more than for Kasis to be able to see, I sent a thread of power into my hand. I gripped the decayed, rotting organ, and sent the aether straight into its body, the heart melting in my hands.

The wraith stopped moving, stopped fighting against me, and fell uselessly to the side. Pulling my hand free, I stopped, staring down at the gaping hole in the creature's chest. A green and black ooze slowly seeped from its body, the same liquid that now dripped from my hand. The hand I had just used to break through its ribs and destroy its heart. Slivers of bone stuck out from between my knuckles, piercing my skin until my blood mixed with its.

I let out a shaky breath, easing the shards out, gritting my teeth as the jagged edges tugged at my flesh. A relieved breath burst from my chest as I dropped them to the floor, and I searched the nearby tables frantically until I found a rag to wipe away the red and black blood dripping down my hand. Rubbing as much of it off as I could, I tossed the cloth onto the still corpse to be burned later.

I looked on the ground, spotting my dagger a few feet away. I snatched it up and wiped the hilt on my dress.

Gods, I missed my thigh sheaths.

The thin material that covered my form was in tatters, hanging off in strips and barely holding itself together by threads.

Why was I never fucking prepared for these things?

I hustled over to the stacked boxes off to the side, aware of every second that passed by as I rifled through their contents. After what felt like an hour, I finally found one filled with linen clothes.

They weren't leathers, but given my current circumstances they were better than what I had. Whipping off the remains of the night dress, I took a quick glance at the wounds on my abdomen. The deep cuts were slowly leaking blood, rivulets running down my stomach, marring my pale skin. A dark green—near black—liquid stuck to the edges where the cat's claws had pierced my skin.

"Fuck." My face twisted in disgust. The thought of Kasis's poison seeping into my body had bile rising in the back of my throat.

Thankfully, my magic was all over it. Streaks of gold carved across my body, racing over sleek curves to the openings. The cracks spread out from my chest, breaking my skin to allow the magic more room. Eventually my entire body was covered in them, the nebulous storm peeking out through its cage.

I would have to hope being a goddess exempted me from illness, even if it had been created by another god.

I pushed away the anxiety that threatened to overwhelm me, shoving my legs into a pair of linen pants. The matching top followed, covering the glowing lines that painted my body as I ignored the sizzling burn that radiated from the wounds and instead ran out through the back entrance.

A gust of wind threatened to knock me to the ground as I exited, a miniature tornado sweeping across the open area surrounding the tent. In the center, commanding it like a queen of ice and wind, was Zanaya.

Her curls were pulled back tight, but strays had pulled free and flew around her beautifully serene face. Her ice blue eyes glowed, their color burning through the gathered wind.

Wraiths were dragged into her tempest. They clawed and bucked against the force, but none could overpower the blows that swept them off their feet. I reached for the tent post behind me, sending my power into the ground to anchor myself as the funnel stretched higher.

An endless stream of air fed the twister, its mistress pulling from every whistling breeze along the plains. Beasts were thrown around inside, broken beams, shredded canvas, and the destroyed camp were all sucked in along with them.

Branches groaned from the surrounding willows, their switches pulled taut as the wind tugged at them. Zanaya's form blurred inside the tornado, but I watched as she raised a hand high into the air and with a resounding scream that was lost to the wind, she yanked her hand down.

The funnel collapsed inward. Everything, all the wraiths, it had pulled hit the ground with a boom that sent a plume of dust in every direction. Shielding my eyes, I only turned back as the air stilled.

There was no movement, no sound. My hands shook as I released the tent pole. My heart pounded relentlessly as I tried to find my friend amongst the destruction.

One beat.

Two.

Dust rained down upon the carnage, and from its depths Zanaya bolted out, blood-covered and welding twin blades of ice. A savage look crossed her face as she fell upon the disoriented wraiths without an ounce of mercy in her heart.

I briefly closed my eyes, before I ran for her, my badass friend who was going to get herself killed taking all of them on.

The maniac let out a battle cry that ripped through the air, startling everyone, who had been stunned by her display, into action. All of the wraiths' attention were on her, their angry snarls and screeches enough to understand that they didn't appreciate being thrown around.

Leaping over the ring of broken shit that had gotten sucked in, I tackled the first wraith I saw shooting off a bolt of energy at another that was circling around behind her. I went rolling to the side with the large beast, somehow landing on top.

I wrestled with its writhing form, attempting to avoid the clawed swipes and kicks as I slammed my hand into the ground next to its exposed skull. I jerked back just in time to miss being impaled by the spike of rock that I'd summoned, the creature's spine severing as its head was ripped free. The decapitated skull dangled on the rock, pierced by the sharp point right through one of its eye sockets.

I pushed on until I was back to back with Zanaya. "A tornado, huh?"

"It was the only thing I could think of," she grunted, shards of ice appearing out of thin air to shred an attacking coyote.

"Did the others find you," I yelled over the roar of battle. Movement on my peripheral had my hand shooting out before I could even turn to look. I felt a resounding pulse from beneath my feet at the same time, an answer to a subconscious call.

I clenched my fingers into a fist, blue vines and gray willow roots erupting from the ground. The earth crumbled and broke away, more and more rising from beneath, nearly swallowing several Descendents.

Oops. Still too much.

They whipped around on their own accord as they burst free, entangling several wraiths within their limbs. Tightening as they captured their prey, the beasts struggled to escape, but the roots and vines held strong.

They clamped down hard and I heard the wraiths' ribs begin to break, their chests caving in from the pressure as they were dragged into the ground.

"Yeah, they're around here somewhere," she replied back. We both pulled away at the same time, each taking a wraith head on.

I somersaulted out of the way, the grizzled creature passing overhead. Rolling back onto my feet, I dodged to the side as another one joined the fun. Both were all bone, the skin having long ago peeled away from their frames.

One dug its claws into the dirt, bunching together as it jumped. I braced myself for impact, only for two ginormous fangs to come down upon it.

Black blood sprayed as the snake's mouth crushed the beast. The size of a small house and as thick as a tree trunk, the serpent's body separated me from the other wraith. Its dark iridescent scales shimmered with all kinds of hues in the moonlight. Small spike-like scales lifted up from its body in a sort of protective armor.

The great viper turned, glancing down, her bright green eyes stabbing straight through me just as they did in her human form. A pale, thin scar cut across the top of her right eye, a menacing wound coupled with the tips of twin fangs that peeked out, her large forked tongue tasting the air.

Saanvi.

A Primal.

In my months with the Descendents I had only ever seen a few. The prehistoric, mythical forms they took were often too large to shift into in normal settings.

The quietest of our group, I wasn't exactly surprised she hadn't said anything, but given the power that Primals could often garner I was surprised she didn't lead her own battalion. With a form like hers, she could have been a commander right alongside Zanaya. A question I would have to ask her another time.

Turning back to her prey, she pulled back, her angular head

rearing high above the now wary wraith. Letting out a horrible hiss, she struck. Flinging the wraith into a nearby tree, several snaps echoing as it slid to the ground.

The wraith shook its head, pieces of muscle and skin flying from its neck as it did so. The broken creature began crawling along the ground. A mindless monster uncaring of the certain demise that was falling quickly upon it, dragging its back legs to reach Saanvi and I.

It was a wretched, pitiful sight, and a part of me broke inside for the person it could have once been. How had this become their ending? Maybe it was Kasis's way of getting back at his brother, forcing Kanan to quicken the deaths of his own people.

And quicken them he did, as the blade of his great sword carved the broken wraith in two.

Shadows dragged themselves out from between the trees as a darkness unlike any other fell over the field. Tendrils of stark ebony snapped out in anger, their rage a diluted mimic of their master's.

Forming from nothing, Kanan's hulking body stepped back from the severed parts of the wraith at his feet. His eyes burned like hot coals, his face a mask of cold, unrelenting death. Taking in the carnage, the bodies of friend and foe, he snarled.

The battle stopped, everyone brutally aware of the predator that had just stepped onto the field. No one moved, not even the wraiths, as Death looked them over. I could almost hear the prayers, to the Cosmos...to me. Pleas to keep his gaze swift and moving, for him to not settle those blood rubies upon their lives.

Smoke curled from his flared nostrils as a wave of heat emanated from his body so strongly I could feel it across the distance that separated us. He surveyed everything before him, until our eyes finally locked and the unbridled fury inside us both was mirrored by the other. He nodded in acknowledgement, the understanding there even when the words were not.

His clawed hand gripped his sword tight, blood dripping from its sharp edge, before releasing it to the shadows. The darkness swallowed the blade and then began to crawl over his body, expanding outward in a never ending void.

The trees groaned from within the darkness. People and wraiths alike ran away from the growing darkness, trying to avoid being swallowed by it, but it inevitably took them all.

As it came upon Saanvi and I, I smiled. Wicked and full of a righteous fury, I welcomed the darkness and was left blinded.

Only the faint outline of golden cracks along my skin broke through the sheer pitch and even then it wasn't enough. There was just...

Nothing.

And then a roar that made the ground tremble and the sky rear back in fear, was set loose into the air.

CHAPTER NINETEEN

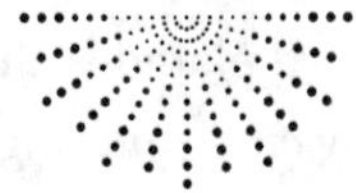

The shadows peeled away almost as fast they had come. Descendents gasped and the wraiths wailed, already running before the last of the shade could lift.

Standing above us all, his crown of horns held high, was the dragon of legends. Death incarnate. His first form, unleashed upon the enemies that sought to take what was his. His people. His land. His throne.

And they would die for it.

One of the wraiths, already sprinting out across the open plains, let out a sharp trill. The sound striked the air, a broken call, but bone-chilling all the same.

As one, the remaining wraiths turned tail and ran. Coming from all around, abandoning their fights and possible meals, they bolted out across the moonlit grasslands.

Twisting his heavy muscular head toward me, Kanan let out a low rumble. Loud crashing came as trees were taken down by his swinging tail, sharp barbs smashing through thick trunks. People scrambled out of the way as the large needle tip came barreling at me.

Already guessing his next move, I ran around Saanvi's sleek form, headed straight for the impossibly sharp barb. I leapt as it came around, landing in a crouch and reached to hold on to one of the small spikes at the end of his tail.

My muscles tensed as I felt his tail dip. With a powerful flick, he flung me high. I rose over his back, suspended in the air, before everything started rushing up towards me.

Pushing my gathered power into my feet, praying to whoever would listen that the few things I had learned would save me, I let out a pulse. Just because I couldn't die, didn't mean my legs wouldn't shatter on impact with the hard plated scales.

Gods, that would be the icing on the fucking cake.

I felt resistance beneath me, slowing my fall as I closed in on the sharp spines that ran along his back.

Finally, with the air cushioning my blow, I landed atop his heavily muscled back with a jarring force. Nearly losing my balance I grabbed the nearest spine. Sharp pains ran through my legs, knees shaking, no doubt in my mind small fractures now dotted the bones.

I really need more practice.

Ignoring the pain, I gritted my teeth, moving in and out of the sharp spines until I got into position. Finding my seat, I wasted no time as I grabbed hold of the spikes that lined his neck.

I patted his scales, the fire in his chest heating the dark plates. "Go, we need to follow them."

That was all he needed as he raised his tremendous wings. With two powerful beats, the wind knocking the Descendents over, we were in the air.

Catching the retreating wraiths was no problem, Kanan's wings crossing the distance in mere seconds as soon as he took flight.

The horde was at least fifty in number even after all the ones that had been killed. We glided high above them and watched as they raced over the plains, either unaware or uncaring of what lay in wait above them.

"We need to see where they go," I shouted over the wind.

Darkness brushed against the walls of my mind, waiting patiently to be invited in. Opening the mental door, the shadows billowed in like smoke, no longer hesitating at the doorway.

"We can't stray too far from the others, it could be a trap."

He wasn't wrong, everything up to this point had only shown how deep Kasis's plans went. Every little thing was a smoke screen for something much bigger. Two thousand years and a lifetime of hatred had given him as much time as he needed to put everything into place.

"This might be our only chance to find out where they're coming from." I pushed the thought towards him.

A growl of frustration was his only answer. The vibrations shook me to my core, rattling my nerves.

"If we can see where they came from, we might be able to figure out Kasis's whereabouts. We're out on an open plain, and yet they still managed to sneak up on the camp, how?" The question had been lingering in my mind since the hoard had attacked. *"I don't like it anymore than you do, but we don't have many options here."*

This time he let out a grumble, one of annoyance, and the scales against my legs warmed.

"Stop growling, you overgrown lizard, it's not helping anything," I snapped. *"I know you're pissed, so am I, but it does us no good if we don't know what our next move is. What would you have us do? Once we get back to Eskira we'll have no idea where to start in order to find Kasis or figure out the rest of his plans. We need something to go on."*

It was silent inside my mind, until his dark voice echoed throughout, *"Agreed."*

It wasn't long, however, until our question was answered. We must have been barely a few miles from the lake, when Kanan shouted into my mind. *"Look."*

He angled his right wing, allowing me to see the wraiths below. Beneath us, the mutilated creatures barreled headlong through the tall grasses, before disappearing into thin air.

I blinked twice thinking I had missed it, but no, as more and more of them fled to the same spot they each hit a point where they were just…gone.

My pulse picked up until it once again pounded away in my ears, the realization hitting me like a jolt of lightning.

"Get us down there Kanan," I yelled in urgency, not even bothering to say it in my mind. The hoard was quickly vanishing before our eyes, along with any chance of figuring out where they came from.

Kanan dove quickly, circling around until we could see the faint ripple in the air where the wraiths were moving through.

"What is that?" Kanan asked.

The fifty or so wraiths had swiftly turned to twenty, and more were rushing into the rift that somehow linked the plains to somewhere else entirely.

"There's not enough time to explain, but we have to get down there. Now!"

Without hesitating, he tucked his wings into his side and dove, air rushed past until the distance between us and the ground became concerning. I tucked my head down as the wind battered my body, bracing as Kanan swept his wings out at the last second, catching the remaining breeze with a jerk.

My knuckles were white from the tight grip on his spines, the strength in my legs put to the test as I clenched hard on his scales as we hit the ground like a meteor.

Dirt sprayed as we came to a sliding stop, the jarring descent nearly knocking me from my seat. I was up and moving even as drops of blood ran through my fingers.

Already guessing my next move, Kanan angled his wing. Sliding down the thick leathery membrane that covered the bony structures beneath, I hit the ground running. Sharp pains shot up and down my legs, my knees complaining with each pounding step.

I raced across the few hundred feet that separated us from the wavering portal until I could finally see the other side.

Trees. Color. Dozens of wraiths rushing off into the distance towards familiar buildings that had the air inside my lungs freezing.

"Light it up," I whispered into the darkness that hovered inside the doorway of my thoughts. My mind raced with thousands of possibilities, and not one made sense. How? Where?

Kanan's lumbering steps came up behind me as his enormous shadow fell across the grass. Watching as the last few wraiths entered the tear, a loud stream of fire chased after them. The blast of heat from above nearly forced me to look away, but I kept my eyes on the flames as they hit the rift and didn't come out the other side.

Screams. Piercing wails that came from somewhere inside the incinerating hellfire. The horrendous noise kept going until it was abruptly cut off.

Like someone had simply closed the door, Kanan's fire swept out across the plains in front of us, no longer sucked in by the ripple.

Kanan closed his massive jaws with a clank, his fangs clenched as he let out a harsh growl.

Faster than my eyes could track, shadows—pulled from the blades of grass around us—covered him entirely. An undulating, writhing mass of darkness that covered his form.

They peeled away, leaving Kanan inches away from me. His face was hard as stone, brow thunderous as he stared out to where his fire now crackled and burned away at the sun-dried grass.

"You were wondering how Kasis escaped," I said as smoke filled the air. "This is how. One of those things appeared behind him beneath the mountain, and he disappeared through it. I don't know where too, the ripple kept changing. I honestly don't think *he* knew where he was going, or cared, but he definitely wasn't surprised by it."

Kanan said nothing, yet I could see his mind playing over every word I said.

"I think this might be how the wraiths were getting away with the kidnappings so easily, even with your soldiers so close by," I continued, waiting for him to say something.

The sky had begun to lighten, turning from a star-lit night to a radiant dawn unhindered. I had always found it funny how that worked. No matter how much you wished the world would slow down, it continued on as if you didn't exist. So far beyond a simple mind, beyond one person, that even as lives changed forever, it was never deterred from its singular purpose. A constant amongst the chaos.

"Have you ever seen anything like this Kanan?" I pressed in hopes we weren't as screwed as I thought.

He shook his head, eyes still locked to the spot as if it would open up again at any moment. "No, love, this is something new. Something I haven't seen in all my years."

And as we watched the flames lick away at the fields, slowly dying by some unknown hand, I was left wondering what had changed during the years we had been gone. What forces were at work to bring about an unknown that not even the God of Endings could remember.

CHAPTER TWENTY

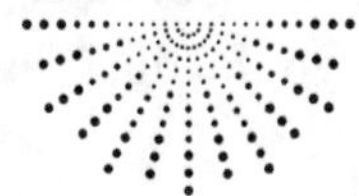

The flight back to camp took eons, the billowing smoke in the distance an ominous sign for what we would find. And as we circled over the destruction, the damage was worse than I feared.

Tents were in shreds, blackened edges and ash-stained blood smeared across the fabric, like some gruesome painting telling the tale of the battle. Crates holding our desperately needed supplies had been smashed, their contents somewhere within the mess of it.

Torn flags, the shafts cracked and splintered, lay useless against the ground. The tails of one had caught fire in the embers of a dirt covered hearth, the place of rest and stories trampled in the fighting.

The Descendents were scattered. Those who were able tended to the newly wounded or gathered the strewn, dirt-covered supplies. Others, however, had been left in some kind of trance, their eyes blank as the world continued to move around them.

We did a fly over, low enough to spot any lingering wraiths, but high enough not to disturb the wreckage any more than necessary. That's when we noticed the frantic waving.

"Kanan—" I shouted, dread setting in as I saw who it was.

Already angling for a landing, he replied, *"I see her."*

I jumped up as soon as he landed, barely looking in my panic, and slipped, saved from hitting the hard ground by the wing Kanan held aloft. It caught my falling body before I could plummet a couple hundred feet, allowing me to slide down unhurt. I took off running as soon as my feet hit the ground, trusting Kanan to follow behind. Bolting towards Zanaya, moving fast enough to blur around the edges, I crashed into her sobbing body.

I held her to me tightly, pulling back enough to see her tear stained face, the water carving through the dust that covered her from head to toes. "Who? Who is it?"

She sucked in a choked breath, pointing behind her to the gathered group, already half dragging me. "It's Nala. Please, please, you have to help."

I was already sprinting before she could finish getting the words out, my legs carrying me across the distance. Breaking through the group of my friends, horror on every single one of their faces, I skidded to a stop, falling to my knees.

"Oh gods," I panted, taking her in, "No, no, no, no."

Nala, sweet, crazy Nala lay crumpled on the ashen floor, intestines spilling from her body. Eviscerated. Slashed side to side. Blood spread, poured, from the gaping wound, in a delicate pattern of death. Even worse…she was awake.

The red-headed pyro was holding the vital organs to her, keeping them from touching the ground, a tired grin curling at her lips. "Bastards got me," she joked on a wheezing rasp of a breath. "Don't worry I got them back. Blew their asses up."

She giggled, the sound a fake imitation of her usually giddy, infectious laugh. The twinkling embers that marked the ends of her hair, and were so unique to her, had cooled to an ash gray. They spilled around her in a shadow of a halo, lacking the light they, and their mistress, were known for.

I shoved my shock aside and pushed her hands away, taking hold of the organs that threatened to spill into my lap. "Cosmos, Nala," I gasped as her blood drenched my hands. As I carefully placed her intestines back inside her exposed abdominal cavity, the skin flaps with their serrated edges hung as useless as the torn muscle that lay exposed to the air.

I nearly lost my grip on her entrails, the blood-slick innards doing their best to come back out. "Shit," I gasped, pressing down in order to keep them in place, shouting orders. "I need another set of hands. Now. Gauze, someone find me gauze."

"He-he-here, I have them."

The shaky voice gave me pause. I glanced up, catching Zander's hazel eyes, filled to the brim with tears, his normal boyish grin nowhere in sight. As he placed his larger hands over mine, the only thing holding his friend's organs in place, he looked like he was going to be sick. His face lost what little color had remained, but with a sniff and a nod at me, he held it together.

"You won't let me become one of those things, will you Zan?" Nala's quiet question had the blood in my veins running cold. The grim request, in what could be her last moments, was one between friends, as integral to each other as their own souls.

Zander swallowed hard, his face twisting in pain as he choked on a sob. Tears dripped from his chin, falling between his blood-covered fingers. "Great Divine, Nala," he ground the words out, "shut up, don't say that. Don't—don't say that. You don't get to say that, you aren't going anywhere."

Nala's yellow eyes gazed into Zander's, a single tear falling from the corner. She smiled, a beautiful, sad thing that was only for him. Zander pressed his lips together, smothering the keening cry that tried to rise from his throat, dropping his head between his shoulders instead, avoiding the pain of watching the light fade from her eyes.

The gauze I asked for was passed from behind, and I went to work unfolding the torn strings of skin and muscle, swallowing the bile that rose as more and more of her blood painted my skin. Breathing through the smell of it all, iron thick in the smoky air, I laid the white material over her exposed organs.

I tore the gauze with my teeth, zoning out the sniffles and cries, and falling deep within the nebula of gold and color. It ran free in a way I had never allowed it before, zipping through me, tearing away at its restraints until my skin glowed like a thousand suns.

Zander and Nala were taking one last moment, words said in between heartbeats as I listened to the hum of my power, the steady rhythm growing louder. A flicker of darkness in the corner of my eye caught my attention.

Kanan kneeled beside me, his hulking form throwing a shadow over Nala, black tendrils curling off him like the smoke that blanketed the sky, he appeared ever the dark god. A reaper, come to take the souls he was due. Laying his palm against a section of Nala's unmarred skin, he breathed deep as something settled over him.

His eyes flicked towards mine, the golden hue that took over my vision flaring as our power-filled gazes met. "Her death is not mine, love. None of them are."

And with those few words an understanding washed over me. As I placed my hands over Nala's heart, guiding my aether into her, my intention was clear. Fix what had been broken. What should not be.

Death himself did not stake a claim to her, to any of them. These injuries, deadly as they were, were never meant to be her ending. This was a premeditated attack, one meant to force these deaths.

This was Kasis's way of getting even with Kanan. Taking everything that his adoptive brother protected and twisting it into something revolting. When Death came, it was to be expected. There was the knowledge that it was time to cross that invisible barrier that separated the living from the afterlife. A new beginning taking flight. The balance never to be broken.

Now Kasis saw fit to mess with something that could have innumerable repercussions, the likes of which I don't think any of us would understand until it was too late.

If this wasn't Nala's time, then I sure as hell wasn't going to let her go. Not when she had so much life left to live, her family ready and waiting to go through all of it with her.

My golden power rippled through her, tearing away at the darkness, narrowing in on the wounds that threatened to take her from this world. A rush of magic turned to the abdomen, knitting together the ripped muscle, the tears in her major arteries, stopping more of that life-giving blood from gushing out.

My mind's eyes, however, followed by a thin trail of gilded energy, headed inward deep into the heart of Nala's magic. A smoldering blaze of yellow light, fiery embers that matched the ones adorning her hair, flew in every direction.

The magic was dazzlingly bright, flares of energy bursting out from within. It was as untamed as the woman it embodied, encapsulating Nala's wild fire perfectly.

An aura hung around the yellow fire, a gray haze tinged with that all too familiar festering green. The barest hint of the diseased magic that terrorized us at every turn, taking our people and changing them into unrecognizable monsters.

Nala's spark fought back, snapping at the foreign magic. Blazing whips of energy attacked with bloodthirsty steel, refusing to yield. I urged my own magic forward, rushing to help. As my power wrapped the bristling yellow flames in a shield of gold, I stood sentry over Nala's healing body, giving the rest of my energy the chance to heal the damage.

There was little sign of the Warp anywhere else. The insidious illness lingered like tar wherever it went, taking over until there was nothing left but its suffocating presence. The small bits that were trying to infiltrate their way into Nala's magic would stand no chance once her body was healed, her spark no longer distracted by the impending weight of death.

With no foothold to begin its invasion, the murkiness began to fade, the last persistent remnants of putrid rot disappearing into nothing against my unstoppable combustion of power. Her skin knit together under the gentle hand of pure aether, threads of power acting as stitches, her body fighting to catch up and remove the parasite.

As the taint lifted, flaming magic that burned like the sun shining through, there was a tug in my chest. A song playing in my ears. A rhythmic lullaby that swayed in tune with Nala's lively energy and rekindled its burning heart.

I drew closer to the lovely noise, a perfect harmony that was hypnotic in a way I couldn't explain. The balance of sweet notes tangled with the abundant zeal of Nala's spark. In the illuminated darkness, a thin red band, nearly invisible, stretched out toward the daunting flames.

Just out of reach, both yellow and red nearly touching but unable to make the connection, I felt compelled. So when a tendril of gilded light took hold of the red cord, I didn't stop it. Nor did I stop when the line of power yanked on the end, dragging forward whatever it was attached to.

Then the world exploded with light.

Thrown back, I hit the ground a couple feet away, my connection to Nala broken. I covered my eyes, blinking back the spots that had taken over my vision. Squinting through the pain, I was left speechless.

A swirling mass of yellow and red magic blocked out everything and everyone. The powers twined together, growing brighter and more powerful as they became one. Rolling over each other, like ripples in a lake, the colors became an aegis of salvation, defending against anything that might try to break them, protection from a world that could very well separate them forever.

And in the middle of that incandescent shield, their forms blurred and coated in magic, Zander held Nala to his chest. He had his face buried in her neck, seemingly unable to let go of the best friend he nearly lost. Nala gripped him just as tight. With her arms wrapped around him, all but choking him, they were lost to an unbreakable embrace.

Someone beside me gasped. Rough hands reached out, pulling me up from the ground and away from the intertwined magic. Narrowing my eyes through the glare, I was able to make out Kanan and Saanvi next to me, moving us all back.

"Is this what I think it is?" I asked, touching my mind to Kanan's, his velvet darkness a living, breathing thing in my head.

He curved a hand around my abdomen, pulling me in closer as his shadows curled around us, blocking out some of the burning light. *"They're bonding. A pair."*

"I didn't mean to," I confessed, *"It was like they were stuck."*

"So you unstuck them," he said with conviction, his chuckle resonating deep within me, bold and so very him. I would never confuse the sound with anyone else.

"I didn't know that's what I was doing," I retorted. He said nothing, but the shadows in the corners of my mind laughed.

"It makes sense though. Zanaya mentioned that some think the reason so few pairs have been found is because we weren't around." The thought had some merit. I mean if we created the Descendents, an integral part of them came from us. *"What if she was right?"*

"A compelling theory," he replied, deep in thought. *"Makes you wonder how much of ourselves we left behind when we made them."*

"How did we create them?" I realized I had never asked. Out of all the crazy things I learned, I never put together what it actually meant to be a goddess. *The* goddess. The Descendents were my people, they had been ever since they accepted me with open arms, but I had forgotten what that actually meant.

"It's a long story, but the gist is that we did something akin to our own creator. He separated the fragments of his power, allowing them to take the shape they wished," he answered, waving a hand down his body. *"Whereas we took a single shard from ourselves and imbued the animals, the plants, the pieces of this world we loved with our power. It took very little for our people to take form. They were there, just waiting for us to come along and give them the push they needed."*

"Well fuck me."

He laughed, this time out loud, "Yeah that about sums it up."

"How long will they be like this?" I nodded to Nala and Zander, their magic enveloping them completely.

"Could be minutes. Could be hours," Saanvi answered, appearing over my shoulder. "When Fayla and I bonded, it took four hours before the magic subsided."

"You've never talked about her before. Or your other partners," I voiced in shock.

She looked at me, tilting her head at me. Moonlight hit her striking eyes, turning them into jade gemstones, with the stark white scar cutting into her eyebrow, she appeared a specter in the darkness. "You never asked."

She was right, I hadn't thought to ask. In the months that I had gotten to know her, what little she had been willing to share at least, I hadn't learned anything about her other half. Or quarters, I guess, the she-viper and her pair being in a long term relationship with another bonded pair of women.

"I'm sorry," I said sheepishly.

She grinned, her two fangs on display, "Don't worry, golden girl, it's not like I'm a forthcoming person."

"Well I would like to meet them, if you think they'd be okay with that."

"Just try and keep them away." Laughing, she knocked her shoulder against mine, turning to walk back over to the others. "Go on, queenie. I'm sure Moian is looking for you, we'll keep watch over these two."

Strutting over to the others, she joined in on the vigil, Orion throwing his tree trunk of an arm over her shoulders.

"She's right," I sighed, "I need to go find Moian, see if I can help. Seems like if we catch it early enough, we can stop the Warp from setting in. I need to let her know."

"She'll be in the thick of it." He looked off past the infirmary tents, shadows curling near his ears. Placing a hand on the small of my back, we started off towards the chaos Kasis's creatures had left behind. "Come, there's more to be done."

As we headed for the main source of chaos, I took a second to look over my shoulder, catching Zanaya's eye, silently ensuring everyone would be okay. Jerking her chin, she ushered me on.

It didn't take long before we hit the devastation, blood and ruin all around us. The warriors were disordered in a way I had never seen. I had gotten so used to the orderly procession in Eskira, guards coming and going like clockwork. Everything running without a hitch that the total disarray was as demoralizing as the battle itself.

The uninjured soldiers that traveled from the Gravelands had been drained, the only thing keeping them from joining those under Moian's care was the fact that they were on their feet. Now, there wasn't a single person who didn't look haggard.

Some had dropped where they stood, curled against the cinders that littered the ground like snow. Others struggled to drag unconscious bodies from the debris, eyes frantic and bloodshot.

One Aetherian, the bark-like pattern along his bare arms giving him away, waded through the wreckage, his eyes unseeing, staring ahead at nothing. The cuts and bruises that marred his face were healing before my eyes as he passed by unblinking.

A teal-haired woman, only a few feet away, desperately pushed at a tree that had fallen during the fight, crushing someone beneath. Even the strength near-immortality lent couldn't save you from exhaustion. Before I could move to help, Kanan rushed over, lifting the tree with ease, shadows bolting in to grab the downed man.

A healer appeared from nowhere before anyone could call, jumping in without a thought. The young man's apron was smeared in grime and blood, the wraith's black tar sticking to his skin.

"Great Cosmos," I breathed, taking in the awfulness around me as Kanan came to a stop by my side. "Where do we even start?"

"One thing at a time, love," he gritted out. The skin of his face was tight against his razor-sharp cheekbones, red eyes aflame. I knew this was eating at him as it was me, tearing away at something crucial inside him.

His dark pets dug into his biceps, hissing and spitting at the air. My own magic answered in kind, going from a smolder to a blaze in seconds. The whirring hum returned with a fury, growing louder and louder as I glanced out over the destroyed camp.

The air was laden with pain, wails of grief rising in a crescendo with the drone of my power. Everything else fell away, the thrum becoming louder, harsher, deeper, until it was all I heard. It boomed inside my head, beating against my skull, forcing my entire being to listen.

And then I heard it.

Goddess please...

Life be with me...

I know I haven't always deserved it, but, Goddess, I need you...

Goddess of Beginnings, I honor thee, I need your help...

A golden aura grew around me as the words filtered into my head, each one stabbing me deep in the heart.

No, no, please, my queen, I'm not ready to live without him...

Queen Atallia, if you can hear me...

Eyes turned to me as my skin cracked, my golden spark blasting through in rays of startling light. Hope, faith, shone through those weary eyes. More and more words hit me, each one from a different person, their voice unique to them.

Goddess of Beginnings, Lady of Life, Consort of Death, I need your help...

Please, My Lady, help me...

Please...

Please..

Please.

Hundreds of desperate calls, all of them begging for me to help. There was no turning away from it, from them.

"Oh gods," I whispered, a halo of aether around me, preparing for what was needed of me. A single glinting tear ran down my cheek. "They're prayers. They're all prayers."

CHAPTER TWENTY-ONE

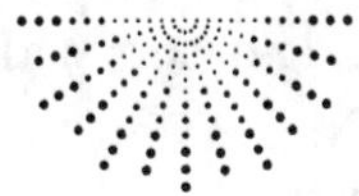

"Are you insane?" Bron paced back and forth in front of the blazing fire that had been thrown together from the broken scraps of the camp.

I leaned against a half-charred log, my body weary, muscles trembling, and a bone-deep ache had settled in deep. A mental fatigue came with it, one that made moving any part of my body, let alone argue with Bron, feel like an insurmountable feat. That sure as hell didn't mean my sparkling personality didn't shine through. Lifting an impertinent eyebrow at him, I asked, "Do you actually want me to answer that?"

He scoffed, shaking his head in aggravation. His pale, white hair had come undone from his bun, long strands hanging around his face. The loose tresses were stained gray from wraith blood, and the scars on his neck and arms stood out starkly against the dark goo covering his washed out skin.

He threw an arm out toward me as he turned to Cashim, the most reasonable of us all, and begged, "Can you please talk some sense into her?"

The night had turned long, a new prayer, a new person, there to take the place of each one I answered. I carried on even as dirt and blood began streaking my face, running down my face alongside the silent tears I shed for each lost soul. Hours of work had broken my nails, the chipped plates ripping off, leaving lines of fire, and then immediately healing. Still, I kept going through the night until even I began to feel the burn of exhaustion. Even as I became entangled in countless lives, each one leaving a mark on my soul.

Ribbons of power had extended from my body, attending to multiple patients at a time, acting as extra arms. Kanan had been right by my side, acting as aid, taking orders without fault.

As soon as we ensured Moian and the other healers wouldn't be swamped, the newly wounded and the old under their watchful care, we called for the councilors. All of them had shown up in minutes, disheveled and covered in gore.

"I'm being perfectly sensible," I retorted. "It might be our only chance, Bron. Look around you, it's not exactly like we're winning any wars here. We're barely surviving."

Oakina chimed in from across the roaring fire, her gray leathers shredded and bloodied. "Our queen is right. It might be a risk we'll have to take."

"Losing you and the king at the same time could be the opening Kasis is looking for, My Lady. We have gone to blows twice with the Chaos's forces, in a matter of days. I don't know if our people can handle much more," Elaric interjected.

I would be lying if I didn't say I was shocked by how much Lord Pyke had spoken. The usually reserved man had listened intently, a calculative look in his eyes I never would have expected, as Kanan and I filled them in on what we had seen.

"Are you sure you saw Rhaera in this portal, My Lady?" The question came from Yeva. Despite her normally demure appearance, her sharp nose and keen look in her eyes made her appear particularly hawkish. The chunks of wraith stuck in her plaited hair and speckling her warm brown skin, quickly turned demure into dangerous.

"It was the same village in the distance," I confirmed, the taste of smoke thick on my tongue. "I remember it quite clearly."

Bron snarled, a rumbling feline sound that had the hairs on the back of my arms raising. "Yes, where you were kidnapped and then taken to Kasis's house of torture."

"Bron," Kanan's quiet command cracked through the air. The dark god had taken up position behind me, stationed against the trunk of a willow with his arms crossed. He hadn't said much since the meeting had started, but I had a feeling he was saving all of it for when we were alone.

"Are you kidding me, Kanan?" he argued. "You can't seriously be considering going back there?"

Kanan simply stared at his best-friend, millennia allowing them wordless conversation.

Bron shook his head, jaw clenched as he ground his teeth. He huffed, his silver eyes flashing in the early morning light as he walked off into the unorganized madness around us. "Fine, do whatever the hell you want. What do I care."

I rubbed my eyes as pressure grew behind them, dread surfacing at the headache I knew was brewing on the horizon. I let my hands slap against my thighs with a sigh as I looked over the gathered Council.

"Lady Yeva, we need you to fly back to Hassere, alert them to what has happened. Take up stewardship of the city again in our stead; we can only guess Kasis's plans, and while we may assume he'll focus his attention on Kanan and I, there's no reason to give him our other cities on a silver platter."

The avian primal nodded, her eyes honed onto my every word.

"Lady Lilyi will be accompanying Cashim, Lars, and the remaining war party back to Eskira to assist in the search for answers on the Warp." The delicate woman dipped her head in agreement, her endlessly dark eyes watching the proceedings with an unblinking gaze.

"Oakina and Elaric, you will go with them as well, but as soon as Eskira is settled, we need you back to Ophineas protecting our northern border. Who knows if Kasis has infiltrated our seas."

"Kan—"

Lars snorted quietly, interrupting me as he muttered under his breath.

"What was that?" I quipped, but Kanan's low growl covered it.

The Council froze, shooting daggers at Lars. No doubt for opening his fat mouth and garnering Kanan's anger. The rumble was that of a predator, lazy and tired, but in no way incapable of meting out quick death.

I peeked over my shoulder and saw the dragon's attention focused solely on the now admonished worm.

"Careful," he warned in that low tone that was whispered in the darkness of dungeons. "I would hate for your usefulness to wear out so soon."

A silence hovered over the area, none of the Council daring to look at Lars. Most chose to look at their feet, head bowed instinctively. Cashim peered up through his thick eyelashes, watching everything in that shrewd way his niece had acquired and utilized to be the commander she was today.

Lady Lilyi was the only one watching Kanan, her black eyes gleaming in the light as she took him in, her face impassive.

Clearing my throat, I broke the tension. "Kanan and I will head for Rhaera from here in the morning. Hopefully, if we find what we need, we should be back when you arrive in Eskira."

"We wish you luck, my queen." Cashim's solemn face said anything but, and I had no doubt he agreed with Bron that this was a bad idea. Thankfully, instead of arguing he simply bowed his head before heading for the infirmaries.

The rest quickly followed, leaving just me and Kanan standing by the fast growing fire.

"Bron's not wrong, you know," he said from behind me. "This is a horrible idea. The last time you went to Rhaera, you were kidnapped."

"I know."

"Kasis had his henchmen take you through one of those rips and hold you captive in one of his cells."

"I know."

"He tortured you," he spat. "Hurt your family."

I whipped around, facing him. "Kanan! I know, okay?"

Breathing hard, I blinked back the tears of frustration. "I know. Don't you think I know what I did? I'm at fault here."

His face dropped, "Atallia."

"No," I let out a miserable laugh. "It's true. I'm the reason all of that happened. I went with you to Rhaera despite both you and Cashim telling me not to. I was stubborn and stupid and naive, and I went even knowing I was powerless against the things in this world. *I'm* the reason they set a trap for us. *I* got myself captured."

I looked away, unable to meet his gaze. "*I* got that little girl killed. I did that."

He stepped closer, reaching out, but I backed away. He stopped as I shook my head at him. "I did that, Kanan. I play those moments in my head, over and over, and had I just fucking listened she might still be alive. I wouldn't have gotten captured, and the Descendants wouldn't have had to come rescue me."

And there lay my problem. My jumbled mess of emotions all stemmed from the absolute shame that lay rotting away inside me. Self-loathing and disgust ate away at any sense of confidence I had in myself.

"How much of this do you think would be happening if it weren't for me? Huh? How can I be expected to be a queen—a fucking goddess—when everything I do is one big mistake after another? I need to do this, Kanan. I need to try and do something right, find some way to fix this before it gets everyone killed."

He stared down at me, a short laugh leaving him. "Get over yourself, love."

I leaned back in shock. "Excuse me?"

"Get over yourself," he repeated. "Yes, you were a catalyst for a lot of things, and maybe you've made some questionable choices, but if you think for one second that Kasis wasn't already an obsessive fuck before you came into being, then you're wrong. When I look back on our earliest times, long before you, he was always off. Not in the way he is now, but he was never *right*."

There wasn't much I knew about the time before my past self had come down to Irropia, even the little book of history Wrynn had given me had only spoken of the Time of Nightmares briefly.

"What do you mean?"

He shifted closer, easing into my space until his dark scent engulfed me. "I mean he was always experimenting, seeing what made certain things tick the way they do. When he realized his power was less than mine for no apparent reason, he started pushing himself to his limits to see what he could do. Illusions, tricks, manipulation… chaos."

"He hid it well, but he reveled in the power we wielded over others, and knowing I held more twisted something inside him long before you came around. And when you did, you simply became another one of his obsessions."

He peered down at me, the corner of his lips lifting. "For good reason, to be fair; neither of us ever had much restraint when it came to you, but whereas my obsession stems from devotion, his was born of greed and jealousy."

My heart stumbled and the air in my lungs sawed out of me as he gripped my chin between his thumb and forefinger

"You may be a goddess, my love," he said, dragging his thumb over my lower lip, watching it with a hungry expression, "but don't let that inflate your ego. I have no doubt anymore that my brother was going to be an evil fuck with or without you. A few bad mistakes made in this life doesn't mean you deserve to put the full weight of that on your shoulders."

I could feel that burden lingering, eager to weigh down my every decision like sunken vessels taken by the perilous swells of sea. In the time between finding out who I was and now, I had taken on the blame for every one of Kasis's decisions, something I was beginning to see was a bit arrogant of me.

"Does this mean we're about to fight on whether I'm going to Rhaera?" I asked teasingly. A grin pulled at my mouth, even as a warmth burned from where his hand still cupped my chin and spread through me like wildfire.

Sensing my mood change, he grinned back, those two dimples

putting in more work to get me wet than any dirty words. "I don't know, are you going to let me kiss you again?"

The way he said it sounded like he had a lot more than that in mind, and damn if that wasn't starting to seem like a grand idea. My core clenched in anticipation. The stupid bitch.

"I need this, Kanan," I said in all seriousness. "Maybe it isn't all my fault, but I can't keep seeing our people get hurt like this. I may not have expected it, or even wanted it, but they look at me and see their queen. I don't think I can keep failing in protecting them."

He rubbed his thumb against my jaw, his eyes hard as stone. "I know, love, we won't. Kasis is ahead of us, but not for long. We're going to do everything in our power to keep them safe, aren't we?"

"Everything," I agreed with a nod.

He smiled then, playful and full of fang. His pupils split into the vertical slits of his dragon form before returning to normal, but a draconian look stayed put in those swirling blood red eyes. "Now about that kiss…"

I laughed, backing out of his grip. Shaking my head as I went, I glanced over my shoulder, "I'm still mad at you, asshole."

"Sure didn't feel like you were mad at me," he retorted smugly. Despite the light tone, his eyes bore into mine, a possessive adoration shining brightly. The dragon staring through those red irises, admiring what he considered his.

What we'd done had been a lapse in judgment, a delicious one, but a lapse nonetheless. Despite my softening anger, I was still hesitant to trust him again. I wasn't fully sure of his reason to withhold everything from me, and it's what stopped me from going to him every time.

There was a very real, very instant, part of me that looked past the hard exterior and the secrets that cloaked him and saw my other half. I saw a very real possibility of what we could be, of what we had been before.

I just couldn't tell if that was me, or my past life. I didn't know what was real anymore and what wasn't.

I didn't even know if I was real. This life I thought was mine, but that had never been the truth in the first place. Was it real, or would it fade away like the rest of my memories?

CHAPTER TWENTY-TWO

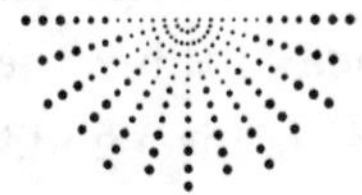

"Remember to always keep them with you, even if you need to sleep. Don't separate, you're both stronger together, and Kasis will be less likely to take you if you stay with the king," Zanaya rambled, passing me several black blades. The heartsglass sucked in all the light being thrown off by the fire, the surrounding area dimming until the extra daggers were safely stored inside my pack.

I'd already strapped two to my thighs, and after Zanaya's insistence, two blade-filled gauntlets now covered my forearms. Each of the small throwing knives that she had sheathed in the leather guards were only the length of my palm, but despite their size the onyx crystal would do more than enough damage against anything magical.

And if that didn't work…well a blade to the eye always had a way of fucking up someone's day.

"He would be an idiot to try that again, but nonetheless, don't let him get the slip on you just because we might be underestimating him. From what you've told us, you cloud his judgment, he might try it simply because you're in play."

A warmth filled my chest as she continued, stressing on common sense things. The minute I had told them that we'd be separating,

Zanaya had become a mother hen. Quickly switching between Commander and worried friend, she'd been both ordering me not to get hurt and also making sure I had packed everything I needed.

"Don't forget to keep your balance. If you get ambushed, don't let them take you to the ground if you can help it, you'll be at an immediate disadvantage."

Zander cleared his throat from where he was leaning back against a log, his long legs stretched out before him. A tired, placating grin curled across his devilish face, "I think she knows that already, Zani. Besides, our golden warrior here is a goddess, I'm sure she has tricks up her sleeve not even she's aware of."

He shot me a wink, crossing his muscled arms over his chest, before glancing back into the fire. His handsome face, with all of its angles and sharp lines, was alight in the fire. The flames had turned his hair into a rich red that matched the fur of his fox, until sitting next to a resting Nala they looked like twin infernos.

I appreciated the vote of confidence, but even Zander's normal swagger was dull. The normally exuberant trickster had spent the entire night by Nala's side, ensuring her chest continued to rise and fall. Everyone was exhausted, the hours she'd spent unconscious long and hard, all of us sitting vigil until she woke in the early morning.

No one had found sleep easily, some didn't find it at all. Gathering the newly dead and mutilated, the healers were more overwhelmed than ever, and those still standing had been pulling double shifts on watch to ensure another attack didn't happen at our most vulnerable.

Most hadn't even fully recovered from the Gravelands, and the hard journey was not helping the matter either. We were nearing the end of our strength, both physically and in power.

It was the worst time for Kanan and I to be leaving them, but our options were becoming more limited by the day.

We couldn't risk only sending one of us. Kasis was showing us by the day that in the time we'd been gone, he had been finding new ways to get around what he lacked in power, and it was becoming clearer that any chance we had at stopping him would need both Kanan and I.

At the same time, by leaving, we risked the war party being taken by surprise again. The rips, portals, whatever they were, changed things.

It seemed like nothing was going our way, but if Kanan and I could find anything about Kasis's plans, then we might have some chance to stop what was coming. We had been on the defense for so long that if we didn't start hitting back, we might lose before the war had even begun.

It was a gamble, a huge fucking gamble, but all we could do was hope we'd picked the lesser of two evils and that something would come of us going back to Rhaera.

No one had liked the plan, even after seeing the merit in it. If the fight had shown us anything it was that we worked better together. Splitting up was the last thing any of us wanted at the moment. Even the mysterious Saanvi and quiet Orion had been visibly uneasy with my plan.

A weird sensation had been building since they had all circled up around me as I packed, giving me their support during the little downtime they had. A tightening in my chest that made it hard to breathe, and yet I felt like a weight had been lifted from my chest.

I had never had this before. Never had friendships that needed no words, only each other's presence to flourish, and that's what I felt was slowly building between me and this tight knit group of warriors. Each of them different in their own way, but together they fit like puzzle pieces, better together than they ever were apart.

The emotions clogged my throat and forbade me from speaking them out loud, but the more time I spent encircled in the bonds of friendship, the less I felt that they were necessary.

I buckled the straps of my pack before reaching out for Zanaya's hand. We gripped each other tight, a look passing between us that conveyed far more than I could voice.

I had only known her for a short time, but even I could recognize a kindred spirit. Someone I knew I could rely on no matter what. Even amongst the chaos, a voice in the back of mind echoed that thought repeatedly until it might as well have been engraved into my brain.

"I'll be okay," I promised, speaking the words to everyone. "This won't be like last time. I was naive, thinking I would be fine even without my power."

I shook my head at my own stupidity and pride, the two things that had led to my capture. I straightened, taking her with me. Squeezing her hand tighter, I said the words I prayed were true. "This time I'm ready, and I won't make the same mistakes."

She nodded her regal head, releasing my hand and rushing me with open arms. I froze, hesitant for only a second, before locking my arms around her.

"You're our last piece, Atallia," she whispered into my ear so only I could hear it. "Don't take that away from us when we've only just found you."

Tears welled in my eyes as her words struck true, hitting me right in the heart and crushing the cynical voice that said this was temporary. That they'd get sick of me, eventually fear me like everyone always had.

If I had nothing else, I knew I would always have them, and that nearly broke me. Pressing my wobbling lips together to stop the sob that wanted to tear free, I blinked the tears from my eyes and held on as tight as I could to her slender form.

Finally breaking apart with one last look, I moved to the rest of them.

"Now, I know just how much you'll miss all of this, " Zander joked, waving his hand up and down his body, "but don't worry, it'll be here when you get back."

I laughed, holding on to the sound in my heart and memorizing his boyish smile.

"Oh come on Zander, you can't tell me you think you could compete with a god." Nala shuffled up beside him, her short frame buzzing with barely contained energy despite the burnout I knew she was still facing. The bandages around her abdomen were tinged pink, and when her knees nearly gave way, Zander's arm was there to support her.

The fox shot her a wobbly smile, worry mixing with loving familiarity. "You tell me Nals. I think between him and I, I could put up quite the competition."

The live-wire tilted her head in contemplation, eyes squinting as she looked him over. "Maybe if all those muscles of his are fake."

She turned her gaze to me, open curiosity on her wan face. "What do you think, Talli? Is it all a show? Even I would be disappointed if all that yumminess turned out to be a fake."

"Oh gods, please tell me it's not," Zander begged in genuine concern. "That would ruin all my fantasies. I swear that man could get me pregnant with just a look, and I will be extremely disappointed if I can't have that anymore."

"You can't get pregnant, Zander," Saanvi muttered from behind him, pinching the bridge of her nose.

"Semantics. I would let that man do some very dirty things to me," he replied huskily and without a shred of embarrassment.

His eyes were unfocused as the others groaned their reproach like he was remembering those fantasies. Not that I could blame him. Blinking rapidly, he returned his attention to me, lifting his eyebrows, "So?"

I chuckled as the redheads watched me intently. "All real, I promise."

They both let out actual sighs of relief, making the entire group laugh at their absurdity.

"Here," Nala said, offering me a small gray pouch with a shaky hand.

The sack rattled, the stiff material rough against my fingers as I took it. Undoing the leather tie, I opened the cinched bag. A dozen glaring red stones rested inside. Barely larger than the pebbles that lined the bank of the lake, they buzzed happily as I took one in my hand.

Heat and something far more volatile zapped at my skin. The casing rattled unpredictably, shaking as the magic inside quivered in anticipation.

"Shattershells," I exclaimed in disbelief. Slowly lowering the smooth stone back inside the sack, the erratic energy that mimicked its maker calming as I closed the sack. "I thought you used up your supply last night?"

The pyro shrugged her shoulders, the embers from her wild curls closer to ash in color as they fell around her. "I had Orion help me make some for you a few days ago, figured you'd need them at some point. You know in case you need to blow some shit up. No biggie."

Except it was.

Nala created the shells from her own magic, encasing them in a special material Orion pulled and crafted from the earth. It was why many didn't use them, even with their ingenious design, it took time and power to create the small explosive shells, so it often wasn't worth it for those who didn't have the excess.

Even just the twelve she made would have pulled from her reserves, from both of their reserves, which were as dangerously low as everyone else's from the constant fighting.

"Thank you," I whispered, tying the pouch on a belt loop before gently pulling her in for a hug, careful of her still healing wounds.

"Don't mention it," she replied back with a wide smile that transformed her whole face into an even more beautiful version despite the dark circles beneath her eyes.

"You come back to us, golden girl," Saanvi's quiet voice issued. She had closed the distance until she stood right next to me.

Her eyes met mine, withstanding my gaze longer than most, which wasn't shocking now that I knew what she was. I'd been ignorant not to question the power within those verdant green irises, glowing with that magic of the mythical serpent beneath her skin.

I knew I wouldn't get a hug from her like I had from Zanaya or Nala, but I held my arm out in invitation, a warrior's goodbye. "Don't worry I'll be back, just so I can hear your story."

She knew what I meant and smiled, the secrets of her life sealed tightly behind her lips. The tips of her fangs peeked out, and the scar that slashed across her eyebrow rose as she looked me over. She gripped my outstretched arm with her own, her short hair brushing her jaw as she dipped her head.

"A story for another day. One when you come back."

I grinned, “I look forward to it.”

We released each other at the same time and I crossed over to Orion who had stayed further back. The mountain of a man, the quiet, steady rock of the group, was never one to lead the conversation. Instead he preferred to show his emotions with actions, reminding me a bit of Kanan in that way.

“Thank you for the shells.” I looked up at the gray man, his lips pressed thin in agitation as he took in everything around us.

“Whatever I can do to help,” he grunted softly. Reaching into his back pocket he pulled out two leather necklaces. Someone gasped behind me as he pulled them out.

A gemstone dangled from each, the blue-purple colors swirled together like stained glass, dazzling in the early morning light. The rough, jagged stones glowed brightly as they sat together in his large palm.

He took one in hand, slipping the leather over my head. The stone rested gently against my chest, the glow fading away as he pulled the other over his own head.

“They’re amazing,” I whispered in awe. Gently gripping the crystal, I brought it up to my face. The sun hit it as I did so, fracturing the light into a million colorful rays. The one around Orion’s neck flared for a second before dying out. “What are they?”

“They’re beacon stones,” he replied with a gentle smile. “Incredibly rare gems. I only know of a few in existence right now. They come in sets, and are highly sought after because if you shine your magic through it, the other will glow and lead you to its pair.”

A wonder filled me at the small rock I held in my hand. I let myself fall into the storm of power deep inside my chest, feeling the pull to let the power lose to do as it will. With sheer will I contained it and let the tiniest stream out through my hand and into the rock.

Golden light filled the indigo crystal, and exactly like a beacon, the rock around Orion's thick neck flared gold. A brilliant power leaked around the rock and like a puppet on strings it lifted from his chest and strained against its leather cord, reaching out towards the one in my hand.

I couldn't help but laugh, marveling at the magic. A few months ago I would have never been able to guess where I would end up, and I can't say the time in Allasea hadn't had its downsides.

A lot of fucking downsides.

But even as I became desensitized to everything else, the magic—true magic—had never stopped amazing me.

"This way if you get into trouble and need our help, we'll be able to find you. My mother gave them to me before she died, and told me they might come in handy one day. I think she'd get a laugh at how right she was."

"Orion," I stuttered, already reaching to take the cord off. "I can't possibly take this."

He stopped my hand, his gray skin cool against my own. His black eyes, warm and inviting, met mine before looking down with a smile at the gem in my hand. "You're not taking anything, I'm letting you borrow it. Think of it as another reason to get back safe."

"Are you sure?" I asked quietly. My heart hurt for him, the love for his mother so clear in his voice.

His eyes pinched at the corners as his smile widened. "My mother would be proud to know I was using it to help a friend. The returned queen no less."

Dropping the necklace back against my chest as he released my hand, I bowed my head in thanks. "It's coming back to you, Orion. I'll make sure of it, and when I get back I want to hear all about the woman that raised you to be the man you are."

The unmoving rock of a man, a gentle giant when it came to those he cared for, inclined his head respectfully. "I await your and the stone's swift return then."

Reaching up on my tip toes, I pressed a kiss to his cheek. Grinning as his cheeks darkened, what must be a blush for the normally stoic man, I reached down for my pack and slung it over my shoulder.

I took them all in, trying not to let the emotions get to me. Now that I had found somewhere I felt I could one day truly belong, it wasn't easy to give up even if only for a little while.

Zanaya took pity on my plight, shooing everyone off. "Alright get going, we can't keep her to ourselves. The faster she and the king do what they need to do, the faster they'll be back with us."

As I waved goodbye, I prayed it wouldn't be long before I saw them again.

Zanaya glanced over me, her keen gaze missing nothing. "You have everything you need?"

I blew out a breath, my shoulders tense as the comfort of the group dissipated and allowed for reality to sink back in. "Between the two of us we should be fine on supplies, and we plan to stop at the inn before heading to Rhaera. You still good to do what I asked?"

Flipping one of her blades between her hands, the black glass dangerously close to her skin, she tested its razor edge against her thumb.

She couldn't stop the wince as a drop of blood welled, but she seemed pleased nonetheless. I didn't know why she worried, the very same blades had been spinning and slashing wildly last night, taking down wraith after wraith between her ice attacks.

Then again, I hadn't seen her put it in her sheath for more than a few minutes since the wraiths had destroyed camp.

"Yep, I'll make sure Moian gets the message. Hopefully we should have some answers for you by the time you get back."

I shifted the pack higher, putting my arm through the other strap. "Good. Has she seen the corpses yet?"

She shook her head, shrugging as she looked out over what remained of the once organized site. Most had taken to sleeping on the ground, the tents and bedding nearly all destroyed, and many had given up on the venture all together. It wouldn't kill them, but it certainly didn't help morale. Tensions were running high and there wasn't much anyone could do.

"I haven't talked to her since last night, but from what I understand, they had the wraiths moved onto a guarded wagon. She was too busy with the wounded, but the healers seem excited to finally have a specimen to look at. It's the first time the hoards were sloppy enough to leave their dead behind."

"Let's hope it leads to some answers," I added. "Just make sure

Moian gets my message, it might give her a place to start. Oh, and keep an eye out for Wrynn, will you? I'm starting to get worried about him."

"I will," she promised. "You just focus on getting back to us in one piece."

I started walking backwards away from her, a smile spreading across my face. "I'll do my best, multiple pieces just sounds like way too much work for me right now."

I spun around with one last wave, smile firmly in place, and headed for the lake. It didn't take long to get there, the path no longer blocked by tents. Any that had survived had already been picked up, inventoried, and stored on the surviving wagons.

The piles had been pathetically small, and the only saving grace was how close Elona was. It would take the entire party a day and a half to make the trip—maybe two with the overwhelming exhaustion —but once there, Eskira could send aid for the thousand-odd soldiers still with us.

It had been Kanan's idea to send a messenger ahead to the cities so they knew to prepare for their arrival and have the necessary supplies on hand.

Walking over scorched patches of earth, red and black blood dripping down the blades of grass and into the ash-covered ground, I couldn't help but question our decision. We had somehow come out of the battle without losing anyone else, but there were some close calls, and the injured had doubled in number.

Those with wounds had been quarantined, although not one showed signs of being warped. Moian couldn't give any reassurances though; for all we knew, the sickness had mutated, becoming a sleeper inside the bodies of the seemingly healthy.

We knew so little about the Warp, about Kasis and the machinations he had put in place to force us into submission. Our only hope was to go out and find the answers, or else we would be flying blind and our people would be the ones paying for it.

I came over the short rise that led down to the bank, blinking in surprise at Bron waiting near the water's edge. He crossed his hulking arms over his chest and watched my approach with a calculating gaze.

"You come to try and talk me out of this again?" I came to a stop beside him, his silver eyes watching the small jewel-toned birds flying over the water, their reflection lost within the colorful currents below.

He said nothing, both of us soaking in the silence as the breeze blew across the plains, carrying with it the lingering smell of blood and ash. The world was one big contradiction. The beauty of it clashing with the horrors.

Finally, after what seemed like forever, he broke the tension, sighing heavily. "You weren't there, Atallia. You weren't there when he lost you."

The words that sprung up in answer died in my throat.

"Not during the Year of Sorrow, not after you reincarnated, and not when Kasis had you kidnapped. You weren't there," he paused, shoulders dropping as if a weight had dropped around him. "But I was. I saw what it did to him, and I don't think you could ever truly grasp just what you mean to him."

Kicking my foot into the dirt, I crossed my arms tightly, fighting off the chill that tried to overtake me. The lies. It always came back to the lies. My heart wrenched painfully inside my chest. I still couldn't see how you could lie about something so important to someone you apparently cared for, good intentions or not.

"Even if he does have a good reason, what if I'm not the same person from his memories? Have you thought about that?" I asked, my own insecurities coming to the forefront.

He laughed, his big shoulders shaking. "You're not the same."

A pit opened up in the bottom of my stomach, my heart sinking rapidly into the gaping chasm.

"Not in a bad way," he continued on without noticing my crisis, "and not in every way, but different nonetheless."

"Then why does he care?" It had been a question on my mind, echoing those stabbing insecurities since my world had been blown to hell and back.

"Don't you think the first person to notice a difference would be him? You may not want to hear it," he said, giving me a look, "but he was your mate for nearly fifteen thousand years. After you reincarnated, there wasn't even a full week between your loss and him following you."

I hadn't heard much about the time directly after the War of Three, after I escaped Kasis the first time and decided to give up my previous life. I still didn't know why I had done that in the first place, but the screams I had heard in my nightmares, the ones I still heard, gave me some idea.

"Maybe it's time to start asking yourself why you're trying to find reasons for people to not want you. Because it looks to me that he sees those differences and doesn't care."

It was a good thing that Kanan walked out from between the trees then, because I had no words to refute those claims.

And as I began to walk over to the man in question, watching us from the shadow of the willows, Bron whispered one last thing that put my perception of everything at risk.

"You know...he's different too."

CHAPTER TWENTY-THREE

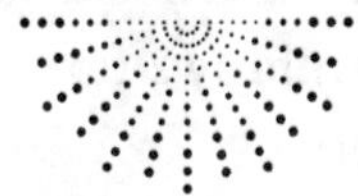

With Kanan's swift wings carrying us, and Allasea's skies on our side, we reached Ellenia's inn only a few hours after our departure. The large, countryside cottage exuded comfort and warmth as we landed in the pastures it overlooked.

I slid down Kanan's wing, taking in the surrounding woodland that circled the back of the inn. Rhaera, with its empty homes and buildings reduced to cinders, was locked inside the malevolence that slithered between those trunks. The answers we searched for could be right before our eyes.

I just wished it hadn't been at the cost of an entire village.

"It's worse," I said as Kanan walked up beside me. Shadows scurried off to their corners except for the ones that almost always hung around him. "Like it's grown."

Shivers ran down my spine, the same cold chill from the plains seeping into my bones.

"Something is definitely here." His eyes scanned the tree-line searching for a cause. More wraiths or something far worse.

"Let's get inside," he murmured, putting his hand on the small of my back and leading me forward. His shadows trailed behind, alert and cautious, watching our backs like guard dogs.

We kept our heads on a swivel as we made our way to the front door. Gods or not, until we knew the depths of Kasis's plans, we didn't know what he might throw at us.

We entered through the front, the inn's comforting interior laid out before us. Surprisingly, it was empty.

No guests lingered in the living room, dozing near the fire, or sat bundled on the couches as they waited for dinner. No sounds of conversation reached our ears, the house as silent as a graveyard.

We glanced at each other, brows furrowed, but as our suspicions rose, Elena turned the corner.

"Oh, your majesties," she said, dipping into a bow. "A pleasure to have you with us again."

"I see news spreads fast." Kanan smiled, stepping forward to greet the innkeeper.

The soft woman smiled back, looking a little strained, but answered all the same, "You know how gossip spreads. It rides the wind and reaches willing ears all around."

Face drawn and paler than the last time we had seen her, Ellenia looked sick. Dark circles marred the skin under her eyes. Her beautiful dark brown curls held a sheen, like she hadn't yet bathed today, and the lines around her eyes that I had once thought were from laughter appeared instead to be the result of tension.

Kanan hummed, scanning over her face, clearly noticing what I had. "That it does."

"Are you alright, Ellenia?" I asked, stepping up to the woman in concern.

She startled, as if unused to anyone being worried for her. "Yes, yes, thank you, My Lady. I'm sorry," she said running her hands down her light blue dress, "I must look a mess. This whole sickness has really taken it out of everyone, most people don't want to leave their towns and cities to travel. Not even the merchants."

She waved her hand around the empty room with a pinched look. "I haven't seen a single soul in weeks. Not since you two came to visit. I guess it's just wearing on me."

"You'll let us know if there's anything we can do, won't you?" I felt bad for the poor woman, her very livelihood being threatened before her eyes.

She smiled sweetly, reaching out to grasp my hand, "I appreciate your concern, My Lady, but this inn has been in my family for hundreds of years. I'll do everything in my power to ensure its survival. We'll both be fine."

I nodded in concession, allowing her her pride, although the darkness in her eyes still lingered.

She shook it off, brightening as her inner hostess came to the forefront. "Well, you both must be starving, let's get you something to warm up. Flying all the way from the south must be taxing."

As she turned back down the hall, indicating for us to follow, Kanan and I exchanged a look. I saw the same question echoed on his face. Narrowing my eyes, I dipped my head to where Elena had disappeared down the hall.

"Let's see what happens," I sent down our tether. The bond, one entirely unique to us I had found, often reminded me of a rope. Black and gold strands winding together until they formed a bridge between us, a connection that only seemed to grow the more we used it. As if it had only needed to be acknowledged to become stronger.

He shrugged his hulking shoulders, *"Why not, could be fun."*

Shadows peeled off the walls, encircling his large biceps and gently wrapping around my ankles. *"I'm right behind you, love."*

With his support, I moved through the hall lined with the portraits of past innkeepers, following the sounds of pots and bowls clanking together.

As we walked, more and more shadows followed, crawling along the floor like a fog. One curious shade pushed open one of the room doors, the old hinges letting out a small creak.

My heart thudded as we passed, the unremarkable room nearly identical to the one we stayed in last time. I almost walked past completely, but the flash of a golden timepiece, half tossed under the bed, pulled me up short.

The dark tendrils around my ankles squeezed as I tensed, reminding me of their presence. Another coiled out, snaking through the room until it reached the long chain, looping beneath it and carrying it back to Kanan.

Flipping it over in his hand, his eyes flicked over the back. His eyes hardened, becoming cut gemstones. He glanced down at me before flipping the clock face in hand to show me.

On the back of the pristine gold was an engraving.

For the spark that keeps my fire alive

Until the end of time, it is you and I

Come back to me always

Larissa

My stomach dropped, denial burning like acid in my throat. I looked up at Kanan, desperately wishing what we thought wasn't true.

Shoving the timepiece and its chain into his pocket, he lightly brushed his thumb across my chin.

"Everything alright?" Elena's voice called from the direction of the kitchen.

Giving me a nod, he urged us forward. "We got distracted by the paintings," he called back, his voice not wavering in the slightest. "How many previous keepers do you have hanging?"

We followed her voice as she responded, watching our steps as we walked. The dining area and kitchen were one big room, a counter and half wall separating the two. Standing in the open arch, darkness climbing along the walls and ceiling behind, I flexed my hands as power began to build.

A tingling spread from my heart, motivated by what that watch meant, and swept throughout my entire body until the hair on my arms prickled. Golden bursts of light roved across my sight and the roar of power slowly built to a crescendo in my ears.

"There are so many now I can barely count them all, there's… uhmmm—" She turned around, the number evading her, and as she looked up, panic flashed across her features.

I didn't need a mirror to know what she saw. Me, a burning star of golden power, standing in her kitchen; and over my shoulder—Kanan. No longer the Champion of Death, but Death himself.

"How did you know we came from the south, Ellenia?" I asked

softly, the words echoing each other until my magic made it sound like a hundred voices all at once.

Shadows filled in through the archway, winding up to the ceiling, staring down menacingly from their perch.

"Wh-what do you mean?" she stuttered out, her eyes going wide as darkness began to overtake the room.

"We never told you where we were coming from," I continued, stepping further into the room. The shadows followed, hissing and spitting, entwining with the wisps of gold power that sizzled off my skin.

The soft candlelight was no match for the ever growing black fog moving in, Kanan's form only half visible in the door. His glowing eyes stared out from within, bloody and on fire. His expression was flat—patient—waiting for his prey to inevitably mess up.

Her brown eyes flickered in the shifting light. Glancing wildly around, as the creeping midnight shadows above and below grew closer, she inched backwards. The fire at her back forced her to a stop, until she had no choice but to face us.

"I-I told you," she stammered, "People like t-to gossip. It even reaches me, despite being this far north."

"You also said you hadn't seen a soul in weeks."

"My queen, please," she pleaded, desperation entering her voice, "I don't know what this is about, but it must be a misunderstanding. Please."

Her eyes flickered again. Tilting my head, I let out a chuckle. It was a disturbing sound, one that surprised me, but even still I pulled one of my daggers from its sheath. "You're better than Jasco, I'll give you that."

A muscle along their cheek twitched. Blinking rapidly they shook their head, denial sitting on the tip of their tongue like a blade. "I d-don't know what you're ta-talking about. Please."

Pacing back and forth in front of them, protected by the shadows that had all but engulfed the room, I balanced my blade on the tip of my finger.

"See, when I met him, his face kept shifting. Maybe he was trying to protect his identity, or maybe he did it just to be confusing, who knows, but one thing I noticed was that he couldn't seem to keep one mask in place," I said pragmatically, watching the beautiful black blade rest perfectly on my finger.

The slight burn from the crystal was enough to keep me anchored. The zing that raced from my fingertip all the way to my chest was a bare pinprick to the wild cosmic storm that lived inside, but it centered me all the same.

Dropping my finger, I snatched the blade from the air, my movement invisible to the naked eye. I turned to face them, the fire at their back radiating the only heat left in the room, and pointed my blade at the imposter.

I gripped the hilt tighter, the golden aura around me illuminating the space in between us. "Like I said, you're better than him…but not perfect."

A second's pause, so silent save for the crackles of fire that I could hear my heart beating away in my chest like a drum and the whooshing of air in and out of my lungs. The cool sensation of darkness swept along my arms as the shadows behind me moved, stalking around the room to lie in wait.

And then, like a waterfall, the panic fell from the image of Ellenia's face, followed swiftly by an eerie, twisted smile. Wicked delight shown through those eyes, nowhere near the kindness and compassion that the real innkeeper showed each and every one of her guests.

"Well," the illusionist drawled, the word sounding wrong coming from Ellenia's mouth, "at least you're not a complete idiot. Seems I underestimated you."

Swallowing the bile that threatened to rise, I glared at the fake and snarled, "What have you done with Ellenia?"

They laughed, and the distorted noise was sickening. Disgust twisted my lips, as a slimy feeling settled over me.

"Poor, poor, Ellenia," they mocked, running hands down one of her blue dresses. "How she fought. Fought for her guests. Her inn."

Clucking their tongue, a sardonic wince of pain on Ellenia's swollen face, they stared unblinking at me.

"But she was easy, and she sang like a bird with a little—" they grinned, "a little persuasion."

I stood there, shaking, rage roaring inside me. My feet were planted into the ground, unable to move from the sheer force that had reared its head, snarling in fury. A monstrous creature that clawed its way forth from where it had settled deep inside the dark pits of my soul.

"Once you left for Rhaera, it wasn't difficult to take her and alert the others of your position. Setting a trap was too easy. That little girl," the imposter laughed, the cruel lilt enraging me even more.

A sneer, a sadistic twist of Ellenia's beautiful face. "I heard you screamed when they killed the pathetic wretch. Was it as glorious as they say, the blade sticking up through her mouth?"The monster let out a forlorn sigh, "I wish I hadn't missed it."

Whether it was the nonchalant way they spoke of hurting, torturing, the sweet innkeeper who had shown nothing but kindness to us, or the sickening delight on his face as he described the little girl's death, I'm not sure, but something in me snapped.

A cold, detached sensation washed over me. The fake kept talking, gloating, but I heard none of it.

Such corruption. That an evil of this magnitude had taken root inside that they relished in others' pain like that, enjoyed it. There had always been those that sought to hurt those around them, they liked the power it gave them.

Kasis had somehow created a people entirely dedicated to seeking that hurt, that pain. The maliciousness had become sentient in a way, crawling inside to roost, spreading just like the plague he had fathered.

And as the shock wore away, the surprise at the lengths this rot would go if left unchecked crumbled to ashes. Left standing amongst the ruin of my naivety was an insurmountable will, built upon a foundation of wrath and love and ancient power, that would stop at nothing to crush the hell that sought to destroy everything we cherished.

I slashed my empty hand out, a ribbon of blistering energy whipping across the illusion of Ellenia.

Jerking back with a satisfying scream, the coward was singed by the gathered flames. Falling to their knees with heaving breaths, the edges of the mask began to peel away like burning paper.

Curling inwards, the person's shape blurred, changing from one thing to the next. Woman, no, man. Re—brown hair. A slender build one second, large and muscular the next.

My eyes throbbed as it all happened at once, like my brain couldn't comprehend what was and wasn't happening.

Finally, the phasing stopped. On the ground, choking on air as he drew in heaving, painful breaths, was a man. Average build, average height, average everything except for his eyes.

A startling green gaze looked up at me from beneath shaggy brown hair, hatred brewing deep inside them.

"You pack a punch, but then again, most of the bitches I've met do."

I lifted an eyebrow, staring him down until he was forced to drop his gaze. "Now it makes sense. With that fucked up face of yours, I wondered who had used it as a punching bag."

Nostrils flaring, the man spit in my direction. Thankfully from his position on the floor it landed next to my foot. Looking from it to him in boredom, I crossed my arms across my chest, dagger still in hand.

"Are you done?"

Slowly getting to his feet, he used the back of his hand to wipe his mouth. Painful grunts forced their way out of his mouth and a grimace carved lines around his eyes as he straightened. "You're gonna have to do better than that if you want to kill me."

Now it was my turn to laugh, "Kill you? Why would I want to do that? You have information I need and I think with a little...persuasion it'll be you singing like a bird."

The man went still, and despite the mask he tried his best to keep in place, a touch of fear licked his heels. Eyes darting wildly around, the pure darkness rippling around us in patient fury, I simply smiled as he realized all too late what he'd gotten himself into.

As predictable as his insults, he rushed me, and emerging from the endless shadows next to him a clawed hand reached out and caught him by the neck.

Demonic black claws, gleaming wickedly in the mix of fire and aether, dug in. Dark blood rolled down his neck from the punctures. The man gasped, choking for air that would not come.

Stepping out from the impenetrable wall of shadow like a dark god of hell, savage red eyes glowing bright, Kanan watched impassively as the man in his grasp struggled. His patience had worn thin while I handled the situation, something that hadn't escaped my notice or appreciation, but now it was Death's turn to enact his vengeance. "My, my, my," he purred, his voice like the slow chill of death. "What an unwise choice to make, when surrounded by gods."

Eyes bulging out of his head, the fear bled through until it radiated from him, spicing the air. Ropes of shade reached up from the floor, climbing up his kicking legs and swallowing him. Kanan unclenched his fist, dropping the man into the abyss of swirling black fog that covered the floor, his choking gurgles cut off.

Leading us into the connected room, his shadows drawing back and filling in the spaces they had abandoned, Kanan pulled out a chair for me before heading back into the kitchen. I shot him an appreciative smile as I sat and waited for the murkiness to clear.

Chained by nothing more than ebony bands, the illusionist was forced into a kneel before me. He stared up at me, both fear and rage within his gaze, nostrils flaring as he fought to break free. Straining his neck as the cords tightened, the one over his mouth began to cut into his black, tan, white skin.

The illusionist's features continued to shift even after my blow, slow and sluggish, but changing all the same.

"What are your people called?" I asked in genuine curiosity. Calling them Kasis's goons worked fine, but the stupid assholes had to have a name. Kasis was too egotistical to not call them something.

The gag drew back just as Kanan walked back in, two steaming bowls in his hands. Placing one before me, he gently tugged on one of my loose curls, playing it between his fingers before moving to sit on my left.

It was such a casual touch, a simple tug, a reminder of support, but the voice in the back of my head, that would've liked nothing more than to reciprocate, grew louder. It was when he did things like that, that my walls started chipping, crumbling against him and the unshakable care he showed me.

"You dragon-fucking bitch," the man spit.

Faster than a whip, the shadow lashed around his mouth and neck, squeezing tightly. Face turning red, there was no noise as he choked. He tried breathing through his nose, but whatever Kanan was doing wouldn't allow the air to feed his depleted lungs.

Second after second, his body desperately needing that nourishing breath, he struggled until even I wondered if Kanan would just kill him here and now.

Unbothered beside me, the dragon god shoveled spoonful after spoonful of stew into his mouth. He didn't bother to look up as the man slowly died, enjoying his meal with live entertainment.

"It would be good if we got some information out of him before you kill him," I teased with a shrug of my shoulders. "Just a thought."

Finally glancing down at the kneeling man, a bored expression fixed to his face, he blinked in that predatory way. The look reminded me so much of a cat watching a mouse, fascinated by its puny existence. Great, now I was thinking about dragon-sized cats.

Seeming to find some kind of reason in my statement, the shadows pulled back, allowing him to drag in harsh gulps of air.

"Speak," Kanan ordered gruffly, his pupils turning to slits, before shoving another bite of stew in his mouth.

The man swallowed, shifting slightly away from where Kanan's long outstretched legs nearly reached him. "We're the Kin of Chaos, and our hoards will wipe your outdated people from this world."

"Mmmmm," I hummed, nodding along as I ate some of the stew. "And just how do you plan on doing this?"

The man stayed silent even as his restraints buried deeper into his skin.

I shrugged, eating another surprisingly good bite. "Okay, how about Rhaera? What does Kasis have hiding there?"

He chuckled, shaking his head derisively, "The king is going to enjoy killing you two."

Kanan's shoulders quacked against mine, his low quiet laugh more terrifying than anything the kinsman had done. Scraping his spoon against the bowl for every last bit, he crooned mockingly, "King."

"Rhaera," I demanded, passing Kanan my half eaten bowl.

Again the man clammed up, refusing to answer.

Sighing, I leaned back in my chair, crossing my arms over my chest and settled in. "Okay, you can talk to him then."

The kinsman paled in terror, and out of the corner of my eye I saw Kanan's sharp fangs flash in the light as he smiled viciously.

Ruthless satisfaction had my lips curling as the man began to scream.

CHAPTER TWENTY-FOUR

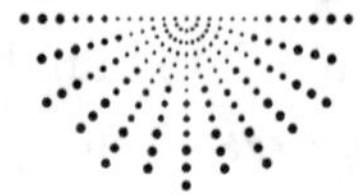

"Did you have to make such a mess?" I snarked, careful to step around the pool of blood where the kinsman's—whose name had been revealed to be Naruk—body now lay.

Kanan looked over from where he was rifling through our packs, glancing around unbothered at the blood staining the walls and floor. "Not my fault he was a bleeder," he said with a shrug.

"Ellenia's going to be pissed at you," I replied with a raised eyebrow.

Continuing to move anything necessary from his pack into mine, he replied in a hard voice, "If she's still alive."

I crouched beside the corpse, a gaping hole where his black heart had once been. After getting what we needed, one of Kanan's shadows had pierced through his ribs, ripping it to pieces. "You said so yourself, the last time Naruk returned to Rhaera he saw her. Still alive, I might add."

"Doesn't mean they haven't killed her, or done worse, in that time," he spoke plainly, buckling my sack once again. "Who knows what manner of things Kasis keeps stored in his little crypt."

It was astounding how Kasis had done it, building an underground base within the crypts that lay below Rhaera and the surrounding forest. Deep underground, the labyrinth of tunnels were a perfect hiding spot, but for an operation as large as his to be at least partially hidden under the Descendents' noses stung like salt in a wound.

I guess for a people of illusionists, whose existence was unknown for the longest time, it wouldn't have been that hard to set up the small fortress little by little over the years. When no one was looking, completely unaware there was a threat at large, let alone one lurking so close, a slow meticulous approach could go unnoticed.

Patting down Naruk's pants, the stiff material was unforgiving as I searched his pockets. There was something rough that scratched the palm of my hand, the uneven surface cool to the touch. Pulling it out, the irregularly shaped stone resembled a strange kind of key.

The mottled green color was a mix of vibrant and dull, cracks marring its exterior, causing splinters to form throughout. Small, near imperceptible pulses emanated from it, like the key was alive.

Finishing my search of the dead man's clothes, I made my way to Kanan, handing it to him. "The guards at the Gravelands had these, they used them to open the cells."

Rolling it in his palm, he inspected the shard. "Ellenia's, perhaps," he surmised, "or some other door."

Stuffing it into the front pocket of my pack, he held the straps out, situating it along my back.

"We'll go in on foot, but if we need a quick escape, I'll shift. I don't want to leave anything behind for them to get their hands on, so all the important things are in here. If we get separated and you think they may capture you again, destroy it. Nothing in here should lead back to our people, or give them any kind of advantage, but I don't want to leave anything up to chance."

"What about you?" I asked in concern, his lack of supplies doing very little to ease my worries. I had faith we could both handle ourselves, but it wasn't like Kasis to be predictable. I had no doubt in my mind he had many, many more cards hidden up his sleeve.

"Are you worried about me love? I'm touched. Here I was thinking you were still mad at me."

I scoffed, rolling my eyes at him, "I am still mad, asshole."

"At least I know you care," he continued with a wink that set butterflies off in my stomach.

"About as much as I care about my left pinky toe," I retorted.

"Hey now, the pinky is pretty important. It's the cutest toe and without it feet just look weird. So the way I see it, you think I'm cute and important."

"This conversation took a very strange turn," I replied, bemused by the whole thing. "You're ridiculous."

His face turned serious once more, losing the playful attitude as he leaned in. Pulling me by the straps towards him, our faces only inches apart, he murmured, "And you're worried."

He stated it like it was an irrefutable fact, and he wasn't wrong. I was worried. This was no longer just about disappearing Descendents and mysterious illnesses. This fight, this war, was personal and had been the entire time. We had just been playing catch-up without knowing it, and I didn't like what that meant for us and the rest of Irropia one bit.

Easily picking up on my doubts, the anxiety probably burning his sensitive nose, he tugged me even closer so our bodies touched. I did my best not to focus on how perfectly we fit, slotting together like two pieces of a singular whole.

"I'll be fine. I have no doubt Kasis has something planned for me, but the likelihood of that happening here and now is low. He'll want an audience when he takes me on."

Tipping my chin up, he grinned in that wicked way that had my insides clenching like it was my first time. "If there's one thing I know about my brother, it is his need to feel superior. He would never waste his chance to show that with no one around to witness it."

"You're doing a horrible job of making me feel better about this," I muttered, fiddling absentmindedly with one of the buckles at the bottom of his leather jerkin. The tunic fit his chest like a second skin, plastering itself over his rippling muscles.

"Are you planning on doing something more with that buckle?" he teased. His voice was husky though, an undercurrent of something far more intimate.

Dropping my hands like they were on fire, I wrung them together behind my back. Maybe I could rid myself of the urge to touch him if I rubbed the skin of them raw. "Sorry."

His chest shook silently. "I'm not, I just think you'd enjoy what's underneath far more."

Peering up at him through lowered lashes, I caught the heated look he gave me. "Last time that happened, I ended up in battle, fighting in a slip with my boobs hanging out."

A rumble made its way from his chest, his hooded eyes still watching me. "Mmmm, what a sight that must have been. You should take better care when divesting yourself of your clothing."

I narrowed my eyes at him, "Dick."

The corner of his lips curled in satisfaction. Backing off though, he swiped the remaining items off the table and into his own sack. He walked over to the backdoor, setting it down just inside the entryway.

I made my way past him and out into the night air, mumbling away about arrogant, overgrown lizards—earning myself an amused, devilish smirk—and we set off into the sinister forest.

The eerie stillness hadn't subsided. If anything, it had grown worse in the dark, more bold. A sickness had taken root, it was obvious in the way I felt watched. The quiet in the air and the lingering scent of rot was a dead giveaway.

Maybe it had gotten too powerful to stay lurking within the forest, or maybe Kasis was just done hiding his depravity. I didn't know which one was worse.

Feeling it just as strongly, tension lined Kanan's shoulders. Shadows pulled from their spots beneath the trees, pooling at our feet as we walked, acting as our guards.

It took under an hour to reach the edge of Rhaera, both of us hanging back several yards as we carefully watched. We had crossed several trails and footpaths, each likely used by the original townspeople. They were gone, however, and yet footprints had been pressed into the damp earth, fresh and undisturbed by the forest.

Seems the Kin of Chaos were just as done hiding as their patron god.

Shrouded in shadows and silence, allowing our muscles to go stiff, we waited. The ghost town had been left untouched, burned buildings and all. Dust now covered the windows and the forest had begun to take it over, vines crawling along the boards and in through the cracks.

Had we not been so certain the kinsmen were somewhere underground, I would have laughed at the ridiculousness of the situation. The village appeared long since abandoned, not a soul alive lurking within its borders.

There was a disease, not yet visible to our eyes, but here nonetheless. It was near perfect in its camouflage. Everything but the town appeared as it should, not a leaf or blade of grass out of place.

That was the giveaway though. How perfect everything was. No birds whistling to break up the silence or faint whispers of wind. No grumbles or paw prints from the predators who had made this patch of woods their home. Not even a stray hare running this way and that, dashing about in a hurry.

And then there was the rot, the seeping foulness that lingered just enough to notice if you were looking for it. It creeped beneath the earth, plaguing the whole forest with whatever Kasis had done to make it so vile.

I felt dirtier by the second as we crouched in the darkness, like the air itself carried with it a sickness, one that created a film on your skin and soaked into your very being. Nausea rose at the thought, but I forced it down.

Knowing my luck, I would puke and alert someone to our presence. Gods, wouldn't that be a way to go. Captured because I couldn't keep my shit together.

Thankfully I was saved from that reality as soon after two men walked out from the main lodge.

Talking animatedly at each other, they were distracted as Kanan pulled the shadows closer to us, using them and the exceptionally dark night to conceal our position entirely.

The two kinsmen walked quickly along the footpath to our left, their voices steadily growing louder.

"When are we getting out of this godsforsaken hellhole?" one of them snapped. "It's bad enough we're not working in the distillery, but now we're stuck underground all day in the kennels of all places."

There was a subtle flash at the edge of my vision and Kanan's broadsword appeared in his hand. The two rubies in the eyes of the dragon's head winked even in the pure darkness, while the blade itself disappeared completely.

Catching each other's eye, a plan formed without words. At his subtle nod, I quietly pulled a dagger from the sheath on my thigh.

"I know, that fucking smell sticks to my skin like shit," the second said in disgust. "Do you know how long it takes before I can stop tasting it in my mouth? Days. Fucking days."

"The screams are what get me," the one closest to us laughed. "No one can hear their screams, but they do it anyway. These Cynths are supposed to be formidable, but they're all a bunch of fucking pussies."

We moved like stalking panthers, slowly pushing through the bush, sizing up our prey. A cold swept through me, the indifference soaking my soul. These deaths would not haunt my nightmares, they would live in my dreams.

They walked right past us, unaware of the danger that lay in wait. We struck together, Kanan moving swiftly to the one on the far side. They barely had a chance to scream as we reached them.

Going low, I swept the man's legs out from underneath him. Falling with a thud, the dazed kinsman sucked in air. Stepping forward, I flicked my eyes up just as Kanan shoved his blade through the chest of his target.

There was a wet squelch as muscle tore. The sharp point pierced out the front, droplets of dark blood dripped from its edge and spilled down the dark blade.

Shadows poured from the open wound as Kanan wrapped his hand around the man's throat, squeezing down. With a broken cry, the kinsman's skin began to crack, flaking off like ash. He withered slowly, nails and teeth falling to the ground as his useless struggles ceased.

I felt nothing, except a fascination at his power, as Kanan dropped the husk to the ground. Who was I to judge a righteous kill made by the God of Endings? Death was calling for both of these men's souls. If they had one left to begin with.

Peering down at my downed victim, I tilt my head in bored indifference as his shocked green eyes looked up at me. "Boo."

Deep down, beneath all the cruelty and hatred and evil, I had to believe there was a small part of these men that hadn't always been so twisted. That Kasis had somehow warped them just as he had our wounded.

Maybe it was still there, buried under the oppressive corruption Kasis inspired.

Too bad we would never get to see it.

And with that, I brought my foot down hard upon his neck, relishing in the satisfying crunch of his trachea beneath my boot and the wheezing breath of air that was forced from him.

I smiled politely, although cold rage coated my every word. "So no one can hear you scream."

His skin paled, the threads of fear that had crept in taking over completely. If watching his comrade die by the hands of Death wasn't enough, the black blade I now held over his eye certainly did the trick.

I looked into that verdant gaze, though he was unable to do the same, instead he lay trembling beneath me. I was enjoying—maybe a little too much—watching him come to the same conclusion as I had. That there was absolutely nothing he could do to stop this, just like the townspeople of Rhaera hadn't been able to stop their own destruction.

And it was with those people, my people, in mind that I shoved the blade through the kinsman's eye.

Standing, yanking the blade free, I ignored the brain matter splattered on its pristine surface. Bending over to wipe it on the illusionist's tunic, I quickly sheathed it.

I waited for the inevitable feelings of regret, knowing I had probably taken it too far, but nothing came. Instead I felt nothing but a sense of calm and satisfaction knowing there were two less monsters walking the planet.

Finally, I glanced up at Kanan, who was looking down at my kill, head tilted and eyes narrowed. I waited for the disgust, but he just clicked his tongue. "Might have been fun to cut out his tongue before you killed him," he threw out, something like disappointment in his tone.

I couldn't help the self-deprecating, half insane giggle that left me. "You're a psychopath."

He smiled, a bit of fang flashing. "Love, I never said I wasn't."

Stepping up to me, he lifted my chin until our breath mixed. He looked down at me with a look so heated my blood might as well have been on fire. All too pleased with himself, he held me still as he whispered against my lips, "But let's be honest with ourselves, little goddess, you're just as crazy as me."

Electricity raced through me, the soft brush of his skin against mine sending me into overdrive. My heart rate picked up, the air in my lungs leaving me in panting breaths. Something in the back of my mind urged me on, pushed me to give in to him. I barely felt myself lean forward, needing something. What, I had no idea.

But as we stood there over the cooling bodies, raw desire between us, I couldn't help but ask the question that had been nagging at me this whole time. "Bron told me that I'm different."

He stepped back at that, the tension cut for now, and tilted his head as his brow furrowed. "From before," I clarified, the words rushing out of me. I swallowed hard, biting my bottom lip as I waited for him to answer.

His face turned contemplative as he let out a sigh. He turned inward, mulling the question over as he reached down and grabbed onto both corpses. Dragging them behind him, one in each hand, he easily moved them off the trail and into the woods.

"Don't keep me in suspense." I tried to laugh it off, but the nervousness in my tone could have been picked up by a deaf man. I hated it, the vulnerability that was peeking through the barriers I had constructed over the years, but there was something inside me—a part that I wasn't even sure was the real me—that crumbled at the thought of being unrecognizable to him.

Fucking pathetic.

"It's a complicated subject," he answered. Licking his lips, which did something to me that I didn't really want to analyze, he stood before me with his hands on his hips. "But yes, you are different."

He might as well have stabbed me, it would have hurt less. It was a mind-fuck, this bond between us. I couldn't tell what was me or it, new me or old. Some days it felt like my soul was split in three. Two parts broken up between different lives, and the other residing inside Kanan.

It was driving me crazy, never knowing whether my feelings were my own. What was real and what wasn't. Because despite everything we'd gone through, all the lies and secrets, the pain felt real.

"Good to know," I replied with a strained smile. Going to walk past him, he stopped me with a hand against my stomach.

He looked down at me in confusion, a muscle popping along his jaw. "Not in a bad way, " he said with a shake of his head. He let out an aggravated breath, "You are so concerned that I don't know you, but you've been mine for millennia, love. I know you better than you know yourself. Even now when you're so against acknowledging that fact."

I narrowed my eyes at that, both hating and loving the blatant possessiveness. He said it with such conviction, anyone would have believed him, drawn in by his confidence and overwhelming allure. My body seemed to agree. The traitor.

He let out a dark chuckle, as if he knew just how effective he was, smoke and velvet rolling over me. "Don't deny it. I wouldn't believe you even if you did."

I ran my tongue over my teeth, but said nothing. Glaring up at him, I simply raised an imperious eyebrow and waited.

Mouth curling into a shadow of a smile, his dragon eyes briefly emerged. The predator inside him seemed pleased by my lack of argument. The cocky bastard better watch it or I might decide to take my blade to him next.

His grin grew as if sensing my thoughts. "You're stronger, more discerning. Not that you were weak in your past life, but the way I see it, you've adapted to this new world."

He glanced over to where he'd left the bodies, eyeing the carnage we had left behind. "The old you would have never done that. Oh, you were capable of it for sure, but you would have killed quickly. You would have gotten justice for the people they had wronged, but you wouldn't have enjoyed it."

And this me had enjoyed it when I crushed his throat beneath my boot, slid that dagger into his eye. Not in an overly cruel way, but in the way I knew they could no longer hurt our people. The ones who had lost their lives to those men who had such blatant disregard for their lives, could now lie in peace knowing their assailants no longer walked these woods.

"The differences aren't bad, you had it all in you before, but you didn't need it then," he said with a shrug. "We lived most of that life in a golden age, where fear and malicious intentions were rare."

We began to walk back towards the town, shadows once again concealing us. "You were kinder, less jaded. We both were, if I'm being honest."

I soaked up his words, in all the time we'd spent since everything had been revealed, we hadn't spoken much about our life together before. It sounded serene and peaceful, so unlike the world we lived in today.

"But we were able to be that way, you see. It wasn't until the very end when things changed. You still have that kindness, the compassion that makes you a formidable healer. Now you guard it all with cynicism and mistrust, and I don't blame you for it one bit. Maybe you became that way because of how you were treated so early on in this life, but I think your soul knew. Knew that it had been taken advantage of, your decency exploited. Even without your past memories, you are still a goddess, some part of you must be aware of what happened."

"What do you mean by that?"

"That's how he took you," he said with a viciousness that both chilled and burned me. Primal rage poured off him, the shadows covering us hissed in support of the violence that I could almost hear thrumming inside him.

Moving closer to him in hopes it would help settle the wild, instinctual rancor, I wasn't the least bit surprised when his shadows latched on to me, twining up my arm until we were essentially cuffed together.

"Kasis had been pulling away from us for a while. We thought he was going into a depression of sorts. Being as old as we were, it was not surprising to me that he might retreat. Sometimes the endless time bites away at you when you've lived for so long, but whereas I had you to keep me from feeling the strain of immortality, he did not."

Both of us went silent as we reached Rhaera once more, the meeting hall now right in front of us. Only a few trees and Kanan's shadows hid us; our element of surprise would have been ruined if more kinsmen came out. Kanan turned his head slightly, listening as a small breeze blew past us. "I don't hear anything, " he said finally, using the night to hide us as we stalked forward.

Making it inside, the barren room was exactly the same as before. I couldn't escape the sorrow that rose from the abandoned pieces of so many lives.

"But he had his people, didn't he?" I whispered so that only he would hear me. "I read it in the book Wrynn gave me."

"Sprites," he rolled his eyes. "They were always incredibly loyal to you, and of course that means they were the only ones able to withstand my mind wipe. I tied the strings of its power to you figuring out who you were, thinking that would keep us safe until we were both ready. Shame on me for thinking sprites would ever play by any rules but their own."

"It's a good thing too, or I would have never figured out who I was," I said icily, giving him a death stare. "Not like you would've told me."

We were both looking for an entrance to the crypt, an entire room separating us, but I could still feel his eyes tracing over me. It was like he was actually touching me with the way they drug over me, leaving a trail of sparks that shook me to the core.

"I have my reasons," he muttered.

I sniffed, mumbling more to myself than anything, "So you keep saying."

Continuing to search, he ignored my grumbles and kept talking. "Kasis has been a perfectionist for as long as I've known him, so when his people weren't even close to the power of our own, he all but washed his hands of them. They were servants to him, carrying out his wishes, but he never allowed them to become close. We built friendships with our kind, some of which have lasted into this lifetime."

Moving on to the raised platform at the front, I listened intently to everything he was saying. It was so unlike him to be this open, but I wasn't complaining, too afraid he'd stop.

"Kasis had no one other than us, and while I didn't know the depths of his delusions I knew he harbored some kind of feeling towards you. That's why I thought he was pulling away, I figured it was getting too hard for him to see us happy."

My heart was heavy in my chest, slowly beating to an almost painful tune. We were happy. Other than the time spent with my foster parents, I didn't know if I had ever been truly happy before coming to Allasea. I believed him, and that made it so much worse, because I desperately wanted that happiness to be a reality.

I shoved everything back into its box, the sad, lonely girl I had pretended not to be trying to rear her head. There was a task at hand and this was no time to reminisce on old wounds. I ran my hands along the edges of the lectern on the stage, feeling for a mechanism or button to push.

"So what happened then?" I walked the boards, paying attention to each step I took.

"You noticed all of this, saw how it was affecting our relationship, so you went to check on him. And in my ignorance, I didn't push to go with you, despite feeling like I should. You told me you wanted to talk to him without making his heartache worse. I stupidly agreed, never once thinking my brother would harm you, and I paid dearly for that blind trust."

There was anger in his voice, it rippled in waves across the space despite his low pitch. I knew had we not been in danger of being found, his true voice might have broken free. The power it held was undeniable.

Despite the anger though, there was also sadness. "We weren't brothers by blood, obviously. None of us were born to true parents, we were created. But still, we had a bond that kept us sane when it was just the two of us, and I naively believed mere envy wouldn't be able to break that. I was wrong."

I felt for him, hating how this whole nightmare began from such a small thing. A mouse against a ratheon, a tree against a tornado; but I guess not even a god could escape the whims of fate.

"So what ended up happening to his people?" I stepped carefully along the carpet that covered the middle of the dais. The people of Rhaera would have had no reason to hide their entrance in a hard to reach place, just enough that naughty children wouldn't go looking for trouble and end up getting lost down there.

"I'm surprised you haven't figured it out yet," he said with a secretive smile.

"What—" A creak echoed beneath my foot, a bare hint of a sound. Kanan's head whipped up, a dangerous gleam in his eyes, like the creature inside him had scented blood in the air. Quickly striding over to me, he leapt silently onto the dais. I backed out of his way as he whipped the rug back, revealing a trap door.

He pulled on the rung with little effort and the old wooden door lifted. A ladder disappeared into a dark hole, leading into nothing. Or so it seemed. We both glanced down before looking at each other with mirrored wariness.

"At least we found it," he said ominously.

"Yeah, but what's waiting for us at the bottom?"

His brows lifted in interest, "Only one way to find out."

"Wait," I stopped him with an open hand. "Kasis's people?"

He chuckled then, menacing and a little evil. "They lost their power over generations, getting weaker and weaker, until their magic was almost nonexistent."

He looked at me expectantly, waiting, and it was then that the realization hit me. "Does that mean..."

He nodded his head, truth clear on his face, "They're humans, love."

CHAPTER TWENTY-FIVE

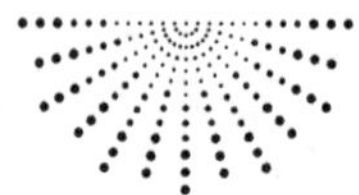

"How is that possible?" I gaped at him, unsure what to do with that knowledge. If humans were descended from Kasis's original creations, how did they know nothing about it? I mean, sure, a few random people ended up having magic of some kind, but it was rare and the children were usually taken away before it even had time to develop.

He shrugged, crouching down to inspect the seemingly bottomless pit. "I have no idea, but even within the first generation of newborns, their power was already weaker than that of their parents. By the time great-great-grandchildren were a thing, the power levels had nearly bottomed out."

"How do they not know?"

Kanan snorted, "Like I said, Kasis is obsessed with everything being perfect. When his creations were, in fact, not perfect, they became all but obsolete to him. They were servants, footmen, and in the end, canon fodder. I didn't agree with it, but by that point he had already pulled away from my confidence, situating himself in southern Irropia."

"What about the Tearing? The children in Rhaelyth?" Their little tear-stained cheeks had poked out from behind drawn curtains in the king's carriages, fear turning their bloodshot eyes manic as they were taken away to the capital. "Or these Kin of Chaos?"

"I wish I had answers for you, love," he replied genuinely, stepping onto the first rung of the ladder. "It'll have to be a question for another time, right now we need to figure out what they have going on down below."

Silently agreeing, I followed him down into the pit. Taking one last look around the abandoned hall, I made sure to bring the door back down with us, cloaking the shaft in darkness. I was thankful my eyesight was better than a human's, because I could barely make out the bars gripped in my hands.

The metal was cool to the touch and slightly weathered, if the rough rust spots were any indication. I followed by feel, having to trust my footing as we slowly descended the small shaft. It wasn't until at least a minute had passed, the only sound that of the clang of our feet on the bars, that a flicker of light appeared.

Barely visible, the soft glow was coming from an unknown source. As we grew closer, the light became brighter, the bottom finally visible. After a few more rungs, the top of Kanan's head came into view as his feet touched down onto a smooth stone floor.

I jumped the last few feet to the ground, hitting with a soft slap. The enclosed shaft opened up into a singular wide tunnel. The light gray stone was worn and scratched from time, waterlines rolling down from in between the crevices. Sconces near the ceiling lined the walls every few feet, a muted yellow light illuminating the space.

A faint dripping of water broke the otherwise eerie silence. Cobwebs hung in the corners, the long-legged spiders watching us warily as we tread closer.

There was a musty, putrid scent that lingered in the air, like damp clothes that had been left to sit for too long. The source was even more disgusting. Crusted chunks of flesh and dried pools of black goo had been pushed off to the side, maggots crawling over the piles.

"At least we know we're in the right place," I muttered, holding my breath as we walked past the rancid gore.

The darkness shivered, the only indication that the shadows were with us. My eyes scanned the tunnel as we prowled forward, taking note of the dried streaks of blood on the walls, like someone had been dragged and fought for something to hold on to.

It was when the blood trail ended abruptly that my heart dropped into my stomach, despair-soaked claws tearing it to shreds.

Swallowing against my dry throat, I looked past it. I couldn't allow the echoes of pain that had seeped into this place distract me. It would help nobody if I was rendered useless because my own feelings got in the way of things. What right did I have to allow myself to be swallowed by the pain of others? I wasn't the one who had been subjected to this nightmare. The only thing I could do for them now was destroy the thing that had hurt them.

Kanan grew tense next to me. "What is it?" I asked, my voice barely a whisper.

"Death," he answered ominously. "It's everywhere."

I studied him, his red eyes glowing in the dim light. "Why do you make that sound like a bad thing?"

He glanced over at me, his expression clouded by shadows. "I may *be* Death, love, but there's a balance that needs to be followed for the universe to exist. Death should come at the right moment, not too early or too late. Same goes for you as Life, there comes a moment when souls have to give up their time on this plane, and it's not for you to interfere with that."

He nodded into the darkness that awaited us, "What I'm feeling is both death and life, but in no way is it an existence. We weren't meant to be separated, you and I, that was a mistake made by our creator. Our original purpose was that of *Existence* in its entirety, you would think it would be a good thing to sense it."

"But it's not," I guessed apprehensively, not liking where he was going.

Shaking his head, dark coils snaked through his hair and around his arms protectively, likely picking up on some unseen force. "No, what I'm feeling is nothing we have any part of. Neither fully life or death. It's a purgatory."

It hit me like a slap to the face. "The wraiths," I breathed.

"That's what I'm thinking, I don't see how it could be anything else."

"He's corrupted what Descendents try so hard to protect." Running a hand down my face, I let out a hard laugh, uncaring if anyone heard. "It's his big 'fuck you' to us. Perverting everything we and our people stand for."

A muscle in Kanan's cheek twitched, his jaw clenched so hard I could hear his teeth grinding. For a second I thought I saw the shadow of wings along the wall, but they disappeared as the lights sputtered and plunged us into darkness.

Instinctively I grabbed Kanan, holding onto his wrist with a white knuckled grip. The cool slide of shadow against my skin brought me comfort as he pulled me in closer to his body.

I pulled one of the blade's on my thigh, watching closely for signs of movement in the darkness.

A gentle breeze blew across my cheeks, as a red glow began steadily flashing within the sconces, making the tunnel even more foreboding. Kanan glanced around suspiciously, his body as tightly strung as one of his piano wires. Running a finger absentmindedly over his strong pulse, the steady thumps calming my own, I glanced over my shoulder, ensuring nothing was following us.

A sensual, dark hand ran across my mental barriers. *"We move carefully. Stay close."*

I followed behind, moving with him off to one side, keeping the wall on our left until we came to a crossroads. Nothing indicated which way we should go, each path looking exactly the same in the foreboding light.

Centering myself in my power, I tried to remember what I had done at the Gravelands to sense living beings inside the mountain. That day was mostly a haze, the memories clouded in a golden fog. My power had exerted control that day—exhausted and emotionally drained, I hadn't fought the overwhelming presence, allowing it to drag me underneath.

Now, instead of surrendering to the unending primordial power, I concentrated on it. It was as brilliant as the sun, as endless as the universe, and as far-reaching as an exploding star. It was beautiful and it was mine.

I allowed it to envelop me, but instead of giving myself over to it, it gave itself over to me. My lips curved in a small, secretive smile as we melded together, becoming one. Exactly as it was meant to be.

I wasn't a person with power. I *was* power.

Exhaling, cutting down the thoughts of failure that tried to taint the connection with a steely ferocity, I trusted myself for once, and let the magic fly.

Bursting free, a near invisible wave of golden energy shot down the tunnels and throughout the entire crypt. A prickling feeling came at me from every direction, tiny pings that echoed in my mind.

"There are people down each tunnel, but the closest are to our right." Using the bond to communicate was becoming as easy as breathing. Kanan's presence at the edge of my thoughts was as distinctive as the man himself. Carnal, primal, and almost violent in its strength, there was no confusion as to who would so boldly assert themselves. Even as he kept to the periphery.

"Right, then," he said without hesitation. Keeping close, we moved silently, continuously scanning our surroundings for any signs of wraiths or kinsmen. The red light cast shadows onto the limestone, every flicker and flare making me tense.

As we made our way further down, rooms began to appear, carved into the walls like nestled nooks. I peeked into one, dagger at the ready, but instead of finding monsters, I found six identical indentions dug into the wall. Smashed pots, crushed flowers, and melted candles were strewn about the floor. Half-burnt portraits were torn to pieces and thrown carelessly on the once pristine death beds.

And in the middle of the mess was a pile of shattered bones.

Cracked femurs and broken skulls. The small bones that had once made up the hands and feet had been turned to dust. Teeth lay chipped at the bottom of the mound.

A familiar smell hit my nose. Face scrunched in disgust, my teeth ground together as my anger built. *"They pissed on them."*

Silence.

I looked over at Kanan and froze. His eyes glowed red, slitted pupils glaring at the desecrated graves, as a deadly growl made its way out of his chest. A wave of hot energy grew around him, scalding my skin. The dimly lit catacombs darkened as ink-black shadows threatened to consume the space.

With each destroyed room we passed, his ire rose until I was almost choking on it. It would have been intimidating if I wasn't feeling the exact same way. Defiling the crypts wasn't an act of war, it wasn't public or in the throes of battle. It was calculated, premeditated, done for the sheer fact that it would bring the Descendants pain.

This was a sacred space and it had been sullied. Thousands of years of history lay amongst these bones, and now the last remaining piece of that had been destroyed. Some of the first Descendents were no doubt laid to rest here, and many had died during the first war. It was a senseless act, one aimed to derive pleasure from sorrow.

And with the wrath of those who had been wronged behind us—we hunted.

No longer sticking to the shadows or dark crevices, we followed our instincts to our prey, stalking them down like the rabid animals they were. Raucous laughter echoed through the chambers, leading us directly to them.

We honed in on our targets, scenting the blood that would spill, tasting the rich iron that would seep into the air. Like vengeful spirits, we ate the distance between us and them, unable to resist the thrill of the hunt.

Excitement thrummed through my veins as the noise grew louder. Groans and low hums, mixed with the conversation of unaware kinsmen. Loudest of all, however, was the screeching. Broken thrills and wheezes, demonic chittering and sharp, piercing screams.

We slowed as the end of the tunnel came into view and stopped at the edge. Two twin staircases spiraled down into the large room below. Barred-off cells lined the walls on each side, hungry snarls coming from the darkness.

As we crept closer, several wraiths charged into view, smashing their bodies against their cages until parts of their skin peeled away and oily blood stained the ground. A foul odor wafted into the air with each hit, the sickening smell enough to make my stomach turn.

Dozens of men milled throughout the room, coming in and out from different directions. One cracked a silver cane against the bars of a cell, his guttural voice bouncing off the walls as he yelled, "Quiet!"

The wraiths backed away from the bars, but grew louder still as more and more crowded to the front.

"What has gotten into them today?" one man asked, his sandy-blonde hair shifting to a burnt red before my eyes.

The original man chuckled, dragging his cane across the floor as he walked. "Can't you tell? They're hungry."

Another kinsman sneered at the slobbering wraiths. "Disgusting things. Can't wait to be rid of them."

"Have Demo and the others made it out of the tunnels with the last batch?"

"Cleared," a lanky boy replied, entering from the tunnel on the left. His face was young, even as parts of it phased in and out. A nasty scar carved down his right cheek, the jagged wound the only part of him that stayed the same. "They popped through the fissure just a minute ago. They're Vallenia's problem now."

The one with the cane snorted. Walking down the rows of cells, he peered into each, examining the wraiths that screeched at him. Black and green foam lined their mouths as they yelped, nipping and biting at each other.

"Time," he called, watching impassively as two wraiths attacked one another. The smaller of the two was in trouble quickly, its back leg snapping in two like a dried twig with one good bite. The others in the cell circled around the fighting pair, the clicking of their bones haunting as they yipped excitedly.

"Two minutes until the tunnels are cleared, Commander," someone out of view yelled out.

As the fight came to an end with a resounding snap of the smaller wraith's neck, the others in the cell descended upon its body, ripping into it with abandon. Muscle and skin tore quickly as limbs and blood went flying.

Some of these were no doubt former Cynthonians. Our people. Or at least they used to be, and now they had been turned into mindless monsters, feasting on each other's flesh. As they fought over the body, it was hard to believe they had once been people at all.

"Let's get a move on," the cane wielder shouted forcefully. "We don't need any more of them turning on each other before we get them out the gate."

Some of the workers began filing out of the room, leaving a dozen or so behind. Kanan and I looked at each other. This was our chance. We couldn't allow more of these things to be released, not if we could stop it.

"We need at least one of them alive," I warned Kanan, giving him a look.

Watching his prey's every move, there was the tiniest curl to his lips. *"Now where's the fun in that?"*

"What's the quota, Rast?"

Completing his inspection, the commander—Rast—spit on the ground. "The king expects at least half of these babies to be at capacity and back to Vallenia by the end of the week. Ver told me he's getting tired of the lack of production we have going on here."

"What does he expect?" one of them griped. "It's not like we have the element of surprise anymore."

"Yeah, well we all know what happens when *he* gets mad, so let's try not to fuck this up, yeah? Keep to the edges. Unless we're ordered otherwise, I don't want to hear anything about there being an attack on the larger cities. You fuckers hear me?" Rast commanded, no room for argument in his tone. "No messing with those pussies hiding in the main three, the last thing we need is to bring any more attention to ourselves."

Oops. Too late.

As the others voiced their agreement, I gripped my dagger, the muscles in my hand twitching with barely contained anticipation.

"What are they gonna do?" The young boy scoffed, pulling a piece of twine he had over his head. A short silver tube dangled from the string. He handed it over to Rast, the apparent leader of this little group.

"Well, I don't know about you, kid," he replied in an almost fatherly manner, "but I don't particularly want to be face to face with a pair of angry gods, do you? At least not until everything is in place."

And that's when we stepped out.

"Then today is a really unlucky day for you," Kanan stressed, as we appeared from the shadows. He strolled down one set of stairs, I the other. Hands in his pockets, he was the portrait of casual boredom.

The kinsmen stilled and the wraiths watched through their expressionless eyes, only sheer hunger shining through the black that had taken over.

Kanan chuckled, the sound cold enough to send chills down my spine. Empty-handed and unarmed, one would think he posed no threat at all, but he wasn't a man anyone would ever underestimate.

Towering at least two heads over the tallest kinsman and packed with so much muscle he made them look prepubescent by comparison, there wasn't a single inch of him that spoke of weakness.

If his physical strength didn't deter people, the natural aura he radiated would. Blood and violence. The fiery strength and cold determination that stood at the center of his being. The echoing roar of the creature that lived just beneath his skin, choosing a more human facade to fool its prey.

They had sealed their fate by playing part in Kasis's horrors against our people, but in violating the catacombs, the graves of so many dead, they had ensured themselves a painful ending.

As the kinsmen came to this realization right before our eyes, untouched darkness peeled itself from the walls, hanging over them like a drawn sword. They had unleashed a hellish, nightmare of a god upon themselves, and I savored their fear.

The remaining kinsmen in the room didn't seem to know what to do, glancing between the two of us as we took the final steps into the pit. Sweat ran down their faces, no one moving an inch.

"Now," Kanan began, striding forward into the middle of the room. "Who wants to die first?"

There was a beat of silence, so quiet I could hear their pounding hearts, and then a man on my right charged Kanan with a mighty yell.

With a flick of the wrist my throwing knife embedded itself in his eye. He stopped dead, mouth parted wide, and with one hand frozen half way to his face, he fell to his knees. I stoically pulled another knife from my gauntlet, watching as the man's body slid to the floor, the light in his green gaze going out.

Kanan *tsked,* drawing my attention. He gave me a bemused look before releasing a sigh, "You took my kill, love."

"Aww," I cooed teasingly, "I'm sorry. I couldn't let you have all the fun now, could I? If you're a good boy though, I'll let you have most of them."

He gave me a downright sinful smile, his red eyes gleaming with naughty promises. "Oh, don't you worry, I'll show you just how good I can be."

It was all kinds of wrong how much that turned me on. Damn dragon and his stupidly erotic voice.

"But first," he growled, locking in on the kinsmen, "I need to deal with you."

Fight or flight kicked in at that moment as the cool whisper of Death's breath curled down their necks.

Almost simultaneously, they broke free of their paralyzing fear. I had to give them some credit, over half the group surged towards us, weapons at the ready. Others chose to flee. Disappearing down the two tunnels on either side of the pit, they abandoned their comrades. Cowardly…but smart.

I was a little offended that most of the kinsmen were aiming for Kanan, their various blades drawn, but if nothing else, it allowed me to slip in behind as they tried to take him on.

I grabbed hold of one's shoulder as he completely bypassed me and slashed my black dagger across his throat. Whipping around before he had even hit the ground, I flung my second throwing knife with a precision that spoke of all the early mornings in the sandlot with Geoff.

Hitting a man twenty feet away, I leaned back as a saber swiped dangerously close to my throat. I pulled my second dagger free of its sheath, fisting both blades tightly as I steadied myself.

I let the background noise fade. The hungry snarls of the wraiths and the cacophonous booms as they slammed their bodies into the bars, trying to break free. Grunts and wheezes, fists hitting flesh, the hissing shadows that watched from above waiting to be called upon, and even Kanan's dark laughter.

It all fell away as the swordsman squared off against me, his blade held aloft. Six-foot and solid, he was impressively balanced on his feet as we parried blows. The serrations of crystal hitting crystal sliced through the space around us. The reverberating power from his blows shook their way through me.

"My king will reward me handsomely when I bring you to him. He'll be impressed, and I'll finally get out of this fucking place," the dark-skinned man gritted out as I crossed my daggers in front of me, locking with his hilt to stop a devastating blow.

I sneered, pushing back against the pressure. "Kasis couldn't give two shits about who you are. You'll be lucky if you don't piss yourself when you die."

He grunted, rage and something like pain filling his jade eyes. Blinded by his emotions, he didn't see the crack in the floor behind him growing. Pushing just enough of my power into it, the hairline fractures in the stone split.

Planting my foot into his chest, I sent him stumbling back. Heel catching, he slammed onto his back. I'd learned to take an opportunity when it was presented to me, and so I leapt atop him, driving one of my daggers down through his heart. I felt the hard rock under him give way as my blade staked him to the floor.

Hard breaths pushed their way out of my chest, and I spared the man one look before I pushed to my feet. Stepping over his body, I left him pinned to the floor like some butterfly on display.

Kanan still fought at the opposite end of the room. His shirt was ripped and the two wet patches that clung to his skin were concerning, but he fought like a mad man. He dodged killing blows like everyone else was standing still, striking hard and fast with claw and sword. The latter of which he must have called from wherever he kept it.

A flash of movement caught my eye, forcing my attention away. The young boy that had been talking to the commander darted out from the tunnel behind Kanan, rushing over to the wall next to the cells. With rapid, jerky movements, he pulled something from his pocket before shoving it into a small recess I hadn't seen before.

Looking over his shoulder, he caught my eye. His pupils had swallowed his irises whole and he was damn near hyperventilating. I almost felt bad for the boy, but then he smiled. A terrible, villainous smile.

And the bars on the cells lifted.

CHAPTER TWENTY-SIX

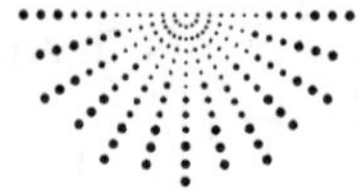

"Oh shit," I cursed as the wraiths were set free. The boy dashed back down the tunnel, disappearing into the darkness.

Having heard me, Kanan fought harder as the wraiths sprung free of their confines. It was too late though, as at least fifty of the decaying monsters were set loose. Under normal circumstances, we could have taken them, but here, now, as they all swarmed together, we'd be buried in seconds.

Who knew what they would be capable of with the power of a god in their system. As the group split in half, heading for either of us, Kanan seemed to come to the same realization.

As he dragged the edge of his sword through the last of his attackers, his sharp eyes swept over the situation with a strategic gaze. "Go!" he shouted across the room, the wraiths having nearly reached him. "Into the tunnels, find a way out."

Everything in me rebelled against leaving him. Separating had never gone well for us, but with a wave of wraiths seconds from slamming into me, I had no choice.

I grit my teeth in frustration, letting out a shaky, "Fuck," and then ran. Sprinting into the tunnel behind me, the snarls and growls grew louder. A sob tried to bubble up from my chest as a roar of fury shook the catacombs behind me.

Paws pounded the stone behind me, claws as sharp as blades scraping against the rough surface. The *clip-clop* of formerly cloven animals bounced in the tight space as their brutal, vicious sounds forced me forward.

My heart hammered inside my chest like it was trying to break free. Gasping breaths rushed out of my lungs as more and more bodies entered the tunnel. I whipped my head over my shoulder as I raced down the endless path, my pack slapping against my back, and was met with a rushing mass of snapping jaws and melted flesh.

They fought for position, snapping and biting at each other for the front spot. Fighting for who reached me first. Bodies were flung against the walls, slowing the ones in the back. The limited room was my only advantage. I don't think I had ever been so thankful to be stuck under thousands of pounds of rock.

I skidded to a stop as a plan formulated in my mind, my hand going to the small pouch at my side. I prayed to who knows what—myself maybe—as I took hold of a singular red shattershell, the stone shaking with untamed energy, and dropped into my power.

"I'm sorry," I whispered to the souls of the dead that were gathered here as I lobbed the vibrating shell at the amassing horde. A blazing inferno burst outward as manic fire magic erupted through the catacombs. As the wraiths screamed in terror, some incinerating on the spot, I allowed the golden supernova that lived inside me to break free. It tore through my body so fast the air was sucked from my lungs as I dropped all pretense of control and slammed my hands into the ground.

A golden shockwave hit the wall of flames, the wraiths engulfed within were sent flying back from the impact. Dust puffed out of the cracks that had formed all around me, spider webbing along the ceiling and down the sides of the tunnel. The stone gave a low groan as chunks of rock began to fall. Pebbles and debris rained from above and then, like a tidal-wave smashing through a dam, the ceiling gave way.

Diving out from underneath, the centuries-old crypt came crashing down atop the half-melted wraiths. They shrieked, bellowing in pain as their flaming bodies were crushed under the weight of Rhaera's crypt.

I hit the ground hard, curling into a ball and bringing my arms up to protect my head from the falling wreckage.

Several minutes went by before the last rock settled and the whimpering moans quieted. I rolled onto my knees, coughing up the dust and dirt that filled my throat. I spit, unsurprised by the pink tinge to the saliva. Laving my tongue over the inside of my mouth, I winced as it ran over a spot I must have accidentally bit.

Slowly getting to my feet, I got a look at the destruction. As I sucked in a breath, all I could think was: *Daily reminder—Keep Nala on your good side.*

Taking up the entire width of the tunnel, stone and rock and dirt were now piled high, completely blocking off access to the other side. Black blood seeped out near the base of the cave-in, a charred limb or two sticking out from the carnage. Bile rose in the back of my throat as a few limbs twitched sporadically.

Grief threatened to consume me, not for the monstrous creatures that would have torn me apart, but for the people they once could have been. At least they had been stopped.

I now, however, had no way of getting back to the entrance shaft. I knew there had to be exits spread throughout the forest, or how else would the kinsmen have been able to sneak around for so long? Question was, were the fuck were they?

Placing my hands on my hips, I stared at the blocked-off tunnel. "In hindsight, I probably should have thought about how to get out first, huh?" I asked…no one?

An ethereal breeze blew across my cheek, which wasn't suspicious at all. "I'm sorry your resting place was destroyed." I didn't know who I was apologizing to, but it seemed like the right thing to do. "I'll come back and fix it, I promise."

I pushed back the baby hairs that were hanging in my face, wiping away the sweat beading along my brow as I blew out a breath. "You wouldn't happen to know where I should go, would you?"

Nothing.

I snorted at myself. "Of course not, Atallia, because you're talking to no one."

A hard gust of wind hit me at full force, as if to show its ire, and nearly knocked me on my ass.

Licking my lips, I turned around wide-eyed to face the only option I had. "Got it," I said with a respectful nod. "This way it is."

I eyed the air around me as I walked, though I wasn't even sure what I was even looking for. Specters. Ghosts. All I knew was that when the path suddenly forked in two different directions, a current of air—that raised the hair at the back of my neck—pushed me to the left.

"Are you sure?"

The force became stronger, more insistent. After everything I had seen and been through, I wasn't about to ignore signs from the universe. No matter how crazy they seemed.

I was led through several more turns, the crypt even larger than I could have imagined. Burial chambers lined each of the halls. There were so many I had lost count, but each was as destroyed as the next.

Offerings spilled out into the walkway, a white-gray powder coating the gifts. A skull was pushed up against the wall, cracked beyond recognition, like Kasis's vermin had used it as some kind of ball to kick up and down the tunnel.

Large prayer rooms that had been stuffed to the brim with candles were now destroyed, wax covering the floor. Black marks marred the stone from where the flames had burned against it. The columns inside were chipped and broken. Parts near the ceiling had been left untouched, the beautiful carvings telling a story. A story that might now be lost forever.

My hair was blown back by the impossible wind, the souls' anger nearly palpable. In the silence of the tunnels, I almost thought I could hear their overlapping voices, yelling their outrage into the whistling air.

"Do you think we should go check it out?" a male voice asked faintly from somewhere down a connecting tunnel. I whipped my head around as the sound of footsteps grew louder. Shadows moved along the far wall, growing closer. Ducking into a prayer room, I put my back up to the wall by the archway. I silently drew a blade, thankful Zanaya had insisted on me carrying so many.

Another male snorted, "Fuck that, we're assigned to her. You go see what happened if you have such a hard-on for getting killed."

I listened as their footsteps grew louder, the clanking swish of chains accompanying them.

"Cowards," a familiar voice coughed out.

"Shut up, bitch," one of them barked back.

The other sighed in annoyance, "Why can't we just kill her already?"

"Unfortunately, Rast thinks we still need her. I think she only has one use at this point." The two shared a look and chuckled as they dragged Ellenia past the opening to the prayer room. The innkeeper was trying to keep up, but her two captors kept their stride long, causing her to trip every few steps as they hauled her down the corridor.

Advancing on them from behind, I aimed for the stockier man on the left. I grabbed a fistful of hair and yanked his head back. He yelled out in shock, a mere sliver of a cry as I slid my blade across his throat. Blood poured down his front as he folded over.

Letting Ellenia fall to the floor, the second kinsman pulled a thin rapier from his belt. We went blow for blow, me slashing with my dagger, him stabbing out with his blade, the clang of metal like a melody for our dance. Both of us were fighting our hearts out, though only one could be the victor. And it sure as hell wasn't going to be him.

A gale came from behind me, showering the man with dust. He shouted in pain as the grit sliced into his eyes, and it was just enough for him to lose his guard. Slipping away from his flailing arms, I slashed at his hand, making him drop the thin sword.

I went to finish him off, and didn't see Ellenia move until she'd shot up from the floor, rapier in hand. She stabbed out with the sword, albeit clumsily, pushing against it with all her strength. The man's mouth fell open as he was slowly skewered with his own blade.

"Get fucked, you bastard," the sweet innkeeper ground out, face savage as she watched her jailor die. She stood over his body as he fell into the wall, making sure she was the last thing he saw as the air left his lungs.

I waited in silence as she gazed down at the dead man, but then her shoulders started to shake.

"Ellenia?"

I touched her shoulder gently, turning her around. Tears streamed down her bruised face, mixing with the blood from a split lip. Sobs wracked her body. Pulling her to me, I closed my arms around her as she broke.

"I'm-I'm so," she sniffled, taking in a gasping breath, "so sorry. I thought they w-were travelers. I-I couldn't stop them. They as-asked questions and I tried, I promised I tried, but they wouldn't stop. Why wouldn't they stop?"

I held her closer as her words dropped off. She didn't need to say anything more. "Shhh, shh, I have you," I comforted, stroking a hand down her dirty, matted hair. I was glad my words came out calmly, because the scorching heat that erupted in my chest had me nearly shaking with rage.

I glared at the dead men, gold sparks flickering along the edges of my vision. "They won't hurt you again."

It took a couple of minutes before she calmed, her cries quieting. Releasing her, I lifted her wrists, getting a look at the crystal shackles. If my power existed outside of my body it would have snarled at the heartsglass, the restricting magic pulsing with a desire to control.

A lock on both cuffs kept her manacled. A long chain in the middle connected them to the ones around her ankles. "Which one has the key?"

She bit her lip, uncaring as more blood dripped from the cut, and dipped her head towards her kill. "Back pocket."

Not wanting her to touch him, I kicked the man over onto his front, rummaging in his pockets until I found the key. Quickly unlocking her, the strain on her face eased as I tossed the horrid chains away from us.

Bruises circled her wrists and the inflamed scabs around them looked infected. She cleared her throat, voice raspy from crying, "I tried to get out of them, but they were too tight."

My lips pressed into a tight line, memories of my own time spent as a captive surfacing. I too had felt like a trapped animal, but I'd been so beaten at the time I wasn't able to fight the shackles.

Sweat dripped down my back and my lungs burned as the air suddenly became thinner. A few cracks opened up on my skin, gleaming filaments floating into the air. I forced the thoughts away, swallowing the scream that wanted to rise. I couldn't do this here, not now, not in front of Ellenia.

Instead, I directed the wild energy elsewhere. Cupping Ellenia's cheek, I eased the power into her, careful not to overload her spark. I had found that healing was the easiest form to control my magic in. It was like a part of it knew we were trying to repair something, not destroy.

The glittering energy flowed beneath her skin, moving from one injury to the next. Her bleeding lip closed and the bruises all over her body changed from black to blue, green then yellow, until they finally disappeared completely.

She sighed as the pain she'd obviously been feeling eased. Her shoulders relaxed as the aether worked through her, eyes fluttering close in a spare moment of peace. "Thank you."

Removing my hand, I smiled through my own agony. "Of course. Now let's get out of here."

"I don't know the way," she admitted. "They blindfolded me on the way here, and I was never allowed outside."

A slight stirring in the air made me smile. "That's okay, I have a few friends who can help."

I took us back the way I had come, this time, however, with a few nudges in a different direction, making me think whatever souls lingered here wanted me to find Ellenia. Perhaps they were compassionate souls not wishing to add to their numbers, especially from one with so much life left to live.

It wasn't long before we came upon another ladder, this one much older than the one in the main lodge. I eyed it warily, but I didn't see what choice we had. There was no going back to the pit, not with the cave-in. So, dangerous ladder it was.

As we began the climb, red rust broke off onto our hands, but it held under our weight. *Thank the Cosmos.*

Holding on tightly with one hand as we reached the top, I felt for a door. Cool metal met my fingertips, so I gave it a hearty push, bowing my head as dirt fell in through the cracks. "Watch out," I called to Ellenia below.

I flung the door back and crawled out of the hole. A singular sweep of the woods around us and my heart dropped.

"Do you know where we are?" I asked as Ellenia climbed out, scanning for anything to point us in the right direction. Dawn had just broken if the gentle hues of the sky were any indicator.

Breathing heavily, she took in the woods around us. She smiled as she steadied herself. "Yes, actually. I grew up playing in this forest. If I'm correct, we're not too far from the inn."

"Thank fuck," I groaned, straightening. At least one thing was going our way. "Can you get us back to Rhaera?"

She blinked at me in confusion. "You want to go back there? Why?"

"Kanan was with me. We got separated, and I'm not leaving without him. If you want to point me in the right direction and then head to the inn, I understand, but I need to make sure he got out. If those wraiths were able to feed on him, who knows what they could do."

She pressed her lips together, folding her trembling hands behind her back as she glanced off in the distance. "You saved me. You both did, I guess," she replied in a shaky voice. "The least I can do is make sure you find him. I'll take you there."

Relief flooded through me, now I wouldn't be wandering the

forest searching for another entrance to the underground crypt. "Thank you."

I peered down into the dark shaft. I didn't know if the spirits could hear me, or if there were any spirits at all, but I felt like they were there. Watching me. "I'll be back," I whispered, making the promise for both them and for me.

Closing the trap door, I kicked the displaced leaves back over it. I didn't know how long this war would take, but even if it took years, I would come back and fix what had been broken.

With my promise in mind, I nodded to Ellenia. "Lead the way."

CHAPTER TWENTY-SEVEN

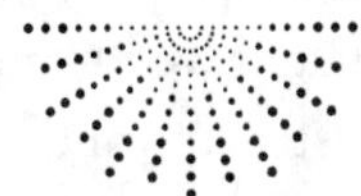

We trudged along in silence, mostly in case any wraiths had broken free, but also because we both seemed lost in thought. Ellenia's face was drawn tight, the once beautiful laugh lines that spoke of a life full of smiles had been replaced by stress and a haunted look in her eyes.

Some would have called her gaunt, her eyes slightly sunken in, cheek bones more pronounced. Her plump, voluptuous curves were hidden beneath the saggy gray cloth that must have been the only thing they offered her. Descendants couldn't die of starvation, but in some cases, that was a curse.

Whether they starved her or not, she was haggard and exhausted. Guilt ate at me, chewing away at my heart little by little. She shouldn't be out here. Shouldn't have to be going back to the same place that had become her personal hell. But I was desperate.

Kanan could be stuck down there, fighting against wraiths and kinsmen. He was more than capable, and I would bet on him in any fight, but a number of things could have happened. What if the cave-in had spread further? What if he was buried beneath a hundred tons of rock? *What if it's my fault?*

My chest felt like it might be crushed by the pressure, lungs and heart burning from the effort to continue beating. Failure and worry burned my throat like acid. Angry as I might be, if he was hurt or worse…I wouldn't know what to do with myself.

"My Lady, may I ask you a question?" Ellenia asked softly beside me.

Stepping over a fallen log, I held a hand out to help her over. "You may, so long as I can ask you one. And I insist you call me Atallia."

The innkeeper who I had originally passed off as a sweet summer flower, delicate and beautiful and worth cherishing, was stronger than I gave her credit for. Exhausted beyond belief, magic depleted, and emotionally distraught, she still fought.

Taking my hand with a grateful smile she yanked the loose fabric of her slip up as she clambered over. "I couldn't possibly. You are my queen. The Goddess."

"Which leads me to my question," I say, choosing to ignore her distraught look at my request. "How do you know who I am if you've been stuck in the catacombs this whole time? Even if you weren't taken until days after, it is unlikely the news would have spread this far north so quickly."

"Those men have big mouths. They brag and curse and joke. In those tunnels, everything echos, so even when they weren't taunting me or…hurting me," she swallowed hard, "I could overhear them. They weren't stupid enough to discuss anything important, unfortunately, but when I heard them talking about how a 'gilded whore' was somehow the long lost queen, it didn't take much for me to figure out who they were talking about."

She glanced at me from the corner of her eye. "There was something about you when you stepped into my inn, I couldn't tell you what it was, but I just knew it was unlike anything I had ever felt. It's heavy and old, and it hangs around like a halo, radiating from you without you even noticing. I'm not sure what that is, but it's intoxicating to be around so much power."

I wasn't sure what to say to that, the awe in her voice stirring an uneasy feeling deep inside, but I was saved from answering as a blast of air hit us so hard we fell to the ground. Riding the gale force came a wave of darkness, spreading out in every direction, an unstoppable power descending upon us without restraint.

Ellenia gasped as it swallowed us, but I smiled, embracing the dark power. I was blinded as it rushed over us as thick bands of shadow wrapped tight around my ankles, crawling up and over my legs. All sight and sound of Ellenia disappeared with the rest of the world, a magical night overtaking the dusk.

A soft whoosh came from somewhere in the darkness, the impenetrable depths making it impossible to figure out from where. Getting to my feet, the ropes of shadows unrelenting in their hold, I swiveled around in every direction.

I couldn't see anything, the power so smothering not a single fleck of light was able to break through. Even my metallic hair had disappeared into the darkness, not a single strand visible. I might as well have been floating in a starless sky, nothing but pure black surrounding me.

The harsh breaths I took were loud, louder than they should have been, every one of my senses more on edge. My skin prickled in awareness as the onyx fog swept across my skin in caress.

Taking a step back, my heart trying its damndest to break through my ribs, I slammed into a hard chest. I gasped as a thick arm, corded in muscle, curled around my waist. Leaning into him, I closed my eyes, dragging in his drugging scent like an addict.

I squeezed my eyes tight, biting my lip as a shaky breath tore free. His other arm came around, wrapping me up tight. Grabbing hold of it, I dug my nails in as a soul-crushing desperation crashed through.

Going up on my tip-toes as he leaned down into my neck, I reached behind and dragged my hand through his silk hair, holding him to me. Standing there, finally able to breathe, our hearts beating as one, the realization of just how fucking gone I might be for this man hit me.

I turned in his arms, wrapping mine around him and held on for dear life. He dragged his hands up my back, one clenching the nape of my neck as his ragged breaths warmed my skin. I couldn't see him, but pressed up against him like this, both of us grasping on to the other, I didn't need to.

I knew every hard line and curved muscle, had studied them far too often to be considered sane. His arms were strong bands around me, that finely-honed power tempered into warmth and protection. Long, thick legs were spread wide to accommodate our height difference, boxing in my own. The slight prick of his stubble gently grazed my skin, the sensation making my thighs clench. His soft curls tickled my ear, chiseled face pressing in tighter.

His scent, his touch, the feel of him against me. The relief that he was okay, that the person I was unquestionably tied to hadn't been taken from me. It was all too much. I had tried, tried so fucking hard not to let him back in, to stay mad and hate him for his decisions, despite whatever reasoning he thought he had, but I couldn't pretend anymore. Pretend that he didn't mean something to me.

Trust was another thing entirely, and I wasn't sure how we were going to overcome that particular obstacle, but as I trembled in his arms, for the time being, that was the least of my concerns.

Then I realized, I wasn't the one trembling.

Pulling him back, I touched my forehead to his. "Kanan, you're shaking," I whispered on a gasping breath, cupping his cheek. "Are you hurt? Did the wraiths get you?"

I ran my hands down his biceps, feeling for any wounds or blood. My fingers met nothing but warmth and worn leather. I looked up at him, everything still shrouded in darkness save for the smallest glow of red, rubbing my nose against his. "What is it? What's wrong?"

The silence stretched between us, and before I could say another word, his lips crashed into mine. He took advantage of my shock, plunging in with his deft tongue and taking without mercy. I thought about backing away, the rampant emotions of the past few hours clearly running high between us. The unbridled pleasure coursing through me made the decision for me though.

Kissing him back, I pressed myself up against every perfect inch of him. My nails dragged down his neck, my other hand sliding down his shoulder, digging into his biceps as he roughly pushed me into a tree.

When I went to pull away, breathless, he racked his hands into my hair, holding me to him as he delved deeper. I couldn't do anything but answer in return. A ragged, depraved groan tore free from his throat as we dueled. He licked and bit, kissing me with a wild, reckless abandon I wasn't used to seeing from him.

So controlled, always holding back out of necessity, the king had well and truly lost control. Every touch, every kiss since I had learned the truth up until this point had been initiated by me, but that restraint was gone. Pulverized beneath a long coming desperation that matched my own, the tether between us glowing with the strength of the connection. Its own heart was beating madly, contained within the embrace of the bond that transcended any worldly meaning. It yanked and tugged, pulling at us until there was no discerning the difference between his end and mine.

Blinded, surrounded by his scent, his power, *him* I could do nothing but submit to the raw ecstasy that consumed us both. Letting out a small, aching moan, I nipped his lower lip between my teeth, enjoying the hungry sound that rumbled in his chest.

He took long sips from my mouth, catching every keening cry and eager noise. Like a starved man, he feasted on me. Made me feel like I was the last drops of water in the desert, an oasis amidst parched, scorched land.

His hands roamed as he pressed me harder into the sturdy trunk, the bark biting into my back. Savoring it, they traced and worshiped every dip and curve, uncaring of the leathers that separated him from my skin. They continued down until he cupped my ass, lifting me against him without warning.

Wrapping my legs around his trim waist, he stepped fully between my thighs. Naked heat rolled between us as his hard length met my soft core, the gods-forsaken trousers doing little to stop the lust that roared inside me like some rabid beast.

Encircling my throat, every inch of skin sensitive to him, he snarled into my mouth at the hot touch. Rolling his hips into mine, I whimpered as a near painful need pulsed between my clenched thighs.

His thumb raised my chin into his addictive kiss. The sharp points of his claws pricked the skin of my neck, the ones on my thigh twitching in barely withheld strength. The power in his finely-honed body called out to mine, the golden storm that lived and breathed inside me reached out in longing.

Kanan's kiss turned slow and consuming. Savage need turned into a gentle, heady seduction. Light presses against my lips, small bites that he laved his tongue over to soothe the sting. It was as if he had led us to a precipice, the dive into carnal oblivion right there in front of us, a bare step away, only to ease us back from the edge and into something far more dangerous.

Unhurried strokes, long drugging pulls that did more than just reel me in. Each caress, every brush, all meant to ensnare me into this web of history that connected us. Thousands of years, cosmic entanglements steering us together no matter the obstacles in the way.

He finally leaned back, his fangs biting into his lower lip as he watched my tongue dart out to wet my own. He touched his forehead to mine as our ragged, panting breaths mixed, his air becoming mine and mine his.

"I thought I'd lost you," he breathed, voice shaking with something I had never heard in his voice before. Fear. An emotion I hadn't thought possible for the dark god to feel.

Opening his eyes, bright fire burning wildly, he took me in. Memorizing every inch that only he could see. With a low groan, wrenched from deep within, he kissed me again. A flash of pleasure as he ripped the air from my lungs, leaving me breathless.

He broke the connection quickly, but I followed after him, leaning in for more. Pulling myself together, I swallowed hard as I caught my breath. My eyes traced over the small parts of him I could see, which wasn't much.

I knew he could see perfectly well, his eyes attuned to all kinds of darkness. Which meant he could see the blush I could feel working its way over my cheeks. The crazed, starved look in his eyes was no doubt a reflection of my own.

"Are you okay?" I whispered, careful not to stir the taut tension that had settled between us. A single move and I felt like I would set us off, lost to the hedonism that lingered just on the horizon.

His thumb swept down the column of my throat. A sweet caress as he placed his hands under my thighs, supporting my weight against him. "Love, I haven't been okay for a while."

Confused by the answer, I went to question him on it, but in classic Kanan fashion, he chose that moment to move on from the subject. Lowering me, my hyperaware body sliding slowly against his, he made sure I had my footing before drawing back.

I was infuriated and turned on beyond belief, which was doing wonders for the emotional turmoil I had going on. It was like for every step we took forward, we took two steps back. I didn't have a chance to argue it with him though because in the next breath, I was blinded.

Turning away as light washed over us, I blinked away the spots in my vision. The noon sun hung high above us, the canopy blocking most of the light, but compared to the pure ebony of Kanan's power, it was downright blinding.

A cool summer breeze blew through just as I faced him, the gleaming strands that had come loose from my braid flying across my face. His heated gaze ran over me as mine did his. Nothing was said as we watched each other.

Words were somehow incomparable to the understanding that flowed between us on a soul-deep level. That damned connection that had always been there, pair bond or no, allowed for a far more efficient way of communicating.

I didn't need to say anything, and neither did he, for both of us to know that whatever had just happened wasn't even close to being done. There were things that we couldn't put off in order to deal with whatever the fuck was between us, but it would come. The determined, single-minded look in Kanan's eyes made sure that was read loud and clear.

No more running, it was time for us to figure out our shit.

CHAPTER TWENTY-EIGHT

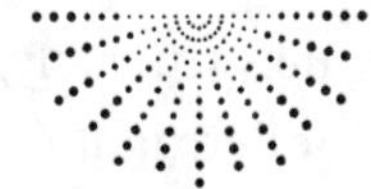

Our next move was an obvious one. There was nothing else in Rhaera for us, the wraiths either dead or buried and any remaining kinsmen alongside them. If we wanted to find one of them, we would have had to locate another tunnel entrance, and the risks far outweighed anything we might have found.

Small pieces of the puzzle were finally beginning to come together, and we needed all the information to figure it out. I could only hope that Zanaya had relayed my idea, and that Moian had followed through.

Getting home was more urgent than ever, a sentiment Kanan seemed to share. We flew fast, every wingbeat bringing us closer and closer to the mountain citadel, our eyes on the horizon looking for the gleaming capital. He covered miles of beautiful, untouched land in minutes, eating away at the distance that separated us from our home.

"My eardrums will never be the same."

I stretched in my seat, rolling my eyes despite the chuckle that left my lips, barely catching a glimpse of our passenger over his heavily muscled shoulder. The midnight darkness that had settled over the world had turned her into a blob of shadow.

Poor Ellenia was having the fright of her life. Grasped in Kanan's claws, she dangled hundreds of feet above the air. Curses on Kanan's name that would have made a sailor blush, interspersed with the panicked screams she seemed unable to contain, ripped through the air around us.

The argument on whether she would come with us or not had lasted all of two minutes. To her credit, she had stood her ground, insisting she would never abandon her inn. That is, right up until an already-shifted Kanan had let out a disgruntled grumble and snatched her up between his claws. I, unfortunately, agreed with the arrogant lizard. It was too dangerous for her right now. For anyone, really.

"Poor, poor baby," I teased, *"I didn't know you were so sensitive."*

I smiled in delight as a growl shook between my legs, thighs clenching around him as he dipped to the right. *"It's just a little screaming."*

His voice, normally velvety smooth, rolled through my mind in a dark caress.*"The only person I want screaming my name this loudly, is you. Preferably as I'm doing things that make you forget your own."*

I couldn't help the little jerk I made against him as those carnal words washed over me, their meaning not lost on me. Sex coated his every breath, nothing but hot desire stirring between us like a raging, unstoppable fire. Ready to consume us both.

I wasn't sure I would survive if it came to that. A lot of our problems weren't even close to being solved, but damn if letting him do all kinds of naughty things to me didn't sound fucking fantastic right now.

The rational part of me knew I should have backed off, but the other part, the one who wouldn't mind stripping naked and seeing just how a god liked to fuck, had a much bigger mouth. *"Is that right, and just what would you do to me?"* The words were a purr down the mental bond, husky and heavy with sensual promise.

Silence.

"Careful, sweet goddess," he murmured the sinful warning, *"I don't think you know who you're playing with."*

"Who said I was playing?"

A growl vibrated his onyx scales, the heat that radiated from them getting hotter. *"There aren't many things I want more than that, but there is one; and no matter how badly I want you hot and panting under me,"* a pained, needy groan escaped into his voice and had my soft bits tightening, *"I won't give that one thing up."*

"And what is that?" I asked, waiting with bated breath.

"You," he answered without hesitation. *"I want you. Every single piece, because I won't have any less than that. Not when it would just torture us both."*

My heart stopped beating. At least, that's what it felt like as he came out from behind those impenetrable walls he always kept up, separating him from the rest of the world.

"Your smiles. I want them to be because of me. Your laugh. That fierce anger and scathing tongue. The resilience you carry in your heart like an inextinguishable flame. I want them all," he said with powerful conviction, every word breaking through my lust and hitting somewhere far deeper.

"When I look into those piercing eyes, I want every part of you looking back at me. When you come to me, I don't want it to be just for my body, my touch. I want it to be because you see every part of me, every good, bad, and downright dark part of me and take me as I am."

"Kanan," I whispered weakly down the bond. Never in a million years would I have expected such declarations from anyone, and as he bared his heart and soul, I was speechless.

"You've been mine since the universe was a thought in our creator's mind, Atallia, and I desperately want to be yours. The Divine. God and goddess. King and queen. Whatever they called us, our names were always synonymous with each other. There was no me without you."

I was grateful for the shearing wind that blew into me as we raced across the skies, carrying away the tears that rolled down my face. Raising a hand, I wiped the salty streaks from my face, only for them to be replaced by more.

"Maybe it's not fair of me to say any of this, you don't have the memories I do, but you have to understand, there is no after you for me. I wouldn't blame you for wanting nothing to do with me, I know I've done things. Things I'm not proud of, and no matter how much I wish I could change that,

I can't. If you come to me, it'll have to be with trust and an open heart. I want it all, love. Every. Single. Piece. Until the stars are dust in our hands."

My chest tightened painfully, my lungs struggling to expand, until it felt like I couldn't breath. Suffocated by the emotions that were both my own and not, but the more I was stuck with this dual reality, my soul seemingly split in half, the more everything aligned.

The lines were beginning to blur, muddling together until I couldn't tell what was what. Closing my eyes, I tilted my head back to the dark sky. The wet streaks that marked my face cooling in the night air, and as I opened my tear-clouded eyes, I was met by the wordless wonder of Allasea's night sky.

Heis was especially brilliant, larger and closer than I had ever seen it, the elder moon's blue surface unmatched in color. It was unlike anything I had ever seen even in Allasea's magic-filled lands. The turquoise blue, swirled with cloudy white, and speckles of green, was downright blinding in its brilliance.

Taipea wasn't far behind, the ice-white sibling nearly as prominent. The two silver rings that spun around were barely slivers in the sky, but their sparkling light turned Taipea's rays dazzling.

Ayu and Sessa, the younger and smaller moons, weren't nearly as pronounced tonight, but that didn't make them any less stunning. With Ayu's three spectacular bands of golden red light that cut the moon in all directions, and Sessa's mighty black and silver craters that melded with its startling green hue, they were both magnificent.

It was these siblings that Allasea's nightlife could thank for the enviable beauty that not even the daylight could dispute. It was also the grounding presence I needed to center myself once more.

You will not break.

It was something I was saying far too often, but it was nonetheless true. It felt like the world was against us right now, everything piling on top in order to crush any sense of stability or self-confidence.

But maybe that's where I had been going wrong this whole time, searching for answers in the darkness and hoping it would shine and fix all of my problems. Instead, I should have been looking to myself, trusting in myself.

I didn't have all the answers, that was for fucking sure, but I had also given up on myself. Allowing a sense of failure to take root and rot my self-confidence from the inside out. Kasis didn't need to infect or kill me, I was doing a great job of it all on my own.

It wasn't an easy pill to swallow to realize you had become your own worst enemy.

I became so focused on who I had been before, what was expected of me because of that, that I had forgotten about who I was now.

Some things had changed, there was no denying that, and I wouldn't want to. There was so much that I had gained. Friends that saw me for me, and expected nothing in return. A place that finally felt like I could call home, where I wouldn't be judged or shamed. So much good.

Queen. Goddess. At the end of the day, I was still me. Still that cynical, jaded girl from the Outskirts who had a knife problem.

I think it was time to start reminding myself of that fact.

CHAPTER TWENTY-NINE

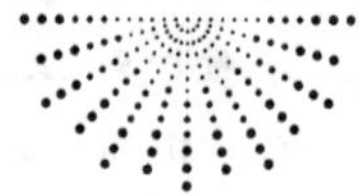

Even with Kanan flying at full force, it still took us half the night to reach Elona. The land had quickly changed from forests and flatland to the steep, rocky terrain that the Crians were known for.

Jagged, snow-capped peaks raced by underneath, the dark stone nearly blending in with the night. Off in the distance to our right, twinkling lights and the barest hint of a jutting summit illuminated by the moons' rays, had a strange twinge plucking at my heart.

Eskira.

As much as I knew both Kanan and I would love nothing more than to fly to the capital jewel, our people would have only just made it to Elona. The ferrymen carrying the soldiers upstream in an orderly fashion.

The seaport town was based in the basin of Eskira's patron mountain, running along the coastline that made up the Strait of Laos. Many of the seafaring locals ran ships up and down the Falla River's many branches, bringing supplies and goods to Eskiran markets.

Unless someone thought they could scale the Crians to reach Eskira, a mistake they would realize very quickly when the treacherous nature of the mountain range made itself known, any army would first have to take Elona.

It was why Eskira was so perfectly positioned. Protected by shearing, dangerous mountains, the only habitable land occupied by the capital city, and only accessible by air or the singular waterway.

Those wishing to take the Falla upstream, would find themselves dealing with a relentless battle. Anyone unaccustomed or unprepared would struggle against the powerful rapids that made up the lower sections, and if caught unaware their boat would shatter against the jutting crystal boulders that lined the bottom. The pieces of rubble and anyone on board would be swept under and taken out to sea.

Eskira was inhospitable to those she did not trust.

And the seamen and captains of Elona had years of experience, and an innate knowledge of the Falla. One passed down through the generations of the seaside village that granted them the ability to ferry passengers through safely.

"How much farther?"

We had been flying since the sun had set. Hours of holding on to Kanan's rough spines, the hard scaling biting into the flesh of my hands. My legs ached from holding my seat, and every muscle along my back begged to be stretched. I couldn't imagine Ellenia was doing much better.

"Look out in the distance," he replied smoothly. *"We'll be there in minutes."*

I arched to see around his thick neck, but his crown of ebony horns blocked the view. Before I could even think to ask, he dipped his shoulder. Flaring his impressive wings out wide, we began our slow, gliding descent. Holding on tight, I finally got my first look at Elona.

Far below us, cloaked in darkness, the sea-town was barely distinguishable save for the odd lamplight burning away in a window. The moon-rays glinted off the Straight of Laos, the dark water shining like one of Kanan's onyx scales.

The wide expanse of the Falla cut through the hillside, carving into the mountain valley as it made its way out to the ocean. The two other branches sparkled in the distance, colors dancing through their waters unhindered by the night's darkness.

The masts of boats dotted the edge of the water, where the sea touched the land. Long docks jutted out into the gentle waves, ropes anchoring large ships to the moorings. Smaller vessels were rigged up closer to the mouth of the river.

There wasn't much detail I could pick out from the town, the long row houses—that appeared made of stone—perfectly blended in with the surrounding landscape at this time of night.

The one thing that did stand out was the field of tents set up right outside the town's borders. Fires burned throughout the camp, restless warriors sitting around the warm hearths. Those on watch noticed us first, a signal spreading throughout the camp, alerting everyone to our return.

Circling lower, Kanan swung us around to an open patch of land on the far side of the valley. With a few back beats of his wings, my legs straining to hold on, we landed. Flung forward with the force of the vibrations, the ground shaking under his might, I threw my hand out to catch myself before I was impaled on the many spines that decorated his sinuous neck.

"You alright, love?" His voice wove through my mind as he stretched his massive leg out, unfurling his claws. Ellenia tumbled out and onto the ground haplessly.

"Better than her," I groaned, bones aching as he shifted away from where Ellenia was keeled over. *"Did you have to drop her?"*

He stepped away, each stride shaking the ground. Bending his knee for me, I half slid, half climbed down his scaled side.

"My ears are bleeding. It's annoying." His muttered grumble brought a smile to my face.

Ruby red eyes, alight with an endless fire, glared down at me unamused. He lowered his head, unimaginable in size, and those snake-like pupils constricted tightly, as dark and endless as his shadows. Smoke curled from his nostrils, coiling up like he was a living flame. *"I saw that."*

"I have no idea what you mean," I teased. *"Besides you like Ellenia, remember?"*

"Yes...when she's quieter."

I rolled my eyes at the dramatics, leaving him to shift, stretching out my stiff muscles as I walked over to where Ellenia, and those that had come to meet us, stood away from Kanan's hulking form.

Zanaya smiled, shooting me a wink as her hands were currently occupied holding Ellenia's hair back as she lost the contents of her stomach.

The innkeeper looked up from where she was bent over her knees, panting and a sickly green color, "Can we never do that again?"

"I don't think flight suits her." Stating the obvious, Saanvi sauntered from the surrounding darkness, Bron by her side.

I massaged the inside of my thighs and let out a tired laugh, "I don't think flight really suits anyone."

"Whatever do you mean, my darling queen?" Kanan teased, appearing by my side. "I'm a perfect steed."

I snorted, "Yeah, if that perfect steed was a hundred thousand pound, scaled, flying liz—"

"Don't say it," he grumbled.

"Lizard," I mouthed to Zanaya, who giggled. At Kanan's glare, she choked it down, covering it up by clearing her throat. Pressing my lips together to stop my own laughter, I got a look at our friends.

Visibly tired, even in the darkness, but no worse for wear since we had left. A huge weight lifted off my shoulders, the relief hitting me hard. I worried we had made a mistake in leaving, taking away the army's biggest weapons, during a time when Kasis could seemingly attack from anywhere.

After pulling Ellenia to her feet, Zanaya dragged me into a hug, holding me to her tight. I returned it, reaching a hand out to grasp Saanvi's at the same time, the corners of her mouth curling in her version of a smile. Bron and Kanan clasped forearms, coming together in a back-slapping hold.

"How is everyone?" I asked the two women as we separated. "Nala? Zander?"

"Both great," Zanaya answered honestly, squeezing my arm in support, "although they're even more inseparable than ever."

Saanvi snorted, "They're driving everyone insane with their antics while we wait for the riverboats."

"Why does that not surprise me?" I chuckled. The two redheads weren't known for being troublemakers for nothing. Now that their pair bond had settled into place, they were going to be an even more efficient team at causing mayhem.

"How have things been?" Kanan inquired as we all began walking back towards the temporary camp. "Any problems?"

"Other than the burnout we're all facing, no. The trek here was long, but thankfully the few airborne we could spare were able to alert Eskira, they had supplies waiting for us." Bron ran a hand through his pale hair, a roguish grin spreading across his face. "Morale is up. So close to home, everyone's gotten a second wind. We can taste it, smell it in the air."

"Seems as though something happened to you," Saanvi joined in, glancing at the disheveled Ellenia. We had stopped long enough for her to change out of the tattered piece of fabric the kinsmen had considered clothing, but grime still covered her from head to toe.

My heart clenched, looking over at Ellenia, the innkeeper's unfocused gaze staring ahead as I replied, "You could say that."

Zanaya and Saanvi gave me a look, asking me with their eyes what no one wanted to say out loud. I averted my gaze. Ellenia's story wasn't mine to tell.

"The warped?" I questioned tentatively, changing the subject. The status of the sick warriors had been on my mind since we'd left for Rhaera.

"Stable for now," Zanaya answered, "the Warp hasn't progressed any farther in the ones you were able to help, but the new cases…it's not looking good."

"How many?" Kanan pressed, glancing over his shoulder, our eyes meeting, the worry eating at us both.

"Ten new ones after the attack at the lake, a lot less than Moian was predicting thanks to whatever Atallia did," Zanaya sighed, a curse falling from her mouth. "But that still takes us to sixty in total."

Too many lives that might never recover, taken far too early because of some evil god's plans they had no part of. "Has Moian made any progress with figuring it out? You told her what I asked?"

Zanaya nodded, a grave air taking over, "She asked you be brought right to her, or that she speak with the entire Council once you arrived."

Kanan looked over at me, questions in his eyes, "What did you ask of the Mender?"

"If I'm right, then everyone needs to be there to hear it," I said with a shake of my head. Gods, I hope I wasn't right.

"Commander Zuberi hasn't been very informative about her dealings with the Mender," Bron shared, glaring at the unimpressed Zanaya.

Although she was shorter, she looked down her nose at him, sniffing in dismissal, "Lord Bron doesn't seem to understand that, despite what he may believe, not everything is his business."

"I was put in charge for a reason," he argued, "Everything is my business."

"And I," she retorted sourly, "was given a task by my queen and friend, so you can shove your big fat ego right up your ass."

I glanced at Kanan, eyes wide. He shot me a look, brow furrowed as his red gaze bounced between the bickering duo.

"Uh...what's going on with them?" I asked, sending the question down the bond.

He peered at me from the corner of his eye, bewildered by the argument unfolding before us, *"You think I know?"*

"Should we stop them?" A curse flew from Zanaya's mouth so crude, my mouth dropped. Even as I struggled to contain my laughter, I continued, *"I think we should stop them."*

"Enough," Kanan growled. "We don't have time for this. Commander, find Ellenia some sustenance and a place to sleep, and then come join us. Bron, call the Council to a meeting. The queen and I will be washing up in my tent, we expect them to be there in ten minutes. You two as well, *without* the arguing."

Zanaya shot Bron a scathing look and stomped off with a huff. Saanvi followed behind her, cackling all the way. Ellenia trailed after them, the sea breeze blowing her matted hair off her neck, cooling the sweat that had beaded along her skin.

Swiveling around, I lifted a suspicious eyebrow at Bron, a thunderous expression carving across his broad features, thick arms folded over his chest. "Don't look at me like that," he glared, prowling off in the opposite direction.

Kanan and I watched them go, matching expressions of confusion on our faces. Rubbing his brow, he sighed, wrapping an arm around me, leading me further into the camp. "Welcome home."

CHAPTER THIRTY

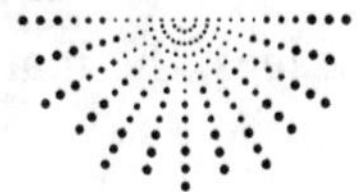

Kanan's tent had apparently taken a hit back at Lake Thesian, the large black structure torn to pieces, shredded beyond compare, by the attacking wraiths. Suspecting we would be riding in on the night's wind, Bron had a newer, albeit smaller, one already set up for us.

The fact that only one had been put up, a glaringly obvious ploy by the moon-kissed primal, had me contemplating setting Zanaya loose on his presumptuous ass. See how highly he thought of himself then.

Thankfully for him, I was too tired to carry out my evil plans, more focused on wiping away the sweat that had collected at the nape of my neck than I was on wiping that feline grin Bron had secreted away as soon as he pointed us to our tent.

He was at least smart enough to have set up two basins of water, a point that only slightly lessened my ire as I now had to somehow exist in a small, confined space with a half-undressed Kanan without spontaneously combusting.

Slowly peeking over my shoulder, I glimpsed the scarred skin of his back as he pulled his tunic over his head. Every muscle in the smooth strength of his arms, from his massive shoulders to the smallest tendon in his hands, was on display as he tossed the leather to the side.

I knew I should look away. Despite the…progress we had made, I had no business leering at him, but I couldn't help but watch as his back rippled with power beneath the layers of scars as he bent over his basin, washing his face of the past few days.

Dragging my gaze down the length of him, every part of him a feast for my eyes, I noticed he had loosened the ties on the black leather that cloaked his thick legs, the material now hanging dangerously low on his hips.

What would happen if I went over there and tugged them down just a little further?

"If you want to come over here and help me, love, instead of just watching, I wouldn't complain." I whipped back around, jumping at having been caught as his deep voice rocketed through me.

"I have no idea what you're talking about," I snarked, leaning over to wipe my own face, the water still warm. I would have to remember to thank whoever had brought it, because despite summer having fully rolled in, the nights could still be cold. Especially so close to Eskira, the mountain winds competed with the sea breeze, chilling the valley as soon as the sun dropped into the ocean.

"Is that right?" he mused, "So I just imagined feeling your eyes on me?"

"It wouldn't be the first time you acted delusional." Taking a quick glance to see if he was looking, although I couldn't really blame him if he did since I was doing it to him, I stripped off my own top. Orion's beacon crystal dangled between my wrapped breast, the necklace cool to the touch as I ran my fingers over its rough surface.

He chuckled, the sound soft and husky, "Delusional am I?"

"You've admitted yourself that you have obsessive tendencies," I taunted, gathering the cloth that had been left on the side of the wash bin, dipping it into the water and quickly swiping it across my skin. There was more splashing behind me, the tension taut enough to cut as we both stood bare only feet away from each other.

I wiped down my arms, biting my lip, a warmth building in my chest and in other places as my mind strayed to dangerous ideas, imagining what it would be like to run my hands down the same path as the water that now coated his skin.

"I have said that haven't I," he hummed, the natural heat he released radiating across the space that separated us. "In all fairness my obsessive…tendencies are typically worsened by a certain golden-haired goddess."

"It's not my fault you have control issues," I ribbed even as my heart stuttered in my chest. Finishing up with the washcloth, I donned the oversized, gauzy tunic that had been folded and left inside one of the few chests that had made it into the tent. The white material hung past my leather-clad knees, the sleeves dangling well below my wrists.

The neckline was left open, and if it plunged any further it would have been considered indecent, but as the smoke and amber scent wafted from it, that unmistakable hint of dark, burning warmth hidden underneath, I decided it didn't matter all that much to me if I ended up flashing the Council.

I've done it so many times already, they're probably used to it by now.

"Oh but see here, little goddess," he started, the room darkening slightly as the shadows in the corners stirred, "that's where you are very, very wrong. I hate to put more responsibility on you, but my control is most definitely tied to you."

My hands trembled as I rolled my sleeves up, waiting with bated breath as he continued. "I suggest you be careful, love, because if you asked me to plunge this world into darkness, I don't think I would be able to say no. If you were taken from me again, I might very well decide the entire world doesn't deserve to go on if you're not in it."

The silence stretched thin between us as I detangled my wind-blown hair, the seriousness of his statement not lost on me. "You wouldn't do that, Kanan, not when so many count on us."

He sighed heavily, "I wish I had your faith, but I'm not that altruistic. The truth of the matter is, if I don't have you then I don't want anything else. Not a crown or a throne, not power, certainly not a world without you"

I barely felt it as my fingers threaded through my hair, gathering the long sections to braid it back, my entire being focused on his words, hanging on to every breath.

"I lived alone for a long time," he murmured. "Long before Kasis, even longer before you. I began to feel as our creator did when he made us. The Cosmos was a power, but no power in the world could have cured the loneliness inside him."

A shadow came down from above, the dark tendril snaking in front of me, watching. I lifted a finger and let it curl around my wrist, lick at my skin, almost like it was tasting me. It carefully pulled back as its master continued ripping my heart out of my chest.

"I felt it, that loneliness, even when Kasis appeared. Then came the Time of Nightmares," he voiced, torturous memories thick in his words, "but you came along and fixed all of that. And for the first time in my life, I didn't feel alone."

I twisted the ends of my braid as I listened to him scrub his hands over his face and through his hair. I couldn't bring myself to turn, to look at his hunched shoulders as he dropped those impregnable walls, allowing himself to be vulnerable.

"But nothing, *nothing*," he stressed, "compares to that year without you. When I couldn't find you, our bond silent. Gods, it was so silent. I wanted to rage against the world, take my anger and grief out on anything I could get my hands on, but the only thing I could focus on for long enough was getting to you. So, while I would love to believe like you do that I wouldn't lose myself again, I know in my heart that I wouldn't survive that silence again."

Air caught in my throat as I closed my eyes, fighting the tears that wanted to flow free. His defeated sigh had me turning to see him toss his washcloth into the bowl, water splashing out onto the side of the table.

His back was still streaked with blood, both red and black. I was moving before I could even think to stop myself. He stiffened as I reached an arm around him to grab the soaked rag, squeezing out the water.

"Here, let me" I whispered, brushing the rag gently against his heated skin. I worried my lip as the white material turned red. "Did you get hurt?"

"Mmm," he replied noncommittally, "those beasts got a few good swipes in."

"You don't feel any different, right?"

"No," he grunted, his muscle flexing under my hand as I placed it on his shoulder.

"Okay," I sighed in relief, "that's good. The Warp isn't subtle, so you would know by now. I don't think Kasis's plague can affect us."

"Not yet anyway," he muttered grimly.

That was a sobering thought, because who knew what Kasis was playing at. Things weren't acting as they should anymore, and if anyone could figure out a way to kill true immortals, it would be Kasis's hatred-fueled self.

Kanan dropped his head between his shoulders, gripping on to the small wooden table in front of him, the muscles along his arms tightening as I continued my task. A bead of water dripped from his damp curls, rolling down his neck and in between his broad shoulders.

That tempestuous droplet gave me all the permission I needed to memorize every inch of him, imprinting it into my mind, uncaring if he caught me again. My empty hand was unhurried as it traced over the scars mottling his back.

His vulnerability sat close to my heart, the organ throbbing in a way I wasn't used to. Maybe it was his willingness to share, or perhaps I was being driven insane by his closeness, the heady feeling cascading through me wherever we touched enough to send me into a spiral of need. Either way, whatever the reason, my own walls dropped slightly.

"I know what it's like to feel alone," I said in a hushed tone, as if a sense of quiet had fallen around us, separating us from the rest of the world as we bared part of our hearts, our fears.

"I know," he uttered, something like self-loathing in his voice. "I heard you with Moian back in Hassere."

Now it was my turn to hum in response, and because of his unjudging silence—turning his head to the side as he waited, wanting to hear what I had to say—I felt myself open up. "I had Maris and Geoff, of course, but," I blew out a shaky breath, "I don't know, it just never felt the same. There was always this hole inside of me, a big gaping pit that never stopped searching for I never knew what."

Dipping the cloth back into the bowl, watching as the water turned pink, I kept talking, knowing if I stopped I wouldn't start again. "I got very good at ignoring it, shoving it deep down inside me until most days I couldn't feel it anymore. But it was there. It was always there, peering up at me like some monster beneath the bed, just as desperate and desolate as it had always been."

Hearing the emotion in my voice, he went to turn around, but stopped at the hand I placed on his hip. If he looked at me, I would cry, and I couldn't handle seeing those stupid sparkling tears, shining up at me like twinkling stars as they hit the ground.

He didn't move again, but one hand did reach behind to take hold of my hip, bunching up the hanging tails of my shirt so that a finger could stroke my skin underneath.

I kept cleaning, careful around the new pink skin that must have been where the wraiths had sunk their teeth in. The steady, rhythmic movement helped calm me as I spoke. "I spent my whole life thinking I would never get to fulfill that need inside of me, and after a while, I was used to the idea. Figured at least I had my parents, or whatever the hell Maris and Geoff are, which is more than some people.

"Then I came to Eskira," I paused, "and everything was different. I wasn't hated, people weren't disgusted by me. I found friends who genuinely care, and even when I had no idea what the future would hold, I discovered a certain kind of peace. The kind of peace that comes with knowing that though not everything is going as expected, I would be alright."

I blinked as realization swept through me. "I knew that even if I couldn't find Maris and Geoff, couldn't untangle the secrets that seem to stick to me wherever I go, that I would survive. It wouldn't break me."

"And did that fill the hole?" he asked huskily. "Did it make the loneliness go away?"

"That's the thing," I replied with a laugh. "It didn't. You would think it would, and in a way it fulfilled another ache inside me, but that gaping abyss was still there. I don't know if it was seeing all the couples around me, seeing Saanvi with her partners, who I still haven't met," I complained, "unacceptable if you ask me. But regardless, I realized I needed that connection with someone. Needed to feel loved and cared for. Someone who would compliment me in every way, who would stand beside me, holding me up when I need it and cheering me on when I don't."

He tensed beneath my hands, swiftly going from relaxed to hard as the onyx scales that covered his other form. I swallowed as the emotions I tried so damn hard to keep under control started to seep through. "I want to go to bed every night knowing I'm loved and wake up every morning to see that love shining in someone's eyes. Kisses behind closed doors, arguments that could wake the dead, secret touches that only we can understand...all of it Kanan, I want it all."

"I get it," he ground out, the veins in his neck protruding angrily. Releasing my hip he placed his hand back on the table next to its twin. Shadows crawled along the inside of the tent, sending the tent into further darkness. The small flames in the oil lamps stood no chance against the starless ebony.

"I wish you well on your search," the words were polite to the point of being diplomatic, but even as he spoke, the wood cracked under his palms.

"Kanan, you're missing my point," I breathed, tossing the pink-stained rag onto the table before turning him around to face me.

I stepped closer, perfectly lining up my curves with his hard planes, glancing up beneath lowered lashes into those scarlett daggers.

"What I'm trying to say," I admitted, letting him see the emotion my scarred heart had finally set free, "is that I don't feel so alone anymore."

The world paused as he stared down at me. For once it seemed like the king—the god—was stumped.

After what felt like an eternity, he let out a shaky breath, eyes softening in a way that was so unlike him it stunned me enough to be caught off guard when he gripped my hip and pulled me in tight.

A nearly soundless gasp escaped me, my skin flushing beneath his gaze. Lifting a hand, he took hold of my chin, dragging his thumb over my lower lip. Fangs digging into his supple lip, that magnetic gaze swept over my face with a burning intensity that threatened to set me on fire.

His pupils were blown, a savage look of need taking over the blood red irises. I went up on my toes as he leaned down, our noses brushing in a soft caress. We both paused, breathing the other in

Watching my lips, he swallowed hard, wetting his own before asking in the most sin-filled voice, "Do you want this?"

My emotions warred with my mind. We may have our problems, but I'd be lying to myself if I said there weren't more emotions involved than just anger. And I hated liars.

I pressed up into him, needing the contact, my lips grazing his as I answered truthfully, "Yes."

We came together, not in a clash, but in a sweet melding of lips and tongue. I moaned as he swept in, the delicious taste of him, all smoke and warmth, drowning me under the pleasure of it.

Whipping us around, with one arm still holding on to my hip, he knocked the basin of water off the table, sending it shattering onto the ground next to us. He lifted me into the air without thought and settled me on the once occupied table before pushing between my thighs, arching me over his arm as he opened my mouth further to his conquest.

His other hand slid higher up my thigh, digging into the thick leather that separated us. He growled into my mouth at the interference, stroking me with his tongue.

Whereas our previous kisses had been hot and desperate, more a battle of wills than anything, this one was full of a different kind of need. A slow, seducing kind, where we pretended we had all the time in the world. Long, sipping pulls from each other's lips. Light nips from his fangs, slightly harder ones from my own dull teeth that had him chuckling into the next kiss.

Running my hand through his hair, I tugged until he purred, smiling against his lips as the sound broke free from his chest. Pulling back only slightly, dragging my bottom lip with him until he let it go with a *pop*. I tugged harder on the midnight strands.

Half chuckle, half growl, he glanced at me through lowered lids, his glazed look telling me he was as drugged on the erotic feeling of it all as I was. "Careful, love," he rasped, watching my reaction as I felt his claws prick through my leathers, smiling wickedly as my breath caught in my throat, "I might decide to stop playing nice."

"This is you playing nice?" I panted, a sensual grin lifting the corners of my lips. "What about when you're not so nice?"

A rumble shook his chest. One large hand came up to collar my throat, yanking me to him as he took my mouth with a fervor. He was no longer being sweet and slow, instead demanding I give him everything with each rough stroke, in the slight pressure around my neck, and the barest taste of iron-rich blood as his fangs scraped over my tongue.

The hand on my thigh moved closer and closer to the junction of my legs, rubbing against the leather in his way. Too distracted by his mind-numbing kiss, I didn't see what it was that caused it, but in the span of a second my pants had been rendered to dust.

Gasping for breath as I pulled away in shock, his calloused hand set off a flurry of sensations as it rubbed against the skin of my thigh. Only a few thin, black strings were left to remind me that I was once wearing trousers.

"How did you do that?" I groaned, throwing my head back as he transferred his attention to that spot where my neck met my shoulder, running his fangs down the sensitive skin. My legs trembled as his claws pricked my hip slightly, the coarse grain of the wooden table biting into my ass.

"I have quite a few tricks up my sleeve," he rumbled, a smile in his voice, "and I find myself particularly persuaded to use them to rid you of your clothing."

"How generous of you," I muttered distractedly. My eyes rolled back in my head as those dangerous fingers came close to the center of all my desire. So damn close.

"Well, you know me," he said against my lips, "I can be very, very generous."

Kissing me like it was his salvation, he cupped the back of my head, wrapping my braid around his fist. Giving as good as I received, I scraped my nails down his chest. I tightened my legs around his hips and dragged him closer until I wasn't sure where I started and he ended.

"Kanan," Bron boomed from outside, breaking through the impassioned bubble we had found ourselves in.

We broke apart, breathing hard, our chests brushing with every inhale. I dropped my head to his shoulder, heart pounding against my ribs. His hands tightened on my hips, holding me closer as he rested his chin against me. A growl made its way out of his throat, a puff of smoke curling around us.

"I could send them away," he mused quietly.

Chuckling, I lifted my head, "You know we can't do that."

"Worth a try," he grumbled.

Pushing him back, I gave him a look as I said, "It's for the best anyway, I think you and I have a lot to talk about."

He stood to his full height, the walls that surrounded his heart coming back up with an almost audible slam. He dipped his head, holding out his hand. Grasping it, I jumped off the table, thankful that Kanan's dark power hadn't shredded my boots, the ceramic shards of the basin crunching underfoot.

I was pants-less, but at least I had my shoes. Which was progress in my opinion. I never had my fucking shoes.

I kicked the broken pieces to the side, hiding them behind the table. I tipped my chin up at the front flap of the tent, "Let them in."

"Enter," Kanan commanded, pouring two glasses of water from the pitcher on the circular table in the center of the tent.

I came up next to him, accepting the goblet from his hand as Moian entered first. I froze with the water halfway to my lips. The grave expression on her drawn face told me all I needed to know. My theory was right.

Fuck me.

CHAPTER THIRTY-ONE

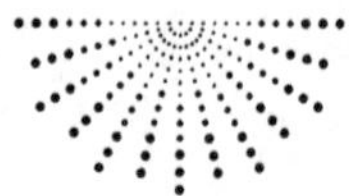

"Shit," I muttered, setting the goblet down on the table as the others filed in. Going around to Moian's side, I guided the healer to a chair, pulling it out for her.

She collapsed into it, her dirty apron fluttering around her. Her shoulders drooped with the new profound sense of dread that had been weighing on my mind for days. Fingers stained black, crusted bits of wraith blood stuck beneath her nails, I knew she had completed what I'd asked. Had learned what I suspected.

I shared a solemn look with her, the knowledge in those deep brown eyes, that was once the cause of such confidence in the wise Mender, now a source of great worry.

Taking the offered cup from Kanan's outstretched arm, I set it down in front of her, squeezing her shoulder in support. "Drink," I ordered, lifting an eyebrow when she went to wave it off.

She relented, bringing the cup to her lips and swallowing the chilled water. "Thank you," she sighed, sitting back in the chair.

Assured she wasn't going to fall unconscious, I stepped back, turning to meet the rest of the group.

"Kanan," Bron greeted, "put a shirt on, man, you're going to make everyone else feel inadequate."

I glanced over, Kanan's wide stance making him even more of a dominating presence inside the small tent, his heavily corded arms crossed over his chest, the muscles popping more than usual. Bands of darkness coiled over his forearms, crawling down his carved abs to wrap around his leather-clad thighs. The ties of the trousers were still loosened from earlier, the breeches hanging lower than ever, showcasing that dangerous v-shaped line of muscle.

Everything about him screamed of power. There wasn't a single part of him that was soft or forgiving. The merciless God of Endings. Death personified.

Snorting, the dark god rolled his eyes at the only man likely to get away with talking to him like that. He strode to a random chest, digging through it to pull free a black version of the same thin shirt I wore.

He pulled it on, covering the wide array of scars that covered his back. The fine material settled along the hills and valleys of his body, coating him like a second skin. Spreading his arms wide, he asked, "Better?"

Thick, white brows came down as Bron pressed his lips together to smother the feline grin trying to break across his face. Nodding seriously, he replied, "Oh yes, the tortured king look is so much better."

I had to look away from Kanan's annoyed visage before I broke out into laughter, my shoulders shaking in restraint.

"And you, my dearest queen," the white haired menace quipped, an all too knowing smile on his face, "shall I ask why you have no pants?"

"Oh bite me, Bron," I retorted, flipping him my middle finger.

His grin grew wider, the firelight bouncing off his twin fangs, "That can be arranged."

A low, near-imperceptible growl rolled through the space. Bron's smile fell marginally, covering those sharp teeth, but mine grew in response.

"Don't listen to the pussy-cat, Atallia," Zanaya mocked, stepping out from behind Bron's sizable form. "He's all talk, very little bite."

This time the growl came from Bron, his silver eyes flashing in the light, reminding me of the feral cats that had wandered the alleys at night back in the Outskirts. He tracked her path around the table, watching her sleek figure with an intensity that had me narrowing my eyes at him.

Catching my look, he glanced away, that annoying smile once again firmly in place. He took his place at the table across from Zanaya, the two continuing to snipe at each other. Kanan watched on, looking between the two with a bored countenance, a tic in his jaw the only indicator of his annoyance.

"Let's get this over with," Kanan commanded, the quiet cadence of his voice still able to break through the impending argument between our two friends.

"My queen," Cashim addressed me, bowing his head as he passed. The guilt surrounding him was thick enough to clog the air, and as much as I wanted to keep being mad at him, I knew I would have to convince his niece to talk to him before the remorse ate him alive.

Lilyi, Oakina, Elaric, and even Lars, joined the table with similar greetings. It was cramped with all of us squeezing into the small space, but it would have to do. We needed to make some decisions about what our next move would be.

"Any word from Lady Yeva?" I asked, taking my seat. Zanaya was seated on my right, Kanan to my left.

"She arrived back in Hassere not long after we began our journey here," Elaric said. "She and her convoy sent word the second they made it into the city."

"She didn't fight the escort?" Kanan questioned.

Lilyi answered, "She took it happily. I think we can all agree these are not normal times, what with new nightmares around every corner, even a primal needs backup nowadays."

"I believe the unfortunate circumstances we are being forced to deal with are changing all of our perspectives," Cashim added, shifting his attention to Kanan and I, "Tell us, Your Majesties, what did you find at Rhaera? Bron mentioned Ellenia arrived with you."

The innkeeper was well known amongst the Council it seemed, their attention focused on what we had to say. It made sense. As diplomatic envoys of the three major cities, they would have traveled around Allasea and had most likely stayed at her inn more than once.

"Before we get into that," I started, "I would like Moian to speak. If what I believe she has to say is correct, then we all need to hear it."

Lars shifted forward in his seat, bracing his forearms on the table. "What do you mean?" he demanded, quickly adding, "My queen," when Kanan shifted his glare to him.

Taking a deep breath, twisting my hands together beneath the table, I recounted everything. "Back at the lake, I encountered a wraith that did something I wasn't expecting. Of course it tried to kill me, and I fought it, but once I had killed it, a strange thing happened. A thin strand of energy was released from its body."

Shaking my head, the memory of that shining wisp was still fresh in my mind. "I barely saw it, it was so small, but it got me thinking. What we know about the wraiths isn't much, but what we do know is that they're corrupted versions of Cynthonians, or the animals that populate this world," I added, having seen creatures from both Allasea and Rhaelyth in those cells underneath Rhaera, "and we know they feed on our sparks. The magic in our blood."

"Right," Bron stressed, "but what does that have to do with what you had Moian looking into?"

Everyone looked at me as I made the connection. "Tell me why, when these beasts rot, skin literally sloughing from their bodies if they don't feed from us, would they not consume every last drop they can get their teeth into? When they're so crazed and rabid from hunger, that their only thought is to drain us dry. Why was there even a hint of magic left to be released from that wraith's body when I killed it?"

"That's where I come in," Moian began. "The queen had Commander Zuberi relay her theory, and since this was the first and only time we have had access to wraith corpses, we were in a position to find the answer."

"And what exactly is your theory?" Oakina asked warily.

I looked around the table, everyone's gaze fixated on me. On my left, Kanan took a deep breath, shifted in his seat, and that was all I needed to know he had figured it out.

"I think Kasis is collecting our magic," I proposed. "For what, I have no idea, but it's the only thing that makes sense. Why would he create these creatures who fall apart without an influx of energy? Energy he could never ensure would be available unless he had access to a large collection. It's completely inefficient."

"Unless it's a smoke screen," Kanan considered, glancing over at me with appreciation in his eyes. "It's all an illusion," he continued, letting out a hollow chuckle. "My brother's favorite game."

I gave him a pressed smile, hating how many painful memories this must bring up for him, all the while wishing I could remember my own. At least then I could comfort him with the knowledge that I understood where the betrayal came from.

Cashim cleared his throat, rubbing a hand across his brow, "So you think the wraiths don't actually need to take our magic to survive?"

"Well no, not exactly," I explained. "I think they need some form of energy to survive, but not nearly what we thought they did. I suspect it's more like bees to a hive. Collecting pollen from flowers, sometimes from miles away, then bringing it back. Bees still need to eat, but they always offer more to the hive than what they need to survive."

"So they're containers," Bron suggested, pulling a wickedly curved blade out of nowhere, playing it between his fingers. "Vessels to hold our energy until they can bring it back."

"Vessels that want to claw our faces off and eat our insides," Zanaya chirped sarcastically.

"Exactly. I assume that's why they always collect their dead if they can," I said in speculation, shrugging my shoulders. "I mean, out of how many wraiths we've killed collectively, and this is the first time anyone's seen or heard or talked about this, it seemed suspicious to me. So I asked Moian to get her hands a little dirty."

The Mender laughed dryly, showing off the black smudges on her hands. "And dirty I got, but it was worth it."

She reached into the pocket of her apron, a clinking sound

piquing everyone's interest. Pulling out her bounty, dropping three cylindrical objects in the middle of the table, she leaned back in her seat. Her face twisted into a sneer as they pulsed with a familiar, unpleasant power.

They couldn't have been longer than six inches and not even half the width of my palm. Both ends were capped in a shiny, silver metal, but the main body was a dazzling, crystalline white. If I squinted hard I could just make out streaks of color zipping through the smooth stone.

"I found those inside the three bodies I dissected. Heartsglass. White, obviously, " she snipped, a burning hatred, so unlike the healer, sprouting from her words. "Queen Atallia is right, even dead, I believe these canisters are still holding on to the energy those three wraiths took."

"Your blade must have cracked the one inside the wraith you killed," she tipped her head in my direction. "The black heartsglass could have easily chipped it, allowing some of the energy inside to escape."

"How are they alive with heartsglass inside them? That's what we use to kill them," Lars interjected.

"The sludge," I formulated, pursing my lips as the thought struck me. "Black kills them, but this is white. Which by Descendent standards contains and dampens magic, but wraiths don't really have any magic of their own, do they? Even the ones who used to be Cynths are stuck in their animal form. Who's to say Kasis doesn't force the shift and then do whatever it is he does to make them stay that way, taking away what makes them a Descendent?"

Moian picked up on where I was going, her healer's mind running a mile a minute, "White heartsglass wouldn't affect them in the same way, not like it does us, but if Kasis used magic to turn them into those things, prolonged exposure could cause the crystal to start attacking their bodies instead. Turning their blood and organs into this filth."

She glanced down at her hands, her face turned green. "Basin," I pointed behind me.

"Thank you," she replied in a rush, jumping up from the table to scrub her hands.

We waited for her to finish, no one judging as she rubbed her skin raw. Healers were used to blood and guts, they had to be, but I don't think anyone could stomach knowing a putrid, liquified mixture of both was drying on their skin, crusting under their nails.

Collecting herself, she rejoined the group. Her hands were noticeably red from scrubbing, but no one made a comment.

"So if the wraiths act like bees," Lilyi reasoned, her sharp mind picking up on the real problem at hand, "then where is the hive?"

"Vallenia," Kanan announced, shooting me a knowing look. The pieces finally coming together. "We have to go to Rhaelyth."

And because I was just full of fun surprises tonight, I didn't hold anything back as things started to connect. "Where magic has been steadily disappearing for centuries."

CHAPTER THIRTY-TWO

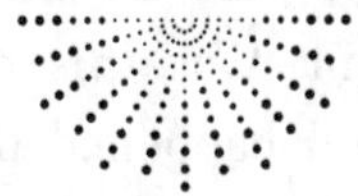

The tent erupted with questions, everyone speaking over each other, trying to understand the possible relation between Rhaelyth's dire situation and the one we now faced.

"Quiet, please!" Cashim shouted over the noise, "This isn't helping anything."

Lady Lilyi, her calm and collected nature undeterred in the face of panic, stepped in to help manage the unrest.

I shared in their worry. It ate away at me more and more as Kasis's attacks ramped up. The reality of our situation was suddenly becoming all too real, nipping at our heels just enough to remind us of our impending demise if we weren't careful.

A barren world, starved of all its beauty.

Magic-less, save for the few precious drops that persevered against all odds. At least until they were found and taken away.

If I was right, and Kasis was somehow behind the depletion of magic in the mortal homeland, then we had a firsthand look at what our future, Allasea's future, could look like.

Cosmos, I hoped I was wrong, that the coincidences were just that. But, gods, why were they starting to look like connected pieces of a much bigger plan?

I scratched the arm of my chair and watched the thin, curled shavings float to the ground like fallen leaves. It made me wonder how easy it would be for us to be wiped away like that, how effortlessly our existence could become nothing more than a passing season in the unstoppable timeline of this world. A single beat in the millennia of the universe.

Perhaps that was what was needed. Maybe Irropia deserved better, a fresh start. The old me was the one who decided to start this whole mess over again. Was this my punishment for being unable to face whatever had happened to me all those years ago? Had I been a coward? Too damaged to fight for my people, my world, when they needed me most? Am I still broken? Did the same weak heart still beat in my chest, but only now covered in different scars?

No, a voice—my voice—snarled inside my head. *Not weak. Not broken. Scarred and cracked, but not broken. Never broken.*

I jumped, shaken from my thoughts as Kanan placed his hand over mine, stilling my hand. It shook beneath his, a sharp, fiery pain spearing through my finger. It wasn't until he lifted it from the armrest that I realized my nail had snapped from the pressure. A single drop of blood, bright red and glistening in the firelight, rolled off the pad of my finger, dropping to the ground next to the pile of shavings.

Blinking rapidly, I swallowed hard, wetting my dry throat as I glanced down at the chair. A divot, stained with my blood, now marked the left arm.

He took hold of my hand, pulling it into his lap. A shadow reached up from beneath our chairs, a square of gauze held out to Kanan.

Where the hell did it find that?

Accepting the offering, Kanan gently wiped the blood away, careful not to swipe over the exposed nail bed, as we waited for the table to quiet. He was engrossed in his task, mindful of every little tremor in my hand as the minuscule wound began to heal.

There was a tug on the end of my hair. I had to smother a laugh as I glanced down. Another dark coil had snuck up into my lap without me noticing, and now played with the piece of leather that tied off my braid.

I peeked over at Kanan out of the corner of my eye. He had frozen, watching the naughty shadow with a reproachful glare. It stilled too, as if realizing it had been caught, but then quickly decided it didn't care and went back to twining through the bottom of my hair.

I bit my lip to stop the giggle that wanted to escape. My shoulders shook from the effort of it.

Kanan stroked his thumb over the back of my hand, and then I felt him stalk down the mental bond, stroking the edges of my mind, asking for entry.

As Cashim finally reeled everyone in, I opened the doorway that only Kanan had access to.

"They don't like you hurting yourself," he said before I could ask.

A smile tried to spring forth. Looking down at my lap, the shadow reluctantly slipped back under the table as I replied, *"Is that right?"*

Silence.

Glancing over I watched a pink tinge sweep over the sharp edges of his cheekbones. *"Are you blushing?"* I gasped in surprise.

"Of course not," he snapped, shifting in his seat, angling away slightly although he didn't release my hand.

"Oh my gods, you are. This is a momentous occasion," I teased, a ripe satisfaction warming my chest at the thought of making the big, scary dragon blush. *"I feel like I need to have this documented in our history books."*

I could feel his glare in my mind as he threatened, *"If you do I will set the whole damn archive on fire."*

"You wouldn't dare, that's just criminal to burn books," I lamented in faux shock. *"The historians would have your hide. They're probably after your head already after all the mind tricks you've played."*

"The historians will have to learn to move on, they don't need to know everything. Sometimes history is better off left in the past."

"And what about me?" I asked after a pause. *"Will I ever get to know everything?"*

He stiffened beside me, and I felt his mind retreat from mine. My jaw clenched, my nails digging into my palm as I took the hand he held back. He flexed his own before curling it into a fist on his thigh, and I couldn't tell if he was trying to shake away the feeling or if he was trying to hold on to what was no longer there.

He was saved from answering to my anger by Bron questioning why we thought Vallenia was the origin of our problems.

And so we began from the beginning. Starting with finding a kinsmen posing as Ellenia, the two guards we killed, finding the catacombs beneath the dais, the cells of wraiths. Everything.

I left out the part about being led out by the spirits of the desecrated crypts, half sure I had imagined them, but I stressed the importance of restoring the sacred grounds. I made the souls a promise—whether they lingered in this realm or not, their bodies deserved to have their resting place rebuilt.

"So this *factory*," Elaric questioned suspiciously, "you think this is where the wraiths are coming from?"

"All we know is that the kinsmen in charge of the wraiths beneath Rhaera mentioned a horde that had just left, and how they were 'Vallenia's problem now,'" I repeated, rubbing a finger over my brow. "Which could mean anything, but given what we saw and heard, it seems likely that they're coming from there."

Zanaya leaned against the table, arms crossed, "How would they be able to move that far without anyone noticing?"

"That's where it gets weird," I answered, crossing my leg over the other. Might as well get comfortable, it was going to be a long night.

"Oh, *this* is when it gets weird," she raised her eyebrow at me. "Funny, I thought we were already there."

"This is not the time for jokes girl," Lars barked from across the table.

"Careful how you speak to my niece, Braxix." Cashim spoke calmly even as his ice-blue eyes flared in anger. Too absorbed with the brewing aggression, no one seemed to notice the water inside the glass pitcher freeze in response to that cool response.

It was often easy to forget that Cashim stood as the Aether of House Zuberi for a reason. His calm and wise demeanor had a way of putting people at ease. Full of advice and diplomatic solutions, a warm, inviting smile, and a compassion that was rooted deep in his soul. I often forgot that he too wore blades, his gold-handled cutlass, the red gem in the hilt gleaming, was always strapped to his side.

But as a hairline crack marred the pristine glass carafe—the water turned ice now so cold it had fractured the vessel—I saw not a sage healer or discerning councilman when I looked at him, but a warrior. A blizzard of tremendous power in those extraordinary eyes that marked him and Zanaya as family.

"Don't worry Uncle," Zanaya interjected, carefully disarming the situation with her words, "I'm sure Lord Braxix doesn't wish to continue making an ass of himself."

"You little—" Lars ground out between clenched, his face quickly turning a bright red. Embarrassed or enraged, I wasn't sure, but it looked like his head was about to explode. Which was a fun thought.

"Little what?" she taunted, a no-nonsense tone that had even my spine straightening. Lars looked around the table, no one coming to his aid nor speaking up. Weighing his options, witnessing the same tornado of power residing in Zanaya as it did Cashim, he wisely remained quiet.

She looked him up and down in disdain, turning away dismissively. Grabbing my attention, the picture of innocence, all batting lashes and pleasant smile, she broke the tension, "As you were saying, Your Majesty."

Bron grinned from beside Kanan. One filled with promises and something else entirely that made me worry my friend didn't know what she had gotten herself into.

I couldn't help the smirk that spread at her antics as I continued on with the conversation. "The kinsmen mentioned the rifts, called them fissures. The way they spoke about them, they were obviously accustomed to using them."

"What do we even know about these *fissures?*" Oakina spoke up, her keen gray eyes as dark and tumultuous as a thunderstorm, but underneath the fury of that storm lay a mind of steel. One that made me glad she was on our side.

"Not much," Kanan spoke shortly from my side, "but if Kasis is able to use them to transport his creatures across Allasea, let alone across the Blackwood and into Rhaelyth, then it's a priority we figure them out. Last thing we need is his army stepping through one directly within our city gates."

It was Moian, surprisingly, who asked the question, "How do we fight, and win, a war when we don't even know where our enemies are?"

A long silence settled over the meeting as everyone mulled over our ever growing list of problems. The main one being a lack of information. Every time something new came to light, it was followed by even more questions we had no way of answering.

Kasis had years on us. Centuries of planning and scheming, coming up with every contingency to thwart us in mounting an attack. Hell, he had Kanan and I running around chasing leads. It was exactly what he wanted. A confused and unorganized people made much easier prey.

"We can't keep leaving," I spoke directly to Kanan, resting my head on my fist. "Sooner or later he'll take notice and strike when we're away. Our being here is everyone's best defense."

He breathed heavily through his nose, shadows rising behind his chair. "I know, but we might not have much of a choice. Vallenia is our only lead."

"We need to know more," I countered. "More about Kasis, his plans, these fissures. We're flying blind and it's getting us nowhere."

He scrubbed his face, running his hands through his ebony hair, threads of shadow lifting from the strands as he did so.

"You could always ask *her*," Bron supplied vaguely. He watched Kanan like a hawk, his attention utterly fixed on his friend.

Kanan went still. Deathly still.

Bron held his hands up in surrender as Kanan shifted that searing gaze, alight with murderous intent, in his direction. "You know I'm right, Kanan. She's our best option."

"Who is?" I glanced between the two men, a conversation happening without words.

Bron opened his mouth to answer, but Kanan cut him off with a growled, "No."

"Kanan," the silver Cynth implored, "what other choice do we have?"

The room darkened, the shadows that had flooded the floor beneath the table rose from amidst the chairs, suffocating the room with an immense power. It was like sparks of lightning hitting water, whipping arches of violent energy, the air buzzing with pressure.

"Any choice but that," he snarled. The sound was as inhuman as the beast that he truly was, a grating, rumbling sound that had the hairs on the backs of my arms standing straight. "Anyone but her."

"Will someone please tell me who we're talking about?" I demanded. If there was a person who could help us against Kasis, I didn't see why they wouldn't immediately share it.

Bron shifted in his seat warily, the draconian glare on him downright deadly, as he turned to me and said, "The Orama."

Kanan's growl turned into a thunderous roar that had all of us covering our ears for fear we'd go deaf. Shadows tore from the wall, snapping at the air uncontrollably. The flames in the lamp and torches died down to embers, as if unable to withstand the overwhelming darkness ready to consume them. Thrown into near pitch black, Kanan's authority shined.

Gripping onto his chair's armrests, shining onyx claws ripped into the wood with an ease that was equal parts frightening and impressive. He had always been massive, it was a hard thing to forget even sitting, but right then, as pain-tinged anger poured off of him in waves that threatened to choke me, it was like he had grown in size.

I must have been imagining it, but even then the cloak of blood and war and death that surrounded him pushed against everyone one of my senses, and I wasn't the only one feeling it.

The others, every single one, had shifted as far away from the God of Death as they could without drawing attention to themselves. No one wanted to be a dragon's prey, so they had all rooted themselves to their seats. Silent. Unmoving. Unable to take their eyes from the predator in their midst, they waited with bated breath to see what he would do.

"Enough," Kanan breathed in warning and the air in front of him rippled with heat.

Bron's jaw clenched hard, a muscle twitching along his cheek. Eyeing Kanan, he knocked his chin up, steadying himself as if preparing for a blow. "As your oldest friend, I say this because I know if you were rational about this topic, you would see the wisdom in what I have to say. I know you have your issues with her, valid ones indeed, but not even you can deny that she could help us."

"For a price," Kanan sneered, hatred burning deep in his veins. "It's always for a fucking price."

Bron, who must have had brass balls, growled in frustration before hurling back, "Maybe the godsdamn price is worth it. Let go of your anger for a fucking minute, Kanan, and think. You're too smart to throw away a good plan because you have problems with her."

"That witch has cost me much more than simple problems and you know it. Asking her a question is never what it seems. She's cryptic with her reward and exacting in her payment." Kanan scoffed in derision. "We could ask her a hundred questions and get nowhere, or we could ask one and have everything we need, that's the problem with her. You never know what you will get, or if it is worth the expense she's due. That she'll take."

"If this Orama can give us any information that we need, don't you think the risk is worth it?" I interrupted, and his attention turned to me.

Eyes as bright as the burning center of a hot coal, swirling rivulets of blood streaking through that fire. They were beautiful as they were terrifying and I couldn't help but wish there was more time to memorize their brutal ferocity.

I gave him my full attention, knowing he was the one who needed convincing. "I don't know what issues you may have with this woman, but we are in jeopardy here, our people are at risk every day from an attack. If Kasis can use the fissures to get anywhere in the world, we could fall under siege at any moment. Day or night.

Behind city walls or out on the open plains. He has an advantage, as well as time to prepare. There are no other options left for us to explore."

He said nothing, his roiling anger thick in the air, but he also didn't cut me off so I took it as a sign to continue. "What would you have us do? Fly around the world looking for answers? We could," I surmised, shrugging my shoulders, "but that would leave Eskira and the other cities open to attack as well as ourselves. And if Kasis has found a way to siphon *our* energy fully…then it's game over, he's won. He'll be able to supercharge his beasts and whatever other hellish things he's drummed up. The world will end, the universe will crash down around us, and he gets what he wants. Whatever the hell that is. The only reason he didn't do it two thousand years ago when he had me the first time is because he didn't have everything in place like he does now," I explain, the foggy memories that I had once considered nightmares coming to mind.

Kanan watched me, but I could see that cool, calculative mind at work, and I knew a hundred million things were going through it. "You know all of this. Have probably been running it through your head for days. So I don't need to explain to you the situation we are in, nor that we have run out of viable options."

He looked down into his lap, every inch of him rigid and unyielding as stone. A statue of a king hardened by the thousands of years he's lived, the memories that haunt his every waking moment.

With a shake of his head, he spoke, his voice sounding more human, which was a positive in my book, "You don't know what that senile old witch is like, love. What she'll demand from us if we ask her our questions."

Cashim cleared his throat, sensing the danger had passed, his lyrical cadence at odds with tension in the room. "He does have a point, My Lady. When you both disappeared after the end of the war, I went to her in hopes she could tell us when you and the king would come to be again. Of course only a few of us knew there would be a reincarnation, but not even the king could tell us when to expect it."

"When was this?" Lilyi asked in shock, something like anger

flashing in those unfathomable black eyes. “You vaguely mentioned asking her a question but never gave us an answer.”

Cashim glanced over at the petite, beautiful woman, an apology in his eyes as her musical voice turned frosty. “I’m sorry, my friend, but I was under orders not to share what I knew, and the Orama’s foretelling would have only caused premature alarm.”

“I see,” she sniffed haughtily.

He sighed as Lady Jai turned from him, warm skin seemingly darker under the flickering light as it pulled tightly over the sharp bones of her face. Her endless black eyes, reflective like a mirror, darkened impossibly further, hardening in a way that was shocking to see from the aloof councilwoman.

“And what did she say?” I asked cautiously, glancing from Cashim to Lady Jai as some connection strained amongst them.

With one last guilt-ridden look at the upset Lilyi, he wiped his hand over his mouth, body tensing as he responded, she said ‘The pillars of Life and Death will rise on a tide of blood and sorrow, when power rots from within and the darkness between stars triggers the calamity. The beginning of the end to end all beginnings.’”

A silence fell over the tent, no one daring to break it as the seer’s words sunk in. The beginning of the end to end all beginnings.

What the fuck.

“How is it that this is the first time we’re hearing about it?” Kanan accused, shaken from his anger.

Cashim dipped his head. “I had all but forgotten until recently, the only reason I’m bringing it up now is when parts of it started coming to pass, I always assumed the calamity meant inevitable war with whoever was creating and controlling the wraiths. I never expected it to be Kasis. A war with Chaos, a repeat of history, when we all thought he was dead.”

“What was her price for that knowledge?” Kanan questioned snidely, his dislike for the seer a stinging venom with every word spoken of her.

“Nearly two thousand years and I still don’t have the answer,” he smiled grimly "Just that there would come a day where she would ask a favor from me and I wouldn't say no."

He seemed understandably nervous about the idea. If a clairvoyant witch who is known for demanding payment for her services, instead only warns me of a favor she may one day ask, I would dread it every morning I woke up, quietly exhaling in relief as I go to sleep that same night.

Laughing dryly, Kanan raked his hand through his hair. "This is my point. You've had this favor held over your head for so long, been tormented by it, chances are she hasn't taken her debt just to fuck with you."

Cashim didn't seem so convinced, in fact, he looked anything but as a haunted expression flashed across his face. He was a smart man to fear such a favor. Whatever the Orama would take as payment for a two-thousand-year-old debt couldn't be good.

"Capricious as she may be," Oakina said quietly, a far away look in her eyes, "she follows her own kind of code. When my daughter was born, she was incredibly ill. A very rare occurrence for our kind, but it has happened before and so I brought her to the healers in Ophineas. I figured they would be able to fix whatever it was that thought to take her from me. When they couldn't—" She swallowed hard, and we all watched in silence as the honed blade that was Oakina Vyn fell speechless.

A single tear swept down her face, the smallest showing of vulnerability. She wiped it away immediately, straightening in her seat. The unshakeable mask of impartiality, strength, and ferocity was firmly shoved back into place as she proceeded. "I went to the Orama, asked her what I could do to save Alda, and she gave me exactly what I needed. Asked only for a single drop of blood in return. So yes, be wary of the seer, but given the circumstances, she might just show leniency. Irropia is her home too, I doubt she would wish to lose it."

"Well, I will have to disagree with you Oakina," Lady Jai chipped in, crossing her legs together and placing her interlocked fingers over them. "I believe the king is right. She is too unpredictable to waste our time on."

Cashim shot his closest friend and ally an astonished look. He stayed quiet, but kept sending her confused glances, as if he didn't quite understand something. Poor man was struggling with both the women in his life.

Debate took over the table, everyone having a differing opinion on the matter at hand. That wasn't the battle I was looking to win though.

"You know I'm right," I sent down the link that connected my mind to Kanan's. The bridge pulsed with an energy I couldn't see but knew was there all the same. The same energy connected me to the man himself, regardless of a pair bond or not. One and the same. That's what we were. I needed him on my side.

"Doesn't mean I have to like it." His voice was thick with so many emotions it was hard to catch them all.

"No, it doesn't," I agreed. Leaning my head back against the chair, I twisted to look at him, our gazes locked together. *"But it does mean that we have to try. I don't plan on letting Kasis win without a fight. Do you?"*

He looked at me for a long time, before closing his eyes, and as he leaned back in his chair, letting out a big sigh of defeat, I knew I had him.

"Brat."

I smiled in victory, a silent, drained chuckle shaking my ribs at his lush grumble. The rest of the group were still arguing amongst themselves, Cashim playing mediator, as always. Arguing seemed to be one of their biggest talents, Oakina and Lars trading snipes that had quickly moved away from the original topic. I was almost tempted to leave them be, see how long they could go without noticing, but as Kanan's shadows finally lifted and the light from the small fires grew, everyone's attention turned to us.

"The queen and I will visit the Orama," he began, reluctance in his every word. "After we arrive in Eskira, we'll ensure the warped and the wounded have been safely transported to the infirmary, the remainder of the army checked on to ensure no illness has spread. Once I have been assured of the border's security, and our people's safety, we will leave—no sooner than that."

No one objected to his demands, none of which were unreasonable save for the fact that I wouldn't put it past him to use Eskira's safety as a reason not to go, but that was a battle for tomorrow.

Everyone was exhausted, Moian had all but fallen asleep in her chair, her eyelids closing of their own volition. There were decisions to be made, plans to hatch, and an unavoidable war to prepare for, but my mind was falling prey to the exhaustion that whispered in everyone's ear. We could worry about calamities and war tomorrow.

For now I just hoped for a night of restful sleep. I couldn't remember the last time I had laid my head down. Had it been two nights ago, three? The magic thrumming through my veins was the only reason I was still standing, and although the risk of nightmarish memories stalking my dreams was high, I desired the sweet moments of oblivion sleep could bring me.

So long as the horrors stayed in my head, I could accept the inevitable screams that would claw free from my throat, and cherish the few precious hours where the world fell away and only the realm of dreams existed.

CHAPTER THIRTY-THREE

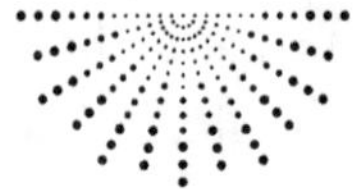

Mornings started early in Elona, the entire town following the rhythm of the waters. No carefully placed dials or marking the sun-casted shadows, time was defined by the rising and falling tides of the Divinian Sea.

Seasons were evident from the ever-changing water levels. The shift from the warm and plentiful months, where fish were caught by the netfuls and the Falla flowed freely from the spring rains, into the cold, scarcer ones was celebrated with the rest of Irropia during the Rising and Setting Eclipses.

The shifting of the moons marked a time of repair, rest, and gathering of family. Where hearths were lit and children began to learn the trades of their mothers and fathers.

As it was still weeks away from the beloved celebration, the day was in full swing even though the sky had barely begun to lighten. No one minded the darkness, tall lamp posts containing Aetherian fire lit up the cobblestone streets every few feet. The differently colored flames illuminated the entire town in a prism of color.

The work ethic of the seamen and women of Elona put the entirety of Allasea to shame. Everyone had a purpose; even the children, who scurried along behind their mothers, helping carry nets and spears aboard the barges. An entire swath of older kids, who couldn't have been more than fifteen, sat along the river as they sewed tears in an enormous sail that covered the bank.

Supplies were loaded onto the giant ships in the harbor, sailors preparing for departure. Some would only be gone for the day while others may venture out into the vast, mostly undiscovered Western Reaches.

Wares and goods were separated onto the more compact riverboats, their destination set for the markets of Eskira. Many would have been wary of sending their work on such a dangerous journey, when weeks of stock could be lost with one blow to the wooden siding of the ships, but the people of Elona had magic on their side.

Most of those we passed were attuned to the sea and river in a way I would never understand. The Aetherians with their water-marbled skin and blue toned hair, and the Cynthonians whose sharp teeth and gills gave away their aquatic proclivities. Not all of the working Descendents had such natures, but the few I saw who differed from the majority had no problem working around the disadvantage they might have had.

The efficiency with which the day's goods were sorted and the boats filled with soldiers waiting to return home was astounding. Captains commanded their ships and crews with the authority of war generals, quickly grouping our shuffled ranks onto the floating vessels headed upstream.

I was impressed, and it must have clearly shown as Zanaya snorted in laughter beside me. Smirking, I knocked my shoulder against hers in jest as we walked down the water-logged planks that led to the riverboats. Rhythmic waves rocked the dock from side to side, the iridescent water from the Falla splashing through the slats to wet our boots.

A breeze tugged at my hair, inviting it to dance, as it carried the signature salty scent of the ocean throughout the seaside village. Even across the other side of town it was recognizable, joined by the constant whooshing swell of ocean waves that combined with the mellow lapping of the river against the bank.

"Why does this town have to be so fucking wet?" I chuckled at Saanvi's familiar surly cadence as we approached the last river boat moored at the end of the dock.

"I could make a really inappropriate joke right now, but I'm not going to," teased Nala, the redhead skipping over the low-lying gangway onto the ship's main deck. "I've found in having a near-death experience, that I've,"—she paused for dramatic effect—"matured. Wisened. All that fancy shi—ooh pretty fish."

Saanvi snickered as she crossed over into the boat, "Oh yeah, you've matured all right."

I looked up as Zander popped his head over the railing of the small crow's nest like some deranged bird. "Don't listen to her, Nals, you're absolutely perfect."

"Damn right I am," came the shouted response, sounding far off in the other direction. A loud bang followed shortly by a cursed remark had several sailors rushing towards the back of the boat.

Zanaya's head dropped as she threw up her hands and, in a mix of incredulity and defeat, asked, "How the hell did he even get up there?"

Orion appeared over our shoulders, spookily quiet for a man his size. "Just think how different your life would be without us, Commander," he joked, patting her shoulder as he passed to reach the ship.

"I wouldn't be prematurely graying, for one," she shouted at his retreating back before mumbling to herself, "Which shouldn't be possible, given I'm a godsdamn immortal."

Glancing at me, my lips pressed together to hold in the cackling laughter, she scowled as a growl built in the back of her throat. "Oh, shut up, Atallia."

Heads whipped around, wide-eyed and gaping in our direction. The crew members had gathered near their boats to discuss the day's events, but at the familiarly-spoken chide the conversations slowly died as their attention turned towards us.

Raising an impetuous black brow, her ice-blue eyes scathing as they skated over the sailors, she waited until they turned their judgment from her. "Mind your own damn business," she bit out with a dismissive wave, swiveling around to board the ship, her tight, sleek curls swaying behind her.

I walked behind her, crossing over the short gap that kept the vessel from smashing into the dock, cackling as the disparaging group scattered under her cutting remark.

I stepped down onto the busy deck, several others clambering aboard behind me, and together we shuffled through the crowd until we made it to the side that overlooked the river. Several other docks jutted out over the water, lines of soldiers waiting their turn to step onto a ship that would take them home.

Moian and the healers had already been sent ahead with the wounded, escorted by several guards to ensure their safety should the warped ones turn on them. Several ships had gone with, convoys of our most rested warriors to provide back up.

The riverboat captains had taken one look at the bedraggled, brutalized ranks of the army and began ordering them onto ships. As soon as one was filled, it took off towards the white-capped rapids in the distance, the Crian Mountains rising high above as if to give hope to the weary; Eskira's embrace awaited only a few short hours away.

"My Lady," the confidently spoken words had me swiveling around to find a well-dressed man standing behind us. Standing militantly straight, arms clasped primly behind his back, he held himself with a conviction that spoke of someone perfectly at ease in their environment— aware that they had the knowledge to adapt to any situation. "Rudrik Brassa at your service, captain of the *River's Dream*. My crew and I are honored to have you sailing with us today."

"Thank you, Captain," I answered kindly, even though the discomfort at how everyone treated me rose in response as well. I tried to not let it show for fear I would insult him and his crew, though they would never say as such. Zanaya's mouth twitched out of the corner of my eye, no doubt picking up on the feigned display of poise as I said, "Your ship is beautiful and I find myself eager to experience the trek up river for myself."

He smiled genuinely at the compliment. The captain was a handsome man with sun-kissed blonde hair that was streaked through with startling teal, the ends looking like they had been dipped into the river and came out coated in the shimmering water. Dark tan skin spoke of hours out beneath the Allasean sun, the white heat bearing down on the seaman. Tall and muscled from the hard labor that he must have endured every day to keep the *River's Dream* afloat, I wasn't surprised to see several others around us giving the captain a second look. "We appreciate the compliment, she is the crew's pride and joy."

It wasn't hard to see why. *River's Dream* was a stunning vessel, all dark wood and light blue sails. The shine on the deck, the glinting metal of the anchor as it was hauled up from the riverbed, and the meticulously cared for figurehead—a stunningly detailed sea serpent —that guarded the bow of the ship—it all spoke of love and patience, every inch of the vessel carefully tended to.

"How much longer do you think Captain?" Zanaya asked from where she leaned against the side railing.

Taking a look around at the gathered group of warriors, all finding spots along the deck to wait out the journey, he replied, "I believe we are only waiting on the king. I received word right before that one of the sea boats headed for the Divinian had a mast collapse and the king was near; he stopped to assist."

As if speaking his name had pulled him from the shadows that were as much a part of him as the fire that scorched his veins, he appeared on the gangway. The crowd parted for him with ease as he strode through. He was the biggest predator on the ship and the wide berth they gave him reflected that.

Shadows trailed behind him. Crawling across the deck in search of something, tendrils snaked through the masses, uncaring as people jumped out of their way. As they reached the far side where I had stationed myself, a single wisp of that darkness touched my boot. Curling around my ankle in caress, reminding me more and more of loving pets, they retreated back to Kanan.

Catching the quick flash of red through the throng of people, he dipped his head in acknowledgment, confirming his shadows had indeed found me. He finished making his way to the bow, positioning himself at the front. Unruffled by the stares that followed his every move, he leaned against the railing, resting his weight on his forearms.

"I guess that's my cue, excuse me," Captain Brassa finished with a bow, retreating to his station at the helm. I wasn't sure that I responded, distracted by the picture Kanan painted.

The sun had finally begun to rise over the horizon, the first rays of light glancing off Kanan's loose curls. Darker than the night itself, they were stark, striking, as they absorbed the radiant glow. I could only see half his face, but the morning light caressed his features like a lover; every hollow and dip and carved piece in perfect splendor. The red of his eyes were a living wildfire as he glanced out over the river.

"Oh you have it so bad," Zanaya chided, her all-too-knowing gaze roving over my face as I watched him.

Tearing my gaze off his form, I forced myself to turn around, watching as boats began to take off on swells for the white waters upstream. "I don't know what you're talking about," I scoffed, but even I could hear the tremble in my voice.

"Okay," she played along, situating herself next to me. Her shoulder brushed mine as the boat's crew took their positions at different points along the ship's deck. She said nothing else, allowing the silence to speak for her. An offer from a friend. Holding her tongue, if that's what I wished, but willing to listen if needed.

I blew out a heavy breath. Maybe I needed someone to listen. "He could hurt me again."

"He could," she replied, her tone neutral and without judgment.

"He could lie again; break that small bit of trust that he's built back up." I ran a hand over my mouth, my stomach turning at the thought.

"He could," she repeated.

I was quiet, my mind spinning with thoughts of the unknown, my heart with those of the future. I whispered, so only she could hear the desires, the hopes, of the stupid organ in my chest. "But what if he doesn't? What if we give this a shot and it's glorious?"

Tilting her head at me, she smiled in sympathetic understanding. "I can't say I judge you for holding on to your anger." She looked down sadly, "I still haven't talked to my uncle about any of this. I'm afraid of what I'll say when I do. As mad as I am, I don't want to lose what we have, he's the only family I have left. The last piece of my mother and father."

I reached over to squeeze her hand, waiting patiently for her to finish. Swallowing, eyes glassy as she glanced over at me, she said, "What I can say, though, is that you might regret it if you don't. Immortal or not, given everything that is happening, life is too short to live it full of regrets."

We were silent for a long time, holding on to each other in support. There was a risk in everything and sometimes the reward wasn't worth it; but this…if I didn't make up my mind soon, I might run out of time before there's ever a chance to enjoy that happiness I had only just begun to glimpse.

In a world that was on the verge of ending at any moment, I could wallow in my anger or bask in the glow of love that had survived two millennia apart.

A shout came from Rudrik, a hand in the air forming a sign that must have signaled our take off. As one, the waiting crew, balancing atop the side railings without difficulty, lifted their arms and performed a singular rowing motion.

With the combined strength of the water Aetherians, the Falla, already filled to the brim with magic, rose beneath the ship, lifting the stern and carrying us out of the port on a wave. The blue sails snapped taut as a sharp wind blasted the fabric open, keeping with the momentum of the river. And like that, we were off, and headed for home.

For Eskira.

CHAPTER THIRTY-FOUR

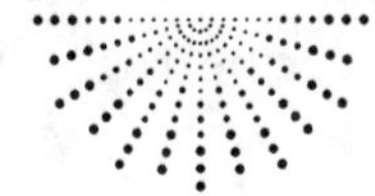

Beautiful as it may have been, the boat ride up the Falla was brutal. Even with the Aetherians helping control the wind and water, the tumultuous, rolling rapids proved difficult to navigate. The cascading drops, where the sparkling water fell from above, were the most difficult; both magic and Captain Brassa's skills at the helm needed to crest the down-rushes.

The river water sprayed over the railings, providing a cool mist as the sun began to warm the valley. Some had moved inward on the deck, moving away from the shower. I didn't mind it even as I occasionally needed to wipe the moisture from my face. After a night of tossing and turning, it was refreshing to shake off the grog.

The haunting, broken cries from inside that bleak cell rang in my ears the whole night. My weak voice, destroyed from the screams, hummed an agonizingly somber lullaby. I had given up on getting any rest hours before dawn had broken. When Saanvi had come to find me, I'd been sitting on the docks overlooking the sea, listening to the waves break along the rocky shore.

A jolt had the ship lurching precariously, some people hitting the deck as it teetered back and forth. Holding on tightly, I set my feet wide to compensate as another rush hit the bow.

A roll went through the boat as the Aetherians raised a wave underneath to lift the vessel over a small waterfall. Bumping into Zanaya as I lost my balance, I shouted over the crashing of the water, "It's getting rough!"

"No shit!" she replied sarcastically just before *River's Dream* pitched one last time, throwing her from the railing.

Before I could even move to grab her, solid pale arms wrapped around her waist as she crashed into Bron. He held her tightly to his chest, gripping the rope ladder nearby as the ship righted itself, the waters finally calming.

As soon as she regained her balance, catching a glimpse of the remarkably pale skin that lay stark against the ebony of her own, she tore free of his grasp. "I had it," she snapped, wiping her face of any emotion. "I didn't need your help."

Bron watched her like he couldn't quite figure out what to do with her. Narrowing his eyes, he ran a hand over the back of his neck before letting out a huffed laugh. Shaking his head at her, he walked off in Kanan's direction.

Rolling my head towards Zanaya, I waited expectantly. She turned that glare at me, growling, "What?"

"Oh, we're playing that game are we?" I teased, "Okay I'll go along with it… What was he doing grabbing you like that when you obviously *weren't* about to go flying across the ship?"

She rolled her eyes at my spectacular performance. "I was fine."

"Okay," I remarked unbelievingly.

"I was."

I looked at her with raised eyebrows, nodding along. "Mhmm, totally fine. You and fine are actually the same thing, I see it now."

"Oh my gods, you're such a bitch," she laughed. Dropping her head into her hands, she groaned.

"Do you want to tell me why you two have been at each other's throats since we got back?" I asked cooly, "Or do you want to keep pretending like everything is fine?"

If looks could kill, I'd have been a pile of ash, but her shoulders dropped in resignation. "We slept together."

I pressed my lips together, swallowing the shriek that rose in my throat. I needed to give her the same nonjudgemental ear she had given me. *Calm down, Atallia.*

"Okay," I say passively. I balanced my hip casually against the balustrade. "And how do you feel about that?"

She shot me an unamused look. "You can tell me how you really feel, I can handle it."

"Oh my fucking Cosmos, Zanaya." I moved closer so only the two of us could hear before asking, "When did this happen?"

"The night you and Kanan left for Rhaera."

"Wha—how?" I asked in shock.

She looked at me from the corner of her eye, raising a brow. "I don't think I need to explain the how to you." Her face fell flat, turning serious as she looked at me, "Do I?"

Smacking her with the back of my hand as she chuckled, I pressed on, "You know what I mean. I didn't realize you two were…you know."

She shrugged, "I didn't really either. I mean he's obviously a handsome man, and we've seen each other in passing before, but it had never really crossed my mind either. It wasn't really until you arrived that I started noticing him more." Flipping around, she crossed her arms and kicked her legs out. "He's always been a very elusive person, and he wasn't around much until Kanan appeared, which makes more sense now, but even when I was young I would hear about him. He acted as a discrete seventh member of the Council, brought in for tie-breaking decisions and such."

"I didn't know that." Even now, Bron was still a big mystery to me, just like a lot of things. He was Kanan's closest friend, whether the two men would admit it or not, and had apparently acted in our interests when we hadn't been around.

"Yeah, it wasn't often, but his vote held the most sway amongst the Council. Other than that, he did his own thing."

"Still kind of does." The water, now serene and calm, rippled around the boat. As clear as glass I could see all the way to the bottom, large chunks of brilliant crystal jutting up from the riverbed. It was a wonder they didn't tear through the ship. Then again, the ride wasn't over just yet, so maybe I shouldn't be giving it any ideas.

Looking over to where Bron and Kanan braced themselves near the bow, she cracked a smile. "You can say that again."

"So you slept with him, and then what?" I asked, tracking a silver-scaled fish as it darted around us, surfing the wake.

She scrubbed at her face, pinching the bridge of her nose. "I screwed up. He was a perfect gentleman…well, afterwards," she said with a suggestive grin before it slowly slipped away, "But then I started getting scared. I haven't felt like that with anyone before. I've had my fair share of lovers, but I've always kept them at a distance for a reason."

I didn't need her to explain why. "Your parents."

A grim air hung around her as she looked down at the deck, scuffing her boot against the polished wood. "I lost everything because of love. The toxic, poisonous kind that drove my mother's ex-lover to murder, and the all encompassing, soul-tearing kind that ensured my father would never survive her death."

"Oh Zanaya," I murmured. Turning around, my back to the river, I pressed my side into hers hoping she could take some comfort in not being alone.

"He read my mind. Not on purpose of course, I know he sometimes picks up on things whether he likes it or not, but when he tried to talk to me about it…" She drifted off, leaving me to fill in the blanks.

"And I'm guessing it spiraled from there?"

Pursing her lips, she nodded. Her eyes were glazed over, deep in thought. "Yeah that about sums it up."

"We have shitty love lives," I joked after a long pause. "That or we're both fucked up enough to be our own worst enemies."

Laying her head on my shoulder, curls tickling my neck, she let out a big breath. "Both," she muttered.

We sat that way for a while, watching as the towering pines and evergreens that lined the bank went by. Birds, with feathers more stunning than jewels, dove in and out of the water, fish hanging from their beaks, heading into the forest for their nests.

Butterflies fluttered near the banks. Their iridescent wings shimmered, turning them into shooting stars in the dawn light. Bees had just begun to wake from their hives, buzzing and humming the day's song as they collected the newly bloomed pollen.

A stag like no other lifted its pearlescent rack, watching us float by. Its coat was a perfect verdant green, blending into a lighter shade around its elegant face. Gold vines and blush pink flowers grew from the base of those sharp horns, curling up and around the shafts. A small, lavender bird flew down from a branch to perch itself on the top point, the melodic chirping notes of its call carrying across the water.

The sky had turned a deep magenta, streaks of orange and yellow and blue stretched throughout as the sun carried itself higher into the sky. The river of color that mimicked the one we were on had turned a dazzling red, traces of other shocking hues twining together.

Everything was perfect and beautiful and so otherworldly any artist would weep at seeing its majesty. In the few months since being chased over the border, Eskira—the whole of Allasea, really—had wriggled its way into my heart. Digging its roots deep, refusing to leave and only growing stronger by the day.

It was my home. Mine to love. To protect. I might have been doing a shit job of it, but with a certainty that had grown with every sunrise and sunset, not a single one ever the same as the last, I knew I would give my life for it. Lay it down happily for everything beneath its rainbow skies.

"Oh no," Zanaya groaned against my shoulder, "make her go away."

"Hey I heard that," Nala complained as she strode up to us. Her wildfire hair framed her face, a happy wide smile cracking open at Zanaya's torment. Embers drifted from the burnished strands to land on the deck, leaving behind pinpricks of black soot. A sailor tailing behind her, probably to ensure she didn't blow something up, glared at the dark marks that now marred the flawless wood.

"Nala?" I asked, my curiosity peaked.

She jumped to a stop in front of us, her curls bouncing as even more specks fell. "Yes?" she responded cheerfully.

"Why do you have a spear?"

The solid metal weapon stood a foot taller than her. Its black reflective head gleamed, the edges sharp enough to slice air.

"Oh this?" She grinned up at it, spinning the rod in her hand, "I found it lying around."

Zanaya peered around her, raising an eyebrow in question at her impromptu guard. The man gave her an aggrieved look. "She found one of our weapons chests." He shifted his glare to the back of Nala's head. "Our locked weapons chest."

Zanaya pressed her fingers into her eyes, throwing a hand up. "Why?" she questioned, thick brows puckered in bewilderment.

Nala shrugged, smiling proudly, "They should have done a better job of locking these things up if they didn't want me finding them."

Zanaya scowled at her, arms flopping against her side in resignation. "Give it back. Now!"

"Why are you always ruining my fun?" The redhead pouted, but she passed the spear over. A frown grew on her face as the crewman snatched it away, muttering about crazy women as he walked off with the weapon. Swinging around on one heel, nearly falling on her ass in the process, she frowned, "Why was he so mad?"

I chuckled as Zanaya pounded a fist into her forehead over and over again. "Come here crazy," I said in response, pulling her over to the side so she wouldn't get trampled by the group of men running past with a lengthy net thrown over their shoulders.

"How are you doing?" I nodded down at her stomach, covered by a fitted blue tunic and a black leather harness that carried twin long blades. Her bandages had already come off, but I knew the sting of the wounds, a reminder of how close to death she came, would linger for far longer.

Twisting a scarlet strand around her finger she shrugged off the question. "Been better, but I'm finally feeling like myself again."

"And Zander?" I prodded. "How are you two?"

A smile brighter than the sun pulled at her lips, the corners of her eyes creasing as she glowed with happiness. "We're great. I mean I heard about what bonding with your pair could be like, but I never would have expected it to be like this," she beamed, lifting her shoulders, "I'm never alone, not that he hasn't been annoying me for years, growing on my ass like mold."

Zanaya's head snapped back, forehead creasing as she shook her head at the creative imagery. I swallowed my laughter, not the least bit surprised. Nala's mind worked in fascinating ways and we just had to accept that. She'd probably blow us up if we didn't, so it was in everyone's best interest to go along with the madness.

"Did you always know each other?" The two redheaded troublemakers were always so in sync, I had always assumed they'd been friends forever.

"Sort of," she answered. Hopping up onto the railing, she swung her leg over until she straddled it. She didn't seem to care that the boat rocked every few seconds, sometimes dipping closer to the water than I was comfortable with. She rode with the motion though, making some kind of game out of it.

"We grew up in the same village up north, near the Cliffs of Barrae. My family life growing up wasn't the greatest. It was shit if I'm being honest." She bit her lip, worrying it with her teeth. When she glanced away, scratching the side of her neck I saw a horizontal scar, no bigger than the length of my pinkie. It was faded, barely light enough to see anymore, but I knew from what Kanan shared of his own experience, it took a lot to scar a Descendent's skin. Even when they were children.

"My parents were perfectionists. They needed to have everything under their control at all times. Perfect house. Perfect marriage. Jobs, friends, children, all of it. When they had a daughter who liked fire and blowing stuff up, well I'm sure you can guess how that went. When I would get into trouble, that would shame them, " she said miserably. "So I was a disappointment in their eyes, but that wasn't the worst of it."

The air chilled strangely, enough for me to look over at Zanaya.

Eyes hard, she ground her teeth as Nala recounted her childhood. Ice crawled from her fingertips, forming a pair of wicked claws.

Oh I'm not gonna like this.

Nala weathered whatever demons hunted her, wetting her lips as she continued, "My brother was the golden child. My parents' favorite, and he knew it. Relished in it. He was without fault. Except of course that he was a sadist."

My heart dropped into the pit of my stomach; the blood in my veins freezing in a way that had nothing to do with Zanaya's chilling magic.

"He couldn't be open in his…impulses in public, but who would notice him taking them out on his little sister? The girl everyone liked to forget existed."

I clenched my jaw tight, a painful throbbing taking up near my temple. This story was sounding a little too familiar.

Her yellow eyes were dull, the jovial air that hung around her going flat. It was so unlike the pyro that I prayed wherever these people were it was far enough away that my wrath wouldn't find them.

"He liked to hit me, beat me up and humiliate me however he could. He had certain desires that no brother should look at his sister to fulfill," she paused, which I was thankful for because I was going to be sick if she continued.

Shaking off whatever memory gripped her, she tightened her legs against the bannister as the ship swayed. "Anyway, long story short, he eventually convinced our parents I wasn't worth their trouble anymore. They kicked me out without a second thought. No food, no clothes, nothing. I was nothing to them," she whispered to herself, "just the trash they needed to be rid of."

She sighed as if speaking it all out loud had set the demons free, whisking them away on the wind carrying us home. "The one thing that kept me there through all of it was the boy next door." Genuine happiness chased off the remaining taint of the horrible memories. "Zander has been my closest friend for as long as I can remember. He didn't know about what was going on at home, not all of it, and when he found out he lost his damn mind. He saw my parents throw me out and tried to convince his family to take me in. They were an influential part of the village so he figured they could protect me from the scorn I garnered, but while his parents were nothing like mine, they cared about appearances. Taking me in wasn't an option for them."

"What did he do?" There was zero doubt in my mind that Zander wouldn't have stood for that. As unserious as he took life, the people he considered his were everything to him.

She grinned, a hint of the crazy that drove everyone wild, but that we loved all the same because it was a part of her, tipping the corners. "When they said no, he left with me. We were sixteen," she said simply as if they hadn't been children, but she just shook her head in amazement. "Do you know what he said to me, he said, 'If they won't take in someone who I consider family, then they don't deserve to be called mine.' We've been inseparable since, and while I always knew he was my other half, as best friends of course, now it's official."

"So how did you end up in Eskira?" I questioned.

I waited with a smile as she stopped to watch one of the birds swoop down into the water. Then her gaze shifted to a dragonfly as it flashed by, a croak of a frog on the bank. One thing after the other, reminding me a lot of Wrynn, until she finally made her way back to me.

"Sorry, uhmm—" she searched her mind, the wheels turning visibly in her eyes. "Oh, Eskira, right. Well when we both made it through our Awakenings, we enlisted with the Eskiran army. We survived by stealing and relying on each other until then, but then we met Zanaya. Saanvi next, then Orion. Now we have you, and we're finally complete."

She said it so off-handedly, I don't think she realized how hard it hit me. To be included in her little family, a mismatched group of outcasts and loners and people searching for where they belonged.

I opened my mouth, but was cut off by a shouted curse and shocked gasps. "Commander!" an angry Captain Brassa shouted from the helm, waving his hand towards the commotion on the deck. Whipping around, it was to see Zander dangling midway down from the crows nest by a rope that had been wrapped around his ankle. He swung back and forth gently in time with the movements of the ship.

As he slowly spun, turning in our direction, he crooked his head as he caught sight of us. He waved at us upside down, his boisterous laughter echoing over the river.

"Great Divine, take me now," Zanaya pleaded. She strode toward him, shouting, "How the hell did you get stuck up there?"

Nala laughed maniacally, jumping up from her spot to help get her pair down. She'd probably mess with him first, but eventually they would get him down...or leave him up there. I wouldn't be surprised if they left him to hang for a bit.

"Love," the darkly intimate voice called out in my mind. My gaze immediately shot to his spot by the figurehead, a large hand resting on the serpent's tendril-like horns.

I made my way toward him, smirking as Zander yelped, Orion's long reach able to push the sly fox until he swung like a pendulum. Several in the crowd chuckled, aware of the fox's propensity for mayhem, and enjoying the revenge.

I closed the distance, slowing when another man strode up to speak with Kanan. The scuffed leathers and scythe he had hanging from his belt loop marked him as one of the soldiers. A guard perhaps.

After a few brisk words the man nodded solemnly, executing a swift bow. I expected him to walk away, but swiveling hard on his heel, he took a running start towards the edge of the boat. Right as he reached it, my heart leaping into my throat, a cloud of gray magic consumed him.

With a scratchy, high-pitched cry, a bird of prey, larger than any normal raptor, soared out of the dissipating magic. Strong wing beats carried him across the water and high into the air, angling for the mountains in the distance.

"Everything okay?" I prodded, keeping my eyes on the airborne until he became a gray speck against the sky, growing smaller by the second.

"Yes, I sent Keegan ahead to call on Synval, he oversees the city scouts and coordinates with those throughout the rest of the country." He lifted a shoulder at my unspoken question, "A thought I had that he might have some insight on."

"Which is?" I pressed, settling myself on a crate that had been shoved underneath the overhang where the front of the ship came to a point.

He crossed his arms over his chest, straining the material of the shirt he wore. "I created the Cynthonians from the animals of Irropia. All of the animals," he said in answer, strong brow creasing in thought, "including those of prey. The mink and small nesting bird. Squirrels, rabbits, grouse, weasels, all of them. Kasis took them as well when he raided the outer settlements, but we haven't seen them, not on the battlefield at least."

"So where are they?" I finished. What he was insinuating made sense and I was stupid for not seeing it earlier. "You think he's using them to spy?"

"It's what I would do," he glowered. The red of his eyes swirled with fire and fury. "The smaller Cynths have hundreds, thousands, of paths throughout the country that no one would ever notice, including within Eskira. They're experts at not being seen; avoiding detection is their job. It's rooted in their survival instincts, and makes them so damn good at it."

"And if Kasis has been able to tap into that part of them, he might be able to gather information on us that way," I finish for him, putting the pieces together.

Lips set in a grim line, a muscle popping in his jaw, he nodded. "Exactly."

It was yet another problem to add to our ever-growing list. Kasis may have well and truly thought of everything, and if he had found a way to spy on us, he might have won the war before it even started.

Kanan let out a self-deprecating chuckle, and whether it was the bond or because I was becoming more and more attuned to him, I knew the knowledge ate away at him. Every line of his body was bunched tight, as if readying for a fight, his face drawn so the hard lines of his cheek bones cut through his skin. I could almost see the weight of responsibility—the weight of the world—that rested on his shoulders. Each and every decision he made was so that burden never had to fall to anyone else.

"It's not your fault," I say plainly, playfully kicking his leg. "You can't know everything. Not even you are that powerful."

He glanced over at me from where he was looking at his crossed legs, eyes blank. He said nothing, peering into my eyes and catching glimpses of my thoughts, the genuineness of my words. I couldn't tell whether he believed me or not, his eyes shuttered of all emotion other than displeasure.

"Why did you call me over here?" I segued. There would be no prying anything else from him, his vulnerabilities protected by impenetrable walls. Even for me they rarely fell, so I wouldn't push. For now anyway.

"What if I said it was because I missed you?" he mused with a hint of a grin.

I narrowed my eyes at him, pushing loose strands of hair behind my ear as a strong wind came through. "You knew where to find me."

A single arrogant brow lifted as he said in reminder, "Yet you're the one who left our tent last night after the meeting."

"You and I both know it was for the best," I answered quietly. A commotion near the back of the boat piqued my interest, but a shadow crawled up from the side of the crate to dance over my skin.

He shook his head in exasperation as the thin shadow hugged my finger before glancing up at me with that hypnotic, unyielding gaze. "Doesn't mean I can't wish differently."

"I would have made terrible bed company anyway," I said in lieu of responding to that sensuously murmured comment.

He slanted his head in concern. "More nightmares?"

Before I could respond I caught sight of Zanaya leaping from the steps leading up to the helm where Captain Brassa had abandoned his post. I straightened, my pulse jumping in concern as she pulled to a hurried stop in front of us.

"Commander?" Kanan asked. He frowned at her unease, the

expression deepening further as more and more of the soldiers on deck raced up the stairs, looking out behind our ship.

Her eyes were blown wide, the black of her pupils taking over. Pointing behind her she said something that had my heart stopping, the thrum of prayers beginning in my head as magic filtered through me.

"An unknown force has gathered on our southern-side. They're coming in fast and gaining on us."

CHAPTER THIRTY-FIVE

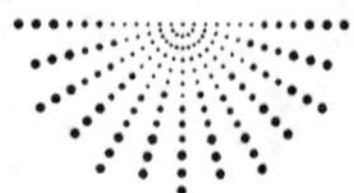

We charged through the mob blocking the way to the stern of the ship, Kanan's enormous breadth knocking the distracted soldiers aside and clearing a path for Zanaya and I to follow behind.

Climbing the stairs to the top deck, we pushed our way to the back railing, Elona a faint speck in the distance. Captain Brassa was already there with several of his crewmen, along with some of Zanaya's squadron who made up a majority of the soldiers on our vessel.

"What in Cosmos's name is that?" one of the sailors asked, his thick brogue reminding me of Bron's.

Out in the distance, a mass of light grew bigger, closer. Explosions of flickering light darted from the trees, sweeping down over the river as they headed directly for us. More and more until the mysterious force was all we could see.

"What fuckery has Kasis created now?" Bron growled from the back of the group.

"Have we received word from Elona?" Kanan's rough growl tore through the panic.

Whatever was headed our way, they were hurtling toward us at considerable speed, the haze of light concealing their forms.

"No correspondence, sir," someone shouted off to the side. Several sailors jumped onto the rope ladders, hanging themselves over the water as they signaled to the other boats. It wasn't necessary though, everyone watching as the thunderous cloud of power grew larger, a relentless whirring reaching our ears from within the storm.

"Defensive formations," Kanan roared, his full voice cracking through the air like a whip. People next to us ducked away from him as the power behind the words smashed through the air, shattering it with a single command. The boom rolled out over the water, disturbing the surface and snapping through the confused stupor afflicting the squadrons, warriors jumping to follow his orders.

"Archers to the front," came another bellow, darkness crawling over the deck to surround him. Sticking a hand into that ebony nothingness, the shadows roiling like snarling wolves, he pulled out his dragon-hilted greatsword, swinging it in a single hand to gain his grip. "Captain, steady the ship."

Rudrik followed through, taking the large wheel in hand even as he tossed looks over his shoulder. Despite the fear in his eyes, he called out his own orders, his men clambering to their positions.

I unsheathed my own daggers, the black blades not far off in color from the darkness that fell over the side of *River's Dream,* surging out over the river until the sparkling water below disappeared beneath the overwhelming eclipse of Kanan's power.

Lengths of that power reached up into the air like arms, claws forming, clenching in anticipation of ripping into its prey.

"Everyone behind me," the dark god shouted over his shoulders, the four fangs of his top teeth flashing in a snarl.

The archers stood in formation two steps behind us, arrows notched and at the ready. The ranks of battle-worn soldiers followed suit, pulling their weapons as the last dregs of energy they could muster went into retaining their defensive positions on the deck below.

"You too, love." His rumble came down the bond, hard and demanding. A general, a warlord, commanding his warriors to fall back as he took the brunt of the damage.

"Fuck that," I snapped back just as hard. I plummeted into my power, pulling up as much as I could from the endless depths that pulsed within my soul. My skin crackled with it and my vision turned golden. An aura of glinting power pooled around me.

"Get back!" he growled in my mind, his dark presence inching further in as if to yell at me better. *"That's an order!"*

I snorted, loud enough for him to hear it and shoot a glare at me, as I lashed back, *"Well that's too fucking bad for you. I'm your queen, not your foot soldier. Try that tone with me again and I'll throw you overboard and let whatever the hell that thing is deal with you, you stupid lizard. Stop being so godsdamn self-sacrificing."*

"Atallia." The sound of my name ground out between his teeth twisted low in my belly, the heated feeling cementing my demented status.

"If you were anyone else this would be grounds for punishment," he cursed, keeping his gaze on the closing force.

"Really? That's a shame," I snarked, letting power fill my hands until the glow broke through my tight grip on the blades, rays of golden light shooting outward. "Sounds like a fun time to me."

He was stopped from answering as the host came over the falls, barely a mile back. "Archers, prepare to fire."

Bron came up to my side, sword in hand. From his pointed look I knew why he was there. I tipped up my chin, shoulders back, and stayed put.

The swarm grew closer, and details started to become visible. From far away it looked like a moving smog, blocking everything out with the intensity of its light, but as it sailed through the air, individual colors started to appear. Reds and pinks, greens and blues. Every hue and shade on display as the orbs moved in toward the ships, the whirring buzz growing louder.

What the hell.

A sense of familiarity crashed over me. It prickled in the back of my mind, annoying, like a misplaced word on the tip of my tongue.

A silver light darted frantically throughout the wave, so different—unique—amongst the coloration that it immediately drew my eye skywards. Soaring high above, the pewter ball of light dove in front of the host. Shock hit me, followed quickly by horror.

"Hold your fire!" I screamed. Woven in with the words was a heavy dose of power, each syllable pounding against my eardrums. I darted forward, dodging the shadows that lunged for me. "Hold your fire, it's Wrynn."

The desperation in my tone must have carried for no arrows were fired as the light crashed into us. Wings filled my view, blocking out the sky. Each set of delicate, pearlescent appendages carried a small body through the air, expertly flying around any obstacle in their path.

"Sprites," came a gasp from behind me as all around us the masters of flight, dragonflies in the flesh, came to a landing. They perched on any available edge, some going as far as touching down on the astonished shoulders of the same warriors who were seconds away from shooting them out of the sky.

A tiny female sprite came to a stop atop Bron's shoulder. Her petal pink glow complemented the Cynth's white and silver coloring, softening the edges of his features with her undeniable femininity. She pushed a strand of short hair, a shade darker than her fluorescent magic, behind her ear and gave Bron, who leaned away in concern as if she were the big bad predator, a blushing smile. As she plopped herself down near the crook of his neck, the war-forged Bron glanced around for help against the tiny, pink woman.

Rope ladders, booms, crows nests, the main figureheads at the front of each ship, even the trees lining the bank, everywhere I looked it glowed, and for a moment the ships resembled shining stars gently riding the celestial waves of some far away galaxy. As the last remaining sprites came in for landing, the flight collectively reeled in their halos.

A shocked silence had fallen over the river, not even a peep from the other ships could be heard. Weapons hung loose in the warriors hands as the sprites watched on with childlike curiosity.

In all my time in Eskira, Wrynn was the only sprite I met, and he rarely ever mentioned them himself. Now, as I spun around, arching my neck to take them all in…there had to be hundreds, maybe even thousands surrounding us.

I searched for those tell-tale wings, shimmering amongst the endless sea of color, but without their halos it was harder to find him within the winged masses. After several passes, a wink of white caught my eye before it disappeared behind one of the spokes along the ship's oversized wheel.

I strode over, giving Captain Brassa a grateful smile as he stepped out of the way. Peeking over the top of the wheel, I spied the top of Wrynn's white hair, his short body crouched behind one of the spindles.

He held his semi-translucent wings, white as fluffy clouds, tight to his back as he peeked around the wheel again. The gossamer membranes sparkled in the sunlight as he shifted, like they had been rolled in crushed diamonds.

"Hi, Wrynn," I said with an expectant grin.

The little sprite jumped in surprise, pink tinging his cheeks as he looked up. He blinked, his dark eyes glancing around uncertainly as he lifted a hand in wave. "Hi, Tali."

"How are you?" I asked casually. "Been busy?"

"Uhmmm," he rocked forward on his tiptoes and wrung his hand, glancing around at the flock of sprites. "Yeah. A little busy."

"Really, busy with what?"

He bit his lip, lifting his tiny muscular shoulders. "This and that."

"Mmmm, I see. Did you let your friends know you were going to be busy?" I tilted my head, lifting a gold brow, "That way they would know you were alright."

His wings drooped behind him in dejection, head dropping to the top of the spoke as he looked up at me with sad eyes. "I thought you'd be mad at me," he murmured miserably. "I don't want you to be mad at me, Tali. The Monarch forbade me from telling you, but I couldn't let them keep hurting you. Those bad people kept hurting you and you still didn't know and I couldn't keep watching. I thought the book would help but it was too late and there was so much blood and it was everywhere and, Tali, you were bleeding so much…"

"Wrynn. Wrynn. Wrynn, breath," I shushed, resting the tips of my fingers on his back, his whole body heaving with effort as he spilled his guts. "You have to breathe."

Hands on his hips, he swallowed hard before sucking in a harsh breath. The poor sprite looked near to tears as his breathing evened out, and my heart hurt seeing how he'd been tearing himself up. "You've have to stop doing that to yourself or you're going to hyperventilate one day and pass out."

With quick fluttering beats, he carried himself up until he reached eye level with me. Looking at me, his heart on his sleeve as he said, "I'm sorry, Tali. So sorry. You're my friend, the bestest one I have, and I kept something from you. You don't hate me right?"

Well if my heart wasn't already melted where he was concerned, that certainly did it. "Of course not," I reassured him, opening my arms for a hug. "I could never hate you Wrynn. I don't know everything that went on, and I'm a little upset that you didn't tell me, but I know despite it all you were there for me when I needed you most. I just wished you had come to me after, I was worried about you."

He fluttered back to hover in front of me, an apology written on his face, a small smile breaking through the regret. "I know. I should have told you where I was going, but I figured if I went and found help, you might not be mad at me anymore."

"Wrynn," I sighed as he somehow wormed his way even further into my heart, "all I care about is that you're safe and unharmed."

His smile widened in glee while his wings beat faster in excitement. "Well," he blushed brighter, "I'm fine, but you should definitely meet the people I brought with me. They have a lot to tell you."

He nodded rapidly, flying around in a circle as he searched through the winged crowd. He must have spotted who he was looking for because he waved someone down from high above. Looking at me over his shoulder, he widened his eyes, whisper yelling, "He's kind of important, okay?"

Pressing my lips to keep the laughter in, I gave him two discreet thumbs up. "Oh," he exclaimed, flying past me quickly.

He stopped in front of Kanan, whose shadows had pulled back

from the river and toiled behind him calmly now that the possibility of a threat had passed. Wrynn's eyes widened as Kanan's blazing gaze locked on to him.

"Hi-hi, uhmm, oh hello, are you friendly?" the sprite asked distractedly to one of the shadows as it reached up to touch the tip of his gray shoes. The dark limb backed away after a quick inspection, which left a totally unfazed Wrynn under Kanan's scrutiny. "Oh sorry, would you like to come be with Tali? The Monarch is going to tell her thingies and, uhmm, you might want to hear them too."

Kanan's eyes shifted to mine, amusement shining through the searing power in them. *"You have interesting friends, love,"* he whispered, the shadows in my mind running a velvet hand along the bond.

A shiver ran down my spine as he made his way over. He came to a stop beside me, my breath catching in my throat as his hand caressed my back.

"Behave," I chided him, ignoring how husky my voice sounded. I knew he caught it though, his answering laughter full of sensual arrogance.

Wrynn wrapped around us, coming to a stop atop the middle spoke along the wheel. Sitting, he let his legs dangle as another sprite made their way closer.

Wings of dazzling azure blue, traces of glittering teal and pink throughout, and skin of warm brown, the male sprite was undoubtedly beautiful. His neatly kept hair was the same shade of blue as finely cut sapphires, the ends dipped in pink. Every angle and curve was soft, as if he was forever in a haze, the edges of his form fuzzy, his multicolored magic emanating around him without thought.

"Your Majesties," the ethereal sprite greeted, each word a lilting song. "It is my pleasure to stand before you. My Lady," he bowed his head slightly, "it is doubly the honor to once again be in your presence."

"Monarch," Kanan addressed the man familiarly. He dipped his head in an acknowledgement of respect which meant this was someone I should know, or had known at a point in time. It wasn't the first time I wished I could curse my previous self for the loss of memory. I was yet again clueless, and the bitterness that followed couldn't be stopped, leaving a sour taste in my mouth as I searched through the endless dark fog for any sense of remembrance.

Nothing.

There was no denying my disappointment. It was a sly, quiet fiend, watching the chaos unfold while it sat beside the jagged, biting demon that was my crushing sense of failure.

My skin tingled as a cool, silky shadow reached over from where it had curled around Kanan's wrist. Squeezing my hand, it fiddled with my fingers, weaving in and out before wrapping around my own wrist in a band of onyx, its presence comforting in a way I didn't know I needed.

"My apologies, Monarch," I said with respect, giving the excuse for what felt like the millionth time, "but I did not regain my memories with the return of my power, so it seems I will have to make your acquaintance again."

"There are no apologies necessary between us, dear goddess," the man smiled faintly. There was an old, serene air that surrounded him, a wisdom gained from a passing of years, a life lived. His eyes, of stunning azure, held so many memories, had seen so much.

They reminded me of my own in a way. I may not remember, but a part of me, a piece of my soul that could not be touched, had been shaped by those millennia I'd spent in a different life.

So it was an odd mix of shock and crushing realization that barreled into me when he declared, "They call me Xotin, Monarch of the Flight."

CHAPTER THIRTY-SIX

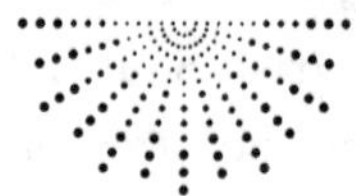

This was the author of the miniature book. The only recount of our actual history that I could find, and the small tome was nondescript enough that the few people I had discreetly asked about it had no clue of its origins. Other than the tiny, scrawling script there had been nothing to identify it. Even the glowing ink hadn't led to anything, several shopkeepers in the lower city marveling at the beautiful artisanship.

"You wrote the book," I asserted, "gave it to Wrynn so he could give it to me."

"Of course I did," he confirmed. The enlightened sprite—Xotin—winged down to the wheel, settling in between the spokes. He stood primly, holding himself with regal aplomb; a direct contrast to Wrynn, who appeared to be holding himself as still as possible in the presence of his Monarch, and unfortunately failing miserably.

Swinging his long legs back and forth from his seat on the helm, Wrynn couldn't help but move some part of his body. Even when he was able to hold still for longer than a second, his dark eyes darted to and fro, glancing from one thing to another. Xotin looked at him in bemusement, a long put-out sigh falling from his lips as Wrynn's wings twitched unwittingly.

Doing my duty as his friend and taking the pressure off him, I asked, "Why would you do that for me?"

"The sprites have served you from the beginning," the Monarch answered deftly. Shifting a panel of his cream robes aside, he revealed a tunic of the same color underneath, cinched by a satin belt. Dangling from the corded rope was a chain pouch, pure white light shining through the links of silver metal.

As he loosened the ties around the pouch, a blaze of light broke free and lit up the sky. The sprites around us shifted in their seats to get a closer look, leaning forward to witness what he pulled from the sac. Those along the shore flew closer in a buzzing of wings. Excitement spread through their ranks, a soft stirring of noise as the light pulsed upwards.

Even the Descendents picked up on the significance of what was happening. They too moved closer, shuffling around to hear what Xotin had to say.

"The sprites were one of the few creatures who existed on this world before the goddess came to be," he recited, a profound sense of time entering his voice, "but before the goddess's light shined upon us…we were dying."

An all encompassing chill worked its way through the crowd. The harsh cold burned in spite of the warm sun beating down upon us.

"A great evil took us one by one. Its identity, that we have simply called The Devourer, was shrouded in an otherworldly gloom, and it was that secrecy that kept us from fighting back as it snuffed out our light. We know not what it is. A disease, a mad creature that has chosen to slumber and that we all fear may one day rise again." Every word had a deep, profound sense of sorrow, tense lines creasing his otherwise refined features as he continued, "All we know is that it has taken eons of rebuilding to restore what was taken from us. With every light it consumed, every soul taken, it further ensured our extinction."

"How did I not know about this?" Kanan asked gruffly, "I would have helped if you had come to me."

"Ahh, but dear king you were enduring your own battle at the time." A grim smile overtook the Monarch's face, one of understanding and shared grief.

Kanan tensed beside me, going as still as a statue, frozen back in time, as he muttered, "My madness."

Xotin dipped his head before answering, "Precisely. I believe our greatest adversary took advantage of your incapacitation and attacked us at will, most likely assuming any death would be explained away by your unfortunate circumstances."

Shadows tightened around Kanan like a suit of armor, the band on my wrist flexing in agitation. I knew from the outside he appeared merely peeved by this information, annoyed and perhaps indignant that someone would dare use him in such a way, but there was no show of emotion beyond the hiss of his shadows.

A clenched jaw, a fisted hand, very little to give away his true feelings because if those were on display...the world might not survive.

Our bond, however, was turmoil, stretched thin between us as emotion after painful emotion hit me in full. I could feel him trying to hide it, erecting walls to separate me from the self-loathing ripping through him. No matter how much he tried though, there was no stopping me from picking up on the heartbreaking realization that there was a part of Kanan that hated himself.

"It's not your fault," I murmured to him, careful not to dismiss the serrating emotions that sliced away like blades. *"No one could have known, not even the Cosmos."*

There was no response save for the silent churning of contempt, a savage seething rebuke to my declaration. Taking hold of his hand, I slotted our fingers together. I grasped onto him tightly when he went to detangle them, refusing to allow him to pull back even as Xotin continued to speak.

"If it had been me?" I prompted without thought, the question a genuine one. *"If I was the one who took form first instead of you; if I lost my mind for reasons outside of my control instead of you, would you have held my actions against me? Would you judge me harshly for those things that still haunt me? Put me in your place for a second and consider whether you would have rejected my plea for help, denied me the mercy of salvation."*

"I could deny you nothing," he replied instantly.

"And would you hate me for the things I unknowingly did? Let me wither and rot away from self-hatred?"

"Of course not," he snapped angrily. Although the rough, outraged words were directed at me, there was no true bite to them, the true emotion was targeted at himself. *"I would never allow you to do that to yourself."*

"Then why the fuck do you think I would allow it of you?" I rebuked, giving him a reproachful look out of the corner of my eye.

There was a long pause, before he said, *"I see your point, my queen. You have my apologies for not considering the prescience of your words. I should know better by now not to question your forethought."*

"You should," I agreed with a smile in my voice. *"Two thousand years has made you rusty in the arts of dealing with women."*

The darkness in my mind shook with brazen laughter. *"Maybe not as rusty as you think."*

It was hard not to chuckle. Or smack him upside the head.*"You're going to get us in trouble with the Monarch,"* I laughed. *"I think we missed something."*

"Just his apologies and condolences," Kanan confirmed. *"Sprites are known for their...theatrics."*

Couldn't really argue with that one. Wrynn could probably out dramatize anyone.

"—and so you have my utmost condolences for the losses you suffered during such awful trials," Xotin finished. His lengthy commiseration seemed to have dulled the honed blade of grief that had sliced through the gathered crowd.

"We thank you, Monarch," Kanan spoke for us. "You have our deepest gratitudes as well as our sympathies for your people."

The flight leader smiled gratefully, bowing his head in acceptance of the platitudes. His robes blew to the side as a calm wind rolled in, his stunning wings lifting as if greeting an old friend.

"How did you and the sprites survive?" I asked, eyeing the beam of light that refused to dim, curious to how everything factored in.

"Well because of this," he answered, reaching into the glowing pouch and pulling out a remarkably pristine diamond. At least I thought it was a diamond.

More clear than glass, the palm of the Monarch's hand was unmistakable through the gemstone. It was unrivaled in its cut, with faint hints of a rainbow of color near the middle that reminded me of shattered rays within frozen lake. A radiant white light that could have rivaled the stars in the pitch black of night, emanated from it.

No bigger than a stone from the riverbed, it sat comfortably in Xotin's hand, but the power it pulsed with should have come from a volcano from how it shook me to my core. Even my power, an integral, instinctual part of who I was, sat up and took notice.

There were tiny gasps from above as the flight caught sight of it. Wrynn, who was the closest, was finally rendered motionless, eyes wide in awe as its energy pulsed outward in waves that nearly knocked me flat. My chest ached as each forceful surge cracked against my ribs. There were dull thumps behind me, some unable to withstand the bursts of power that leaked from the jewel.

"This is the—" his voice flowed into a melodic, song-like language. The flowing clicks and notes interspersed with delicate wing serrations that I almost missed. "Or for your ears, we call it Last Breath."

The diamond, if that's what it even was, gleamed brighter, like it heard its name and wanted to respond. Xotin beamed down at it with a proud, paternal smile. "Last Breath has been recorded throughout our entire history, from the first dawn of the sprites. Every last historian, healer, and scholar within our flight have not been able to decipher its true purpose, only that they all agree that it plays an integral part to our species' survival and ability to thrive. The Devourer was somehow able to tap into the power within and siphon it off bit by bit. There was nothing we could do to stop it." Sadness rippled across his face and was reflected by every sprite, the sorrow shared by all.

"This is where you come in, Tali," Wrynn announced cheerfully, finding a way to work through the devastating power to get the words out.

Xotin looked scandalized at the familiar nickname, but swallowed whatever he would have said when I didn't correct him. "Wrynn is right," he continued smoothly. "We were days away from complete annihilation, those of us still alive were sickly and could barely move, but then you emerged in a shower of gold and we were saved. You heard our pleas, and soon after you saved your mate, you came for us. You were able to galvanize Last Breath, jolting it back to life, all while scaring off The Devourer."

"And that's why you serve me?" I stammered.

"It is an unpayable debt. You saved many lives that day, as well as our species." The Monarch waved around to the sprites who looked on from above. "They would not be here without you."

"There is no debt, Monarch," I stated without hesitancy. "I have had the pleasure of getting to know one of your kind, and he has become one of my closest friends. I may not remember my reasons, but I know that saving the sprites had nothing to do with obtaining a debt from you. Live your lives freely and without an obligation, that was never owed, hanging over you."

Xotin stepped forward to the edge of the wheel, giving me a placating look as he said, "All the more reason. You want nothing from us. No riches or power or servitude. You aided us because that is who you are, and for as long as I rule as Monarch of the Flight, you will have our loyalty. When I fall and my daughter Delia rises," he glanced lovingly towards the beautiful pink sprite on Bron's shoulder, "you will have it then as well."

"You might not win this one, love," Kanan voiced as he looked up. I tilted my head back as hundreds of small adoring faces smiled down at me. I could argue for hours with each and every one of them and still not make a dent in their numbers.

I sighed in defeat. *"Probably not."*

Meeting the Monarch's gaze, unyielding and stubborn, a contrast to his ever-present elegance, I knew I would get nowhere. I sighed again. *"Definitely not."*

"Are you flying with us to Eskira?" I moved on, saving the argument I would be having with Xotin for another day. There was no part of me that wanted the sprites, or anyone for that matter, indebted to me.

"The flight and I will stay with you until the day comes when you no longer need us. Wrynn has informed us of the enemy you face and we would be there by your side if you would have us." Xotin's decree was backed by the resounding whirr of a thousand wings echoing in agreement.

"Eskira would be honored to host the Monarch and his Flight," Kanan responded, surprising me with his diplomatic manner. Cashim would be proud.

"Then to Eskira we go," Xotin assented. He returned Last Breath to its pouch and the translucent stone pulsed wildly one last time as if to prove it could. The last of its light retreated, hidden by Xotin's robes. An inborn knowledge deep inside, ingrained within my magic, couldn't help but think that Last Breath wasn't just some stone imbued with magic.

That wasn't just my magic living within those crystal confines. It was something else entirely.

"Could I steer the ship?" Wrynn asked abruptly to an obviously bemused Captain Brassa, as the man stepped back up to the helm. Xotin shook his head at Wrynn, reminding me of Zanaya in that moment. He let out one last sigh as he departed back up into the sails with the rest of his sprites.

"I don't think so, lad." The captain rested his hands on his hips, tilting his head at the adorable sprite. "It's pretty important the ship stays on course."

Wrynn blinked up at him, nothing but innocence in those brown eyes, as he nodded along...and then he proceeded to lean far to the side from his seat atop the spoke, all of his weight, considerable despite his small stature, following with him. The wheel spun, slowly at first and then gained speed as gravity took hold.

"Captain Wrynn reporting for duty," the menace squealed as the wheel whipped around and around. The ship jolted to the right, throwing everyone into the siding as the rudder snapped to attention in the water.

Brassa lunged for the wheel, jerking it to a halt. Wrynn hung upside down at the bottom, hanging on to his spoke for dear life as he cackled with joy. He darted away, dodging the spinning spokes as the captain righted the ship, getting distracted by one thing and then quickly losing interest when the next showed up. Gods help us if he found Nala and Zander.

One helpless look from Rudrik and I was following behind the trouble-seeking sprite. A loud crash came from below deck, Nala's maniacal laughter carrying through the boards. Zanaya was already moving, leaving behind Zander, who had been tied to the main mast. There was a shout of glee near the stern, shouts and curses following.

This was going to be a long boat ride.

CHAPTER THIRTY-SEVEN

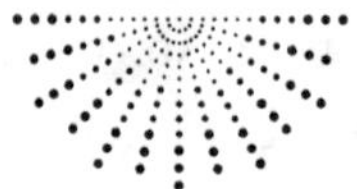

The thing about calling a place home was that it solidified its place in your heart. It was forever ingrained into your person, this place that sang to your soul, calling you back from whatever edge of the world you found yourself on. It was a beacon in the darkness, a guiding light on the foggy sea, beckoning you back to its warm embrace.

That feeling had always eluded me, an ache living in that shred of my soul that was never satisfied with my life in the Outskirts. Even the cottage, the only safe place I had known for the first twenty years of my life, had barely scratched the itch, the longing, for a place to call my own.

And as the first mountain winds rolled down from their peaks, carrying with them the scent of dew and pine and the faintest hint of snow from the highest points, that ache eased away from the painful, lonely limits and shifted into a yearning so profound it was a wonder there wasn't a physical wound to show for it.

It was a weeping, heart-wrenching relief as the beginnings of Eskira's lower city appeared at the edges of our view. We had our first sign of other ships, mere dots on the horizon, their sails lifted proudly in the air, as they came into the port.

"Atallia." Spinning around from where I leaned out over *River's Dream*'s railing, Zanaya waved me over from beneath the forecastle. Nala and Saanvi waited with her, a large trunk held between them.

Moving across the deck, I smirked at where Zander had fallen asleep, still bound to the trunk of the main mast despite his many attempts to cut through the ropes holding him. At some point he had shifted into his fox form, the ropes loose enough for him to escape if he noticed, but the soft snores told me he wouldn't until someone woke him. A wink of white amongst his rose-red fur nearly sent me over the edge.

Wrynn had disappeared an hour ago, no one able to find him, which seemed to be both a relief and a concern for the ship's crew. After nearly sending us crashing into the bank and a whole host of other mishaps, the sailors had nearly rioted against the sprite. The trouble must have worn him out though, his body curled up in Zanders fur. His white wings were cocooned around him like a sparkling blanket, knees pulled to his chest as he too snored.

"You called," I said, coming to a stop in front of the three women, their backs to the door that led to Captain Brass's quarters as well as the stairs leading to the lower decks.

Zanaya took hold of my shoulders, leading me through the door that Nala opened. "Come on," she insisted, pushing me forward and down the hall. She marched me past the spiraling stairs on the right, leading us down the hall to the room I assumed was the captain's.

"Want to fill me in here?" I asked teasingly, amusement dripping from my voice. Nala and Saanvi followed, shutting the heavy door as they carried their burden down the hall behind us.

"Nope. Not until I can lock us inside," she replied flippantly, shoving me ahead of her and into the open room. Holding the door open for Nala and Saanvi to step through, she slammed it closed, blocking the only exit with her body.

Wariness shot through me as they set the trunk down in front of the one desk off to the side. Saanvi stretched her arms high before plopping herself in the hammock hung up in the corner, the frosted window taking up the middle of the wall, bringing in enough light to catch the suspicious looks on all three of their faces.

"What's going on?" I asked, eyeing the door, debating my escape as Zanaya strode over to the chest.

Nala hopped up onto the desk, legs swinging several inches above the ground. She smiled at me, which was always concerning. "We had something flown down for you," she said simply, her eyes gleaming a little too much for my liking.

"Oh yeah?" I asked cautiously. Zanaya undid the lock on the trunk, pocketing the key as she flung the top back. "What did you get me?"

Reaching inside the case, Zanaya carefully lifted out another locked box, handing it to Nala who set it beside her. "You can't say no," she said demandingly, glancing at me over her shoulder with a look that had me even more concerned. "It's not for you, it's for Eskira."

With that worrisome statement she straightened, lifting something shiny from the box. Holding it out in front of her, lifting it high so it wouldn't drag, she presented a length of delicate white material to me like a weapon.

"No." My immediate dismissal was met with a disapproving frown, her narrowed eyes ripping into me as she stepped toward me with the shimmering monstrosity.

"You're wearing it," she declared in a no-nonsense voice. "I asked Brassa if we could use his chambers so that you wouldn't pitch a fit in front of everyone, but if I have to strip you naked and shove you into this, I will."

"Ooo," Nala crooned. "Please do, it would fulfill a fantasy of mine."

We all stopped and stared at her with incredulous looks. Even Saanvi, who picked at her nails with a wicked looking knife, lifted a dark brow at her in question.

Nala froze under the attention, before clucking her tongue. "Don't judge me, a girl can dream. I also have a thing about getting it on in a burning building, it could get weirder."

"You concern me," Zanaya said after a long pause, looking at her as if she was a foreign species. "Like on a very deep spiritual level."

"I know," the pyro smiled proudly, picking up one of the books on the captain's desk. The embers from her hair fell around her, singeing some of the papers scattered across the top. Although she didn't seem to notice. Or care. I couldn't tell.

Shaking her head, Zanaya gave up on convincing the redhead of her own insanity, switching her attention back to me. She thrust the dress into my hands, pointing towards the back corner where an ornately decorated screen had been placed. "Go put it on."

"Come on," I complained. I didn't care if it sounded like I was whining, I already received enough attention as is with the hair, I didn't need any help garnering more. "There's no reason for this."

Zanaya prodded me along until I was backed into the corner, giving me an unsympathetic grin before unfolding the screen and blocking me from the rest of the room. I didn't even have to peek around the divider to know she was still on the other side, probably with her arms crossed, waiting to see if I would try and escape.

"This is ridiculous," I grumbled under my breath, spinning around in the tight corner. Maybe a fissure would appear and take me away from this torture. I waited, peering around for an abnormal shimmer in the air.

Nothing.

I let out a subdued sigh, my plan thwarted. There was no way I could get that lucky.

"It's for the people," Saanvi spoke up surprisingly. "Those who will get one look at the exhausted, burnt-out warriors on these ships and know just how fucked we are. Kasis won't have to do anything to crush our city's morale, you'll do it for him if you don't do your part to show that we haven't been broken."

"We're not broken," I snapped, immediately defensive of the warriors who had fought long and hard to get back here—and the ones who'd come back covered in a death shroud.

"No," the quiet viper spoke softly, "we're not. But we are close, and the people of the city will see that."

I wanted to revolt against her words, tell her that she was wrong, that we weren't even close to being beaten, but that would've been a blatant lie. I saw the constant, painful battle to keep standing on every soldier's face, their energy zapped no matter how hard they tried to hide it. If Kasis and the kinsmen decided to hit us again so soon, there was no guaranteeing anyone would make it out alive.

The hammock squeaked, as if she had shifted forward. "You are a symbol of Eskira's strength. Allasea's strength. If you come into the city dressed in dirty fighting leathers, blades out, it tells everyone in the city that you're expecting another attack."

"I am expecting it," I retorted feebly, even as their point began to make sense. Kanan and I would be the first thing the Eskirans looked for when the ship came into the bay. They would either see strength or weakness.

"And they know that too, but it's not about convincing them that everything is fine, it's about convincing them of our mettle. They may see tired soldiers, bloody and scraped, but when they look at you, untouchable, powerful, standing proudly amongst the men and women that marched for you, they won't see weakness," she explained, her words profound. "They'll see courage and fortitude. An army that went up against a malicious, crazy god and survived, bringing back their lost goddess along with them."

"You give them hope," Nala chimed in. "You give us all hope that we can make it through this alive. When everything seems to be going against us and yet we have our king and queen back for the first time in two thousand years. To many, it'll seem like a sign from the Cosmos, giving us back our strongest protectors in a time of great need."

"So suck it up," Zanaya added shortly with zero pity. "You can hate the attention all you want, but if you plan to help these people and our home, then you need to use it to our advantage."

I blew out a breath, undoing the leather sheaths buckled to my thighs. She had a point, if I could do anything to help us win this war I would, even if it meant putting myself front and center to be gawked at.

Conceding, I began stripping off my leathers and tossing them into the corner. I was patting myself on the back for getting a real bath before we had left because as I picked up the opalescent fabric there was considerably less of it than I would have assumed.

"I can hear you hesitating," Zanaya said from the other side of the panels. "Just trust me and put it on."

I glared at the partition separating us, jumping as her voice snapped through the air. "I can feel you glaring too."

"Fine, I'm putting it on," I grumbled, muttering curses under my breath as I stepped into the shimmering dress. My foot caught on something inside the dress, and I was pleasantly surprised as I fiddled around with it.

"Are these pants?" I asked excitedly. Shifting the fabric around I was able to get my other foot into the side, pulling the fabric up to my hips.

"Please," Zanaya tutted from somewhere farther in the room, "give me some credit. I know you enough to know that a dress would never do for this entrance. We can't have you picking at it every two minutes when we're trying to convince the city of your confidence."

I didn't know if I was insulted or not by that comment, but I settled on grateful as the glistening material fell around my legs perfectly, leaving me free to move as I pleased. When I stood still it looked exactly like a dress. Loose at the ankles, the airy material opened up in one long slit on the outside of my thighs, peeks of ivory skin flashing as I shifted around.

Pulling up the rest of the fabric, it glided over my skin as I stuck my arms through the thin, barely-there straps. The pant-dress hybrid cupped my hips, the silk following the lines of my waist as if it were painted on. It cupped my breasts lightly, leaving my neckline and arms left bare and on display.

I had to admit, from the parts I could see, it was fabulously made and undeniably comfortable. Each thread glittered as if it had been spun from a spider's web, crafted from crushed pearl. It somehow complimented my complexion despite being so pale.

"Throw these on." The offhand comment came right as two softened leather boots of the same glittering shade were thrown over the top of the screen. The finely worked material hit me at the ankle and their small heel brought my height up by a few inches. They molded to my feet, the fit as flawless as the dress, making me question how the tailor and cobbler knew my measurements so well.

I stepped out from behind the panels and tried not to fiddle with the exquisite piece of clothing as the three women took me in.

"It's a lot of skin." I ran my fingers over the areas of my body the fabric hadn't covered. There was no doubt that I would be on display. A lot of me.

Zanaya waved her hand in dismissal. "Descendents don't care about showing skin, that's a human thing. Besides, we're not done with you yet."

I barely had time to protest before she shoved me in front of a floor length mirror. I stilled as I caught a glimpse of myself.

The cloth fell around me in a river of liquid silk, an ethereal shine to it that took my breath away. The smallest of movements caused an array of color to shimmer along the fabric before it settled back into an iridescent white.

It was semi-transparent, teasing hints of my body beneath. Thankfully, it fell just right to ensure nothing I didn't want to be seen could be. Tiny pearl beading added texture, curving along the same line as my ribs, drawing the eye to the smooth lines of the dress.

"Wow, look at you," Nala sang as she appeared over my shoulder. Nudging me, she grinned wickedly. "That dragon of yours isn't going to know what hit him."

I chose to ignore the beat of satisfaction that wound through me, but a smile curled at the edges of my lips nonetheless.

There was a clink of metal as Zanaya pulled something else from the chest. Coming up behind she lifted an intricate set of golden chains over my head, settling them around my neck and shoulders. My skin prickled as they grazed my skin, the cool metal warming after a few seconds.

The links along my back jingled as Saanvi hooked a long train, of the same shimmering material as my dress, onto the layered metal along my shoulders. The fabric dipped low in the middle, leaving my back bare before it joined together and billowed outward.

"Here," Saanvi murmured as she pulled my waist length hair from underneath the chains, taking care that the metal didn't yank at the curly strands.

"Thank you." The gratitude came out quiet. I didn't seem able to look away from my reflection, my swirling honey eyes wide as I searched for who I was underneath the finery.

She squeezed my arm, giving me a rare smile that made her emerald gaze brighten. "It doesn't change you," she said perceptively, looking me in the eye for as long as she could. "None of this changes who you are on the inside. Just think of it as a different kind of armor."

Armor. I could do that. It was protection from the expectant, fervent stares I received. I was giving them something to look at. A distraction from what was really going on underneath, a shield for the scarred heart that I mostly hid from the world. Barricaded by wall after wall of cynicism and mistrust. It wasn't healthy, of that I was sure, but it had kept me alive, so there was that.

If I played the part of untouchable queen, maybe then I could keep the souls of this beautiful city from leaving too deep of a mark on my own. For if I didn't, my heart might not survive when I inevitably lost some of them.

"Nala grab the box will you?" Zanaya asked as she messed with the train until it lay how she wanted it too.

"On it!" She skipped over to where she had left the second box on the captain's desk. It was taller than I originally thought, long and square. The golden lock, masterfully crafted, was in the shape of a starburst.

Keeping her arms underneath, she carried it back carefully. Zanaya slipped a second key from her pocket, undoing the latch with a click. As she lifted the lid, I let out a gasp.

Inside was a crown of stunning gold, the metal buffed to a shine that hurt my eyes if I looked at it for too long. Curved vines made up the main circlet. Crystal thorns, embedded within the metal branches, refracted light and sent a scattering of color throughout the room.

Gorgeous as they were, the barbs looked razor sharp, a single prick enough to draw blood.

Thinly crafted flowers made of pearl sat perched atop the deceptively dangerous vines, making up the body of the decorative headpiece, the tip of each petal gilded with molten gold.

"A crown fit for a queen," I muttered, feeling like an imposter as Zanaya lifted it from its velvet stand. Two threaded chains dangled from the ends of the thorned band, gold and pearl droplets hanging from it every few inches.

Zanaya placed the crown atop my head and a weight, more than just a physical one, settled around me. A responsibility, to myself and to a whole people, coming with the privilege of wearing the crown.

Saanvi and Nala began wrapping two sections of hair around the jeweled chains, pulling them back behind my head to secure the crown. Zanaya took hold of my shoulders and together we looked at my reflection. Smiling, pride and awe entered her words as she said, "No, it's a crown fit for a goddess."

A horn blared in the distance, low and resonating. A signal that we had arrived. Feet clamored on the boards above us as the crew, shuffling down the stairs to the main deck, prepared for docking. I could hear the relieved cries and hoots of joy from here, the passengers primed to leave the *River's Dream* behind for the city of Eskira.

"That's our cue." Zanaya faced me once more, her forehead puckered as she asked, "Are you ready?"

It was a loaded question. One I wasn't sure I could give a good answer to, not with my heart smashing against my chest with every beat, pulse bounding in my golden veins. Air slashed through my lungs, every inhale bordering on painful. My hands trembled, but I clenched them tight. This whole spectacle would be for nothing if I showed any fear.

Surrounded by the three women I had grown to trust the most, I let the truth bleed out. "No. I don't think I am."

"Just remember, you're doing this for the young ones who might have to say goodbye to their parents, the mothers who don't know if their grown children will make it out of this war, the pairs who may be forever separated." Zanaya moved an escaped ringlet behind my ear, resting her chin on my shoulder. Smirking, she shot me a wink in the mirror. "And if all else fails, at least you look damn good."

That broke the tension, Nala and Saanvi grinning as I let out a rough, desperate chuckle. Peering at my image one last time, I straightened my shoulders. I looked the part, now it was time to learn how to act it. "Okay," I say, steeling myself for what's to come. "Let's do this."

CHAPTER THIRTY-EIGHT

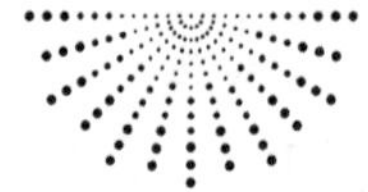

They led the way down the hall, a silent escort as the muffled noises grew louder. I followed, the faint clicks of my heeled shoes against the wood were thunderous booms in my ears. Pushing their way through the door, sunlight shot in through the opening, catching the shimmering silk that flowed over my skin.

I braced myself, taking a deep breath of mountain air. The spray from the river brought in the morning dew, the light mist cooling my warm skin. Stepping from the hall, I blinked away the spots that obscured my view.

Silence.

I tilted my chin up and met the stares of a hundred Descendent warriors. The dozen crewmen of the *River's Dream* froze while completing their duties at my approach, and an endless number of sprites, who were surfing the boat's wake, flew back to their perches and smiled down at me with child-like delight.

The ship lurched and a second horn ripped through the air, Eskira's splendor taking shape as we entered the long passage that cut through the lower and upper segments of the city. No backing out now.

I glided along the deck, moving through the crowd as if on a cloud.

A faint breeze lovingly pulled at the ends of my hair, lifting them into the air in dance. The sun, only now beginning to reach its peak, refracted off the silken gown. The pearly white shifted with blues and pinks and gold and back again.

The chains glittered under the light, their heaviness giving me something to focus on other than the attention falling on me. I hit the first row of tired warriors, their eyes going wide as they took me in. They parted before me, meeting my gaze for a moment, their shoulders straightening as a renewed vigor entered their weary eyes.

A path was created to reach the stairs leading up to the bow. The train tugged on the looped chains, the drag reminding me to keep my back straight as the loose silk floated in the wind behind me.

Ascending the steps, the slits in the dress separated, allowing me to easily climb the short distance to the secondary deck. I blew out a discrete breath as I made it up without face planting, sending out a prayer of thanks to whoever had crafted the slits in the dress because they were obviously the goddess in this situation, not me.

There was a flutter in my chest, a quick beat of wings, like a trapped bird trying to take flight from inside my ribs. The bond burst alive in my chest as I saw the reason why.

The cape came into view first, a counterpart to my own. Draped from the broad expanse of his shoulders it fell like a rain of darkness, like the night itself had been collected and imbued into the threads by some impressive power.

Then there were his shadows. Creations of the very same darkness that lived in his veins. They curled from beneath the loose material, moving like smoke around him. Roving the deck like loyal dogs, they didn't stray too far, but were curious nonetheless.

He sensed me from the way his body shifted, almost tensing, as he took a deep breath. Preparing himself? A shadowy finger reached out to stroke along the toe of my boot, a second one coming to inspect the bottom of my dress, seemingly intrigued as it changed colors. He placed his hands in his pockets, gazing out across the river as the boat sailed past the first buildings.

He turned at my approach and it was a struggle to not let my jaw drop. I had seen him wear many faces in the short time I had known him. A warlord. A warrior. A dragon. But rarely did I see this version of him, the side of himself that maybe he never wanted, but bore without complaint.

A crown of the darkest metals curled in perfect resemblance of his dragon horns. Locks of his raven hair fell around it in flawless waves, the two main branches curving back into points so sharp my skin stung at the thought of touching them. Albeit shorter, the barbs near the front were just as deadly. The sun's rays, shot through with the colors of magic, glanced off their tips. They glinted in temptation as if inviting someone to touch them and reap the consequences. A savage crown for a king who was Death, a burning hellfire of a beast moving beneath his skin, just waiting for the opportunity to stretch its wings.

Right now, however, he was very much the stoic ruler who wouldn't hesitate to shed the civilized charade in order to slaughter those that threatened what was his.

Surprise lit his face before swiftly changing to something darker, more severe, as his gaze swept down my body and back up. His pupils constricted, going vertical, a ring of fire surging outward from them, burning on the edges of his blood red eyes. A ferocious need heated those swirling irises, more brutal than even mine.

It was like a harsh current ran through his body, every muscle locking in place. I could imagine his calloused hands, fisted in the pockets of his black trousers, forced to stay still to keep him from reaching across the distance that separated us and yanking me closer.

Shadows crept over his shoulder, one of them brushing at his ear. They were an impeccable match for the ebony black of his formal tunic. Instead of cutting down in the classic V-shape, the sturdy cloth crossed over his chest, a column of golden buttons on the left fastening the shirt closed.

Deciding they were done playing with my shoes, a curl of dark magic wound its way up my leg. It was soft beyond reason, like being stroked by air. When it snaked a little too close to the juncture of my thigh I looked at Kanan with a fake glare. "Careful, mister."

"They're possessive of you," he answered unapologetically. The shadow did pull back, wrapping around my ankle boldly. Kanan offered me a hand, an unmistakable request.

He gave his pets a reproachful look as they continued doing as they pleased. "They often misbehave if I'm not constantly on guard, which is annoying and makes them restless."

"I don't mind," I assured him, taking his outstretched hand. His fingers curled around mine in a strong grip, not too tight, but firm enough for my pulse to skitter in response. "They're cute, and they make me laugh."

"Cute?" He looked taken aback. Indignation creased his brow, his confusion making me want to laugh. "They are formidable. Vicious. Bloodthirsty," he named off, mouth twisting in distaste. "Not cute."

I hummed in response, then chuckled as a shadow chose that moment to knock over an unlit oil lamp, the clang seeming to spook the wisp of darkness, sending it reeling back. Kanan exhaled smoke from his nose in sigh, a tendril appearing from his hair to twine with the vapor before darting back into hiding.

He glanced over at me as I laughed, watching me with an indescribable look. "Do it again?" he asked softly when I stopped. Tilting my head in question, he whispered in a tone shared between lovers, "Laugh, smile, just keep being happy."

A simple request. He knew we weren't fixed, too many things still needed to be discussed for that to be the case, but as the first bridge came into view, a crowd of Eskiran's ready to judge whether this would be a celebration or a mourning, we were united in our shared uncertainty for the future. To ask for a moment of happiness amidst the turmoil was not a prayer I would deny.

So I smiled, bright as the sun. I let all our problems fall away for a heartbeat in time, allowing a sliver of the happiness we strived for to shine through as I gazed up at him. His face slackened, softening in a way I had never seen from him. "You're beautiful," he whispered, an emotion in his gaze that made my head spin, my heart cracking open under its intensity.

That only made me smile wider, which he answered with his own. As glorious as the city we called home, his eyes crinkled, grasping my hand tighter as he brought it to rest in the crook of his arm.

He cupped my chin up as he scanned my face. His eyes caught on the crown of flowers and thorns, smile turning smug. "Soul of a goddess, heart of a queen."

I scoffed, "I don't know about that, I still feel like a fake. A pretty dress doesn't make me either of those things."

"Come here." He tugged me along, walking us over to the railing overlooking the main deck. Zanaya and my friends, Bron by the commander's side, were at the front. They all wore smiles on their faces. And behind them, row after row of warriors were arranged in faultless formation.

They stared up at us in allegiance. Their faith in us written in the way they carried themselves, backs unbending, weapons straightened, leathers brushed off.

Our closest friends looked on, chins lifted, and as one they bowed, a clenched fist pressed over their hearts, steel in their spines.

The ranks of soldiers after them followed suit, a grizzled determination settling over the squadrons. Pride exploded through me. These men and women who honored us with their sacrifices, their hardships. Every time they lifted their swords, aimed their arrows, they carried us with them. Fight after godsdamn fight and they hadn't given up, not on me, or Kanan. Not on themselves.

And yet they bowed to us.

I swept my glowing gaze over every single one of their faces, and did the only thing I could think of to show my own respect.

I bowed back, Kanan following suit.

I lowered my head, the burden of the crown was heavy but unshakable. A few gasped, but many didn't. The reality of a ruler was not that of being served, but of serving. To protect and cherish and guide, even if that meant taking the agony of the world unto yourself.

I bowed not for a crown. Not for a throne or power, but for hope. Hope in a world where I was everything they needed me to be. A servant. A protector. A queen and goddess. I was theirs as much as they were mine, and by the Cosmos if I wouldn't break the fucking world to save them from the clutches of chaos.

As we lifted our heads that promise burned freely in my eyes. Let the universe see just what I would do to be worthy of the power it granted me. To be worthy of them.

"There she is." Kanan's piercing stare glimpsed the change unlocking within me, and as we turned and looked upon the hundreds gathered along the bridges and streets, sprites soaring overhead and into the crowds, the thunderous roar of a thousand cheers echoed across the city.

CHAPTER THIRTY-NINE

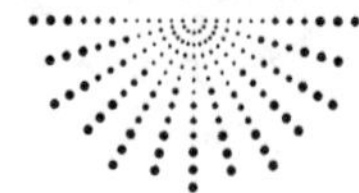

The halls of the citadel were unusually quiet for the time of day. The celebrations had been in full swing since our ships had pulled in to dock around noontime. Dancing and drinking in the streets, mates and mothers meeting weary soldiers with wet eyes, the cacophonous noise of a whole city welcoming us home.

The war party had been dismissed to their homes so long as they passed Moian's checks, those needing healing or who showed signs of the Warp were sentenced to the Mender's care. Several Aetherians, who had collapsed during the ferrying, had grumbled their complaints. Getting stuck with the *warden,* as the squadrons so kindly called the lead healer, was apparently on par with being sent to the dungeons. Their whines had gone unanswered as a horse-drawn cart trudged them up the streets to the infirmary.

Kanan had long since disappeared, having whispered in my ear that he needed to check on the guards stationed along the walls. In lieu of the regularly posted squadrons, several regiments had been left behind to ensure nothing happened in our absence. Eskira could never be left fully defenseless, not as the seat of power in Allasea, but it was down to a skeleton crew with the entire army in various stages of burnout.

That had been hours ago, the sun surely touching the horizon by now if the orange and yellow sky was any indicator. I begged off any assistance with the formal garb, choosing instead to wander the halls. The last thing I needed right now was more people surrounding me, touching me. It felt like I hadn't had a moment to myself in days, and frankly, my nerves were shot.

The last time I had walked the halls of the palace I was the random girl who caused more problems than she was probably worth. Now I was a queen.

Shit was crazy.

Queen or not, I still couldn't find my way around this winding labyrinth of a palace. Each path led to a hundred more, one even bringing me to a staircase that was cut into the side of the mountain, no railing or barrier to keep you from plunging a thousand feet down.

Those memories would really come in handy right now.

My savior came in the form of a petite woman exiting one of the many doors lining the corridors. Her adorable fawn-colored hair was pulled back into braid, small locks curling widely around her soft, heart-shaped face. Looking down at the basket in her hands, she almost ran right into me as I came to a stop before her. Big, brown doe eyes lit with surprise as she glanced up. She gaped at me, her jaw dropping open.

I hadn't yet changed from the shock and awe gown, the crown of iridescent flowers and thorns firmly situated atop my head. "Hello," I said kindly. Maybe that would lessen the shock. "I was hoping you could help me with something?"

Her basket dropped from her hands, clattering to the floor and spilling the sheets inside.

Or not.

I crouched down while the young maid gathered herself. Righting the basket, I began tossing the linens back inside. There was a gasp from above before the woman all but threw herself to the floor.

"Oh my gods, Your Majesty. I am so sorry," she said in a rush. Her voice trembled, round cheeks turning red as she stammered out the apology. "Please let me get those."

"No need," I reassured her, placing the last sheet back in the basket. "I'm sorry if I spooked you." I chuckled lightly, watching as her shoulders eased slightly, a ghost of a smile tipping the corners of her rosebud mouth.

I stood with the basket in hand, handing it over once she straightened. She looked at me like I had three heads, seconds away from dropping her basket again. Her face had frozen in a mask of astonishment and panic.

I needed to get out of here before she froze like that. "I confess I'm quite lost, could you point me in the direction of the throne room?"

She mumbled the directions, and I took off with a swish of my train. She twisted as I walked past, mouth agape, watching me go like she was in a fever dream, unsure if anything was real.

Using her directions, after admittedly a few wrong turns, I made my way down the long runner leading to the copper doors cutting everything off from the throne room. I pushed through them, damn near getting the silk train caught in it as they closed. I came out onto the balcony overlooking the main floor, the darkened space providing cover as an argument hit my ears.

"What would you have had me do?" Cashim demanded, a plea in his voice. "I was under orders. This was to protect them, you, everyone."

"You could have said something," Zanaya retorted in scathing anger. Moving closer to the railing, I looked over and saw them standing on opposite sides of the sturdy table that spanned the middle of the room. Like two opponents in some sad game they volleyed harsh comments at one another, each word spoken in anger finding its mark.

"You spent my childhood telling me stories about the Divine, how gracious and compassionate of rulers they were, and I know you told me the truth because there were fucking blank spots," she spit across at him, "in my memories. What was I to you? Your godsdamn test subject to make sure the block hadn't broken?"

Cashim ran a hand over his close cropped curls, his face puckered in anger and guilt. "Of course not, I told you those stories because you enjoyed them, and it was the only thing that helped you sleep at night after your parents died."

Zanaya stepped back, silencing whatever she would have said. Her body tensed, each breath leaving her in ragged pants. "You never told me that." Her voice lost some of its hard edge as grief lined her face, "You never speak of them."

He looked down, sighing as he placed his hands on his hips. "And maybe that's a fault of mine, but for those first few years, I didn't know what I was doing Zani," he looked at her, wetness gathering in his ice blue eyes. The effect was startling, turning them into twin lakes, frozen over by grief. His pain was stuck in the ice, unable to escape from the agony of what had happened to his family no matter how much time had passed.

"I had just killed my brother, had to set him beside his murdered mate on their pyre," his voice choked off, emotion clogging his throat. He sniffed, steadying himself with a breath. "And then there was you. This child who had just lost her entire world in less than two days. You didn't know what was happening, not really, but you knew it wasn't good. Your father didn't make it long after Sana's death. When I found him, he was covered in blood rocking you by the river. I thought he might hurt you, but some small part of him must have been there at the end."

Tears streamed down my friend's face. The whites of her eyes were bloodshot, her blue irises all the more noticeable. The physical marker that tied the last two members of this broken family together. Their bond was more noticeable though. Forged in grief, strengthened by a love that transcended the blood they shared.

Leaning his forearms against the back of a chair, Cashim dropped his head into his hands, scrubbing them over his ragged, weary face. "I had a traumatized child in my care, I was dealing with a broken Council who couldn't settle on a decision about anything, and I had this...responsibility to the king that ate away at me every day."

He stared up at Kanan's obsidian throne, no less intimidating or majestic as the first time I had seen it. "Only a few people in the entire world knew what I did, and it had to stay that way. They came back as children, can you imagine what would have happened if they'd landed in the wrong hands? The king did," he exploded, waving his hand out towards the imposing seat, "but at least he regained his memories. Think of what would have happened had Maris and Geoff not found Atallia in the woods. They spent years searching for her. No one knew she wouldn't have her memories, and there are a great many people in this world that would have taken advantage of that fact, turned her into their own personal weapon. A goddess, Zani. We are blips in the universe compared to them. Fireflies in the presence of burning stars. She could annihilate us at any point. They both could."

"She would never," Zanaya said in my defense. "That's not who she is."

"You're right," he agreed with a nod, "but she could. And as soon as she learns the true breadth of her power, it would be as easy as lifting a finger. I know the queen would never, but imagine that power in the hands of someone who's been manipulated since childhood, when they're easily impressionable and controlled."

The silence was palpable. The emotional part of me wanted to be hurt by their assumptions, that it would be easy for me to hurt innocents like that, but the logical side knew they were right. Had Maris and Geoff not raised me, had they not shown me that there was such a thing as love and kindness and compassion, I very well could have been a different person entirely. Without my memories there would have been no way for me to find my way back to who I was.

I was a blank canvas waiting for the marks the world would leave on me. That's what reincarnation offered, a chance to start over and begin again. Whether I turned out good or bad was up to the influences that shaped me.

"I understand where you're coming from," she said, breaking the quiet, "but I am your heir. I get not telling me as a child, but I'm no longer the same little girl who clung to your leg so desperately all those years ago. You brought her into my life, watched as she became someone I cared for, and you lied to both of us."

There was a glint of red at Cashim's hip, the ruby jewel in the hilt of his saber flashing as he moved around the table. He halted when she backed away from him, arms crossed, and his face fell.

"You are my family Zanaya, and I know I could never replace your parents, but you've always been my daughter. I would lay down my life for yours in a heartbeat because you are my everything, the only family I have left. It was never my intention to hurt you or cause you to be angry at me. I've done everything for you." His imploring gaze begged her to understand. The love in his voice, his eyes, in every fiber of his being couldn't have been more visible, but I was afraid Zanaya was too blinded by her anger to see it.

"Everyday I work to make this world better. I may not always do things right, and I've made plenty of mistakes. Ones that will stay with me until my last days, but I strive to do right more than wrong..." He paused, swallowing the emotion in his throat. "So I can look you in the eyes and be proud of who stands before you. Simply having you in my life has made me a better person, hurting you is the last thing I would ever want."

She was silent for a long time, a war of emotion playing out on her face. Her brow puckered as she looked at him, eyes watery and full of pain. "That's the thing, Uncle, you have hurt me."

The blow landed, Cashim visibly recoiling from her. She winced, the words paining her just as much, but that didn't stop her. "How can you ever expect me to trust you when you clearly don't have the same trust in me? I get why you did everything." The words were forced out between her lips, no lie in her tone, as each one cut like a glass shard. "And I understand the position you were in, but like you said, we're the only blood family we have left and if that doesn't count for something then I don't know how else to prove to you that you've had my loyalty since the day you took me in."

She didn't wait for him to answer, turning and striding from the room with bowed shoulders. I wanted to go after my friend, comfort her, but I knew she needed this. If anyone understood what she was going through it was me, and offering soft, comforting words wouldn't fix the cracks in her relationship with her uncle no matter how much we both wished they would. It would be her choice whether or not to accept Cashim's decisions, and nothing but her forgiveness would heal the broken man below me, each of his silent sobs a hammer to my heart.

Before I knew what I was doing, I moved down the hidden staircase that led to the bottom. I padded my way over to him, the faint clinking of the metal chainmail alerting him to my presence. His head whipped up, reddened eyes meeting mine for a shocked second before he regained his composure with the speed and experience of a man used to keeping his cards close to his chest.

Bowing low, lower than he ever had, he took a few extra seconds to gather himself, and when he rose I pretended not to notice his shaky breaths. "Your Majesty," he greeted nobly, carefully tucking his trembling hands behind his back. "May I help you with something?"

I stared up at him, watched the pain in his eyes flicker in and out, and pain of my own flared to life. What a mess this whole thing had caused. No one had been left undamaged by the decisions of some long gone version of Kanan and I. It wasn't fair. That others were hurting for reasons outside their control, and whether I had played a part or not, I couldn't help but feel responsible.

Stepping forward as glittering tears filled my eyes, I wrapped my arms around him in apology. He tensed in surprise, which only caused me to tighten my hold, hoping sheer will could mend the chipped, fragile pieces of his heart. He must have recognized that, taking me within his own warm embrace. And that's how we stood for a few moments, withstanding the chaotic torrent of betrayal and hurt and love. Two wounded souls hoping against all odds for a better world.

When we finally pulled away, I looked up at him, cupping his stubbled cheek. "She'll come around."

The air of old wisdom he carried fell away, leaving him open and vulnerable as he looked for guidance in a fellow splintered spirit. "How do you know?"

"Because she loves you. More than you'll ever know," I whispered up to him, keeping those cracks from shattering apart with the knowledge of a love I knew still burned inside his niece. "She may be angry, but you have a bond forged in the fires of shared pain, cooled and shaped and sharpened by the love that you have for each other. Don't give up on her."

He lowered his head, nodding as the words found their mark. "Thank you, Atallia," he said, using my true name and waving off the formalities that were not necessary between us. "I am incredibly sorry for any hurt I may have caused you as well. I hope you know it was never to lead you astray, but to protect you from the forces that would have used you in a way that should never be stood for."

His normally lyrical voice, a harmony intertwined with every sound he made, so similar to his niece, was thick with sincerity. "You were put in a position that you never should have been, Cashim. One way or another, you came out the loser in this situation. Either you lied to those around you, for who knew how long, or you betrayed your king's confidence, possibly putting both of us at risk during our new life. It was a responsibility that should have never fallen to you, but it did. For that you have *my* apologies."

He went to argue, but I didn't allow him any leave. "You have been nothing but loyal to Kanan and I, and while it may have taken me time to comprehend the weight you shouldered, you have done right by us and our people, and for that you have my thanks."

He blinked rapidly as one of the chains holding him down, barely allowing him to breath under the burden of responsibility, fell away. It broke as I recognized its unjust restraint of a man who had done nothing but try to please everyone in order to keep them safe.

He needed time, I could see it in the way he tried to process the newfound freedom. He stood straighter, breathed easier, an invisible pressure that made it impossible to exist comfortably being released.

"Have you seen Kanan?"

"I spoke with him earlier," he offered distractedly. I had never seen Cashim so unsure. There was no situation that I believed he couldn't handle, but at being noticed for what he was—a good man trying his best for those he cared about—and centuries of living his life in the service of others, he seemed lost. "I believe he was headed into the forest."

I nodded in thanks, leaving him to his thoughts, and made my way to the door he motioned to. Hidden behind the thrones, it was clear that it wasn't used often, the hinges desperately needing an oiling as grating creaks split the air. Glancing over my shoulder, I glimpsed the councilman one last time. He stood in a sort of stupor, so small in comparison to the looming grandeur of the room.

I could only hope that uncle and niece would come back together soon, and that Zanaya took her own advice, because she was right. In a world that was threatening to end at any moment, there wasn't any time to waste on regrets.

CHAPTER FORTY

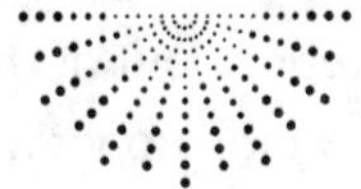

It took some figuring out, but I eventually found the path that led to the mostly inaccessible piece of woodland that Kanan had pointed out that one time in the sunroom. He was out there in the forest, somewhere deep within its depths. The bond quivered with the knowledge that he was close.

With some maneuvering, I carefully removed the delicate chainmail and connecting train, untwisted the crown from my hair, slipped out of my boots, and left the decorative pieces behind as I set off into the forest looking for my dragon.

The moss-covered floor brushed the sensitive arches of my feet as I walked. A wind, cooler than the ones that often blew through the city, caressed my skin like a lover, brought down from the high peaks surrounding me. My skin pebbled in response. I appreciated it all the same, needing the chilly reprieve from the day's activities.

I carried on through the splendid wildwood, careful not to tear the spider silk that was draped along my body in a pearly sheet. The slits in the dress, the illusion unbroken as the colors wavered in rays of light, proved useful once again as I made my path through the brush.

I had long since given up on making sense of the connection between Kanan and I, and as an invisible force pulled me along in a single direction, I decided that I didn't need to know. Sometimes putting a name to something, understanding every little aspect of it, wasn't necessary. There was something to be said about the enigmatic, and maybe the nature of the cosmic powers at play should stay in that veil of mystery. It was better for everyone's sanity that way.

I had some idea where he was. There was only one thing in this part of the woods that would draw him here, and as I came upon the grove my suspicions were proven correct. The thicket thinned and the canopy became sparse as I stepped out of the tree-line.

My mouth dropped as *it* came into view.

Holy shit.

The tree was massive. Bigger than any I had ever seen, even the Blackwood giants paled in comparison. The ebony trunk was as wide as the palace turrets, spiraling high into the air with its crooked, winding branches. It had twisted somewhere in its lifetime, bending to the winds that formed it, but not breaking. Never breaking.

The roots spread far and wide, reaching where I stood at the edge of the grove and probably far past it deep underground. They jutted out of the ground in some places, gnarled and strong, breaking through the moss covered ground in its journey to grow.

A flash of light caught my eyes, dragging them up between the branches to glimpse a few gilded leaves. The size of my palm, they sparkled even in their singularity, but I could imagine that had its crown been full, held high above the forest, it would have shone like a star in the night. Blinded the sun with its magnificence.

Unfortunately, save for the few gossamer leaves, the tree was empty of life. Which was eerie in a way that I couldn't describe. It wasn't how it should be, my head throbbing as I tried to remember why, but nothing rose from the darkness clouding my mind.

"It's doing better than it was." Kanan appeared from behind the wide trunk, his attention fixed on the knife in his hand as he slid it across his palm. He made no outward sign of pain as the white crystal sliced his flesh, blood bubbling up almost immediately.

He flipped his hand over, let his blood flow freely over the knotted roots near the base of the tree until the stream slowed and then stopped completely. His natural healing wouldn't allow more than that, but it didn't stop him from taking the blade in his other hand and making a line down his forearm next. Stepping carefully between the crucial support system of the tree, more of his blood dropped onto the ground, seeping into the soil that fed the Eskalla.

"Kanan," I gasped, already moving forward. "What are you doing?"

He watched me approach, his brow furrowing before he placed the blood slick blade against his skin again, cutting deeply, dark red splattering the base of the trunk. "I'm feeding it," he replied offhandedly, fully focused on his task as he went to slice again, but I snatched his wrist away from his forearm before he could.

"Stop," I panted, stumbling over the last protruding root that separated us. I tightened my grip on his wrist in case he was crazy enough to try and carve into himself again. We both knew he could pull away at any time, but as I glanced up at him from beneath lowered lashes, slowly stroking my thumb against his wrist, he might as well have been powerless.

The way he looked at me… Gods, a girl could get addicted to being looked at like that. Like I was the center of his world, the force that kept it spinning. It made my heart do all sorts of funny flips, stuttering and starting, losing its rhythm entirely when he glanced down at me with such open reverence it was suddenly difficult to breathe.

"Why are you hurting yourself?" I asked quietly, dragging my fingers across his wrist gently, uncaring of the beads of blood that had rolled down the blade and were now staining my skin.

A strand of hair blew into my face as the breeze picked up, the chilly air brushing against my exposed skin. I could barely feel it as heat radiated from him in waves, sinking into my skin with every exhale that left his body.

He took the errant lock between his fingers, seemingly hypnotized by the golden curl, riveted by the shine, and it was at that moment I realized his pupils had become slits.

A dragon and his gold. Isn't that what he said? That not even the Cosmos himself could take the beast of fire and death from his treasure.

"Kanan," I called for him, letting the bond thrum between us to get his attention. His eyes snapped to mine, pupils dilating as he took me in. "Why are you hurting yourself?"

"It's the only way I could save it," he says pensively, almost to himself, distracted by some force I couldn't see. Sliding my hand up, taking advantage of whatever haze he was in, I gingerly pried the blade from his fingers.

"The tree?" I clarified. I stepped closer, pushing into him, a fluster building inside at the faint purr he released. "You're trying to save the tree? Is there something wrong with it?"

He was still watching my gleaming hair with that same beastly, near feline fascination the ancient beast beneath his skin was known for. "It hasn't been the same since we left," he answered, his tone reminiscing on memories I couldn't see. "When I came back, it was sickly, even more than it is now. I thought it was going to die, and there was nothing I could do to stop it."

I snuck a peak at the twisted trunk. Upon closer inspection I could see that the bark was black as night in some places, reminding me of Kanan's shadows, and dull gray in others. The spots where his blood had spilled were the darkest, the roots sucking in the power-filled ichor like it was water.

"It needs blood?" I asked. It seemed an odd requirement for a tree. "Why?"

He curled the lock of hair he held around his finger once more before dropping it, and watched as it fell with a shimmer of light against my chest. That inevitably drew his attention to the shifting rainbow of my dress, the white morphing into iridescent colors with every slight movement.

"Kanan." The words left my lips with a bit more force than I intended, but it did the trick, his eyes snapping to mine in an instant, a dark, consuming desire spreading through them. *What had gotten into him?*

I had rarely ever seen him as anything but in control, and this was seeming more and more like the complete opposite.

A shadow wove in between the roots, appearing out of thin air. It crawled over the moss covered ground, coiling around the trunk in order to reach out and touch the skin along my shoulder.

"The Eskalla Aboritos is the Tree of Balance. A physical manifestation of our pair bond. It is both of life and of death. Without either of us in the world," he answered with more clarity in his gaze, "it began to wither. Only my blood seemed to keep it from completely decaying and rotting away into nothing. It's still alive, but barely. My blood isn't enough, especially since we haven't reinstated that particular aspect of our connection."

There was a slightly bitter note at the end as he watched his shadow lick at the delicate skin of my neck with a covetous, almost jealous, look. "The leaves are new though," he said calmly, even as his entire person was focused on where his power touched me. "So I have some hope it'll recover."

Everything about him seemed on edge, like he was a hair's breadth away from plummeting into some unknown. I was used to the wild electricity that hummed in the air around him like a shield, zapping out at anyone brave enough to get close. The unmatched power he held within had enough of a presence to prickle at the skin even when he was at rest. I found it intoxicating in a not-so-sane kind of way, but that seemed to be the tune in which we danced around each other.

But this was different. Rougher. Less contained than his normal iron-clad control. It was raw and fierce, more enthralling, gripping, in its intensity. It felt like I was on a dangerous precipice, waiting to slip and fall into the abyss with him.

"Why this tree, though? Surely there are plenty of others that are spectacular in their own way? The Blackwood for example. Why hold on to it after all these years?" It was a harsh question, but I needed the answer.

A realization had been building inside me for a while, one that made it feel like the world was simultaneously falling apart all around me, my cage of denial shattering, while also rebuilding into something brand new. My heart weeped, broken and cracked, but the fractures were healing. It was like my chest had been crushed, my lungs unable to fill, while also taking my first breath of fresh air.

He glanced down at me, a curious expression crossing his face as if he could sense the importance of the question. "It was very lonely, those years without you. When I remembered everything, my first instinct was to immediately find you, regardless of the fact that I had no idea whether you had been reborn or not. But then…things," he choked out, frustration darkening his eyes, "stopped me from doing that. So there I was, ridiculously young, without the ability to get to you, and I had nothing. Except for Bron, but I'd never tell the cocky bastard that."

I nearly chuckled at the resigned, sarcastic comment, but his body was so rigid I was afraid anything might set him off. "Knowing you could be out there somewhere, without me, vulnerable and unaware of what we were, nearly sent me into another spiral. I considered it, for far longer than I like to think about, but with Bron's help and some…other things," he snarled this time, "I staved it off. That didn't stop the thoughts from closing in. They were suffocating. Eating away at me whenever I gave them leave. I was hopelessly alone, even surrounded by others, and there was nothing I could do to fix it."

He sounded so vulnerable, so sad, that gold-flecked tears welled up in my eyes. I knew all too well what it felt like to be alone even in a crowd. It was the worst sort of heartache, being visible but still unseen.

"And then I found this," he uttered pathetically, waving his hand at the barren, near-lifeless tree. "It was one of the only things I had left of you, and it was trying to leave me too."

A tear fell and a rumble of thunder followed. The sky had quickly darkened, a melancholic gray that matched how I felt as his words tore through me.

"Your blood is keeping it alive?" I asked weakly, swallowing my emotions.

He nodded slowly, tilting his head back to glance at the brewing storm. "It's the only thing I've found that works."

All this time. He kept it alive all this time. The last piece of who we used to be, a symbol of the bond we had shared…the love that had pulled me from a cosmic slumber and to his side during his darkest moment. An embodiment of everything we were supposed to represent. Life. Death. Balance. And all the things in between.

"Kanan?" I asked softly, tracing the strong lines of his neck.

A drop of rain hit his cheek as the storm clouds roiled above us, rolling down his bobbing throat. "Yes?"

"Do you think we are meant to make it through this together?" It was a question that I had shoved to the back of my mind and tried to ignore. It mocked me every time I thought he and I would make it past all the lies and secrets and dangers. "I mean, if you think about it, Life and Death could very well be enemies instead of lovers. Opposites clash as much as they attract. Perhaps this time around we aren't meant to start over or get our second chance."

He peered down at me, the strange mood that gripped him disappearing in a flash, the fires within sparking to life. Anguish and pain and that emotion that made me lose my breath, broke through the impenetrable walls around his heart and speared directly into mine.

He cupped my cheek with a clawed hand. *When did those come out?* Leaning down from his great height, he pressed his forehead into mine, our noses brushing, both of us aching to be closer as we breathed the other in. "I could never be your enemy."

"How do you know?" I whispered in distress, each word brushing his rain wet lips. A smattering of droplets fell against my shoulders, the cold beads rolling in between my breasts as the icy water turned my nipples into hard points. The gust of wind blew through the clearing, static filling the air, the tiny bolts of electricity prickling against my flesh. The drizzle sped up and it wasn't long before the silk dress stuck to my skin.

"Because I am yours in every way. Everything that makes me who and what I am," he panted roughly, eyes wild and full of need, "is yours. And you are mine. There is no greater certainty in this world than that."

I pressed my lips together, smothering the sob that threatened to rise, my gold flecked tears mixing with the rain that ran down my face. "What if that's not enough anymore?"

"I want you to listen to me, Atallia," he pleaded, sliding his hand through the drenched strands of my hair. "You were right when you said that I didn't know if I wanted you for you or because you reminded me of who we used to be," he said, licking his lips. "I know now."

"There isn't a second, a minute, an hour—day or night—that goes by that I don't think of you. Of your courage and bravery, how you've handled everything that has been unfairly thrown at you with a grace that is beyond reproach. The dueling kindness and blood thirst I see within you, I want them both. You are perfectly imperfect, just as I am, and I want—*need*—every part of you."

The tears were flowing freely now, carving gilded paths down my face. He wrapped a comforting arm around my waist, pulling me flush against him as he continued, "I have spent my entire life, all seventeen thousand fucking years, being feared."

I felt every word like a rough, sensual caress, and it wasn't the man looking at me but the ancient entity that lived inside him. Hungry, downright starved. "And yet you stare me down without flinching. With those eyes of yours that make my heart feel like it's exploding from my chest." His voice was breathy with reverence, a hint of depravity. "Sometimes I wonder if that's your goal. To make me give it to you. Have me rip it out with my own bare hands and present it like some kind of gift, bloody and desperate and on my knees, begging you to never give it back. Would that make this insanity, my obsessive need for you, stop? Tell me so, and I'll do it."

My heart stumbled, unable to catch its rhythm, not knowing what to do as my blood boiled, racing through my veins like the lightning that shattered the sky, igniting every part of me. Biting my lip, I closed my eyes, shaking my head slowly. I rested my hand on his chest, fisting his shirt tightly as a sob broke free with each crack of thunder, every emotion I had shoved into that desolate box in the back of my mind coming back in force.

And that's when he dropped to his knees.

Gripping my hips, he looked up at me, uncaring as the storm raged around us, nothing but devotion in his glazed eyes. A fallen angel, my dark god, kneeling before me like I was the altar at which he prayed, whispering his worship against my skin like I was his own personal salvation.

He took my wrist in hand, eyes never leaving mine, and placed the tip of the dagger I still held against his heart. I tried to pull away, but he was unyielding and pressed harder still until I felt his skin give way underneath.

"Kanan," I gasped, struggling against his strength, but it was no use. I went still, not wanting to accidentally drive the blade deeper.

He blinked through the rain, eyes glassy, and a strangely peaceful smile curling his lips. "If I am to be your enemy, my love, then carve my heart from my chest and end this miserable existence of mine. Because that is what it shall be without you in it. Miserable and lonely and without light. I love you, I have always loved you, and I will continue to love you until the stars are dust in our hands. So take it, little goddess, for it is yours. As it has always been."

He may have been the one declaring his heart, but why was it mine that felt like it had been ripped from my chest? The tattered shreds that remained ached in a way that a dagger through it would have been a mercy.

"I would never want that, Kanan," I cried, clenching the hair at the base of his neck. His powerful shoulders dropped in relief, eyes closing as his expression shifted to one of ecstasy at my touch. "I need you too much."

"Then why, sweet goddess, do you torture the both of us?" he inquired softly, his gaze still hidden. There was no judgment or scorn in his tone. It was a genuine question, one that I'd begun to ask myself more and more, and yet the answer remained the same.

"I don't know who I am anymore," I whimpered, letting go of the blade so that it dropped to the moss in between the tangled roots. Dropping into his lap, I straddled his strong thighs, reveling in the feel of him as he wrapped his arms around my waist. I cupped the back of his neck, pressing our heads together until there was no telling where he ended and I began.

"One minute I feel confident, powerful, and the next I'm second guessing every moment of my life. I can't tell what's me and what is some remnant of who I used to be. The secrets and lies and nightmares. I feel like I'm being split in half and there's nothing I can do about it," I bawled, stabbing pain building behind my eyes as the tears continued to spill. "I'm sorry I don't remember, but I don't know what's real anymore, Kanan." My voice had turned raspy, throat raw from the clawing emotions. I felt exposed on so many levels, helpless to stop feeling…everything.

Entrenched in one another, kneeling under the tree's impressive, but barren, crown, while the rain fell around us in a curtain, we were sheltered, hidden away from the rest of the world. Protected from the outside forces that sought to tear us apart. It didn't, however, save us from ourselves. Which seemed to be our greatest adversary.

He watched the emotions play out across my face, as open as a book to him no doubt, his eyes softened in understanding. Dragging his thumb down my lips, which parted with a shaky breath, he leaned in. Eyes flitting between mine and my lips, a silent question clear in his gaze. One I answered without hesitation.

Closing the distance, our lips met as a crack of lighting, arching wildly, split the sky in half, both of us groaning in relief at the contact. Electricity streaked through me as our mouths moved against each other. The prick of his claws as he gripped my waist through the silk of my gown, so thin it might as well not have been there, sent a heady, thrilling pleasure through me. Shivers coursed down my spine, thighs quivering as my core melted beneath his strong touch.

Every starved pull from my lips, each hot lick from his tongue, sent another wave of that heat coursing between us until I was downright wanton with my need for him. He held on tight, as if he could keep me with him through sheer strength. I wouldn't have put it past him to try.

The scarred, wary girl that had been abused and shunned, turned feral through the acts of others, wanted to buck against his hold, fight what he brought out of us; but there was a reason he was who he was. A warlord turned king, a god of power so immense he couldn't always keep it contained within himself. He was unyielding, conquering, a man who did not give up easily. Or at all.

He may have been a monster to others, but to me…he chased my monsters away. Forced me to face my fears when it was easier to hide behind them, giving me the space to become who I was always meant to be. I never thought I would be thankful for an arrogant, pushy asshole, but I was for him.

Instead of shrinking from his touch, I tightened my own on him, the feelings I had always been too scared to give to anyone else growing by the second. We fought, battled for control, the way we always did when we met like this, the excitement of it making my blood rush, heightening every sensation.

My bite, an amused growl from him, the scratch of my nails down his scalp, his possessive grip digging in, both of us trading sensual blows until we ultimately fell into a senseless, desperate back and forth. A frenzied push and pull that sent us careening off the precipice as we poured everything we had into the other.

We finally pulled apart, deprived of the air we had taken from each other. With each panting breath our chests brushed, steam rising from where the water hit Kanan's bare skin. The heat coming off him would have anyone else backing off, but it only made me want more. I wanted it, him, everything.

Blinking through the rain that washed away my tears, I met his wild gaze. His pupils had blown wide, turning his eyes into black reflective pools, need and love overwhelming anything else. Power raced beneath my skin as he cupped my cheek and spoke three words that healed something broken inside me. "That was real."

CHAPTER FORTY-ONE

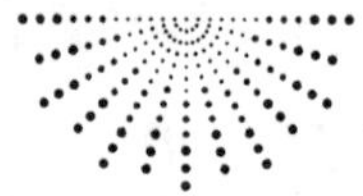

My heart raced as his words hit their mark, leaving a lasting imprint on my battered soul. I bit my trembling lip, tears stinging my eyes as every chipped, broken piece of my heart tried to come to the realization that this was real. That a love that defied the universe could exist, and that it was mine.

"This is real, Atallia," he repeated against my lips. "*You* are real. Different, similar, I don't care, because you are mine and the only thing that matters to me is your happiness. If I could take your worries away I would. I would shoulder every burden if it meant giving you the peace you desire, but I can't," he said with real pain in his voice, as if it truly caused him such. "But this, what's between us, is real. I know that in my heart, because even when the world is in shambles, this feels so godsdamn right that nothing makes sense without it."

Never in a million years had I expected such declarations from anyone, let alone Kanan. He was always so reserved, stoically observing the world from behind those carefully crafted walls of unbreakable will and feral power, yet here he was, baring his soul for me to see.

I knew what it cost him, to be so vulnerable, to put all of himself on display to be judged and hopefully found worthy. There were walls he was building even now, erected around the deepest parts of himself so that if everything came crumbling down, some semblance of himself would remain.

I once told Kanan that some people carried their scars on their skin while others held them on their hearts. It took me until now to realize—he had them on both.

And even now he was trying to make me feel better. This self-sacrificing man who had forgotten what it felt like to be taken care of, to not be single handedly shouldering the weight of the universe. He was still holding things back from me, but the more he refused to share, the more I began to believe there was more at play than I had ever realized.

There was a gaping canyon between us. Him on one side, me on the other, and he was asking me to jump. To meet him halfway and take a chance on something great. It was up to me to believe, to trust. It was the only thing he ever asked of me.

"Say something," he pleaded softly, his large hand coming up to cup my cheek. His eyes were withdrawn, unfocused, as he caressed my skin—like he was bracing for my judgment and expecting the worst.

I leaned into his touch as my cynical mind raced with a million overcomplicated thoughts. How would this work? What if I was hurt again? Over and over they went, but, for the first time, I silenced that cautious voice and let my heart speak instead. "I love you."

He froze, speechless, which suited me just fine because I wasn't sure I would be able to get this all out if he interrupted. "I'm not sure how good I'll be at it," I said, a self-deprecating laugh escaping my lips, "but there will be a lot of things we'll have to face, so maybe we give each other some grace, because truth be told, I'm a disaster, Kanan."

I could see he wanted to argue, but I pushed through, licking away the water on my lips. "I'm a mess, though I'm doing my best to figure it out. If there's one thing I know to be true, it's that my heart is yours. It's been yours for a long time. I just needed time to realize that."

I rubbed my nose against his, smiling at the disbelief on his face.

"You love me?" he whispered hoarsely, his arm around my waist tightened, fist clenching the wet silk of my gown.

Thunder rolled across the sky, a low boom followed by a crack of light streaking through the gray clouds. I nodded, letting out a relieved breath of air, a smile unfurling on my lips. It felt like I had been released from a cage, a bird set free. Chains made from my own jaded self-preservation had kept me from soaring to new heights, but no longer. "I love you. I don't know why you didn't tell me everything before and I don't know why you can't tell me now, but I'm trusting you, Kanan." I scrunched his soaked curls in between my fingers, squeezing my eyes shut, heart pounding outside my chest as I begged him, "Please don't make me regret it, because I don't know if I'll survive if you do. I want this. I want this so bad, Kanan, but there's only so much I can take before there's nothing left to give."

His brow creased and twin tears fell down the chiseled planes of his face, his eyes molten fire. He blew out a breath, a curl of white smoke twining through the air as he wet his lips. "Never." He shook his head, banishing the idea with the confidence of someone who always kept his word, no matter how few were spoken. "Never, Atalia. I'll spend every day for eternity making sure the thought doesn't ever cross your mind."

It was a promise that now lay before us, like a fragile piece of glass, so easily stepped on, broken by indifference and neglect; but it could be strengthened, forged into something new, something stronger, by the desire to keep the love we had for each other alive. Two thousand years we had waited for another chance, and now that it was here, it was up to us to protect the gift we had been given.

He was my other half, a piece of my soul that I never knew was missing other than the ache in my heart that had never been satisfied. I wanted to weep at the time we had lost. Both of us had been so alone in this world, adrift in the chaos, and now we had been found.

We moved at the same time, coming together in a clash, both of us determined to take those lost moments back. We were entrenched, consumed, with one another. Pleasure was our vice, need our master, like puppets on strings unable to break away from the demands of our desire.

The storm let out a deep grumble, rain pouring down on us from above, but neither of us cared, the erotic burn exploding from our tether sparked a fire that threatened to consume if we didn't give in.

Strong hands curved over my ass, sliding up my back. Currents of barely restrained power traveled beneath his skin, sinking through the transparent silk clinging to mine. I arched into him, my core clenching as the small stings heightened the pleasure racking my body.

A low moan escaped my lips, quickly captured by his as he swallowed the sound. I brushed against him, needing more, needing my skin on his. Thank the Cosmos he was so damn perceptive, picking up on every one of my reactions, because damn if he didn't grab my dress, dipping low along my back, and rip it open.

The rain soaked fabric tore like wet parchment, leaving my back bare to a gust of wind blowing through. The cold rain ran along the dips of my spine, a direct contrast to the warmth of Kanan's hands. The soft scrape of his claws played along, tracing the paths of those droplets.

Reaching around with one hand he took hold of the front, tearing away the flimsy gown like it was nothing. He plunged into my mouth, twining with my tongue before pulling back to sip from my bottom lip.

"I hope you didn't like that dress," he breathed without even a hint of apology. His blood ruby eyes were lowered, lids heavy as he looked over me. He took my mouth again before I could answer, sweeping in like a man possessed.

I leaned into it, coming over top of him, using my superior position to my advantage so he had to look up at me as I kissed him back. Cradling his head with both hands, I satiated my hunger for him, sucking on his tongue and drinking in his addictive taste. Smoke and shadow and just everything him.

He growled in appreciation, a hint of smile on his lips as he gave as good as he received. We both knew he was being patient, waiting, letting me have my fun as he enjoyed having me naked atop of him. The prickle of his claws as he dragged them down the length of my body in a carnal tease, the deliciously soft bite on my lip from his wicked fangs—all a reminder of my limited time, his restraint hanging on by a thread.

"Fuck the dress," I panted, pulling away to suck in a breath of air as he turned his attention to my neck. Sucking on the sensitive spot where my shoulder met the curve of my throat, he cupped my breast with blatant possession. I gasped, arching into his rough touch, the breathy noise pathetic with how needy it sounded.

My head dropped back, eyes rolling when he bit down, those deft fingers pinching my sensitive nipple. He played me like a virtuoso, reading me like sheet music, knowing how to wring every note, every crescendo from me until he stole my breath. *Who needs air anyway?*

I rocked against him, the hard lines of his body brushing against the sleek curves of mine in a perfect melody. Even through his thick trousers I could feel his shaft pressing up against me, causing an ache to build in my core. My thighs quivered, shaking from the strength of the desire rocking through me. I spread them wider, situating myself over him as I moved. Anything to lessen the burn.

His hands clenched, digging into my skin. Groaning he leaned his forehead against my shoulder, trembling as I ground against him wantonly. Any semblance of his rigid control was being shredded as I sought my release.

"Not yet you don't," he growled roughly in my ear. Then he *moved*. A cacophony of thunder followed, whips of lightning splitting through the storm clouds, as he lifted me off him and laid me down in between the roots of the Eskalla.

Kneeling between my spread legs, the look in his eyes made the hairs on my body rise. Every bit the satisfied predator, his prey right where he wanted it, a sinful smile kicked up the corners of his mouth.

Cocky as he may have looked at first glance, I could see the truth plain on his face. There was no room for feeling insecure when he looked at me like that. With pure reverence. A blatant hunger, tinged with an instability that had been building for months, years, from before we were even ideas in each other's thoughts. It was a soul-deep need that surpassed the physical, crossed the line of mortal comprehension, stepped over the boundaries that even our own people would never understand.

It was the way he traced every inch of me, as if he was afraid I'd disappear, his pupils dilating until they swallowed his glowing red irises. He licked his lips, mouth open slightly, every ragged breath leaving his chest sharply.

Fuck. He looked as wrecked as I felt.

Reaching up, he carefully undid the buttons along the side of his formal tunic, his eyes, dark as the clouds roiling above us, never leaving mine. Inch by painful inch the tunic was peeled away, the drizzling rain coating his bronze skin in seconds. He tossed it haphazardly behind him without a single glance, crawling over me with naked heat in his gaze.

Gods, he was perfect. I drug my hand over the dip of his hip bone, the dark pants he wore hung low enough for me to trace that line of muscle that never failed to make me lose my thoughts. He growled, the sound vibrating his chest, as I skated a finger along that line, just barely dipping beneath the band.

I smiled, heeding the warning, choosing instead to slide my fingers over his abdomen, tracing a thin scar that I had never noticed before. The faded white line cut across his right side, long enough to make me wonder who had tried to gut him, and if they were still alive. *Doubtful.*

Following it with the tips of my fingers, I scraped my nails up the small muscles in between each of his ribs. I did it again when he shivered under the delicate touch. His biceps tensed beside my head, a shaky breath reaching my ears as he lowered his head.

"Don't play with me, love," he purred, nudging my chin with his nose. Lifting it at the request, he nuzzled against my jaw, placing kisses down the line of my throat. "Or I might just decide to play back."

Uhmmm, yes please. The thought crossed my mind even as a short gasp broke free. His large hand, splayed across my clenched abdomen, stroked my wet skin in distraction before slipping to the crux of my thigh. Fingers dangerously close to the apex of my need, he pushed against my trembling leg. Spread wider, he settled his hips against mine, blocking out the rain with his broad shoulders.

Hand against his chest, I marveled at the contrast. He was the black of night, and I the blazing light of the stars. Separate they were beautiful, but when put together they were magnificent. No star shined as bright as one held in the embrace of endless darkness, and it was often darkness that went unappreciated. For without the stars, would anyone take the time to notice the layers upon layers hidden within?

Desire burned me, running through my veins unhindered. It tore away at my control, leaving me a panting, mindless creature seeking their next fix of dangerous, intoxicating poison. I slid my leg along the outside of his, the leather of his trousers rough against the delicate skin of my thigh, a sensation that had much more sensitive parts of me quivering in need. I curled it over his hip, nudging him closer.

I ran my hand through his mess of curls, the strands dripping wet, dragging his head up and taking his lips with a ferocity that scared me. I could have been the beast out of the two of us by the way I kissed him. Willing to drown in his taste.

A whimper crawled its way from my throat, a pressure building beneath my skin, aching with the need to be closer. Whatever entity had taken over my body, scattered any rational thought from my head, had broken me down to my base desires. I wanted to crawl into his skin and erase any space that separated us.

He groaned into my mouth, the sound pained as he took my lower lip between his fangs before letting it go with a pop. He came back with a punishing force, taking it again without mercy. We were insatiable. The both of us unable to stop, to pull back and rationalize the insanity, the desperation that gripped us.

Shadows crawled along the roots, drops of rain sending wisps of darkness into the air as they snaked through the tangle of moss and bark and thin-stemmed flowers. Placing one clawed hand above my head, he braced himself as he took hold of my throat, tilting my chin up to get a better angle to completely shred my composure. *Not that there was much left anyway.*

Fisting his hair tight, I drug my nails down his chest, hard enough to leave a line of bright red blood as his shadows moved between my spread thighs. If I was lucky he'd speed this along and I'd finally reach that peak he kept teasing me with, so I bit him back just because I could.

He growled in appreciation, but the hand around my neck tightened by a hair, the bite of his claws enough to still any thought of taking back control. *Damn lizard.*

Chuckling against my mouth he pulled back, arching an arrogant eyebrow. "I heard that, love. Patience is a virtue, you know."

Whoops. I was distracted, having sent the thought down the bond accidentally. The bridge connecting us was more present than ever, rippling with unrestrained energy, alive in a way I had never seen. Much like me, it was coiled tight in anticipation, a spring waiting to snap.

"And I hear lust is sinful," I sniped back, arching up and wiping his smug grin from his face by licking a drop of rain off his strong neck. Tracing the tendons that were as rigid as the cock in his pants, I nipped at his jaw in frustration. "I'm still burning up from it anyway, and if you don't do something about it soon, I might just commit another sin and take a knife to you. Maybe it'll encourage you to fix what you've gone and done to me."

"Done to you," he said against my mouth, a bare whisper of a kiss. He looked at my lips and hummed, raking his fangs over his own. His claws dug into the ground above my head, his gaze flitting back to mine, that stare an inferno the sun could never replicate, insatiable and merciless as they watched me shift restlessly beneath him. He smirked devilishly, but his face was stark with a kind of dark hunger that edged his words with a hint of danger. Like he was a breath away from consuming me entirely. "Trust me, love," he purred huskily, "I haven't done anything yet."

His rumble scorched me from the inside out, adding to the mounting need that had me soaking wet for a whole different reason.

I swallowed, wetting my lips as I brushed the blood that had welled from the scratches marring his chiseled chest. Rain fell on us, droplets rolling down his sides as beads of water washed everything away. Rivulets of red coursing down his perfect form. Peering up at him as I skated my fingertips downwards, I smirked. "Well you can start by taking off your pants."

He hummed again, the ambivalent noise making me want to simultaneously kiss him senseless and also smack him upside the head until I received a real response. "Why would I do that?" His hand left my throat and my breath caught as it slid down between my breasts. He may have been stroking my skin, but with every simple touch it felt like he was caressing my soul.

"I think I quite like having you at my mercy," he admitted, satisfaction in every syllable he spoke. "There are just so many fun things for me to do."

That's when his shadows tightened around my thighs. They were jerked back by the dark tendrils, held open as those strong fingers skimmed down the plain of my stomach. They didn't budge even as I struggled just for the hell of it.

Closer and closer, the tip of his claw drawing patterns on my skin as he went. He smiled, secretive and hazy, like he was in some kind of dream, teasing me further. Those wicked fingers dipped low and I held my breath, but he skated them down the inside of my thigh like the bastard he was.

A mewling whimper ripped itself from my chest despite all attempts to smother it, his dark chuckle inciting a flurry of emotions within me, like butterflies flapping their wings to the beat of the wind.

"Kanan," I breathed, voice heavy with want. The muscles in his arm tensed overhead as he leaned even closer, nose brushing mine as he hovered his lips directly over mine. He merely grinned, enjoying the little game he was playing. Heavy lidded eyes followed my every twitch and expression.

"Yes, my love?" he taunted playfully, watching me with the patience of a man who knew he had the woman he desired beneath him and had no intention of rushing anything he wanted to do. I reached for words, but I was rendered speechless by the need that was shattering my world into tiny fragments of existence, my core aching and empty, clenching with each carnal word.

I don't know how many times I tried but anything that came to mind was lost to the storm of desire in my veins, mirrored by the one shaking the skies. As I finally forced the words to my tongue his deft fingers found the source of all my pleasure.

I cried out, throwing my head back as my nerves were set on fire, pure carnal sensation a barrage against my senses. Kanan's lips parted, hovering over mine as if he could swallow the sound.

He stroked me again, rubbing my clit just enough to send me spiraling closer to that edge, barely out of reach, but not enough to send me over.

"Oh gods. Kanan," I moaned, my eyes closing in rapture as raindrops fell onto my face, drowning waves of ecstasy threatening to throw me into utter darkness.

"While I appreciate the prayers, my love," he breathed, leaning his forehead against mine as he licked the water from his lips, "I would much rather worship you."

Any words I might have said were quickly dashed away as he took my mouth, sweeping in with his tongue as that damn finger thrust inside me. I rolled my hips against his hand, bucking up into him as I melted under his lashings.

Moans and whimpers and cries, he took them all without complaint, was starved for more as he plunged his finger in and out of me, going so far as to add another. My thighs shook, the dark restraints holding me open to his ministrations were unyielding. I instinctively wanted to close them as the delicious pressure began to burn.

I pulled his head back despite his disgruntled snarl, gasping for air. Wetting my dry throat, I gave him a look that left no room for argument. "Lose the fucking pants, Kanan."

The dragon seemed inclined to listen for once, his eyes a wildfire of desire as we came back together. I'm not sure what he did, barely shifting an inch above me, and frankly I couldn't care less, because within the span of seconds my leg was wrapped around slick, warm skin instead of the worn fabric of his pants.

I groaned, raking my nails down his back, rippling under my touch, until I dug them into his bare muscled ass. We both fell prey to the other, soft touches replaced by the frantic need to be closer.

My sensitive breasts rubbed against his chest as I arched into him, nipples hard as the bullets of water hitting his back. Pressing his hips in closer to mine, the hard length of him only inches from my entrance, I felt something strange build in my chest.

The rope tethering us together came to mind, a braided bridge of black and gold that transcended any worldly means. It glowed brighter, a galaxy of light and darkness making up each strand, and as every second passed it throbbed with more power as Kanan and I touched.

Stilling above me, Kanan broke our kiss. He rested his forehead against my breast bone and trembled with restraint, shaking those dark curls as if he was banishing something from thought.

I breathed heavily, his fingers still moving inside me, stroking my inner walls in a dangerously slow rhythm that had me close to insanity. Peering down at him as I panted, my entire body vibrating with sensation, I ran a hand through his ebony locks. I leaned back into the waterlogged moss, trying to gather any semblance of thought, and asked, "What is it?"

"Our bond wants to reforge itself. Fully," he voiced quietly. He shuddered as I ran my other hand across the scars decorating his back.

"And that's a bad thing?"

"No." He released a shaky breath, and I could hear the pang of desperation in his voice as he explained, "But I don't want to force that on you if you're not ready. It doesn't always care about what we think, so I'm trying to hold it back."

Before I could respond, his fingers hit a spot that had my eyes rolling back into my head. I pressed my lips together, stifling the moan wanting to burst free. Regaining any sense of composure was like trying to wrangle a flight of sprites, flittering here, there, everywhere, always out of reach.

"What if I don't want you to hold it back?" I murmured, finally getting the lodged words out.

He picked up his head and let out a long breath, faint trails of smoke along with it. "You can't say something like that and not mean it, love. There's no going back once it's done. You'll never be free of me. Two thousand years we were separated and the universe still found a way to bring us back to each other. It seems inevitable one way or another."

The corners of his eyes creased and I could hear the pain in his voice, like the words hurt to say, but say them he did. He would never ask it of me, never push me to bond, I knew that to my very core, but I also knew it must have killed a piece of him every time he staved off the madness. A madness that must have already begun if the unfocused, fixated state he was in early was any indicator.

"And what if I never wanted to?" I asked, because sometimes I had a masochistic streak and liked to make things difficult for myself.

He was silent, and still, so still I thought he might have stopped breathing entirely if it weren't for the nearly imperceptible rise and fall of his chest beneath my hand. His shadows shivered with scarcely contained tension.

"Are you okay?" I questioned, worrying my lip as I watched every emotion under the sun pass over his face. "What are you thinking about?"

He let out a low chuckle, the sound barely human. "Oh, little goddess," he purred, "you really don't want to know what's going on in my fucked up head. It involves things like kidnapping and other unhealthy means of keeping you with me, but I wouldn't worry too much about it until after I completely lose my sanity."

At least he knows it's unhealthy. I arched an eyebrow at the response. "And how, pray tell, do you plan to keep me locked away somewhere?"

"Oh, I have my ways," he said with a smirk that was pure sex, nothing innocent about it.

"Really?" I teased, dragging my foot over his calf, "Because so far I've seen a whole bunch of nothing."

Before he could snark back with some arrogant response that would no doubt set me aflame, I pressed my lips to his. Soft and sweet, and so unlike the others we had bestowed upon one another. Heartache and loneliness and powerfully alluring love, I poured it all into the kiss. Each press of my lips to his was a wound on my heart healed.

"I want this, Kanan," I whispered when we pulled away. "I want you, and I'm not going anywhere. I don't want to be anywhere else in the world but here with you."

He looked down at me, his eyes throwing a red glow against his cheeks as they burned. I had his undivided attention, every ounce of the power he carried focused on me and the bond tying us together. If this is what it felt like to drown, I would happily sink beneath the waves and take in a breath.

"Thank fucking gods," he muttered, bringing our lips together again, and then it was all over. The tether tightened, switching between bliss and that delicious ache that occurred when stretching an unused muscle. Darkness rushed down the bond, wrapping around the corded bridge of energy, pulling to a stop in the middle. Waiting.

Doing what felt right, I let go of the reins and released control of the energy embedded in my soul. I didn't need to look to know gold energy coursed beneath my skin, my glowing core shining through.

Unlike me, my power needed no time to decide anything, immediately rushing down the bond, a cosmic burst of energy barreling towards its end, two undeniable forces seconds away from clashing together.

Removing his fingers from my quaking core, he grabbed hold of my hip. Hard. I was damn near delirious, my sense, my rationality, were lost as he angled his hips, the head of his cock positioned at my entrance. I didn't even care when his claws bit into my skin, a stream of blood rolling to the ground.

It was one moment. One ripple in time that would alter everything. The universe ran on moments like this, where a single decision to love and have hope changed the course of fate. It was astonishing to grasp even a hint of it. How such a small thing, in the grand scheme of incomprehensible powers, could set off a chain reaction of decisions far greater and have the ability to change someone's, everyone's, futures.

It was often pieces of our lives that we would never think twice about that impacted us the most. But this. This was a cataclysmic shift that would shake the world and never be forgotten.

As Kanan pushed forward, thrusting into me fully with one roll of his hips, our magic smashed into each other and the world exploded into nothing and everything. An ending and beginning.

The rain and storm clouds disintegrated, replaced by a sky of black and gold that melded into a stunning mix of oblivion and genesis. Magic spread far and wide, taking over the grove and beyond, and the world suddenly became very small. It had been boiled down until it was just Kanan and I, nothing outside of our shield of much importance as the pair bond forged itself anew, doing its damndest to make us one.

I felt like I was bursting at the seams as Kanan overwhelmed my every sense. The pleasure of it was almost too much as he demanded everything. Took everything like he had been starved of the only thing he needed to survive, and in some ways he had. Swallowing every sob and whimper he wrenched from me like I was his own personal feast. Like he had every right to them, because he did. To him my pleasure was his and he took what was his due.

I felt him under my skin, in my veins, brushing against the edges of my mind in sensual promise as every iota of my being became intertwined with his. He was everywhere all at once, pounding into me without mercy as the pair bond wove itself into the one that would forever connect us. There was no separating the two of us, where he ended I began. Or maybe it was the other way around, there was no telling. Not with the way I felt shadow and flame moving in my blood, through the sinew of my muscles, digging their way deeper until they reached my soul.

His emotions became mine and there was no differentiating

between the two. Everything he felt...gods. The slide of our sickened skin against each other, the grasp I had on his cock, the overwhelming need to possess and protect that was rocketing through him. It was too much, the bond twisting and twining faster and faster, his—my—desperation feeding its own.

It tore into the core of our beings, not the physical ones that were in the throes of passion, but the beings of energy that lay beneath the skin we chose to wear. Walls were ripped away, obstacles incinerated by its otherworldly power, nothing standing a chance as it tied us together on every level possible.

It stung, barbs of dark magic piercing through me, gilded ones fusing to him, as if telling us, reminding us, that it would not stand to be separated again. Ripping free from one another would no doubt shred our souls.

Kanan groaned, crushing the root in his grip to pieces, the intensity of the added connection doubling the fever spreading through every recesses of our bodies, both of us subjected to its gleeful fury.

Lifting his head, he looked down at me with that impossibly bright gaze, an unending, primal hunger that had overtaken any reason flooding the red. He looked ravaged, every drop of tranquility and self-control ripped away from him and replaced by a crazed, savage fervor.

His pupils constricted and dilated, back and forth, the two sides that made up the god pounding away inside me fighting for supremacy. His perfectly crafted mask of humanity was being stripped away from him bit by bit, years of craving his mate and now finally having her wrecking any semblance of logic.

Eyes on me, he nipped and licked his way down until he reached my breasts. Taking a taunt bud in his hot mouth, he sucked hard as I cried out. My nails bit into the back of his neck, gripping the small strands of hair there. He stroked a hand down my trembling body, sliding down to grasp my thigh.

Sweat covered our bodies, and I shook wildly, close to the end I so desperately craved. Each thrust pushing me further along. I bucked against him as he hit a spot inside me that had me going blind, moaning with every shift of his hips.

The pair bond blazed hot as a star, flowing like molten metal into the shimmering tether. They combined, becoming a swirled mass of energy, braided together in a way that made them impossible to separate.

Sliding up my neck, his hand rose to cup my breast as he slammed into me. I yanked his head up and fused our lips together. The kiss was punishing, as punishing as the brutal pace he set. Shadows wrapped around our legs, tying us together as one began circling my clit, pure rapture taking hold as he drove into me.

He settled his weight over me, bracing on his knees just enough so that he could use his other hand to grip my ass, holding me still as he quickened his strokes. Both of us became sloppy, chasing an end that was within reach.

The man kissed with his whole body, every thrust of his tongue matched by his cock. I could feel every pulsing inch of him as he thrust, my moans turning to sobs. Snarls of pleasure told he wasn't far behind, and as the last fragment of magic eased itself into place, slotting in perfectly, I came apart beneath him.

Magic erupted around us, light and darkness, black and gold, all flashing before my eyes as wave after wave of pleasure took me under. It was never ending, crashing through me so all I could do was hold on and submit to the intoxicating euphoria.

He lifted my knee higher, pushing in deeper, which only made the ebbing pleasure flare again. He thrust harder. Once. Twice, and on the third he growled, shuddering against me. Lost to the surge of release and the connection between us, I wasn't surprised when I started hallucinating.

The delicate golden leaf unfurling on the branch above me was a beautiful mirage, sparkling like the embers of magic floating to the ground around us. And when a dozen more burst to life, I couldn't help the dreamy, satiated smile that broke free at the sight of them.

CHAPTER FORTY-TWO

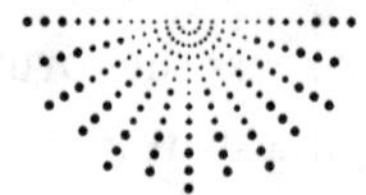

The next morning, light filtered in through open archways, slashing across my eyes and waking me long before the rest of the world. The faintest hint of the sun pierced the fading darkness of the sky. The deep navy of night blending slowly into the soft hues of sunrise. Light blues and pale oranges, the iridescent white of a blazing star only just pushing past the horizon somewhere far in the distance.

It would be an hour or two yet before anyone else woke, the few moving around at this time of day were a hell of a lot more productive then I. Wallowing in a warm bed sounded like the better option to me, at least for a few more minutes.

It didn't help that it was the most comfortable bed I had ever indulged in, although this was the first time truly seeing it. The second Kanan had used his shadows to portal us to his—our—rooms, he threw me onto the overly large bed, and from there we lost ourselves in one another. Over and over again, until eventually exhaustion forced the both of us to sleep. The compulsive need singeing our every nerve had made everything else irrelevant. The second he put those talented fingers and wicked tongue to work, the room didn't seem all that important.

It had taken me months, and a hell of a lot of revealed secrets, but I finally figured out what the gigantic tower, amidst the spires that decorated the front of the fortified palace, was for. I originally believed it was part of the disarming facade that made the citadel appear a lovely show piece of a city. A delicate jewel in our crown of power, easily attacked because a god's pride knew no bounds, and no one would dare launch an assault against it.

How wrong those enemies would be. Every inch of Eskira was armed to the teeth, soldiers and weapons alike were hidden in plain sight, and kept well oiled at all times.

However, amongst the other towers—which were all used as launch points for the airborne Cynths and for enormous contraptions that could shoot armored bolts, enhanced by Aetherian magic, miles into the distance—were the rooms of the Divine.

It was a haven in which we could escape the rest of the world. High above the city, fluffy clouds and a river of magic within reach, a wall of doorless archways that led onto the balcony carried in the cool breeze. The scent of the mountains, pine and snow, and the ocean winds, laden with salt and static, filled the space. White gossamer curtains framed each of the three entries, fluttering into the room with every gentle current.

The heavily reinforced balcony was a perfect perch from which Kanan could look down upon the whole city in his dragon form. The stunning view that I could see from here was a shock to the senses. I would only have to step out onto the sleek cream stone and I'd be standing amongst the clouds, the last remaining rays of moonlight caressing my skin.

The room itself was thoroughly lived in, with pieces of Kanan everywhere I looked. An elegant piano, polished to a shine, was stationed by the three steps leading up to the balcony. Stone turned to a fine grained wood, a rich mahogany that highlighted the handwoven rugs covering the floor, the black detailing as striking from afar as it was up close.

Stacks of books and sheet music lay scattered across the room, sheathed blades were lined up against the far wall, including his giant greatsword, the black blade a void of color along the wall, and a cart, loaded with sparkling glasses and a decanter of his favorite drink, was parked near the seating area in the middle.

What was even more curious though, were the touches of femininity throughout the room. The finely crafted furnishings, all bearing carvings of Allasea's flourishing nature, the slender pitcher of lunai next to his drink of choice, the metal forged sconces that looked like large golden leaves, smaller decorative versions covering the walls around them; even the vase of extraordinary blooms, blood red and drooping from their stems like tiny bells, sitting on the low table were all signs of a woman living in the space.

All signs of me living in it.

He wouldn't have… *Would he?*

A glint caught the corner of my eye, pulling my attention, and there, placed casually on the bed's side table like it hadn't been weeks since I'd thought about it, weeks since it should have died, was a flower.

Six diamond-encrusted petals, dipped in pure starlight, lay against the dark wood propped up by gilded thorns. Gold specks dusted the wood, the three small stamens in the center dropping the shimmering pollen. Gently brushing my fingers along the nearest petal, the flower seeming to lean into my touch, the same scent from that small infirmary room came crashing back to mind. A night's breeze, filled with the energy of the stars, a hint of iron-laced blood mixed with the bloom of wildflowers. New life, death, it hit me all at once, the flower a mere vessel of an idea. The potential for something different.

Last I'd seen, the otherworldly flower had been shoved to the bottom of my trunk alongside the Monarch's history book. At least a week had passed since I stepped foot in that room, if not more. *Where did it come from?*

The bed dipped as a heavy weight shifted next to me. A smile, intimate and genuine, blossomed on my lips. *That's where it came from.*

Rolling into his side, I rested my chin on his shoulder so I could look up at his sleeping face. I placed a hand on his chest, careful not to wake him, and had to smother a laugh when the soft purr vibrating his chest with every exhale—a constant throughout the night—grew louder.

I squeezed my eyes shut, pressing my lips together as my shoulders quaked with restrained hysterics. I couldn't wait to tell this ginormous man, a dragon turned god that sparked fear and respect into the hearts of everyone who looked upon him, who wielded a sword larger than some men, and found joy in slaughtering our enemies, that he purred in his sleep.

I had never seen him so relaxed. The sharp lines of his face had softened, his full lips settled in a pout, so unlike the usual blank mask he wore. The militant way he held himself was nowhere to be seen, the rigid set of his shoulders having fallen. As the first rays of sun began pouring in, casting his honey brown skin into light, I couldn't help but think he was a dream come to life. A conjured hallucination, beautiful beyond compare. The intensity of it making it hard to breathe.

The bed covers had fallen to his hips, exposing the strength of his body. Power and hard work honing every inch of him into a weapon built for war. Had someone told me he was human, I would have laughed in their faces. He was too unearthly, the primordial being he truly was sat too close to the surface to ever be considered human.

The facade he put on for people was just that, a facade. A costume meant to put the rest of the world at ease. He spoke, walked, acted exactly how he was supposed to in order to keep the sheep from realizing a wolf…a dragon was amongst them. The few times he let it slip, fear was instilled into their hearts and minds, just enough to keep everyone in line without much work. A perfectly crafted way to keep order and peace.

But here and now, no one around to witness exactly who and what he was, when he didn't have to force the mask into place, it fell away and left the truth of him behind. Looking at him was like staring into endless darkness, floating through the absence of space, where color and light were nonexistent. The beast living inside him was a breadth away, skating beneath the mortal skin of a man. Fire and shadow and death. The ice cold of the universe matched by the inferno of an exploding star. A contradiction in every way, yet somehow perfectly compounded inside him.

And he was mine. All mine.

It was crazy to think, but it was a truth instilled in me so deep there was no room for any other possibility. It was something I knew without thought. My memories had eluded me thus far, but some things were beyond that, etched into my soul and out of reach of even my own meddling.

I didn't know how long I lay there, tracing meaningless designs on his chest as I listened to the relentless pound of his heart, the beat of a war drum against my ear. My breaths had long since matched to his, until I felt every inhale and exhale keenly. An ache in my chest had been building since waking. A need to talk to him, see those fiery eyes peering down at me through the glaze of sleep.

It was scary, how badly I desired him even when he was so close. If he felt this every time I was around, I couldn't imagine how he had restrained himself. The newly forged addition to our bond certainly didn't help. Even now, almost ready to surface from the last dregs of sleep, I could feel him as if he were inside my mind, body, and soul.

There was a certain kind of relief that came from resolving years of loneliness, that bleeding gash in my heart suddenly gone. All the anxiety and hopelessness, the feeling of being lost in the middle of nowhere, fading away along with it. It was like I could breathe for the first time, no pain or heartache in sight.

He shifted again, turning his head away from the morning light. The faint stubble covering his jaw gave him a more ruffled appearance, his hair mused from where I ran my fingers through it countless times in the night. I wondered how many people had seen him like this. Disheveled and unprotected from the world, his walls of stoicism and boredom having dropped from exhaustion.

What would he look like when he woke? When he glanced down and saw me next to him? My lips curled deviously, my fingers stroking down his chest, past the exquisite view of his abdomen, and dipped beneath the sheet covering his hips. His breathing jerked as I skated along his naked thigh, following the long lines of muscle, before drawing back towards my target.

Sliding down his long frame, a wicked pleasure rolled through me as his brow puckered, body tensing at my loss. I ducked under the covers as he released a sleep riddled groan, rough from disuse. I scraped my teeth softly against his thigh, and giggled when he jerked. I continued playing, stroking a teasing finger along his warm skin, enjoying my uncontested time to do so. When he sucked in a startled breath, I knew I had finally woken him.

Taking his cock in hand before he could so much as mutter my name, I wrapped my lips around the head and sucked. He jerked in surprise, a pained groan tearing through the air as his hips thrust up instinctively, pushing him further into my mouth.

"What do you think you're doing, love?" came his husky voice in my mind. Instead of answering I tightened my hand around the thick base of him, using my tongue on the rest of his impressive length. His hips bucked again, every delicious muscle flexing under my touch.

I moaned as the flavor of his skin hit my tongue, salty and somehow so very him. It wasn't surprising in the least that this part of him was as hot as the rest. Heavy and warm against my lips I brushed my tongue along the underside of his cock, relishing the shuddered breaths and the curses I forced from him.

It didn't take long for him to take back control. Reaching down blindly, he tossed the sheets back before wrapping a fist in my hair. He glanced down at me, panting with each hard drag of my mouth, thrusting up into them with abandon.

"Harder," he snarled, a trace of that inhumanness in his words, as I dragged my teeth over him. Doing as told, I squeezed harder as I took more of him into the hot recesses of my mouth, tugging carefully with my hand before pressing back up. Jaw tensing as a strained groan made its way free of his throat, he looked down at me with such hunger I felt it to my core. "That's it, love," he grunted, rocking harder, faster. "Gods, you feel so good wrapped around my cock like that."

A thrill zipped through my body, almost as good as the feeling of when he gripped my hair tighter, his hips losing their steady rhythm and becoming choppier as we chased his release. Determined to get him there, I took him as far as I could without choking and swallowed, closing my throat around him.

Every muscle of his body tensed, his spine going straight as his release hit him. He threw his head back and roared in pleasure, shaking as I swallowed every drop of him. I licked him clean, smiling with every quivering jerk and twitching muscle as he came down from the high.

Looking up at him, I squealed in surprise as he yanked me up towards him, rolling us over until I was flat on my back. I let out a proud chuckle as he wrapped an arm around my waist and pressed his weight into me.

"Good m—"

I was cut off as he forced my mouth open, sweeping in and swallowing any sound I would've made. The kiss was quick and full of promising retribution that made my toes curl.

We came apart panting, and I glanced up into his heavy gaze, a serene half-grin plastered on his face. "Good morning." Lips brushed mine in a small peck, his smile growing as I shivered with desire.

"Morning," I whispered shyly, unsure where we went from here.

He chuckled, deep and strong, pressing kisses to my neck in gentle affection. "You can't act all timid now, love. Not when you just woke me up with my cock in your mouth."

He kissed me again before I could answer, taking his sweet time. Sedated passion flamed across our bond from both sides, neither of us ready for the rest of the world to catch up.

"How long do you think they'll leave us be?" I asked, savoring these moments of doting attention.

Nipping at my neck until I turned it in invitation, he placed a smattering of tender pecks along the arch of my throat. "For as long as I tell them to," he replied arrogantly, laving his dexterous tongue over his small bites.

I snorted, teeth digging into my lip as he continued indulging himself. "Yeah right. I doubt we get an hour before someone comes knocking."

"They wouldn't dare," he assured me, a thread of something darker in his tone. *Something tells me this dragon doesn't like sharing. Here's to hoping no one is stupid enough to interrupt.*

Even he didn't seem convinced of that though. Rolling us, he settled me against his massive chest, the cavern of fire inside his ribs making him perfect to cuddle up to as another gust of wind blew in from the balcony.

I rested an arm on his shoulder and leaned my head against it so I could watch him. His dark brow was furrowed in deep thought, and I could almost see the cogs of his mind turning over his thoughts. "What is it?"

"I met with Synval after we arrived, he was waiting for me on the wall." Tucking an arm beneath his head, he stared up at the ceiling as he drew lines up and down my bare back.

"And?" I prompted. "What did he say?"

He glanced at me from the corner of his eye. "He thinks I'm right, asked around the barracks to confirm and apparently there have been very few sightings of the prey Cynths that were taken. As in none at all." A shadow crawled up from the floor, slithering over the bed erratically. "As far as he's aware, the passageways his scouts use in and around Eskira are secure, but if anyone could find them and get past our safety measures, it would be our own people…no matter how far gone they are to Kasis's corruption."

It definitely posed a problem for Eskira's security, poked holes in our defenses where we couldn't afford them, but plugging all the passageways would be both pointless and ineffective. Not only would it be nearly impossible to find them all if they were as extensive as Kanan described—even with the scouts help I doubted they could recall them all, and old paths left abandoned from disuse could still lead into the city—but it would also hit us severely, the influx of information we received from all over the world mostly came from the runners using those very same routes.

I ran my lips over the back of my arm in thought. "Does he have any ideas?"

He shrugged, jaw clenched. "Close off any nonessential roadways, alert the entire network, and then it seems the smallest of us will have to enter this fight. Guarding the entries themselves, allowing any incoming messages to make their way in, whilst warding off any wraiths that may try to sneak through. Hold the line long enough that the army can be alerted."

It was like he was already watching them die and could do nothing to stop it. An army in itself, made entirely of the prey Cynths, keeping the knife that hunted us in the dark from hitting its mark. If Kasis tried to catch us off guard, use his scouting parties as a way to infiltrate behind our walls without much notice, it would be the ferociously fanged mink, the ground mice and grouse, dashing hares and arrowing birds, that would meet his forces first. Prey keeping the predators at bay.

I could smell the spilt blood now.

"We'll do everything we can to make sure that doesn't happen," I asserted, there was no other option. Forces were at play though, far more than we thought. Malicious ones that would happily see us fail.

He shifted beneath me, turning more to look at me. "What's that anger for?"

Startling, I tried not to be unsettled by how much he could feel now. *Vulnerability can be a good thing so long as it's with a person you trust.* I just had to keep reminding myself of that. I twisted onto my side, slid my leg over his, and put words to the feeling, thoughts threading through my mind on an endless loop. "Do you remember what that kinsman said to us in Ellenia's lodge? The way he spoke to us? He knew things, said they knew when we had left for Rhaera and were able to prepare. The fissure, the girl they used to reel us in, enough wraiths to keep you occupied while they took me." I shook my head, the pieces didn't fit and the why terrified me. "Even if Kasis has been able to get wraiths into Eskira, we were in the dungeon when we decided to leave for Rhaera, only a few people knew where we intended to go."

"Do you know what you're implying, love?" he asked with a raised eyebrow.

I wiped a hand over my mouth, before meeting his smoldering

gaze. "That we have a traitor amongst us. Someone close enough to be a part of our plans. I know what it means, but you can't deny it's the only thing that makes sense."

He sighed, rubbing his eyes. "I'll have the weapon stores moved, shift the patrols around, change up the configurations. We'll keep it quiet until we know more, the generals will understand, and the commanders won't question me."

It was the best we could do without alerting whoever it was that we were on to them, any suspicion and with the fissures possibly at his disposal, Kasis could be at our gates by sundown.

"I wish this wasn't how we had to spend our morning," he whispered. "You deserve the quiet, peaceful mornings. Talks of love instead of war."

I narrowed my eyes at the brittle edge to his voice, so contrary to anything I'd ever heard from him. It was disconcerting to say the least, and something I would need to rectify.

"Then what is this?" I asked, rolling over to reach for the dazzling flower on the side table. I placed it on his chest carefully, ensuring the thorns didn't prick his skin, and glanced up at him with an expectant look. "Unless I'm mistaken, this is the same flower that was on my bedside in the infirmary when I woke up, and the one placed on my balcony the night I met you. Although that can't be right," I said with a shake of my head, strands of golden hair falling around me, "because I distinctly remember placing it in my trunk."

Pink stained his cheeks as he stroked a finger down one of the diamond petals. "Stardews," he murmured.

As the sun continued to rise, transforming the sky from the night's colors, that of raven feathers, to the soft haze of morning, its rays hit the flower. Like the multi-faceted glass domes of Hassere, it captured the light, entrapping it within in order to sparkle.

"They used to cover the Eskalla's grove, you know." He pinched the stem, twirling it between his fingers. Its radiance shattered with the movement, throwing light all around the room. "They began dying as soon as you were taken. The black ones went first, then the white," he explained, eyes shuttering with darkness.

The air turned heavy, brought down by the weight of the memories. In some ways, I guess I was lucky to not remember it all, to only have to deal with a few recurring nightmares instead of lifetimes of them. The weak, keening cries from inside that cell, the soul wrenching pain as the soft notes of a lullaby left my lips, the sounds echoing in my ears well after I had woken, cautioned me that not all memories were good ones.

"I never let anyone into that grove, and I was so far gone that by the time I noticed," he sighed, swallowing the emotion in his voice, "this was the only one left. I couldn't stand the thought of losing that last piece of you, so I put it in stasis, like the Descendents in a way. It'll die eventually, but not for a very long time."

His pain was my pain. A thousand cuts, each slicing through my skin with ease, would have had less of an impact than the battering loss coursing through my heart. Bruised and broken, jagged pieces of glass shoving into the walls of my chest so that every breath felt like a punishment.

"There's a lot of magic in that grove?" I questioned through the agony ripping through me.

He let out a weak chuckle. "It's where we bonded the first time too. I think the only reason the tree hasn't died is because it was born from our joint power. A combination of life and death, a tree that feeds on sacrifice and growth. The flowers were the same, but your absence was felt keenly by the world."

"The Year of Sorrow," I finished.

"Sorrowful indeed," he murmured, running a finger over one of the glinting thorns. Sharp as a spear, it left a thin line of blood behind. "It was always yours, so I wanted you to have it even if we never got our second chance."

I traced his jaw, tipping his head towards me. "All that time. You waited all that time?"

"Always," he answered gently. "I would have loved you through lifetimes, even if you never saw me."

Tears wet the corners of my eyes, the millennia his yearning had withstood, as limitless as the darkness inside him, hit me all at once, and was matched by the fervor of my own, new but built on the foundation of something old. It enabled the words he needed to hear to come forth. "I see you."

He blinked furiously, swallowing hard as he let the stardew drop from his fingers. The flower hung in the air, floating on its own before zipping back to the table as Kanan took my face in hand. Bringing his lips down on mine, I opened without hesitation, melting under his touch. His warmth, the desire he wrought from me, and the absolute devotion with which he looked upon me—like I was his everything—was a craving which I was helpless to resist.

I had never been so thankful to be naked as he shifted over me, skin brushing skin as his tongue tangled with mine. I was dizzy with the potency of our bond, every thrum of pleasure he felt rippled down the bond and compounded on my own, only to be sent back to him. A vicious cycle of rapturous sensation that we could not escape. Gods, who would want to?

Rising to his knees, he stared down at me like he was sin incarnate, a roguish smile lighting his face. The brilliant red of his eyes had been swallowed, turning as dark as the night in which lovers whispered their deepest thoughts to one another, nothing but pure, unadulterated need in his gaze.

He flipped me over onto my stomach, hands gripping my waist, and pulled me up to my knees. I barely had time to gasp in surprise before he thrust into my warmth. It was embarrassing how easily he slid in, but I stopped caring the second his hips rolled into mine. He groaned deep in his throat, the sound ragged, more debauched than anything I had ever heard. Balanced on my elbows, ass in the air, the angle allowed him to push in even further than he had before.

I felt every inch against my inner walls, the slow rocking pace he set stealing every thought from my mind. I had been relegated to mindless pleasure and choked cries. Pressure built in my core, fluttering with every carnal, unrestrained noise that left his mouth.

"I need more, Kanan," I pleaded on a whimper. "Harder."

A deep moan left me as he pushed all the way in, the base of him stretching me almost to pain. The sharp bite, however, was nothing compared to the flash that rocked through me when his hand connected with my bottom. The sting quickly shifted to pleasure as he wrapped the very same hand around to play with my clit.

He carried on with the steady motion, his finger teasing me mercilessly. "Don't tell me how to fuck you, love," he ordered from above, his voice in shreds. "You're forgetting I had thousands of years to learn every inch of your body."

Winding a hand around to my front he pressed me up, my back to his front. I leaned into him even as he continued thrust, I bit my lip, cries still escaping. His large palm slid up until he was cupping my breast possessively. Lips brushing the shell of my ear, he whispered, "You taught me long before you ever taught those pretty fingers of yours. I intend on savoring every second of this so if I want to go slow, I'm going to go fucking slow."

And I'll be damned if he didn't stick to his word. He was unhurried in his movements, every one as agonizingly indulgent as the next, the onslaught was nearly too much, but release was in sight. It built gradually, almost lazily, sluggish waves of pleasure overtaking me, and I knew it was only going to hit me that much harder.

Lost to the feel of him, I hadn't realized anything had happened until the most violent snarl I had ever heard erupted from Kanan. So loud it shook the walls of the room, splitting the air with savage power, I jerked in his grip. He held me tighter to him, barely allowing an inch of space between us.

I looked over to catch him glaring at the door to our left with such ferocity I was surprised it hadn't caught fire. His chest vibrated against my back, a murderous growl tearing through his clenched teeth.

Someone on the opposite side banged on the heavy wooden door until its frame shook. Bron's muffled voice came from the hall. "You know I wouldn't be here unless I needed to be."

Kanan paused for one second before dismissing his friend with a barbaric grunt, turning his attention back to me. Cupping my neck with one head, thumb stroking over my cheek, he angled my head in order to take my mouth from behind. The position pushed me further into his thrusts, his hips pounding furiously into me, hitting every sensitive spot inside me.

Arm around his neck, I fisted the silken strands, each of my cries consumed by his dominating sweep. My nails dug into his forearm as pleasure licked at my every nerve like a whip cracking against the skin. I was wild and unrestrained. The moans stirring from my chest were rough, primitive sounds. His growls even more so.

Bron beat on the door once more, yelling something I couldn't quite make out over the sounds of our combined panting.

"Maybe we should see—" I gasped, eyes rolling to the back of my head, as he rolled my clit between his diligent, talented fingers, stealing my breath all over again, "—what he needs."

He leaned his forehead against mine, his chest brushing into my back with every pull of air he took. "Then you better come quick," he groaned. Each word was punctuated by a hard thrust, the entire length of him filling me until I felt him in my throat. "Because I don't care if the whole damn palace hears, I'm not stopping until I feel you coming around my cock."

With that he redoubled his efforts, fucking me like a mad man. "Spread those legs for me, little goddess," he ordered roughly.

Widening my stance, thighs shaking from the effort, he angled me forward so every roll of his hips had his cock hitting new places inside that I didn't know existed. My core clenched around him, swollen and hot and not ready to let him go.

The bed frame hit the back wall as we moved together seamlessly, a beat to which our crude noises intertwined, becoming steadily rougher, harder, and faster.

My release hit me like a strike of lightning, slamming into me with a force that nearly had me seeing black. I rolled my head into his neck as I hung on desperately, the shockwaves ripping through me and demolishing any sense of self.

His snarl of pleasure was strangled as his own release hit. I knew the grip I had on him was harsh, but I was unable to stop the spasms hitting me.

Pulling out with an exhausted groan, Kanan gently laid me atop the bedsheet, the rest of the covers laying scattered around us, and stood to his full height. After taking a stumbling step, catching himself with far more grace than I would have at the moment, he wiped himself clean using one of the discarded blankets, and tossed it carelessly to the side.

Taking the small fur throw that had been kicked off the edge, he shook it out before tossing it over my limp, naked body. He gave me one last look, the emotion in his burning gaze rousing something warm and fuzzy inside my chest that beat against the ribs that kept it caged.

Bron knocked again. And again. *He has a death wish.*

Expression shifting to one that said he'd delight in peeling Bron's skin back, Kanan stormed over to the door—still naked—and flung it back.

Kanan cursed, "The world better be on fucking fire and falling down around us if you expect me to leave this room, Bron."

The broad shouldered man, pale as Taipea's moonlight, didn't so much as glance down at Kanan's bared form, his molten silver eyes boring into his friend with apprehension. "There's a fissure in the forest. The Orama has requested the queen's presence.

CHAPTER FORTY-THREE

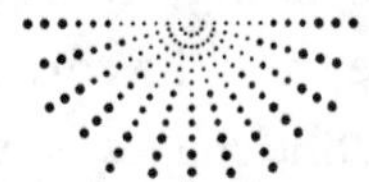

I dressed faster than I ever had, not even questioning how Kanan had tailored clothes that fit me perfectly. I threw on the supple leathers without complaint. The man in question, however, was dragging behind me as we stepped out into the hall, his anger a living thing clawing through the air.

The silver Cynth, and menacer of doors, leaned up against the far wall, arms crossed over his chest as he waited for us, a nonchalant grin pasted on his face, and an arrogant omniscient gleam in his eyes.

"Bron," I said in greeting, flicking my eyes between him and the grumbling giant behind me whose mood had taken a sharp dive off a cliff from peaceful to downright bloodthirsty.

Smile deepening, he dipped his head in deference. "My queen. I hope your morning has been…restful."

I rolled my eyes, passing him on my way to the only other door along the rounded corridor. Unless one wanted to test Kanan's good will by flying up to the balcony, the Aetherian powered lift, with its sparkling copper door, was the singular way to reach the Divine's rooms. *Cosmos, I hope I don't have to keep calling myself that.*

"How did you get roped into collecting us?" I asked as we stepped inside. Kanan stood behind us, a gloomy shadow silently glaring at the constricting walls that jerked with every shifting movement. His hair brushed the top of the enclosed box and the wide berth of his shoulders nearly touched the walls. With both him and Bron packed into the space, I was plastered against the side.

The white-haired saberthor let out a sigh, pulling a thin piece of straw from his pocket. The stalk was no bigger than my smallest finger. "A scout reported the fissure less than an hour ago, they located me first and I happened to be drinking my woes with a few of the generals," he paused, looking at me from the corner of his eyes, "Zani and her squadron were there as well. She suggested we pull straws, and I lost."

"You're a telepath," I scoffed in disbelief, "you wouldn't lose at a game like that."

He quirked an eyebrow at me and then back at Kanan. "Trust me," he chuckled, "no one *wanted* to come up here."

The lift rattled, a concerning noise coming from the side walls. I threw out a hand to steady myself at the same time Kanan's large palm gripped my hip, holding tight until I regained my balance. "Then maybe you shouldn't have," Kanan grunted, furiously burning a hole into Bron's head.

"Stop glaring at your friend," I warned, smacking his chest with the back of my hand. "You don't have that many to choose from if you kill this one."

"Maybe because I don't like that many," he muttered in complaint, eyes narrowing further at Bron's teasing grin. "Fewer by the second."

Bron and I shared an exasperated look. The big warrior looked away and I pressed my lips together to stop the laughter wanting to shake free, both of us leaving the disgruntled dragon to his sulking.

"So you lost, huh?" I couldn't help nagging at him after all of his teasing. His annoyed look told me all I needed to know.

"It made her laugh. Winning, " he clarified after a beat of silence. He shifted uncomfortably from side to side, barely able to reposition in the tight space. "She hasn't done a lot of that recently."

Suspecting that was all I would get from the closed-knit hybrid, I settled with the knowledge that my friend may not realize that she had the original Descenedent, one of the most powerful of his kind, wrapped around her finger.

Making our way through the multiple levels and gates of the palace was enough to make me wish Kanan had flown us instead, but thankfully Bron thought of everything.

Three horses were waiting right outside the towering walls. The dark gate, large and reflective, with its meticulously carved dragon — an exact replica of Kanan's first form—would guard the keep in our absence. Escaping most of the lingering, watchful eyes of the city's citizens due to the early hour of morning, we made it through the streets of the upper city without much hassle.

The guards stationed along the rampart bowed as we approached, keeping silent as the gate master called for the doors to open. The ride didn't last long after passing through, Zanaya's voice reaching us as we entered the tree line.

Nala spun as we approached, smiling wide before dropping into a dramatic curtsey that would have made any court aristocrat proud. "You know, the first time we met, I had a feeling you would make life more interesting."

"I don't know if I should take that as a compliment or not," I remarked, jumping from my saddle.

Kanan and Bron dismounted behind me, quickly knotting off their reins on a low-hanging limb. Kanan had grown more reserved, his anger had turned into a stabbing burn through the center of my body, like a knife that had been sitting in the fire too long. He strode past, a prowling beast on the hunt, bright eyes peering through the brush for its quarry.

"Where is it?" he demanded gruffly, not even sparing the group a glance as he stalked through the trees.

"Through here." Saanvi appeared from behind a large navy oak, waving for us to follow. "Nothing has changed as far as we can tell from the scout's report. It's definitely the island."

Following behind, we reached a tall archway made from the twisted trunks of two trees, their bark a stark white. Pushed together by storm winds, they must have eventually grown into one another, their canopies and root systems becoming one.

But it was the fissure quivering underneath that held my attention. It was a door, an opening to another world...or at least, another part of this one. It was as if someone had taken a blade and sliced through the barriers of the world, splitting space to join the two lands that had a continent separating them. The air shimmered around the sharp lines of the doorway, glittering in the small bits of colored light that broke through the surrounding canopies.

Past that intangible opening lay an expanse of rolling hills, verdant green and shades so pale I could not think of a name, the wondrous sky reminiscent of those above Eskira. The crashing sound of waves against a rocky shore spilled through the rift, the faintest scent of ocean air drifting into the forest. A billow of fog rose in the distance, crawling over the ledge that I could just barely make out along the horizon.

Zanaya glanced over her shoulder as we approached. Squatted next to it, her and Orion were inspecting the fissure, our group's silent giant going so far as to stick his hand into it, his gray skin layered with the pattern of marbled stone. As he pulled it out, the marbling fell away, leaving behind normal supple skin. A dusting of morning dew covered the hairs along his forearm, but only up to where he had stuck it into the fissure's opening.

"Nothing seems amiss," the burly Aetherian announced. Standing at our approach, he bowed as Kanan stormed up to the fissure, barely paying Orion any mind as he glared out across the island hillside, searching for something. Someone.

"We threw in rocks first, My Lord," Zanaya explained, demonstrating with the one she held in her hand. The stone sailed through the gap unhindered, landing in the grasses on the other side before rolling a few feet. "And then Orion turned his arm to stone, we figured it would be the safest way to try and send someone through."

"Where is she?" Kanan growled, ignoring Zanaya's explanation. "That fucking witch. Where is she?"

Zanaya shifted back, self-preservation kicking in as Kanan's shoulders heaved with rage. No one wanted to be near a dragon god when he was in a foul mood. Bron stepped around to her side, positioning himself by her shoulder.

"The scout was the one who relayed the message," she answered. She kept her chin high, spine straight under his misdirected fury. "By the time we arrived, she had already gone."

Kanan snarled, glaring at her as his eyes turned to slits, blood red and murderous. The trees shook from the noises leaving him, leaves rattled on their limbs, and the ground vibrated from the force.

"Hey!" I shouted down the bond, *"I don't know what's gotten into you, or why this seer gets you all twisted up, but don't you dare take it out on my friends."*

He glanced over at me, a storm of emotion in his gaze. There was an inferno building inside him and I was worried what would happen if he didn't get control of it.

"I've never seen you so angry," I whispered calmly to him. Even Kasis rarely elicited this kind of reaction.

He inhaled heavily through his nose and released a smoke filled breath, the tense lines of his body finally relaxing a hair. *"I'm sorry, love. Bad memories."*

"I get it, but I'm not the one you need to apologize to."

"I apologize, Commander," he repeated out loud, voice only marginally less gruff. "I should not be taking my frustrations out on you, that was wrong of me. You and your team have done well."

My friend dipped her head in acceptance, her loose curls brushing the sharp lines of her cheeks. "Thank you, my king, though apologies are unnecessary. Having a fissure this close to the city has me on edge as well."

Kanan and I both knew that wasn't the reason godly wrath was slashing through him, demanding to be released on anyone in his way, but he nodded anyway, accepting Zanaya's worry as his own.

"How long has it been here?" I asked, crossing over to Kanan's side to inspect it myself.

The tension in the air fell away now that the harrowing threat that Kanan's aura produced had passed. "The scout reached us only an hour ago." Zanaya eyed the others uncertainly. "We were, uhmm, incapacitated at the time."

"Drunk off our asses is what she means," Zander interjected, rounding from behind the fissure. "We were still in the Rapscallion, we passed out there last night, and were nursing some killer hangovers," he shivered in horror as his face turned green, "when the scout ran in to find us."

"Oh gods, don't remind me or I'm going to puke again," Nala whined, clutching her stomach for dear life. "It's a good thing we heal fast or someone would need to kill me to stop that headache."

Zanaya shot them a reproachful glare, before shifting her attention back to us. "About two hours now, my queen."

"That's the longest I've seen one stay open," I muttered to Kanan. "Perhaps it means something?"

"It means she's playing games with us," he growled, his narrowed eyes all but daring for the Orama to show herself.

Bron moved to Kanan's side as they investigated the mysterious breach themselves, leaving the rest of us to finally wake up from the night's activities.

Nala and Zander tripped over themselves to get away from Zanaya's burning stare, running to avoid the gust of wind she set to knock them off their feet. I chuckled watching her chase them around with the gales, succeeding on the third try and blowing them into a heap on the ground.

A near-silent shifting caught my attention, Orion and Saanvi casually observing from the edges of the group as they were wont to do. A thought stirred in my mind and I walked over, tugging the leather cord from under my tunic, the gorgeous rough-cut gemstone dangling from it was warm from laying against my skin.

"I believe this is yours," I said on approach, lifting the beacon stone over my head.

He shook his head before I could even offer it back, lifting a hand to stop me. "If this is going how I think it will, then you'll need it again before long. Keep it, I'll have some peace at night knowing you'll be able to reach us even if something happens."

I tilted my head up at him, gratitude for the friendships I'd made settling in my heart. "Are you sure?" I asked softly. "It's your mother's. I wouldn't want to take that from you."

He smiled brightly, black eyes as warm as any others. "She would be proud to know I was using it to help a friend. One day I'll get to tell her about how I was friends with a queen, so really, you're doing me a favor."

Saanvi and I shared a look. Our gentle giant had a heart as big as he was, and it was a shame that more people didn't get to see it.

"Well, if you ever want it back," I explained, pulling the cord back over my head and tucking the crystal beneath my neckline, "all you have to do is ask."

His smile said he never would, but I made him promise nonetheless. "I expect to hear more about her."

His smile somehow grew bigger, laugh lines creasing his cheeks and the corners of his eyes as he agreed. "I would love to."

Shaking my head at him, I switched my attention to Saanvi. "And you," I pressed, raising an eyebrow. "Are you ever going to tell me your story?"

She smirked, secrets dancing in her serpent-like eyes. "Maybe."

I glared at the non-answer. There was an itch in the back of my mind that begged to know more about the puzzling woman, something about her sparked a curiosity within me. "What about your partners? Do I get to meet them?"

Her smirk widened, showing the tips of her fangs as she repeated, "Maybe."

I rolled my eyes, laughing with her at the irking response. I opened my mouth to ask her more about them when a familiar growl cracked the air. Whirling around, I found Kanan pacing in front of the fissure, his hands planted on his hips in frustration.

"What is it?" I called out, forehead furrowing in concern. Bron shot me a pleading look that had me moving quickly. The forest had darkened, shadows crawling out from amidst the trees as they slid closer to their incensed master.

"What?" I whispered to Bron. The both of us watched Kanan pace, back and forth back and forth, like some caged animal snarling against the injustice of being restrained.

Bron sighed, reaching up to undo the bun holding half of his white hair up, and raking a hand through the loose strands. "You were already planning on going to Corosa, this makes it quicker and easier. The Orama has asked for you specifically, which means there's a reason. I told him that maybe you should go."

"She's not going," Kanan barked, spinning around so fast even the shadows trailing behind him reeled back. "It's too dangerous. Who knows what that senile old bat wants with her. Nothing good comes from dealing with that witch. Nothing."

"Kanan," I voiced calmly. "This was the plan. Now we don't have to take the time to reach her, she's come to us." He dropped his head, shaking it back and forth as I spoke. "You know this is the only way we can figure out what Kasis is up to, we talked about it. I'll go, ask her some questions, and then come back."

"She has a price, love," he rumbled, refusing to look up at me. "She always has a price."

"Then I'll pay it," I whispered as I reached him, his body frozen still from the conflicting emotions shredding him apart. He knew I was right, but everything inside him fought against the idea of putting me in danger. It was sweet, how much he cared, but we were facing annihilation. A small sacrifice would be worth it if we saved all that we loved.

His fists clenched and unclenched as shadows crawled up his legs, the pointed ends of the tangible darkness struck at the air like snakes. "Fine," he relented. "We'll go."

"No." I stopped him with a hand to the chest. Pressing my lips together, I took a deep breath as I peered up at him through lowered lashes. His gaze begged me not to, but I had no choice. "Just me."

"Atallia," he warned, emotion thickening his tone. "You know I can't do that. I can't lose you again."

"You won't," I promised. "This is the only way for us to protect the city and get the answers we need. She's requested me, which means you need to stay back and guard against Kasis. If he knows we're gone, he could use it to his advantage and strike while we're weak. You know he will."

His jaw twitched as he ground his teeth together, the grating noise reaching my ears even as I continued, "We would be leaving everyone defenseless if we both left right now. You need to stay behind and prepare the city for what's to come; it's only a matter of time before there's an attack. He's been too quiet. No response after we destroyed one of his outposts? That's strange even for him."

"You can't ask me to put others before you," he begged for only me to hear. *"I don't think I'm capable of it."*

I brushed his jaw sweetly with the tips of my fingers, sweeping them down until my hand rested over his heart. It pounded beneath my touch, steady and ferocious and unbreakable. My fierce mate, never allowing me to be relegated to second place. It was a kind of love that would heal the wounded, lonely child inside me, but today I needed something else from him.

Stepping forward, I leaned in and placed my lips against his heart, letting him into my mind with an ease that spoke of knowing someone so well that they became a part of you.

"You are the first person that has made me feel truly safe, made me feel alive and seen in a way I never thought I would. I know what you feel for me and I can only hope and pray that I can be the same for you. When I'm with you it's like the world is right again. I can't imagine putting anything before you. Before us. But I'm asking you to, and I'm so sorry for that. You are my home, my world, and nothing will change that fact; but we'll need a place to build our life together. This city, our people, they are good. They are good and kind, and they look to us to protect them. I may not always understand what it means to be a queen, but I do understand that. So please, I'm asking you, Kanan, to trust me and protect this piece of my heart."

He closed his eyes and released a pained breath, his chest rising and falling raggedly. When he opened them, they were fire encased in glass, beautiful and wonderful. So much rode on trust, used it as a foundation on which to build something truly indestructible. I had taken that first step, had leaped into the unknown for him, hoping he would catch me, and now it was his turn.

I waited with bated breath, the world seeming to still until it was just him and I, like it had always been. He wet his lips and nodded, leaping in return and taking my hand. I smiled, watching his eyes brighten at the sight.

Pressing up onto my toes, I kissed him gently, taking in the feel of his lips on mine. I brushed my nose against his as I pulled back. "Thank you," I whispered.

His thumb brushed my cheek affectionately. There was a war raging inside him, everything rebelling against the idea of sending me away, but he stayed true to his word and I loved him all the more for it.

"Bron," I called, waving him over from where the group had given us some privacy. "We're ready."

The Primal raced over, unbothered by his friend's earlier mood. "What's the plan?"

"I'm going to go through and speak with the Orama," I informed him. "Kanan will stay here and help guard Eskira and anywhere else Kasis might think to attack."

"I'll go with," Zanaya interrupts, coming up from behind Bron. "Saanvi can take over as interim commander while I'm gone, she knows what she's doing, and that way if we can't get back through the rift, you're not alone."

Kanan visibly relaxed next to me, his relief palpable through the strengthened bond. If taking Zanaya with me would help him feel better about his decision then it was an easy concession to make.

"Thank you," I whispered to my friend, reaching out to squeeze her hand.

She tightened her grip on me back, grinning wickedly. "Can't let you have all the fun can we?"

Bron stepped closer, tightening our circle. "Alright so Zani and the queen will go to Corosa," he clarified, not seeing how Zanaya jumped in surprise at the use of her nickname, "while we fortify our strength for whatever Kasis decides to throw at us next."

"Yes and I think we can use this to our advantage," I added, the thought popping into my head as I glanced over at Kanan. "He can explain later, but make sure to tell the Council we've both left. Hell, let the whole city think we've gone. Kanan can use his shadows and stay hidden."

Bron's brow was furrowed, but he nodded without hesitation. "Do you want me to say anything specific about where you two have supposedly gone?"

"Keep it to the truth," Kanan chimed in, catching on to my idea. "Say we've gone to see the Orama like we planned, make an excuse for the Commander's absence, and leave it at that."

"Easy enough." The saberthor peered over at Zanaya with a confounded expression, a multitude of emotions crossing over his face.

As we moved closer to the fissure, my heartbeat quickened, the rhythm stumbling as it tried to keep up with the faster pace. The last time I had gone through one of these, I had been beaten and kidnapped. That little girl's face, knife protruding through her mouth, still haunted me.

Our group followed behind, watching on in worry as Zanaya and I prepared to cross. Even Nala looked concerned, a stone-faced Zander standing over her shoulder.

"Ready?" I questioned, glancing over at my friend. She had a stubborn tilt to her chin as she tied her hair back, and intense conviction hardening her eyes as she took my hand in hers.

"Let's do this," she declared confidently, and together, hands clasped tight, we stepped through the fissure and into the unknown.

CHAPTER FORTY-FOUR

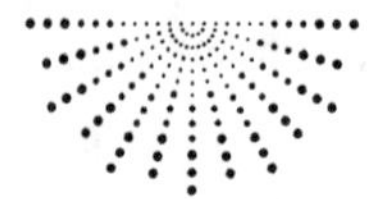

A surge of static energy rolled over me as we passed through, sending all the nerves in my body into a panic. Instinct nearly took over, my grip on the cosmic power living within me loosening as alarm screamed through me. The primal, incorporeal part of me, the one made of energy and light and all things life, roared in agitation as it armed itself against something bigger and far badder.

My foot hit the ankle-high grass of the knolls that spread across the Island of Corosa, and as I stepped out of the fissure and onto a different land than the one I had stood on only two seconds before, the irrational apprehension, a chilling fear I hadn't expected, was washed away.

Whatever had tipped off that inhuman side of my brain lay hidden, showing itself for a split second before retreating into the wind to watch from afar. My magic settled, but the wariness did not completely leave me, the hairs on my arms standing to attention. I kept my eyes peeled as Zanaya joined me, looking for the power that had caused such a reaction.

The aether that made up my being was of the Cosmos, a direct line of his power. If something here made it that jittery, then I needed to be on my guard.

"You okay?" I asked in concern as Zanaya bent over her knees coughing, each harsh sound was followed by her gasping for air. Laying a hand along her back, I allowed some of the excess energy filling me to sweep in and help her adjust. Whether she knew it or not, her spark had sensed something as well and reacted poorly to it. I watched our surroundings, my head on a swivel, ensuring nothing snuck up behind us as she caught her breath.

"Atallia! Can you hear me?" Kanan's voice reached my ears, sounding like he was underwater. Muffled slightly, I watched his lips moving on the other side of the fissure, and could just barely make out the words. "What's wrong?"

"We're okay!" I yelled back, uncertain if he could hear me. "There's something about the fissure—"

Without warning, the rift collapsed, closing in on itself in a blink of an eye. Kanan's fear-filled eyes were the last thing I saw as Eskira's forest disappeared completely. Panic flooded the bond, his emotions overwhelming him to the point of suffocation. Even as I jumped around to look for the culprit, I sent waves of calming energy towards him. There was no way I would be able to concentrate if he was losing it, and I couldn't have him flying here to reach me—we needed our plan to work.

Zanaya sucked in a full breath of air, her chest heaving from the effort as she straightened. "There goes our way back. I guess it's just us." The words were raspy as she filled her lungs with much needed air.

"Are you sure you're okay?" I asked, focusing my attention on what I could fix. Figuring out how to get back to Kanan would have to wait, right now we needed to get our answers and make sure we didn't die in the process.

She nodded, clearing the last of whatever force had struck her from her throat. "All good. I don't know what that was about, it felt like my spark was trying to tear itself out of my body."

What the hell?

I shot an uneasy look her way, alarmed by what that could mean. She shrugged, rubbing her arms as if to chase away a chill. "Trust me, I don't get it either. I mean, Corosa is a paradox in general, so it could be that, but I've also never gone through a fissure before so who knows."

We were atop one of the many hills that covered the island for as far as I could see, the edge of the cliffs that touched the ocean were far in the distance. "What do you mean by that?" I probed, striding towards where the hill began its descent down.

She moved with me, surveying all around us. "Well, Corosa kind of exists as its own entity. Things here are always strange, it's in the air or something. Nothing ever works the way you think it will," she scoffed, "which is probably why the Orama lives here. She's an odd one from what I hear."

"Then let's get what we came here for and get out. We'll have to figure out a way back to the city if another fissure doesn't open, but once we do, we should be able to make it back in a few days."

"Uhmm, that's the thing," she said hesitantly as we crested the hill. "Time doesn't work like it normally does here."

I whipped my head around to look at her. "What! What the hell does that mean?"

Grimacing, she pointed down into the vale. "No one knows for sure, but we think it has to do with those things."

Looking to where she pointed, my jaw dropped. Tearing through the ground, surrounded by hills on all sides, were towering jagged stones that sliced through the sky with their height. *How the hell did I miss those?*

There were seven of them in total, imposing and eerie in their own right. The dark stone was cracked in several places along the sheer faces, light shining from within, giving the appearance of lighting shattering across a stormy sky. As a sharp breeze blew through the valley, a thin, chipped piece fell from the top of one of the great sentries before smashing into a million pieces along the ground.

They stood evenly spaced in a circle, at least a hundred feet separating them from each other. Together they appeared like sentries, guarding whatever was in the middle. From our position atop the hill we couldn't quite see what lay amongst the stone towers, a hedge of protection from those that sought to take a peek.

"What—"

"The Eye Stones," Zanaya answered without prompting. "Before you ask, no one knows what they're for or why they're there. Corosa is usually left alone because of the way it bends reality; even the most curious of scholars are wary of coming here for fear of losing too much time. The Orama doesn't help either, she's been known to chase off anyone brave enough to try and study them further."

"So they're just…there?" I exclaim, waving my hands towards the bizarre structures. They had to have been at least a couple hundred feet tall.

"Pretty much," she answered. "Don't worry, Descendents have been confused by them since the dawn of our time, you're not alone in how you feel."

If no one had figured out what they were—what they did—in the entirety of the Descendents' existence, it might be best to keep it that way. As much as I craved the truth of things, sometimes things were better left alone. There were some answers that weren't worth the trouble they'd bring.

Pivoting on my heel, I turned in a circle, looking over all I could see. "Do you know where we can find her?" I couldn't seem to shake the heavy presence that permeated the air, keeping my magic on edge. "The less time we spend here the better, I think."

"I'm going to go out on a limb here and say we should try the door with the old woman standing next to it," she suggested, shock entering her voice.

Sure enough, off to the right, partially hidden by the black hedge stone, a circular door had been built into the side of a hill. A hunched figure, that I could scarcely make out, stood in front of it, staring in our direction. A chill raced down my spine, that cautionary feeling overtaking me once again as my power lifted its head, aware of something I was not. The figure turned away, as if sensing we'd seen her, and walked through the door. Which remained open.

"I guess we're supposed to follow," Zanaya muttered warily. "Into the dark hole with the creepy seer who likes to take her payment in blood."

"Fantastic," I remarked sarcastically, marching off towards the Orama's cave with a confidence that felt all too fake. I didn't have the time to wait and bolster my nerve. If the island had a way of messing with time, who knows how long we would be gone if we didn't hurry. Kanan and our city could be facing a threat right this moment and I would have no way of helping. Speed was our only hope at this point.

Reaching the Eye Stones was a trek, the valley they took up was easily the size of Eskira's lower city. The grass brushed against our ankles as we plowed on, blowing sideways from the ocean breeze. Loose strands of my hair blew across my face, the salty spray and cool humidity sticking to my skin.

The Sea Smoke, the eastern barrier that hid Allasea from any mortal ships that tried to cross the channel, rose into the air off to our left, swelling high enough to climb over the green hills and touch the clouds in some cases. The fog undulated with the changing air currents, swirling across the sky like a painting.

The Smoke was well known, even in Rhaelyth, for its ability to obscure all sight. The mist could get so thick that any boat that even attempted to enter quickly lost all visibility and never returned. It was one of the many boundaries that separated the two countries, one magical and the other...not. There was a section of the Blackwood that lay to the south, separating the island in half, but as far as I knew, no one ever attempted to lay foot on its rocky banks.

"My gods," Zanaya whispered, drawing my attention. "They're huge."

I tilted my head all the way back, the Eye Stones jutting into the sky like dormant giants, slumbering peacefully for the time being. We were ants in comparison, easily broken under the weight of the power pulsing from them, shaking me to the bone. *So much power.*

"Let's keep our distance," I suggested quietly. There was an unnerving amount of energy bouncing around the stones, pinging off of one another over and over again. It crackled over my skin and small pieces of my hair lifted from my shoulders. I was somehow both terrified and drawn to the mysterious power that flowed through each of the stones.

"Come on," I urged, taking the far route to the cave, around the outside of the stone circle. There was no way in hell we were walking through it. Our luck, the magic would kill us and leave our bodies in piles of charred, smoking bones. Which was a fucking gruesome thought.

We made it to one of the hundred-foot gaps along the circle, finally catching a glimpse of what lay in the middle. Half as tall as the seven stones, though enormous by any definition, a chunk of crystal was embedded in the ground. It was irregularly shaped, craggy and uneven in a lot of areas like someone had taken a hammer to a larger piece and a fragment had broken off.

The pristine crystal was transparent, holding almost no color to it, allowing me to see all the way through to the other side. As I took a step forward, the light hit from a different angle, exposing a kaleidoscope of different shades and hues, unmatched by anything I had ever seen. By the next step, it was gone, vanishing in the blink of an eye and leaving no trace of the mesmerizing display. It disappeared so quickly I was half sure it was just a figment of my imagination.

Doing my best to ignore the power radiating from the glass-like stone, though the pressure was attempting to crush my chest like I had a thousand pound boulder sitting atop my ribs, we finally arrived at the door.

The circular entry had been dug into the mound, carved with an unknown power that had left behind markings. The delicately curved patterns appeared almost intentional with the intricate detail. Swirls were surrounded by tiny individual characters, situated along the arch of each spiral. Dizzying lines, wavering downward along the curvature of the dirt and stone walls, had similar ones as well.

A well-worn trail led right down the middle of the dirt floor, a shallow furrow in the ground, indicating years of use. It led somewhere, that was for certain, but with no light illuminating the eerie space, the trail ran straight into darkness. Whatever lay beyond that was a mystery.

"Do you think we need an invite?" Zanaya pondered out loud. Her voice wavered slightly, and though the bold stare she sent down the tunnel did not yield, I could tell my friend was shaken. I couldn't blame her, I was too.

I was stopped from answering as a chilling voice reached out through the darkness, croaking from somewhere deep within the burrow.

"Brought a friend did we? Hmm, should I be insulted?" The distinctly feminine voice was full of scrutiny. Old as the universe itself, the strings of reality crooned as they were plucked apart by the cutting edge of each word, a chorus of a thousand vocal cords echoing alongside. "I requested Her Majesty's presence, Zanaya Zuberi. You will wait outside."

Zanaya's eyes widened, shooting to mine as my stomach threatened to flip, bile rising in my throat at the thought of being alone with the seer. Reaching out, she took hold of my arm.

"Atallia," she cautioned, shaking her head in doubt. "Maybe we shouldn't."

"I do not like to be kept waiting, especially not by those who are young enough they still need their asses wiped." The bad-tempered derision was shouted down the path. The echoing voices, not all of them human-like, made the churlish comment even more disturbing. Zanaya's disturbed gaze met mine, before we both looked through the unsettling doorway again.

Blowing out a short breath, I gathered my nerve. "I'll be back, stay here and make sure nothing blocks our path out."

I stepped through the door and didn't look back, knowing every instinct inside me was warning me to run, and if given the opportunity, self-preservation would take over. Panic threatened to swarm me as the pair bond with Kanan went dim, the strong pulse of energy across the tethered bridge was my only anchor. Placing one foot in front of the other, never deviating from the worn path, I trusted my feet to lead me through the darkness.

I could have easily summoned some light. Calling my power forward, directing it at will, became easier with every attempt, but I didn't trust it not to react badly and attack whatever it felt was threatening me. Something told me the Orama may not take kindly to any display of aggression. The last thing I needed was a seer—though I was starting to seriously doubt that designation—as an enemy.

The tunnel seemed never-ending, going deeper and farther than I thought possible. The only way I could tell I had even moved forward was the drop in temperature, the air cooling with each step taken. I kept expecting a dank, moist scent to invade my nostrils, but was pleasantly surprised when a vaguely sweet fragrance began to fill the space.

It reminded me of lavender, if the small purple flowers had been dipped in blood and resided in a seamstress' workroom. The needlewomen in town had always smelled similarly, the distinct aroma of freshly spun thread, made from a variety of fibers, clung to their fingers like honey. The smallest hint of iron spiking the air from the small pricks they sustained from their work.

The first glimpse of light finally appeared, the tell-tale burn of a fire. There was a faint lingering of smoke as I approached, but for being underground, the air was mostly clear. A room took shape as I walked out from behind a crevice, a slit in the wall leading into a much larger space.

Circular in nature, and made entirely of dark rock, the cave was larger than I predicted. A vaulted ceiling lent the bonfire roaring in the middle the air it needed to breath, vents all along the rock face taking the resulting smoke away from the main chamber.

Three uneven tunnels around the room broke away in different directions, no end in sight from what little I could see of them. The walls were bare, except for the same patterns that lined the path in, the markings changing in a variety of ways with each detailed pattern.

Then, from somewhere in the darkness, that same eerie voice sang, "I've been waiting for you."

CHAPTER FORTY-FIVE

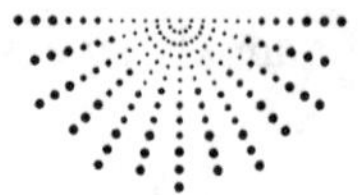

My blood turned to ice in my veins, the world stilling around me, only the faint sound of my breath filling the dead silent room. An ear-splitting shriek, claws raking against stone, rang from the tunnels.

"It's been thousands of years since we've last talked." The voice came again, vibrating against the stone walls until her voice was all around me. Her unhurried footsteps clipped on the surface of the stone, slowly stalking toward me from the darkness. "And now you stand before me once again, young one. Seems little has changed."

Shadows danced along the far walls, the light from the fire creating monsters from the darkness as the panic welled inside me once more. Through the gloom I could just make out the shape of some obscured figure. Hiding in the shadows like a coward.

"Are you done?" I bit out, narrowing my eyes at that short, hunched figure. "I've come for answers."

She chuckled, a raspy broken huff that reminded me of the snippy old women who enjoyed sharing their judgements of others freely. "You ruin my fun." The sharp click of her tongue cracked through the air. "I know why you've come, it was me that summoned you after all."

Shuffling forward into the light, the infamous seer finally came into view. She couldn't have been taller than five feet, the dusty leather sandals she wore, the ties wrapping around her narrow ankles, barely giving her an inch. Old as she looked, her skin was a smooth pale white, such that, even in the poorly lit cave, I could make out the faded black markings crawling across her body.

The tattoos were more intricate than the scribbled designs on the walls, artful strokes crawling down her arms, and I peaked the cryptic symbols that covered her legs through her shift, the airy material showing off her bony form.

The markings continued over her chest, ending with flourish along the curve of her neck like someone had taken a dry paintbrush that had been dipped in black ink and traced some incomprehensible map along her skin.

The slight tilt to her shoulders, the weight of time pushing them inward, did nothing to take away from her presence. There was a magnitude to her that I had rarely felt, similar to what others described Kanan and I of having, yet she didn't seem to notice its effect.

She slanted her head at me, the dull lilac of her hair, dirt streaked throughout, fell past her shoulders. Tiny beaded braids were tangled amongst the rest, the metal catching the sensuous light with a silvery gleam. Her unbelievably pale eyes met mine. Cloudy gray near the pupils, whatever color remained slowly leached away, almost blending in with the white's of her eyes near the edges.

A knowledge unlike anything I would ever know shone through that unsettling gaze like threads on a tapestry. For the longest time I thought I had carried the eons of my lives with me, the passage of time having put its stamp on my soul, but her...she was that time. Looking at her was like looking at the sun, an inevitable, unchanging entity of power that just *was*.

And here I was, sassing her.

"What is your price?" I demanded, my tone sharper than I intended, but then again, I had never done well with my back up against a wall. And that's what this felt like, a beast backed into the corner by some unknown. More powerful or less? It was one answer I didn't want to know.

The old woman chuckled again, staying along the wall as she circled the fire. She reached out to brush her fingers along the surface of an old mirror. Dusty and in desperate need of a polish, it barely reflected anything. The old wooden frame appeared gilded, like handcrafted metal, but it was chipped, worn from years stuck in this cave no doubt.

"Why would you assume there is a price, child?" she asked, glancing over at me curiously. "Isn't it I who requested you come? Perhaps I am feeling benevolent and wish to help simply out of the kindness of my heart."

I caught the snort that wanted to break free. That certainly wouldn't win me any points. Disrespect really didn't seem to be her thing.

"I was told questions always come with a price," I responded. For some stupid reason I moved farther into the cave, inspecting everything within eyesight. "Do you expect me to believe that has suddenly changed?"

"Your mate holds a long grudge. I must say I am quite impressed." She turned her back to me, clearly unbothered, and fiddled around with baskets of gray wool that were lined up in stacks near the back. A broken spinning wheel leaned next to the pile. Several of its spokes were broken off, but the tip of the spindle looked dangerously sharp.

There was a really big part of me that ached to ask her why Kanan hated her so much, but that would require a question and questions came with a price no matter how sly she acted.

"What is your price?" I repeated.

She straightened, scanning me with eyes that did not flinch nor look away when they met mine. A shiver worked its way down my spine, but I held strong, meeting her head on in whatever fucked up mind game she was playing.

The wrinkles around her thin lips deepened as a pleased smile quirked at the corners. "That depends, what have you come to ask?"

"Kasis," I offered in lieu of a question, not willing to test the waters until the terms were set.

If anything, my obstinance seemed to satisfy her more, a gleam sparking somewhere within those near colorless depths.

"Old demons then." She tasted the words, pausing to consider my payment. "Your blood, child, that is what I require. Three questions, three drops."

"Four," I countered immediately. "Three for my questions and one to absolve Lord Cashim Zuberi of his debt to you."

She laughed, but this time it was humorless, dry and a little defeated. "Ahhh, I admire your courage, young one, but unfortunately Cashim Zuberi already knows his price, as does the other, and it is one that can not be taken back."

I had no idea what she meant, but it wasn't good judging by her expression. "You could take it back," I argued. "Tell him that the debt is paid."

"I cannot," she said almost in apology, "but for what it is worth, he accepted without complaint. Three questions, dear one, you may ask me three questions."

I wanted to get angry, yell at her for sweeping my concern under the rug, but it would be no use. Two thousand years she had held onto his debt, and now, all of a sudden, he had been called upon to answer for it. It didn't bode well for whatever it could be.

The Orama shuffled around the room, tidying up random bits and bobs, cracked jars filled with needles and thimbles, spilt wood oil and neat boxes of sewers thread. "You may as well sit," she said offhandedly, gesturing to the feather-filled pillows arranged around the fire. "I would suggest you think carefully about what you plan to ask, I don't do take-backs."

Of course she doesn't.

So I sat. And sat some more, debating what to ask her. The wrong questions and I could leave here with nothing at all. With the right ones, we might finally have what we needed to win this war. A war that Kasis started out of jealousy. Envious of what his brother had that he didn't.

"The only way to stop this war is if we stop Kasis, so," I queried, "how do we kill the God of Chaos?"

"Hmmmm," she hums, shaking her head. "A good question from your perspective, but there are better ones."

She lowered herself onto a cushion across from me, the only thing separating us were the wild flames alive in the hearth. "As Life, Goddess of Beginnings," she began, testing the title on her tongue as if unsure of it, "you technically have the choice to kill anyone you wish. Wipe away their beginning, refuse them access to the living world, and well…they have no ability to impact it."

Hope blossomed in my chest, the first rays of light breaking through the gloom after a year long storm.

"Though I caution you on the consequences of such an act. You need to ask yourself, goddess," she warned," if you *should* kill him. It is a mighty power indeed, but one that has to be used wisely."

The gravity in her voice made me pause, stopping the relief spreading through me with a raised hand. Why wouldn't I want Kasis dead? For all intents and purposes, he was as monstrous as his creations. The pain he caused had hurt so many, whatever good there may have been inside him was long gone.

"If I don't kill him, then he kills Kanan and I, and the world will be doomed."

Pulling a long stretch of yarn from her pocket, she began creating perfectly spaced knots along the main body, several braided rows hanging down into her lap that already looked completed. "Kasis has no way of killing you himself anymore than a human does. It is not within his purview to do so. Whatever he may say, he's as powerless to that as any other. Though…there is always that which is outside his means, should he find a way to access it." She continued her work without so much as a glance up, stringing together designs I wouldn't have thought capable with just her fingers. "That was two, what is your last question girl?"

A triumphant smirk grew. "That was a statement, crone," I contended, returning the chafing sentiment. "Not a question."

Her fingers stilled, and for a second I regretted my comment, but as she peered up at me from her hunched position over her work, she grinned. "Clever, clever girl. I always did like you."

I blew out a silent breath of relief. She could probably make my nightmares look like daydreams with one cryptic remark about my future.

"Second question then," she conceded, going back to her work which is when I noticed her nails. Long and pointed, like the tips of a dagger, they worked together similarly to the knitting sticks I had seen Maris's use whenever she attempted to pick up the "asinine hobby," as she liked to call it. Except these were no dulled wooden needles, no they moved with razor sharp precision, plucking and pulling at the loose threads as she wove, even cutting through the yarn like shears when needed.

The heat from the fire licked at my skin as I thought over my next question. The overwhelming pressure of this place was starting to wear on my senses, the need to hurry up before I became a frazzled, anxious mess building in the back of my mind. It was like something in the walls was telling me to go, to run away and never return. It was unnerving to say the least.

Repositioning myself on the cushion, my boots scraping on the dirt floor, I asked my second question. "How can we find the cure for the Warp?"

"You have already found it," she answered calmly, engrossed in her work.

"That was vague," I couldn't help but snipe.

She huffed, sounding very much like the old woman she looked, though that couldn't have been further from the truth. "Vague questions get vague answers. Ask me better ones and I'll give you better answers. I thought you were clever, please do not insult my judgment by turning out to be an idiot."

Kanan was spot on, I couldn't help but think. *She is a senile old witch.*

Cantankerous as she was, she was also right, however much it irked me. It wasn't a worthy question. I had hoped for more, but at least we now knew the antidote was something we had. Now we just had to figure out what that was.

Question after question popped into my mind, hundreds of variations to ask her. I could ask for clarification on the antidote, but it was a risk. Then there was Kin of Chaos, the wraiths, plans for war. So many things that we needed to figure out.

I ran my hands over my face, relentlessly trying to wash away the stress without much success. Ultimately I went back to Kasis, the start of all of this. "Why is Kasis taking the magic he's collecting from the wraiths to Vallenia?"

She nodded, seeming to like the question, but her face gave away nothing. "Because that is where his stockpile is—the root of his stolen power, if you will. The Sulrin in Rhaelyth was the first to go, wide scale testing to see if absorbing magic into a vessel was possible and then learning how to perfect it. Once he had that, his wraiths were deployed to take the rest."

She must have seen the confusion on my face, the question ready to jump from my tongue if given the chance, because she sighed, weighing her choices. "He may have made you stewards, but you're shit for gods," her derision was more annoyed than cutting. "The Sulrin is the stream of magic in the sky. All magic on this planet was formed from that magic; it is atmospheric. Integral to the planet's ability to sustain itself."

"I never knew it had a name," I admitted. The magical river in the sky—the Sulrin—was always there, it had never occurred to me that it might have had a name. A purpose.

"There are a lot of things that have had their names erased from history," she murmured under her breath, a hint of sadness that I don't think she meant to allow, entering her eyes. Her hands had stopped weaving, the echo returning to her voice, as she sat deep in thought.

There one second and gone the next, she shook herself free of whatever had grasped her. Looking around she caught sight of me. She tutted, setting her work down on the pillow beside her before pushing up off the ground far more smoothly than a woman her age should be able to. "Those are your answers, far more than our agreed upon amount might I add. Time for you to go."

I blinked in shock at the abrupt change in tone, getting to my feet without another word as she muddled about the room.

"Go home to your mate, girl," she said quietly with her back to me. "Enjoy the time you have together, and prepare. Share your joys and losses, hopes and dreams and nightmares. Share your memories and secrets with someone who will hold them tight and never let them go."

Her words struck a nerve, one that I knew was still raw no matter how quickly it was trying to heal, so as I moved back to the cleft in the rock face, I couldn't help muttering, "If only he would share his."

It was silent as I walked off until she suddenly asked, "Are you still mad at him? For how he handled things."

Looking back over my shoulder, her expression was one of genuine curiosity, and it was then that I realized. The Orama, for all her grumpy moods, was nosey. A certified meddler. That or perhaps she got bored, lonely, stuck in this cave all by herself. It had to grate on anyone, even whatever she was.

I'd like to think that's why I answered, or maybe it was because I was hoping for someone to understand. Either way, there was something about the way she asked that made me share what only I knew deep down.

"I love him. I love him so much it hurts sometimes. He's the part of my soul that I'll never be able to replace for fear that it will destroy what's left if I lose him, but," I paused, swallowing, "I think a part of me will always feel hurt that he kept things secret. Important things. I try to look past it, try to understand, because what we have is wondrous, but I don't know why he did it. If I just knew why, there would be nothing that could stop us."

Silence.

An understanding look.

And then…the truth.

"Because I forced him from telling you all those years ago."

CHAPTER FORTY-SIX

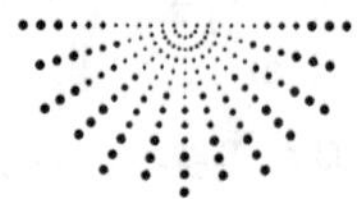

I was stuck, incapable of moving from my spot. My heart stilled within the confines of my chest, ribs constricting upon the organ that had lost its rhythm. A tremble worked its way through me, a full body shake that consumed any semblance of control I had over myself.

"Wh—" I gasped, sucking in a huge gush of air, somehow finding the strength to fill my lungs despite the shards of glass currently stabbing through my chest. A tidal wave of emotion swept me under its powerful crest, rolling through me with unstoppable force, a grief like I had never known spreading through every fiber of my being. Swallowing, pushing through the pressure that squeezed at my throat, I choked out something resembling actual words. "Wh—what do you mean?"

The old woman stepped forward, her nimble hands twisting over each other as she approached. There appeared to be genuine sorrow in her unusual eyes as she gazed up at me, her short frame seeming to hunch even more in the face of my pain. "When he came to me after your departure all those years ago, he did not stop to ask what my price was for his question," she explained, power radiating through her voice as she recalled the memory. "He didn't realize what had happened until it was too late to take it back. I tied his tongue, kept him from revealing anything to you no matter how much time passed, using the blood I took as payment."

The air was knocked from my lungs once again. A broken sob tore free of its restraints, pained and confused, shattering the peace I had crafted from the fragments that were left behind from Kanan's supposed betrayal.

I made myself understand his reasonings, came to realize that what we had, what we could build together through the millennia, was much bigger than any singular heartbreak. Now—*gods, I can't breathe*—now I find out that my dark god, misunderstood and feared by everyone, had been as helpless as me. Unable to share the one thing that would have incinerated the wall that stood between us. The one thing that would have taken away all the anger and hurt that wedged between us.

Can't, he had always said. Never *won't.*

Something clenched at my heart, talons digging in and refusing to let go until it felt like I was dying right then and there.

Years. He had been taking punishment for something out of his control for *years.* Another keening cry ripped from my chest. He'd been taking punishment from me, never once fighting back or denying my rage. He took it without complaint, knowing I needed an outlet for my pain and anger and panic. He took it as if he felt he deserved it.

Tears streamed down my face as my heart broke all over again, but this time it was *for* him. He had come here, asked his question, for me. There would have never been a blood tie without me. He gave everything, took every harsh comment and spite-filled dismissal without complaint *for me*. Everything for me.

Oh gods.

"Why?" I bit out. Anger tore through me, chasing away the bite of agony that filled me with wildfire. "Why would you ever do that to him? To us? What did we ever do to you to deserve that kind of torture?"

The Orama sighed, those eerie eyes flickering to life with things I would never understand, threads of the future that only she could see. "Walk with me, child," she commanded softly, passing by my shoulder to exit through the cleft in the rock wall.

The almost uncontrollable anger boiling my blood made me want to stay still out of spite, but the more logical side of me knew I would never get answers that way. And after everything, all Kanan and I had gone through to get where we were despite her meddling, we deserved answers.

I trailed behind her begrudgingly, her form disappearing into the darkness. The long strands of dirty lavender hair that fell down her curved back were my only guide as we maneuvered our way through the narrow path.

The rock scraped against my sides as we made it out and into the openers of the main tunnel. It was a good thing I had come instead of Kanan—with his broad shoulders and towering height there would have been no way for him to make it deep into the heart of the seer's cave. She would have needed to go to him, met him at the entrance, to answer his question and enact her blood tie.

An image flashed in my mind of a haggard, weary Kanan kneeling outside the wretched witch's hill, days passing as he waited for her to deign to speak with him. The dragon, an unimaginable power in this universe, a power to be reckoned with, forced to abide by the rules of some unknown entity, unable to reach her himself.

Another pulse of anger exploded within me, shaking free of the misery that had settled in my heart. I said nothing though, simply simmered behind the seer like the bubbling volcanic core that rested beneath the planet's crust, capable of detonating at any moment.

I hesitated as the patterns along the walls flared to life as the Orama stepped onto her footpath. A singular line that wrapped around the circular formation of the tunnel glowed with purple light, the core of each design a burning white. As we moved forward, the next line ignited and the first reverted back to stark black, going dormant as we moved on.

On and on it went, each section bringing light to the darkened tunnel as we passed underneath. I desperately wanted to ask about them, but if I hadn't trusted the seer before, I definitely didn't now, and I had already asked one too many questions. Last thing I needed to do was give her anymore power over me lest she do something worse than a blood tie.

"I foresaw your kidnapping." Her dimly lit figure stared forward as she broke the palpable silence between us. "Knew what would happen once Kasis succeeded in taking you."

Gilded cosmic energy rattled against its chains, the hard won restraint I had so carefully built shook beneath its angry touch. "Why wouldn't you tell anyone?" I clenched my jaw tight, far worse words wishing to tear free. I didn't even care that I'd just asked another question. "You could have stopped all of this."

She sighed, this one filled with old exhaustion and reproach. "Child, if I acted upon every bad thing I saw there would be no future for which to aim towards. No progression, no growth, simply a stagnation in existence." She shook her head, an incomprehensible note entering her voice, a thread of importance within the echo of her voice. "As outlandish as it sounds, sometimes bad things are meant to happen. Sometimes they happen to certain people and those people, that event, changes the course of history. So yes, I knew of your abduction and I did nothing about it, but I would do it all over again if I had to. Maybe you should wonder why."

Silence overtook us again as we made our way through the passage. I couldn't tell if she was tempting me, seeing if she could weasel something else from me besides the blood in my veins, but she said nothing, letting her cryptic statement hang like forbidden fruit waiting to be plucked by the curious.

"I will say, your mate almost made me falter that day," she remarked almost to herself. "I am a very hard woman to shock, and yet he did. Heartbroken and begging on his knees, promising me anything I wanted in return for telling him whether you would come back to him."

My heart lurched as she spoke, Kanan's pain as real in my heart as it was to him two thousand years ago. "Many strong men have pleaded with me, offering my heart's desire for answers to questions that have plagued the universe for eons, but a man—a god for all intents and purposes—on his knees for love." Her shuffling steps slowed as she reminisced. "Now that I don't see very often."

"Death without Life is an unstable, unbalanced thing," she continued on, barely registering the spears she was shoving through my heart. "And he was proof of that. Crazed and splintered, broken and nearing his own end if the threads I saw spoke true."

My eyes shuttered close, searing heartache wrecking my nerve. Without my memories, I could only imagine what had driven Kanan to such a point, but the mere thought of him in such a state had me weak in the knees.

I had no idea why she revealed so much. Her end goal was as much a mystery to me as my forgotten memories, but the more she spilled the more I needed to know. Questions pulsed within me, growing stronger with every breath I took, as if being in her presence dug up every inquisitive bone in my body.

Maybe that was the true trick when it came to her. Not the payment itself, but that when you finally had a taste of the answers you desperately desired, you couldn't help but want more.

That desperate curiosity mixed with the seemingly never-ending anguish that perpetuated the sorrows filling the caverns of my soul, created an intoxicating combination. One I was helpless to fight. I needed to know. For myself. For Kanan.

So as the light at the end of the tunnel finally appeared, Zanaya's silhouette a flicker of moving darkness in the distance, I stopped and relented to that burning question. "Why?"

She stopped, only a few paces ahead of me. Her shoulders dropped as she tilted her head to the ceiling, the pale strands of her hair swaying in some invisible breeze. There was no need for clarification. We both had waited patiently, understood the inevitability of that question, that I would be driven to understand. A flaw of mine or perhaps a learned defense against the lies and half-truths and mysteries that surrounded me at every turn.

Turning slowly, she glanced at me with those chilling eyes, seeing far more than anyone should. The lengths of her loose fitting gown fluttered around her as she shifted forward until she stood before me. The power surrounding her roiled and there was a moment of terrifying understanding when her walls shifted just so, allowing me the barest glimpse of the power she kept contained and hidden from the world.

"I needed you strong, young one," she offered up to me. "Stronger than you've ever been for what's to come."

She swallowed, wetting her throat. The purple motifs above us were the only source of light, but they allowed me to see enough of the emotion flashing across her face. Indecision. Regret. Hope. So many more that I couldn't make out, all arrowed at me. "You were something to behold during your first life, but there was a softness, an innocence within, that kept you from seeing the worst in people until it was too late. There are many horrors that haunt this universe, but you became blinded by the good, and it nearly cost you everything."

It felt like my throat was closing up, the walls moving in on us, as my worst fears were realized. It had been me that started this. It was my inability to look past the good, to see the innate bad that some carried with them like a second skin, that had led us to this point.

"You needed to understand pain. Suffering and loneliness and heartache. It was the only way to force your soul to acknowledge that they are just as important to life as all the good moments." There was a heavy weight behind her words that I couldn't fully understand, the meaning just out of reach. "I knew that when you reincarnated you would not survive without learning what *Life* is truly about. You had to face all it had to offer, the good and the bad, if you were to survive this time around. You had to be different. Smarter, harder, stronger, more decisive with your loyalty and kindness, more understanding of the gray areas that linger along the paths of each and every soul, and why sometimes the right choice isn't always an easy nor good one."

She whirled around without further explanation, leaving me there, reeling from the revelations. My head buzzed with the static of unfinished thoughts, whirring relentlessly as I tried to piece myself back together into some functional version of myself. Every muscle I possessed was stiff, tension thrumming through me like a tightly spun wire waiting to snap.

It was only the Orama's expectant cough that broke through my shock. The seer had stopped near the entrance door, Zanaya's dark form swiveling between the old woman and my position, though she likely couldn't see me through the darkness.

A murmured word from the Orama had my friend reluctantly backing away until she faded over the crest of the hill and down into the valley.

I crept forward until I stood side by side with the witch. Blinking away the spots of burning light that danced across my vision, I quickly acclimated to the soft radiance in the sky as the sun began its descent somewhere along the horizon.

A serration of sound pulled my attention to the gleaming silver blade in the Orama's hand, pulled from who knows where, and its glinting handle of carved metal. There were no breaks or hinges along the dagger's length for which the blade and guard became attached, nothing to join the pieces together. No, this blade had been forged in some distant fires as one singular piece. An unbreakable weapon with no weak points in which to shatter the metal.

Stepping forward with the blade, she took my hand in hers, bringing the tip to the pad of one finger. Bright red blood bubbled up immediately as an unexpected jolt of energy jolted through my arm, painful like a strike of lighting, and yet gone within a blink of an eye. I barely had time to register the sharp bite before she had sheathed the unique, masterful dagger and pulled a small vile from her pocket.

"Let me give you one piece of advice, young one," she said quietly as she collected her drops. "Though your memories may be shrouded in loving darkness, do not allow that to wedge its way between you and your mate. Do not be mad at him for things so far out of his control I doubt he even knows of them all. For if the universe threatened to break all around us he would shield you from it without hesitation, and should you wish to face it, he would stand with you against the darkness between the stars."

She capped her vial without any further dramatics—her obscure comments enough to rattle someone's bones.

"That was only three," I said offhandedly, still unsure where her answers left me, but by my count I owed her at least five. Five too many if you asked me, though I had no intention of owing her a debt like Cashim.

The elderly woman smiled, something old and timeless about it that creeped along my skin in warning, though her easy expression appeared genuine. "Consider us even, young goddess, for my interfering with your path, but do not expect it of me again."

I scoffed, relief expanding my chest, "I wouldn't dream of it."

She hummed, smile still firmly attached to her face. "I'll believe it when I see it. Now, it's time for you to go." She pointed one taloned finger towards the hill we had first stepped out on, a pillar of smoke curling in the air above it. "I do believe your city is burning."

CHAPTER FORTY-SEVEN

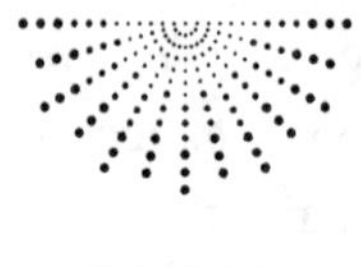

KANAN

Patience was a virtue I took pride in possessing. The ability to watch and wait, to listen for the whispers that spilled from loose lips into the darkness that no one took time to notice, was an invaluable asset that offered many advantages.

It was the camouflaged serpent lying in the long grass, the ferocious saberthor, not a single hair along its sleek coat twitching as it stalked through the bush, who were the most successful hunters. Predators striking down upon their unaware quarries only when the timing was perfect.

That's what it felt like when I crept through the shadows of the castle, jumped between the dark nooks and crannies that were lined with dust from misuse, or stared down at the city full of people, oblivious to the fact that I watched from above, hunting for the corrupt amidst our ranks.

But it had been three days. Three days of shuffling through the conversations and monotonous noise of the castle. Three days of waiting to see if Kasis and his spy would take our bait. Three days since that insufferable witch had sent for Atallia, taking her from me yet again. My patience was running dry and my sanity along with it.

Fortifying our defenses, barking orders at Bron who would then carry them through the ranks, had been my only outlet. Though my friend seemed seconds away from taking his chances and throwing a punch at any moment. The hybrid who had been by my side almost the entirety of my seventeen thousand years was all too used to my dark side, but he knew better than anyone what lay at Atallia's feet, what would happen should I lose her again.

To say my mood had taken a dive off a sheer cliff into morouse and murderous waters would have been an understatement. I was balancing on a razor's edge, every nerve raw and exposed.

Three days.

Three days without her smile, her beautiful laugh, wondrous and full and teaming with something that never failed to make my heart stop and the air flee from my lungs. If she were here she would have skinned me alive with that scathing tongue of hers for acting so beastly, and after pacing a hole into the floor of our rooms, all my attention focused on that braided tether connecting the two of us, I would have welcomed it.

It was only my promise to her that kept me from flying off to Corosa and tearing that fucking seer from her caves. Demand she leave Atallia and I alone. I wouldn't kill the witch, of course, the magic she thought she could hide was enough to stay my hand and consider the consequences of such an act.

There were very few creatures that had walked this world longer than me, and she was one of them. Even if the Orama liked to appear less powerful than she was, there was a different kind of power that came from age and experience. One that was born from standing your ground against the gale force of time. It soaked into your bones, your soul, and left a mark that nothing else could.

The witch carried that mark, as did I, and even Bron to some degree. Atallia, whose memories were lost to her, still bore the stains of old. Haunted eyes, hardened heart, a knowledge that only formed from the labors of a much longer life. The hardships of a growing world, thrown at you one after the other until you had no choice but to fight back and hope there was something left at the end to piece back together.

So no, I wouldn't kill the crone. Imagining her death, however, where her blood stained my hands, dripped from my claws, and the smell of her incinerated flesh wafted into the air...well that was without consequence, and helped settle the rage that stirred the hellfire within my chest.

A shadow snaked down the wall I leaned against, the wisp of darkness paying homage to who—what—I was, bringing me news from all across the city. I lifted an eyebrow as bits of information soaked in, filing them away for later. Sometimes it paid to live partially in the dark, pitiless world of the shadows.

What I couldn't carve from someone's mind myself was easily picked up on by my pets. So few knew to keep their mouths shut, letting secrets fly free into the air as if the wind didn't have ears of its own. No matter if no one was around, there was always someone or something listening. A lesson I was having to relearn myself.

If Atallia was right and we did have a traitor in our midst, hiding amongst the well informed councilors or their families, then we had a much bigger problem, one that needed to be rooted up and destroyed.

There was very little that happened in Eskira that I didn't know about. I had made it my mission long ago to never be taken unaware again, not after my adoptive brother's betrayal against my queen and I. And yet, time and time again, Kasis outplayed us.

The long hours listening from the darkness and finding nothing had driven me into my memories, giving me time to search for the answers to my questions. I didn't often spiral into the thousands of years of memories I kept under lock and key, but after three days of this insanity, my only company for the most part being my own mind, it was a painful inevitability.

It started with the attacks on the outer villages and towns, months in advance to Atallia's reemergence. Kasis had done well by keeping his experiments a secret during the first war, never once openly showing his wraiths, instead utilizing his mostly powerless humans to pester us while he planned for a much longer game.

Then it was the Council's idiotic party where Atallia was nearly taken, his corrupted soldiers somehow sneaking through the halls of the palace without so much as a fight. The one prisoner, *Jasco,* my lips curled into a snarl at the pathetic kinsman's name, had to have been instructed on how to divert me should he be captured.

His mind had been a volatile hellscape, unstable fluctuating layers that slid against each other, never settling, always changing. I had brought my mind down upon those fragile planes like a hammer to glass, shattering them into a million pieces only for a thousand more to take their place.

Each one brought forth a memory. A feeling.

Screams. His or someone else's? Blood. Piss soaking the ground beneath his feet. Manic laughter. Pain. Unfathomable darkness choking him until it felt like his mind was seconds from slipping away forever. A familiar chill I couldn't place that threatened to seep into my bones, taint my soul. Kasis's sickly green eyes. The smell of rotten flesh as it burned and bled. More pain.

Such lovely memories to add to my own collection. I couldn't help the self-deprecating snort that escaped me.

All of it had been useless to me until finally one gave way under the pressure and showed me Rhaera's burning visage. Smoke billowing into the sky. The screams of women. The satisfaction he felt as he watched their children be ripped from their arms.

I nearly broke him then and there. His blood already spilled from his pores, coating the floor in mockery of his feeble attempts to ward me from his splintered mind, seeping into the stone of a chamber meant to hold me back for a few measly minutes. Though those minutes wouldn't do anyone any good, not with what lived inside me.

The primordial monster that I truly was, that chose to stay contained beneath the puny mortal form I had chosen, had rumbled in delight at the thought of his skull bursting from the dark power in my veins. The quiet, slow cracks of snapping bone, the screams of prey sliding over my skin. Not much else could have calmed what I had become after the unsanctioned deaths of my people, the attack on my love. The blood magic I had drawn upon to keep myself restrained had been a breath away from fracturing.

Had it not been for the poorly hidden temptress watching from the second level, I would have done just that. Thankfully for Jasco, my obsession with Atallia ran deeper than my need to end his life, and the little goddess already had too many nightmares to contend with.

So he got to live, and she convinced me to take her to Rhaera. Like a fucking idiot, I agreed, and it quickly became apparent that someone had taught the kinsman how to feed secrets to those with my abilities.

It was then, when wraiths swarmed me from every direction, appearing from thin air, and Atallia's gut-wrenching scream tore through my chest, all chance of keeping up the warlord charade crumbling to pieces, that I knew who was behind this madness. For only Kasis could have prepared Jasco for me. My brother who grew to know my power like no other during those years where it was only him and I, the world at our fingertips.

History had a habit of repeating itself, and we were proof of that. Atallia, Kasis, and I. The three powers of Irropia, bound in a way no one but us would ever understand.

A growl shook my chest, rattling the weak bones that kept the monster caged. It was infuriating, being lost in the darkness, waiting for the sword hanging over our heads to drop. The shadows were my territory, the land I felt most comfortable in, bending to my will with ease; and yet new abominations crawled from those dark recesses, hidden from my view, and hunted those I called mine. I had half a mind to set the world on fire, eradicate this invading disease, and be done with it all.

"How long have we been playing this game?" I called out as the night-kissed darkness fed me information, not bothering to move from my position along the balustrade of the throne room's balcony.

A low feline chuff came from behind me, followed by the swish of Bron's change taking hold. "I nearly had you this time," he said in reply.

I flicked a look at him over my shoulder, lifting an eyebrow. "The shadows tattled on you by the time you reached the lift."

As he shifted out into the open from the shadows of the throne room, the moons' light washed over his pale skin, turning him from a spectral mirage to a colored illusion. Moving between the rays of light, his silver scars glinted in painful reminder. I rubbed my chest where an ache took hold.

"Those nosy fuckers," he grumbled as he came up to my side, leaning his forearms against the carved stone next to me. "I swear they always ruin my fun."

I snorted in response, but my focus was on his arms, bare all the way to his shoulders save for the quilted pattern of wounds long since healed. From the tips of his fingers to his neck he was covered in white marks, even paler than his own washed-out color. The higher up they got the less his skin became visible.

He looked ravaged, like he'd fought a rabid beast and had just barely survived. Cut after cut, layered over each other until you began to wonder how he survived such a brutal attack. I knew his chest was just as bad, the gruesome lines marring his neck, perfectly spaced, were just the tip of the damage.

"Stop staring," he remarked flatly. "It does no good holding on to something you can't change."

I swallowed harshly, grinding my teeth together. My fangs bit into the skin of my mouth, drops of blood hitting my tongue before the small wounds healed, the rich iron taste all too familiar. "You should have never done what you did," I bit out, my anger flaring hotly. Not at him, but at myself, for the pain that I caused.

Probably the only man capable of getting away with it, he rolled his eyes at me, sighing heavily. "What's it been thirteen…fourteen millennia?" he needled, his expression telling me just how ridiculous he thought this was, "And we're still arguing about it. I would do it all over again—you know I would."

I rubbed my hands over my face, skin prickling as the beast shifted in agitation. "I could have killed you."

"You killed a lot of creatures, I don't think either of us need the reminder," he retorted. Shaking his head, he turned his head to look at me. "That wasn't you and you know it. I was the only one that might have caused you to pause, I had to try. And guess what, it worked."

"Barely," I growled. "You almost died anyway."

He knocked my shoulder with his. "Please, you wouldn't have let that happen. You can get all upset about it, but let's be honest here, nothing else could have woken you up long enough to call for Atallia."

He pursed his lips in thought, giving me a contemplative look. "If you really think it through, I'm the reason the world was saved. Decent trade-off if you ask me."

Now it was my turn to roll my eyes. "It was still a stupid plan."

He scoffed, waving my comment off. "Please, I could have taken you had you not been going crazy. Besides, who can say they took on a dragon and lived?"

I knew he meant it as a joke, but I winced regardless.

Don't go there, Kanan. Just don't. Of course the slippery slopes of my mind didn't give a single fuck what I thought and shoved me deeper into the depths of those dark days.

The Time of Nightmares had taken its toll on me. My insanity stained our early history like blood on parchment, and it was something I would carry for the rest of my long life without complaint because of the pain I had caused so many innocents; but knowing I'd nearly killed Bron in my madness, all because he was trying to save whatever part of me remained in that maddened state…that guilt would never dull.

He carried my shame with him everyday, the scars my claws had carved into his body never fully healing, nor would they. Not even Atallia at full strength could heal them completely, and so they remained to this day. A reminder of what I could become if I ever lost control like that again. Some days were closer than others, but never had I allowed myself to reach that endless manic abyss again, not even when I lost *her*.

I forced myself to look at them whenever I could, so that I never forgot what I almost lost when I thought I had nothing. Because despite the horrors I had caused, despite the absolute loss of control I had faced, when everything and nothing became one, and the rational man, even the patient beast, was no more, I had Bron. And for whatever reason, he had stood by my side through it all.

Idiot. Then again, maybe so was I for not forcing the matter more after the incident. He should have never been involved. Not all those years ago and certainly not now. No one should be.

Oblivious to my current state, though I'm sure he would have flipped a finger in my direction at my sentimental thoughts, he shifted beside me. "Women love them, you know, makes me look more rugged."

A chuckle worked its way free at the absurd idea. At any given moment Bron looked like he'd just stepped out of the wilds of Allasea, dirt or blood or some other unknown substance streaking his white skin. His unruly hair was almost always thrown up in some knot at the back of his head or hanging loose around his face. Decorum of any kind rubbed him the wrong way.

Prissy lords often sneered in derision when he walked by, completely oblivious to the looks women gave him as he passed. If he grew any more rugged I'm sure the insufferable aristocrats would stage a coup just to throw him back to the woods he came from.

"It doesn't seem to be helping you with a certain woman," I ribbed, looking out over the city as lights within homes flickered out one by one. "The Commander couldn't care less."

The noise he made was all saberthor, his true form riding high at the mention of Zanaya Zuberi. He flattened me with a glare that had me laughing. "I'll give her credit," I said, pushing my luck, "in all the years I've known you I haven't seen you twisted up about someone like this."

"No comment," he grumbled roughly, peering out into the darkness surrounding the slumbering city.

I smirked, but let him be. Being half Anima, he was used to knowing just about everything about everyone. He never pried without need, but after nearly fourteen thousand years of enhanced mental abilities, most of the time he didn't even need to delve into someone's mind to know things about them.

Even before I gave him the mortal body he carries now, he was no normal saberthor. His parents' mating was almost one of a kind, creating a powerful predator with more sentience than he knew what to do with.

Though he'd never say it, I knew he had been lonely before we met, never truly fitting anywhere. Not with his mother's species—the ferocious, oftentimes vicious, saberthors were mostly solitary, and did not take kindly to unwanted company. He couldn't join his father even if he wanted to, the Anima were mentally talented animal spirits that only gained a physical body once in their entire existence. They did what they pleased and then returned to the world in between.

Gifted with a physical form by his mother, but with the abilities of his father, Bron was a perfect mix of the two. However, it left him without a place to belong. I often think it's why we found each other, both of us not truly understanding our place in the world.

"Anything to report?" I asked glumly, needing something to shake me from my memories. After so many years, thousands of memories, they were often traps that could lead me down paths I never wanted to follow again.

Straightening, he reached back to undo his hair before pulling the leather tie free for his hands to mess with. "Nothing much. The councilors are all behaving as they would for the most part. Cashim has himself locked up in his office, though he mentioned stopping by the dungeons to check in on our friend." He chuckled darkly, pulling the leather tight between two fists before wrapping it around his fingers. "Though, I doubt there's much left of him with Helmina for company."

"She knows not to kill him," I said offhandedly. "The others?"

He shrugged. "Oakina and Elaric set off yesterday, no reports from their travels have come in. Lars is being surprisingly docile, helping the ranks where he can, and Lady Lilyi is pacing the lower levels like she always does. Creepy, but not unlike her. She and Cashim have been in and out of the infirmary with Moian, but other than that not much has changed."

"So nothing to point at any of them being our traitor." A curse flew from my lips. If we did have a traitor on the Council, it was only going to get harder to find them.

"Unfortunately not," Bron sighed, unraveling the leather tie to pull his white hair back into its signature knot. "With everyone more spread out now, if it's one of the councilors leading the other cities, then it'll be almost impossible to dig them up without proof."

I hummed in response. There wasn't much else we could do except keep an eye on their movements, wait for them to make a mistake.

"The warriors are recovered or recovering," he reported faultlessly. After being my second in command in all but name for so many years, he knew what I wanted to know before I even asked. "No one is at their best, but we're better off than we were. There have been some stirrings of nerves within the ranks about you and the queen's supposed absence, but nothing the generals haven't shut down. Mostly it's the waiting game, we can all feel it, the impending battle, but the surge of loyalty from the river boats hasn't abated in the least. We're all with you, just give the word."

"Good. If panic starts to build you let me know," I ordered, both of us stepping away, from friends to the mantle of king and second, with ease. "We might have to cut this ruse short if the rumors start to build. I won't lose the army to an anarchy of our own creation. The chaos will only strengthen Kasis and give him more of a foothold to wage his war."

Bron nodded, running a hand across the railing's smooth stone surface. "It'll be done, though I doubt you have anything to worry about."

"Be that as it may, I lost some of their trust by keeping the knowledge of Atallia and myself a secret, we can't afford for anything to drive a wedge into that crack." Our people were loyal. Loyal to the Divine, their gods and creators, but also to their leaders, who would put everything on the line to protect them. Losing that loyalty would crush us long before Kasis could.

"What of the sprites?" The Flight had taken over the surrounding woods and stables that housed the few whispers within the city limits. From almost any position above the barracks and training fields you could see the combined glow of their magics coming through the trees, wavering in the air as they flew in and out, mostly doing as they pleased, although some were acting as scouts and couriers on Atallia's orders. My mate's silver-winged friend had taken great delight in giving himself the title of Aid to the Queen.

"Nothing much, though the last I heard from Wrynn," Bron chuckled and pinched the bridge of his nose, a common reaction to the excitable sprite, "the Monarch is 'offbeat.' I have no idea what that means, he flew off before I could ask. Said something about the whispers being noisy."

We shared a baffled look, neither of us knowing what to make of that. Shaking his head, Bron threw his hands up. "Don't ask me."

I snorted again, running a hand through my hair as an icy breeze cut its way across the balcony. I could barely feel the cold despite how high up we were, the fire in my blood running hot tonight, an impatient burn taking hold as I held my breath in wait for news of Atallia.

Every second she was away felt like an eternity. A huge crushing weight sat atop my chest, every inhale was painful, and each exhale felt like my last. I didn't think Atallia knew how much rested on her shoulders, how much this world needed her to be okay. Because if she wasn't, despite her faith in me, I would have no qualms plunging it into the void. Without her light, the universe could live in darkness for all I cared.

Bron rested his hand on my shoulder, a quiet show of support. He knew better than anyone what was at stake, what sending her into the uncertainty of that fissure did to me. My queen was fully capable of protecting herself, there was no doubt in my mind about that, but when forces this evil were at play there was very little chance things would be fair; and if I knew Kasis, he would seize any opportunity to take her again.

All I could do was stare out at the horizon, the walls of Eskira's boundaries barely visible despite the dazzling night sky, assisted by the colorful light of moons and magic both.

Where are you, love?

I prayed to the universe, to the Cosmos, to whatever higher power still existed in that vast expanse of space that she would appear. That the flicker of firelight out in the far distance would turn to startling gold and the magnificence that was my other half would show herself.

As that flame flickered brighter in response I almost made myself believe it to be true, that my agonizing wait had ended and she'd returned unharmed.

Except that wasn't the case, and as I stood straighter, Bron's hand falling from my shoulder, a different dread rose to take its place as realization settled in. "Sound the alarms," I roared as the flicker of flames turned into a blaze.

Bron stood to attention, his wide eyes looking out over the city, pinpointing what I had caught only a few seconds earlier. "Wha—"

He didn't get to finish before I launched myself over the railing of the balcony and plummeted hundreds of feet through the air. Darkness pulled away from the mountainside as air whizzed by me, strands of hair whipped against my skin as the shadows enveloped me completely, and without a moment's hesitation, I let the beast tear free.

It broke through the bone and muscle and skin, tearing me apart in order to build me anew. Strength imbued with the power of the Cosmos filled me to the brink. A new shape took hold, sturdier and impenetrable, forged with the flames that seared my cavernous chest.

As my wings snapped out, catching a drift long before I would have crashed to the earth, an ear-splitting roar erupted from my draconian chest, fracturing the air. It shook the world, blanketing the night with my fury, spreading far and wide in warning as an explosion rocked the lower city and caught flame.

Eskira was burning.

CHAPTER FORTY-EIGHT

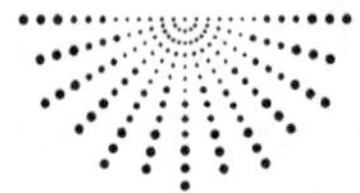

I hesitated, a single second in time as the world around me froze. My muscles stiffened and my feet were rooted to the spot, mouth gaping at what I saw, but as the plume of dark gray smoke grew, drawing me in like a beacon, I broke away from the Orama. I glanced over my shoulder at the seer, her mist-born eyes twinkling in the dim light of the tunnel entrance as she dipped her head, and despite her warning I knew she had just told me what I needed to know.

Eskira was under attack. Kasis's hordes at our gates.

Surging forward, I aimed for the hill as smoke filled the air. I passed Zanaya at the bottom, her eyes blowing wide as I rushed by. Trusting her to understand the dire urgency that gripped me and was no doubt plain on my face, I pushed forward without a word, sprinting faster than I had ever gone before.

Wind whipped around me, picking up the ends of my braid, sending loose strands flying as my legs blurred beneath me. Crossing the valley became my priority. Nothing else mattered as more and more smoke billowed into the air, covering the orange-tinted sky in a cloud of gray.

I could feel Zanaya moving behind me, her panicked breaths as loud as mine as we bolted past the Eye Stones without so much as a glance. I picked up faint flashes of color on the edge of my vision, sparking in and out, but I didn't slow, all my attention on the ascent before me.

I ignored the burn in my legs, the fiery ache in my lungs, as we darted up the hill towards the fissure, sending my thanks to the Cosmos for gifting me the power I had. No matter the burn, the pain, my legs would hold, my lungs would fill. They would carry me across any land, any battlefield. There was no other option.

Faster. Faster. Faster.

I kept repeating the word in hopes that, by some power, I could make Eskira appear. Make Kanan appear. The vibrancy of our bond had snapped back into place only after leaving the Orama's cave, but all I could feel was overwhelming anger. A primordial rage that tasted of his smoke, smelled of his dark amber scent. He must have shifted, the feelings that of the dragon, that was the only answer. His side of the bond felt rawer, more visceral, as if everything was heightened.

I sent a pulse of energy down the braided tether, the pair bond glowing brighter amidst the black and gold bridge. After a few seconds with no response, I sent another, hoping he would understand that I was coming. That I was close.

As we reached the peak, every breath sawing in and out of my chest, I felt his response in my chest. The overwhelming sense of relief and soul-shattering love, followed closely by the need to protect. Every emotion after that was tinged with the flaming anger that was a constant in his current state.

I knew if he could he would have tried to convince me to stay out of the fight, tried to reason with me on why it was safer, but nothing in the world could have stopped me from diving head first through the clean-cut fissure atop the hill.

I didn't even care how it was here in the first place. As the thick smoke hit my eyes, tears welling to combat the painful sting, and the scent of burning wood hit my nose, I darted through the wavering portal without a second thought for anything else.

The buzzing static of the fissure washed over me and I tried to ignore the irrational panic that came with. My power burst to life, flowing unrestrained straight to my hands. Instead of forcing it back, I welcomed it, allowing it closer and holding on to its comforting, unyielding presence. As waves of heat swarmed me from all sides, I knew this would not be the time for restraint.

Taking a gasping breath as I made it out the other side, smoke filled my lungs. No longer breathing the fresh island air of Corosa, I hacked and coughed as the forests of Eskira appeared around me.

Everywhere I looked there was fire, flames as tall as the trees, consuming everything they touched. A forest that was thousands of years old, centuries of stories and memories, incinerating before my eyes. Embers fell from above, pouring down like rain from hell. Branches alight with fire crashed to the forest floor. The young brush got caught in the inferno, the green wood of saplings and summer growth putting off walls of white smoke.

I covered my nose and mouth with an arm, turning around to take hold of Zanaya as she fell through the fissure. Taking choked, gasping breaths, her face was streaked with tears as she pulled in smoke with each drag of the air. She pulled her shirt up to block some of the suffocating vapors and held onto the back of my leathers, the both of us surveying our surroundings.

"We have to get to the city," I shouted over the loud roar of the wildfire. I blinked, tears dripping from them as I tried to clear the fumes threatening to blind me. A tree came crashing down to the right of us without warning, slamming into the ground with a great boom. The charred trunk split apart, sizzling away at the blackened earth beneath.

Before Zanaya could answer, another tree fell, this one nearly as tall as the high walls of black stone that surrounded Eskira. Tearing through the others in its path, it snapped on its way down, spraying us with burning coals and embers.

We ducked, covering our heads as pieces of burnt wood and flaming limbs hit us. Parts of my exposed skin seared as the debris struck me, blisters bubbling to life before quickly healing.

Zanaya screamed beside me, a keening cry that was lost to the rush of flames. Branches hit her right side, striking like steel-ended whips left to smolder in a hearth. Her stunning black skin peeled away, blood seeping from the wounds. I tried to grab hold, heal what I could, but she shook me off. "Go!" she yelled, pointing in the direction of the city walls as more alarming cracks sounded around us. "Go, go, go."

Pulling each other along we dodged burning patches of brush, thermal winds pushing the heat and ash into our mouths, coating our tongues with the destruction of the woodland. We had to squint to see through the thick smog blanketing the forest, the canopy above rapidly disintegrating.

Our feet pounded against the dirt, puffs of char and ash blowing into the firestorm with each hurried step. I threw up a hand as a blast reached out to lick at our skin, the hair along my arm sizzling. Clenching a fist, I took hold of its energy and directed it away, smothering its power and shutting off the force backing it until the small conflagration died off.

Noticing what I'd done, Zanaya quickly took action. Pulling what little water still remained from the air, she aimed to douse the fires in our path. Together we made our way through the burning forest, Zanaya cutting the path, ropes of water curled around her arms like snakes as I protected us from the blazing hellscape consuming every inch of land for miles.

We surged forward, moving like an unstoppable force, a whirlwind of magic breaking the fire-line, leaving behind a smoldering black trail.

Bursting free of the blaze, the great wall of the eastern border loomed over us, its gate blown to pieces. Thick slats of wood and hardened stone were scattered across the field. Blood and bodies lay intermixed throughout, wraiths and Descendents alike. Smoke and the scent of iron mixed with the rot of the corrupt permeated the air, screams—some not entirely human—and the clang of metal came from somewhere inside the walls.

"Check for survivors," I said through harsh breaths, my chest rising and falling with effort as we took in the carnage. Neither of us said anything as we moved from body to body, each bloodier than the next, forever stilled by the evil invading this world.

"I have a few who aren't Descendants," Zanaya called from a few yards over, standing near a pile of bodies. They lay atop each other, almost as if they'd come together in embrace, one final clash, dying as the other died. In the end, nothing and no one could stop that swift darkness. "All dead."

"The Kin of Chaos," I yelled back. "Kasis must have sent them to lead the hordes. We need to get inside, find the others."

She nodded, both of us moving as quickly as we could through the tide of destruction. I looked over my shoulder, the all-encompassing flames slowly following behind, reaching out towards us like a titan of fire. It spread for as far as I could see until my vision burned orange. Its infernal presence rose, taking over the sky, swallowing the Sulrin, as more of Eskira's ethereal forests disappeared under its tyrannical presence.

All that color, the beauty...gone. Nothing would be able to replace the thousands of years that the woodland had stood. Guardians of the earth, connected to the planet from birth, and home to the creatures who chose its welcoming embrace.

"Atallia," Zanaya called from the broken gate, her sweat-covered brow puckering as she waited.

I closed my eyes, moving deeper into myself and away from the physical, the sounds of battle, of heart-wrenching cries and shrill screeches, fading away. Blood, smoke, pain, exhaustion, all of it melted into the background. The bite of heat against my skin became nothing more than a gentle warmth.

I often allowed myself to forget just who and what I was. That the weak, breakable skin I wore was a shell, a mask that allowed me the freedom to roam this world with unfettered access. What truly sat beneath the surface was so much more than that, so instead of restraining it, hiding it, holding on to it for dear life...I surrendered to it. Gave myself over to the relentless power of beginnings.

My mind exploded to life with gold, daring and bright like a star amidst the darkness of space. It coated the world in a sheen as every inch of skin cracked apart from the force rippling through me, undulating beneath the shell, waiting and ready at my command. Boundless. A well of everlasting power.

I was the rain that wetted the ground from which seeds grew. The heat of a burning sun, warming the stones that gave energy to the cold-blooded reptiles that slithered from their caves. I was one with the wind that gave life to dying leaves, carrying them on the breeze as they floated to their resting place, giving their strength to the new and beginning the cycle again. I was formed as the undying cores of planets, of galaxies, were formed.

It was time I accepted that fact. There wasn't any more time to come to terms with it. Not when innocent people, people who believed in me even when I didn't believe in myself, were being unjustly attacked. Not when our way of life was crumbling around us, our peace slipping through our fingers like grains of sand.

I reached out to the intangible flames, felt their fierce spirit pulse through the world, angry and wild and without control. They were kin to the sparks that lived inside the fire Aetherians, to the river of molten power in my mate's blood. As familiar to me as the breath in my lungs, the embers that lived inside my own soul.

Instead of focusing on one, I focused on them all. Peered through the rush of destruction to the wildfire's center and calmed it, put it to sleep like a mother might her child. And like those naughty, tired children, far more exhausted than they realized, the fire quieted.

The flames crawling up the trees and razing the bushland fizzled out, taking their havoc with them, leaving behind cooking embers and a layer of ash from which new growth would one day rise.

I buzzed with renewed energy, left panting not from exhaustion but from the wild excitement of unleashing myself upon the world, breaking free of the demons my own mind had created. Now real demons hunted us and it was up to me to crush them just the same.

I was tired of the back and forth. Acceptance. Denial. Acceptance. Denial. I had opened old wounds and created new ones in my ignorance, and because of it I'd left myself vulnerable to a poison of my own making.

No more.

I was the fucking Queen of Allasea. The Goddess of Beginnings and someone had dared storm my gates.

I wanted my city back, and nothing was going to get in my way of that.

CHAPTER FORTY-NINE

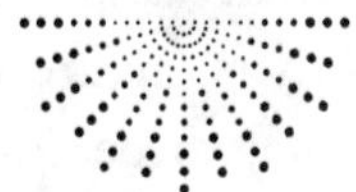

We tore through the open gateway, not a guard or citizen in sight. Blood, red and black alike, seeped through the cracks between the stones, soaking the moss and pooling along the ground. The small wildflowers that grew throughout the streets were trampled, flattened by the ensuing fight that must have occurred shortly after the gate's destruction.

A few armor-clad bodies lay strewn about the side streets. Enormous holes marred their chest plates, blood and bone chips splattering the once pristine metal, no longer a polished black, but instead smeared with dirt and other fluids I couldn't identify.

"Where are the rest of the guards?" I asked Zanaya, sweeping over the fallen and only counting three of our own amongst the bodies.

Bending over, she pulled one lifeless guard onto his back, his unseeing eyes staring up at the smoke-filled sky. His face was twisted in horror, pain creasing lines into his face, while his mouth had frozen mid-scream, the agonizing sound dying off with him.

The gaping hole in his chest was enough to make even my stomach turn, the cooling blood already congealing around the edges. Deep scratches had been clawed into the metal of his arm guards, as if he had attempted to fend the creature off and failed miserably. Whatever wraith had gotten to him had ripped into him with a rabid hunger.

"The fighting might have already moved inward. This could have happened hours ago for all we know," she remarked, closing the guard's eyes before standing straight. "Like I said, Corosa doesn't really work like the rest of the continent does. Sometimes minutes pass, other times days. The bodies are still warm so the fighting couldn't have started too long ago, but that's assuming they attacked here first."

"We need to find the others, figure out what happened." The majority of the clamor seemed to be coming from the lower city, pillars of smoke rising above the buildings to act as beacons.

Tightening the straps of her bracers, the hilts of blades barely bigger than her palm peeking out, Zanaya unsheathed the twin daggers strapped to her thighs with practiced precision. "We'll never find them, not if all the battalions are spread out. I don't even know what day it is, let alone where Saanvi would have everyone stationed."

My heart thundered in my chest, beating faster with every passing second. An explosion chose that moment to shake the ground, vibrations making their way up my legs as fire blasted into the sky, arching high enough for us to see.

I placed a hand to my chest, clenching my tunic in a fist, stomach dropping as resulting screams peeled through the air. Something hard and sharp cut through the material and pressed into my glowing skin.

A startled laugh broke free, relief nearly bringing tears to my eyes as I pulled the beacon stone free, the crude chunk of rock seeming to wink at me. "Orion, I could kiss you."

Sending my light through the indigo crystal, just enough to fill it with the golden rays, I waited for it to respond. Seconds went by with no response and my heart leapt into my throat, but the stone soon lifted from my palm, glowing brighter in response to something out in the middle of all the chaos. I let loose a shaky breath, my lungs filling once again.

"Let's go," I called out to Zanaya, taking off down the street. The beacon stone floated freely in the air, lifting from its place against my breastbone to point us in the direction of the fighting, where the flames of battle were consuming the lower half of Eskira.

The streets were unusually quiet, even for the early time of day. Dew still coated the blades of maroon grass and the lilac petals of wildflowers that bloomed in the windowsills of homes, but now, instead of the sweet fresh scent of a new day, the morning carried with it the lingering smell of rot and smoke, destruction and death.

The farther we ran, getting closer to the fighting with every surge of speed, the more the city changed. Going from deathly still, attempting to escape the notice of evil, to utter mayhem. Doors were flung open along the residential streets, the windows shattered, smoke billowing from inside as unattended hearths caught flame and the fighting raged throughout the city leaving no shop or home unscathed.

We came upon our first fight mere feet from the bridge crossing, the three soldiers being pushed into the upper city by a stag and two wolves, each one more decayed than the last. The warriors were holding their own, lobbing purple fire and spikes of colored ice, pulled from the Falla below, at the wraiths, but they lost ground quickly and were corralled onto the bridge.

"DOWN!" Zanaya shouted across the distance as we charged towards them, her voice turning from lyrical to commanding. With barely a second's pause to look over their shoulders, the three warriors heeded the commander's order and dropped flat. Driven by madness and insatiable hunger the wraiths paid us no heed, seeing only their downed prey and nothing else. Leaving us the perfect opportunity.

With a mighty shove, as if she was pushing against the weight of the world, a gale force wind that sent waves careening into the riverbank tore from behind, nearly knocking us to the ground as it rushed over the warriors and crashed into the advancing wraiths.

Nothing more than skin, bone, and black sludge, the creatures went tumbling back, the wind sending them crashing into the lower city streets. I took my chance, bolting forward and leaping over the three warriors in my path, their shocked faces flashing by as I went down on one knee. Bracing, I unleashed myself upon the beasts.

I flung an arm, and with a roar power exploded from me like a golden scythe. A cutting arc of the Cosmos, aether tearing free of its shell and slicing through the air. Festering flesh met ancient power and disintegrated upon first touch. With no resistance the golden blade slashed into the street, leaving a charred cut along the stone and grass.

I panted wildly, the iron-spiced air coating my throat with each pass as I got to my feet. A gilded halo surrounded me, and I barely had a chance to turn before a scream pierced the air.

Whipping in the direction of the high-pitched noise, I sprinted across the remaining distance separating me from the lower city. Zanaya would check on the soldiers, ensuring they were okay before joining me, so I flew towards the source of the child-like cry.

Everywhere I looked, beautifully crafted buildings were engulfed in flames. Trees that had likely stood for a thousand years and acted as support for many of the homes along the river, smoldered and burned, their colorful leaves, now edged in fire, fell into the streets and river. Embers drifted down on invisible winds, a death snow that singed whatever it touched.

Sweat dripped down my back as I swiveled around, searching for the person who had cried out. I swallowed, my throat as dry as sand. *Come on. Where are you?*

No other sound came, and my heart lurched at the thought that I was too late. Carefully controlling the level of power, I sent a pulse out into the world as a last ditch attempt, hoping one of the small pings in the back of my mind would be near. Closing my eyes, I turned inward. *Come on.*

Ping. Ping. Ping.

Dozens popped up all over, bouncing around my mind like tiny pinpricks along my senses, but it was the one only a dozen feet from me that held my attention. The beacon of light, similar to the stone glowing at my chest, pulled at me like a lifeline.

I followed, finding myself before a collapsing house, the fire pushing out through the door and windows. Easily calming the flames with a wave of my hand I darted through, crouching below the cloud of smoke that hovered near the ceiling.

"Hello? Can you hear me?" I stepped carefully, keeping a watchful eye on the blaze above me, the low groans and cracks throughout the structure were enough to give me pause. Reaching out to the core of the fire like I did with the forest, I calmed its raging spirit. The flames died down, the half burnt furniture and peeling walls turning to red hot coals.

Blackened beams came crashing down from the upper floor and through one of the holes in the ceiling. I jumped at the last second, only barely escaping being hit. Coughing up smoke, I called out again. "Hello?"

A chill raced down my spine as an inhuman growl answered from the room in front of me. Pulling a blade, I kept one hand empty just in case it tried to go for my throat. One step in front of the other, I padded slowly into the space, a bedroom if the smoking remains of bedding were any indication. I tried to peek around the corner, but was met with the cold, blank stare of a wraith.

The creature must have been a fox or some other woodland animal at some point, patches of dull orange fur stuck up oddly from its mangled body, the black tar matting what little remained. It was massive, bigger than any normal creature, making me think it must have been a Descendent at some point.

My heart hurt, but as its heaving shoulders bunched in preparation to attack, lips pulled back to show its razor sharp teeth, I had no choice but to end its misery. Using the fiery energy I gathered from the house, I sent a blast of flame in its direction. Edged in gold, the red hot fire burned through the thin skin and decaying muscle, melting its bones and leaving the vile blood boiling in a pool along the floor. The poor thing screeched, the excruciating noise dying off slowly as the fire ate away at whatever Kasis had done to keep it alive.

When the twisted body of the wraith withered away to nothing more than a pile of ashes amongst the ruins, I finally saw what it had been guarding. Hand over my mouth, bile rose in my throat, the acid scorching away my ability to speak.

Two bodies, mauled beyond recognition, lay among the wreckage of the home. Blood and sinew and muscle scattered around them, their mangled limbs intertwined. The larger of the two seemed to be holding the smaller in embrace, dying together in each other's arms as their lives burned down around them.

I dropped my head, eyes closing as the nightmare of their death imprinted itself into my memories. A whimper escaped me, or so I thought until a rustle drew my attention to the closet. The slatted doors had somehow survived the flames, completely undamaged even as the walls around it were stained coal black.

Moving closer, keeping my blade at the ready, I threw the door open. I couldn't believe it, but as I looked down at the small boy cowering in the corner of the small closet, clothes hanging down, protecting him in the shadows, I wished it had been another wraith.

"H-hi," I cooed softly, sheathing my blade and getting to my knees in order to be on his level. The boy couldn't have been older than five, small teeth biting into his quivering lip as tears raced down his rounded cheeks. Soot smeared his brown skin, leaving dark streaks that the wet droplets carried traces of. "My name is Atallia. What's yours?"

The child gulped, his bloodshot eyes overflowing with fear, but as he took me in, deciding if I was trustworthy, he found some courage to speak. "Sannil."

The name came out shaky, pitiful sadness echoing throughout. I choked back tears, for this poor boy who had just lost so much, needed strength, something he could look to and lean on. My tears would only scare him more.

"Do you want to get out of here, Sannil?" I asked, plastering a gentle smile onto my lips as I reached out a hand. "I know of a safe place for you to go."

I waited with bated breath as the little boy considered my proposal. He must have found something in my eyes, for the few seconds he looked into their iridescent depths, because he unraveled himself from his corner, took my hand in his, and crawled into my arms. Letting out a shaky breath, I sent a silent prayer into the universe to whoever had kept this boy safe, thanking them as I held tightly to his tiny body and pushed to my feet.

"Close your eyes, baby," I murmured into his ear, guiding his head into the crook of my neck. "I don't want the smoke to get in your eyes."

Or for you to see the ravaged bodies of your dead parents. I was too late for them, but I'd be damned if this boy didn't see tomorrow. Striding from the room, ensuring Sannil only saw the closet he'd crawled from, we left the destroyed home.

Zanaya exited from the house across the street at the same time, two bloodied women, both dressed in their nightclothes, following mutely behind her. The three soldiers from the bridge stood near a group of gathered civilians, some covered in blood, others wounded, all of them wearing the same mask of pain and fear and shock.

I watched as Zanaya clocked the boy in my arms, her eyes darting to the empty doorway behind me. An agonizing understanding, one I'm sure she knew all too well, flashed across her face.

"We found about ten in these houses, some were hiding, but others were trying to fight off wraiths," she reported, stopping in front of me. Her eyes hardened as she watched Sannil shake in my arms. Whatever demons this nightmare drug up for her were forced down with a harsh swallow. She pointed at one of the warriors. "Len even found a warped trying to get at one of the women. Looks like Kasis is throwing his latest experiments into the fray."

I seethed, cursing, silently for Sannil's sake, at the unforgivable horrors that had been thrust upon my people by a god who cared so little for their lives he probably didn't even see them as living things, just a means to an end that he would use over and over again until he got what he wanted.

I looked up the street at the dozen or more houses, burning or destroyed in some way, and then back at the group by the bridge. "We need to search the rest, make our way inward and usher everyone we can into the upper city."

"The bridges will be the only way for them to cross," she reminded me. "No one will be there to man the boats."

"Then we'll station Len and the others to guard it, find others to man the rest. We get out as many as we can, enlist the warriors we find along the way to help."

We both knew the odds. The likelihood that many had survived the chaos was slim, even though most Descendents were taught basic self-defense no matter their profession, many lived normal lives. Shopkeepers and seamstresses and fishermen, not warriors. Certainly not capable of fighting off hordes of wraiths, who had both magic and savage hunger on their side.

If we could save just one though…just one person whose life didn't end today, then it would be worth it. I saw that resolve in Zanaya's eyes, the set of her jaw, and knew it was reflected in mine.

We set off, explaining our plan to the soldiers, who were rankled at being left out of the action, but once the importance of their task came over them, they accepted without hesitation.

"Make your way towards the infirmary, the Mender will take you in," I instructed Rena, a voluptuous black woman who appeared to be the only one of the group capable of thinking through her shock. "Follow Len, he'll get you there safely."

"Yes, my queen," she nodded her head in understanding.

As I stroked Sannil's back the boy leaned away from his spot against my chest, peering up at me with big brown eyes. "Sannil, this is Rena," I explained, showing him the kind woman's smile Wan as it was, she tried to put on a brave front for the child. "She's going to take you to that safe place I was talking about, remember?"

"Wha—what about you?" he hiccuped, voice weak from disuse or from the screams that must have clawed at his throat, only self-preservation keeping them at bay.

"I need to stay back so that I can help the others," I answered, hoping my absence wouldn't break the spark of resilience within him. "You need to be brave, can you do that for me? Rena will need a strong knight to help guide the way, do you think you could help her?"

Though his eyes flicked to and fro, nerves making him wary of every shadow that darkened the ground, he nodded. I knew his innocence protected him from the monumental shift in his world, the loss of his parents hidden in the darkness of his naive and young mind, but one day it would hit him. One day he would realize and I could only hope that the strength that filled his heart would stand strong against the barrage of grief that would come for him.

Smiling, I caressed his cheek. The soft, unblemished skin of someone who had seen and been through too much at such a young age. I placed a kiss atop his brown curls and passed him to Rena, giving the woman a nod of thanks before turning away.

Sidling up to Zanaya after one last word with the warriors, I pulled my blades free. Their familiar weight settled my nerves, easing the rising panic and overwhelming sorrow that threatened to take hold of me. There would be time for that later, but right now I needed the steadying presence of a blade, the hum of battle in my veins.

"We'll make our way to wherever the beacon points us, but we'll stop whenever I feel someone. We can hopefully cut down on the time it takes us to get to the others that way."

She dipped her chin and that was all that was needed. And so we went, house by house, fight by fight, sending those we found within the wreckage back towards the bridge. The few warriors that still battled in the street acted as escort, ordered to return to the fighting once the survivors had made it safely across.

Blood splattered my face as I dragged my blade across the throat of a warped, the stinking putrid blood rolling down my chin, collecting in the divot at the base of my throat. We encountered more of Kasis's army the closer we got to the southern wall. Civilians and soldiers and corrupt lay dead at our feet, discarded in the disarray and anarchy taking place.

Sprites flew overhead, joining in however they could. Some released surprisingly powerful magic upon the hordes, while others sought to help the fallen or extinguish the fires consuming the lower city. I tried not to look at the small bodies crumpled on the edges of rooftops and the torn glittering wings that littered the streets.

A chill grazed the back of my neck snapping me to attention. I whirled around just as a spear of ice punched through the chest of a warped sneaking up behind me, the wet slurping of the puncture wound overcome by the shrill cry of the fetid monster.

"Keep your eyes up," Zanaya screamed at me, already moving on to her next target. "I do not have time to save your ass as well as everyone else's."

Exhausted, I barely had enough energy to reply with a "thanks" before the next wraith took its fallen brethren's place. Easily dispatching the boar with a precise strike of piercing stone, bursting up from the street under its exposed belly, I stepped over the two bodies and into open space.

I made to move for my next opponent when a panicked young woman ran into me. Her scream ripped through my eardrum as she took us to the ground, the young man she held by the hand falling to the street with us. Rolling out from under her and onto my back, I barely had time to blink the sunspots from my eyes before the bone white talons of a wraith descended upon us.

With reflexes that still surprised me, I threw myself atop the two, shielding them from the worst of the blow. The pain came immediately, excruciating and searing, as the wraith's claws ripped into my back. Skin tore from muscle and muscle from bone, my nerves screaming as if I had thrown myself into the fires raging through the city, screaming agony racing down my spine as my blood spilled into the streets.

Its heavy weight shifted atop me, serrated teeth clamping down onto my shoulder. My arm buckled, but I caught myself before I could flatten the young woman and her friend. I couldn't help the whimper that escaped my throat as the wraith's massive jaws ground down on my bones. The edges of my vision darkened, even as I fought against my body's need, survival instinct pushing me to fight back.

A scream, this time not from me, broke through my haze, snapping me free of oblivion's grip. Gritting my teeth, bared in a vicious, bloody smile, I flared the energy in my body higher, burning through my own blood and tissue to reach the sickly creature.

After all, this body was only a shell. A casing around what truly lay beneath, it was only about finding the balance. Allowing the power to grow closer without *slipping* away from reality all together.

I hoped the young man and woman closed their eyes as I surrendered to the magic, allowing it to pulse and surge freely. Sounds fell away, the pounding of blood and power in my ears muffling everything else. The hum of a thousand prayers passed by me, as if I'd run straight past them into something else entirely. There was a yelp far in the distance, a weight lifting from my back, as the world flashed and erupted in gold.

Floating to my feet, I vaguely registered gasps, cries of...surprise? Shock? Pain?

Interesting.

Was I breathing? Every inhale barely lifted my chest, the pull of fresh air not there like it usually was.

Why was I weightless? Lifting an arm, I tried to ignore how different it felt, like I existed on some different plane. I glanced down, seeing nothing but glittering gold.

Where's my arm? My eyebrows drew in confusion. At least, I think they were my eyebrows. Arm, Atallia, where's your arm? I looked again.

Still gone. Was I upset by that? Should I be upset by that?

...I think I'm upset.

Panic. That's what this was, right? The whirlwind of thoughts moving a mile a minute. Although everything seemed to be moving slowly, like the molasses that Maris often used to sweeten the tonics she'd give to the young ones. So slow, even the buzzing, frantic emotion couldn't quite reach me.

Maris? I know Maris.

The thought of her slipped away. Her full, warm smile the last thing I saw before she was gone.

Why are my memories so dark? It was beautiful, that darkness, the kind that let the stars shine bright and without restraint. Unblemished onyx. It guarded, protected against something.

I smiled, love spearing through the sluggishness of this reality. It warmed my chest, settled in my soul, deep and unmovable.

Something niggled at the back of my brain, but I couldn't put my finger on it.

"Atallia?"

I turned around, the small voice breaking through the quiet, but saw nothing. The panic came back, using the hole punched through by love, to reach me.

It was uncomfortable. Maybe I needed to see things to make sense of it.

Blinking, the sheet of gold fell away, sticking to the edges.

People. My people.

Tilting my head, I looked around at them. They stared up at me in awe or fear, some with both. Why were they so short?

Rot.

I whipped around, an incomparable fury lashing out of me, blistering from within. A carcass. Multiple. Moving towards my people. Lips twisted in an odd mix of disgust and pity, I threw an arm out. Rays of light peeled away from my position, radiating more power than the sun, shooting between the masses to swallow the abominations whole until there was nothing left, not even a fleck of dust.

Was that my arm? My ivory skin was shredded, splitting at the seams. Broken into pieces to reveal my true form underneath. Gold wisps flew free from the cracks, racing into the open sky to swirl around me.

No, no, no. This was bad. Someone told me this was bad. Kanan! He told me, he told me this was bad.

Why? Why is it bad?

I need to fix this. Fix it. Fix it, pull back, Atallia. This power is yours. It is you. You control it. Come on, take the reins.

I fought my way back to the surface, every step more exhausting than the last, but I pushed through. Step by step I pulled myself from the depths of power. Even when it felt like my knees had been taken out from under me, I crawled forward. Clawing, inching, my way back to...something. What was it? Why was I fighting?

Power pulsed outward in a shockwave from my body, energy slipping through the cracks like a waterfall of molten gold. A torrent of ethereal power, streaked through with color, blasted into the streets. The winds picked up, fire and embers growing in strength. People fell to their knees, screams breaking through the fog around my mind. The power did not hurt them, but their fear resonated all the same.

No!

Digging my nails in, I jerked the aether back with all my strength. Muscles ripped, the iridescent veins in my arms bulged. Whether I breathed or not shards of rock cut my lungs to ribbons.

You. Are. Mine.

YOU.

I climbed higher, away from the mindless well of power at the bottom of this disembodied place.

ARE.

Higher. A gritting scream echoing through my...mind?

ME.

Light. Freedom. Control. The beating heart of galaxies, resonating within this measly chamber of my body.

Now STOP.

The storm of magic obeyed, freezing like a lake in winter. With a gentle tug it came to me, falling in line without defiance. It withdrew from the street, from the people and sky, leaving it all unscathed. Except for the wraiths that had the misfortune of meeting absolute power. The last traces of magic filtered back through the cracks in my skin, collecting just under the surface.

I gasped as the remaining splits sealed closed, taking in a breath of air like I'd burst from beneath the waves of the Divinian, and reality came crashing into me once again. Falling a few feet to the ground I threw out my hands to catch myself, my knees complaining weakly as they hit the cobblestone. *What the fuck was that?*

"Atallia." Zanaya slid to her knees beside me, placing a hand along my heaving back as I panted like I'd run miles without rest. "Are you okay?"

It took me a moment to speak, the conscious ability returning slowly. "I think—" I sucked in a breath, regretting it immediately when ash and smoke were all I could taste. "I have it under control. Did I hurt anyone?"

"No, no everyone's fine," she reassured me. "You're still glowing though. Your eyes too."

Sure enough, light emanated from my body, hovering around

without any signs of dimming. "The wraiths?" I asked, ignoring the obvious halo. There was nothing to be done about it right now.

She looked around, her discerning gaze sweeping the street for any signs of the half-dead. Her curls shifted behind her as she shook her head. "You killed the rest on this street."

"Help the warriors get the civilians to the bridge," I commanded, pushing to my feet. They were shaky, every muscle fiber protesting the movement.

"Where are you going?" She straightened, a hand moving to the crook of my elbow as I wobbled just a hair.

I pointed at the beacon stone, still glowing relentlessly above my chest, the sharp tip aimed at the southern wall. "To find Kanan and our friends."

"You can't expect me to leave you. They're my friends too," she argued adamantly, her gaze burning with an ice cold fire.

She took a firm step forward, but I was already backing away. "I can," I replied with a grim smile. "Because I know you'll help our people before your own interests. I'll find them, Zani, don't worry."

"Godsdamn you, Atallia," she screamed at my back as I broke out into a run.

I looked over my shoulder at her retreating form, the gathered people behind her, their faces somber and soot streaked. "Go!"

With that I tuned in to the power resonating under my skin, pushing it into my legs, my lungs, until I was tearing through the air. All my attention focused on the massive wall looming in front of me, the roars of true battle growing louder with every surge of speed.

"Kanan, I'm coming."

CHAPTER FIFTY

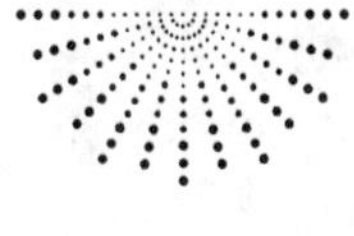

KANAN

"*Kanan, I'm coming.*" Atallia's sweet voice echoed through my head. It was a light shining brightly in the dark of night. Something beautiful amidst the chaos, the ruination Kasis had set upon us and our world. The familiar, welcoming sound warmed my heart even as the screech of metal on metal, blades clanging in opposition, and the wails of wraith hordes frayed my nerves.

I brought my sword down into the neck of a bear whose skeleton was completely exposed on one half of its body, thick slime sliding out from between its ribs. It continued fighting, lifting a listless paw to claw at whatever it could reach. Yanking my blade free, black blood, if you could even call it that, sprayed onto my chest and neck, the strong scent of putrid flesh following quickly.

"Could I convince you not to?" I asked despite knowing how in vain it was. Trying to keep her from the fight would be a fruitless endeavor, a costly one at that, given the force Kasis had thrown at us, but I tried nonetheless.

As I waited for her response, I dodged a kinsman's overarching swing, arrogance making his moves sloppy and open for easy hits. Ducking under his aggressive attack, I knocked his legs out from underneath him, easily taking him to the ground where he's swarmed by the shadows permeating the space around me. Like frenzied snakes they swallow him whole until there's nothing left but pearly white bone.

"I'm not going to even dignify that with an answer."

Cursing her stubbornness, I sent the shadows out to hunt for wraiths, knowing Kasis would have likely ordered a few to hide in case his attack failed. He could still cause havoc, even if he lost the battle. If he infected more people, he could add to his army of warped, the disease, of which we had no cure for, spreading throughout the city like the fires his kinsmen had set. *"I'll take that as a no,"* I grunted in reply, sweeping through a line of warped with a few well placed swings.

She didn't answer, but I had the overwhelming feeling she was flipping me off. Her annoyance burned like acid down the bond, a rippling of thoughts mixed throughout. More present than even that however, was her worry. Unease, a noxious, painful thing, twisted my stomach. It was tearing her up inside.

After nearly four days apart, half of which had been spent with our tether partially blocked, I could feel her again, the bond blazing to life inside my chest like a spark to a never-ending flame, her emotions hitting me in full.

Hours and hours of fighting, making the decision to burn a scar across the grasslands right outside the southern wall in order to cut off the mob of wraiths and warped, commanded by the kinsmen sent with them, from swamping the now destroyed gate, had been worth it as soon as her gleaming light broke through my all-consuming darkness.

Hundreds had still broken through, some half burnt from the fire I spewed. They ran amok in my city, using the confusion caused by their setting fire to the gate to tear down our defenses. Most of the wall's guards had been killed, their blood and magic used to stir the wraiths' maddening hunger.

The sun had risen hours ago and the hordes had only just begun to thin, their endless numbers a mystery in and of itself. The capsules shoved inside their chests were full of stolen Descendent sparks. The few that had broken under sword or claw had exploded with power, streams of energy racing up into the river of color that was mostly hidden by the smog filling the sky.

A male scream rent the air. Whirling around, I nearly missed the sight of Bron pouncing from the rooftop of a half crumbled building onto the back of a retreating kinsman. The ginormous saberthor ripped into the man, foot-long fangs cutting through bone like a blade to skin, and as blood stained his snow white pelt a rosy pink the kinsman's cries died with him.

He stalked over, silent as a phantom, despite being bigger and taller than some of the buildings that had been destroyed. Quite a few had Bron-sized holes tearing through them.

An entire stretch of the lower city was completely demolished, nothing more than cinders and the remains of those who'd gotten caught unknowingly in some twisted man's war. Thinking of the pyres I would have to burn, the number of death shrouds that would be sewn, made me want to throw my head back and roar. Rage at the sky, at the world, at Kasis. Death I may be, but senseless murder had never been to my taste. Especially when this was all just my brother's way of taking his displeasure out on me. These people, my people, meant nothing to him, but hurting me and Atallia did.

Shifting in a burst of silver energy, the shimmering cloud encapsulated his feline form. Bron's face was set in grim lines as he walked out of it, blood and death staining the air around him just as it stained his hands. "The generals have their battalions scoring the upper streets and houses, pushing anything they see back this way."

"Atallia's on her way," I responded, spearing a wraith crawling through the rubble a few yards away with a lance of shadow.

He merely lifted an eyebrow, snorting at my disgruntled tone. He looked down at the ground, bringing a hand up to rub along his jaw only to stop when he noticed the drying blood. Dropping it to his side, he sighed. "Did she mention Zanaya?"

I shook my head, opening my mouth to offer…I don't know what. Comfort? I wasn't exactly the one you went to for soft words and warm feelings. Not that Bron was the soft and warm variety anyway.

We were both saved from that awkwardness though as Commander Zuberi's second, Saanvi, crashed into the southern wall only a few hundred feet behind us. The Primal serpent writhed, hissing in fury at the four wraiths latched onto her.

Shaking off the hit, she lifted half her serpentine body off the ground, the sunlight that was able to break through the smoke caught along her black scales, turning them into an array of chromatic colors. She struck at the pests, unable to reach as the demonic creatures tried to rip into her armored hide.

Gathering the shadows, I succumbed to their call, allowing them to take me where I needed. The world fell away, becoming absolute darkness. In a blink of an eye, I reappeared beside the giant viper, striking out with the heavy weight of my sword, bringing its double edge down upon one wraith, ebony tendrils tearing the other three away.

Sweat dampened my brow, beads of it rolling down as I glanced up at the viper. Jade green eyes peered down at me in return, her second eyelid nictitating in what seemed like thanks. Her slender head whipped up, staring at something behind me. I whirled around as more wraiths bolted from behind a pile of stone and wood, remnants from some structure jutting out at sharp angles.

Gleeful laughter preceded Atallia's redheaded friend, Nala. Her flaming hair flew behind her as she chased a kinsman from behind. Putting on a burst of speed she launched herself onto the man's back, cackling as she wrapped her legs around his waist. Not even his shifting features could hide the sheer panic on his face as Nala plunged her curved blades into his chest over and over again, blood spurting with each stab. Following as he fell to his knees and then flat on the ground, she brought the twin blades down once more into his back for good measure.

I couldn't help but smile at her bloodthirsty grin, eyes glittering with excitement as she looked around for her next target. A ruby red fox followed from behind, leaping over her to chase down the fleeing wraiths.

The ground shook before he could catch them though and a wall of rock ripped from the ground, cutting off the shrieking horde's path and sending them straight into Bron's waiting jaws. Saanvi glided around the fight to catch any trying to escape the bloodbath.

A growl of delight rumbled from my chest, the primordial in me pleased by our enemies' spilt blood. The darkness in my veins hummed, violence as much a part of me as anything else. Violent deaths happened as often as peaceful ones, if not more, and I could not rid myself of one without the other.

Not that I'd want to, I thought as my obsidian claws dug into the throat of a rearing stallion, the underside of its skeletal ribs glowing white. Snarling, I dropped my blade into the shadow realm in order to shove my other hand through its chest. I ignored its broken cries, the fight leaving its body, and yanked free the white heartsglass rattling within.

Tossing the carcass to the side, I glared down at the heinous contraption. I didn't care that it burned my flesh. Didn't care that the cosmic energy I was made of shied away from its controlling, oppressive presence. I crushed it in my fist and let the shards of crystal drop to the ground around my boots. Streams of sage and indigo, twined together, flowed up into the sky. Two souls, gone before their time.

Tug.

My full attention was grabbed, turned inward towards that braided bridge connecting me to my heart.

Tug.

The gilded strands of the tether pulsed again, pulling my gaze to the north. Air rushed into my lungs, each lift of my chest easier than the last.

Tug.

Sprinting into view, her radiant gold eyes locked onto mine. Energy swirled within as they filled with relief. Even covered in soot, blood splattered across her lithe body, strands of her gleaming hair coming loose from her braid, she looked every inch a goddess.

There was an aura of power surrounding her, her smooth ivory skin illuminated from the inside out, but it wasn't that immemorial power that drew me in like a dragon to a flame; no, it was the way she held herself.

Maybe not always confident, though she had more than she gave herself credit for, but courageous. Always willing to put herself in harm's way to save others, to be the mountain that stopped storms from befalling the helpless. Charging in, not always aware or caring of the dangers that would scar her skin and heart, because it might mean saving someone else from the same fate.

It was a wonder she had no idea how under her spell I was. How utterly my world revolved around her. She was the reason the universe kept spinning, the reason my heart beat, although it would much rather be with her than inside my measly chest.

I knew she didn't realize, but I hadn't lied when I offered to rip it out, tear it free of its bone prison and allow it to reside in paradise with her. Sometimes I thought I would beg for it, plead with her to take it, because the insanity of wanting her, needing her, pushed me to my own kind of madness.

Gods. She's mine. It still blew my mind, but nothing in the fucking universe could make me give her up. Even if she wanted to be free of me, banished me from her side, I don't know if I would be able to leave her. The titan grip of the Cosmos couldn't force me from her side, and until the stars were dust in our hands, nothing would. She may be the mountain, but I was the fucking sky itself, and any storm that wished to befall her would contend with me first.

I took a single step forward, restraining myself. My lips twitched upwards, but I grew still as her face morphed from an expression of relief to one of horror.

"KANAN!" she screamed. The light around her flared and turned blinding as it swallowed her. There was a flash, a flickering of energy, and then she was gone.

Gold light flared again, but this time behind me. I spun on my heel, nearly bumping right into Atallia. With a mighty shout, she sent a blast of light straight through the chest of a lunging wraith. The beast must have snuck up on me while I was distracted, taking its chance when it could.

The body flew backwards and slammed into the immovable stone of the boundary wall, falling limply to the charred grass. The field went silent as our friends slaughtered the last of the horde.

I stepped into her, pressing my heaving chest into her back, dropping my forehead to her hair. Breathing in her scent, the familiar sage and vanilla notes igniting something damn near feral inside me. A soft growl worked its way free. The world had gone to shit, but I couldn't find it in me to care all that much as she leaned into me.

Twisting around, she threw her arms around my neck. She ran a hand through my sweat soaked hair and tugged me down to meet her lips. I couldn't stop the groan that tore from me as I pulled her closer by the hips, plunging into her mouth as her taste hit my tongue.

If I ever left this world, I hoped it was with my lips on hers, my cock nestled within the heat between her thighs, the little whimpers and moans she made as I swept my tongue across hers becoming my death song.

She pulled back, far enough for us to catch our breath, but close enough to indulge my need to nip her lower lip. Cupping my cheeks, she drew my gaze to hers, love and understanding overwhelming everything else. My chest ached right above my breastbone, the heavy pounding against my ribs enough to sting.

"The Orama told me everything," she panted, her ethereal eyes growing wide. "I know, Kanan. I know about it all."

I was an idiot if I thought my chest had hurt before, because now it felt like it was splitting open right here and now. That godsdamn organ was shattering and reforming at the same time.

So many years. So many years I had waited to see her again, only to be stopped from going to her, telling her everything, by that witch's fucking blood tie. I had weathered Atallia's anger because I deserved it. Without my blood the Orama never would have been able to stop me from bringing Atallia home as soon as I remembered.

Now she knew why I had kept it all a secret. Why I had to betray her. I didn't even know how to feel. Angry? Relieved? It was like the world had dropped out from under my feet, that weightlessness taking hold, dragging my senses down along with it.

I was pulled back up though when Atallia gently pressed her lips into mine, reminding me all over again why emotions, however irksome they could be, could also be amazing.

"We'll talk about it later," she whispered as we came up for air. Brushing her nose against mine she gave me one last peck before pulling back. "What happened?"

I was glad one of us could remember to put our own selfish desires aside, because it certainly wasn't going to be me. There wasn't a single part of me that didn't want to seclude her away, keep her to myself and tell the rest of the world to fuck off.

"They attacked the southern gate last night," I explained roughly, glancing over at the gaping hole along the wall. "I noticed quickly, had Bron sound the alarm, but hundreds got in before I could burn their ranks."

"What about the eastern?" She swept her gaze over her friends, no doubt looking for serious injuries.

I tilted my head at her. "What about the eastern?" Even as I asked there were shadows creeping through the city, looking for the information I needed. It took seconds, and I stepped back as she replied at the same time as the knowledge hit my mind.

"They attacked the gate there too. Probably set fire to the forest to lure the guards. Though the fighting seemed mostly contained to the wall." She stopped, noticing my face, and peered intently up at me. "You didn't know?"

My brow furrowed as I shook my head. Why attack both, but only stir up trouble at one? A look of puzzlement crossed Atallia's face, her eyes drifting downwards in thought. Squinting in thought she asked, "Where's Cashim?"

"Last I heard he was down in the dungeons." I narrowed my eyes as I watched the wheels turn in her mind.

Her head snapped up, burning gaze locking on to mine. "Did you say the dungeons?"

CHAPTER FIFTY-ONE

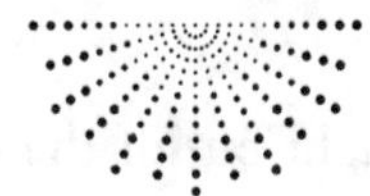

When battle raged and the spark of war ignited, I always thought there would be more noise. Explosions that rocked the ground and sent the world trembling. A crescendo of sounds that would pierce my eardrums and embed themselves into my mind. The clash of armor as the ranks of armies came together. Where two swords crossed and only one came out of it still raised high, the other falling useless to the ground beside its wielder, and the power that turned a blade so deadly fading with the light in their eyes.

I never expected it to be so quiet, and perhaps that made it all that much worse. For when calamitous fighting shifted to the silent aftermath, it left only one question in mind.

Who won?

Kanan and I would have no chance to find out, our fight still ongoing. Using the darkness that permeated the many nooks, Kanan shadow jumped us to the lower halls of the palace. The others were not able to make the jump, that particular skill only capable of beings made from intangible energy, so they would have to follow behind.

I desperately wanted to try phasing through the light again, but time was not on our side, so shadows it was. Within seconds we spanned the miles separating the palace and the border walls, the black smoke lifting to reveal the dim passageways that led to the dungeons. Silence met our ears, this one even more disconcerting than what had settled over the city.

The dungeons were carved deep into the mountain for a reason, the creature—Helmina—that resided within to guard whoever was unlucky enough to be placed inside the cells, was a vocal beast. Her high-pitched screeching could be heard ringing through several floors.

Gods, I hope I'm wrong.

There was a flicker of light out of the corner of my eye, a quick burst of silver pulsing from around the stone corner. I pointed it out to Kanan. His blood red eyes narrowed, power stirring within their depths. With a dip of his chin, we moved.

As we stalked forward, I pulled my heartsglass, letting the familiar weight of their hilts settle into my grip. The darkness of the halls aided us, leaping from the walls to join our hunt. Like pets they stirred around our legs, brushed against our sides in comfort as they fed off our violent energy.

Closing in on the turn, I listened for footsteps smacking against the floor. The echo within the lower passages was horrible, making even the smallest of sound seem like it was coming from every angle, bouncing around and around the stone caverns.

Nothing.

Glancing up at Kanan over my shoulder, I lifted an eyebrow in question. He shook his head after a moment. He couldn't hear anything either. Strange.

"Oh gosh, this is really bad."

My head snapped back as the familiar voice registered. I stepped out from behind the wall. "Wrynn?"

"Tali," he cried out from down the hall, his short frame flittering higher in the air as he caught sight of me. "Oh thank goodness, do you have any idea how scary it is down here?"

He shot over to us, his white pearlescent wings beating faster with every panting breath. Soot was streaked through his hair, turning the white strands gray. "Tali, Tali," he scrambled. "Something is wrong. Very, very wrong."

"What is it? Why are you down here?" I lifted up my open hand, holding steady as his booted feet set down. His wings drooped behind him, exhaustion weighing them down.

"Something is wrong with the Monarch. Bad, bad, bad," he exclaimed breathlessly, bending over to put his hands on his knees. "Air, need air."

"Where Wrynn?" Kanan asked from behind me, the heat radiating from him even hotter than usual.

Still dragging air into his over-exerted lungs, he pointed behind him. To the dungeons. Pulling him in close, Kanan and I raced in that direction. "What's wrong with him, Wrynn?"

He climbed onto my shoulder, holding tight to my tunic as we rushed through the halls. "He feels wrong," the sprite explained cryptically. "Scared."

"You can feel him?" The question probably wasn't the one to worry about at present, but his words seemed profound for some reason.

"The Monarch carries the Last Breath. Last Breath is like a heart, it keeps the Flight alive. Whoever holds it has a direct line to all sprites and us to them." His unusually serious tone had me pushing my legs faster, tearing through the distance to reach the dark plummet into the dungeons.

"Why is he even down here?" Kanan voiced the question that had been pressing on my mind. What reason would the Monarch have to enter the dungeons? Cashim wouldn't either, except to check on Jasco, but he could have sent a guard to do that. What could have possibly sent them both down here? Horror spread through me as a thought popped into mind.

"Wrynn, did Xotin owe the Orama a debt?" I inquired uneasily, dipping my chin to glance at him. "Please say no."

The sprite gulped, his dark eyes wide and swimming with fear. "I'm not allowed to say."

"Wrynn!" I yelled, a pang of guilt stabbing through me when he jumped. "Did he owe a debt?"

He nodded, wringing his hands one over the other. "Fuck," I cursed, grimacing as it rang down the hall. I peered over at Kanan who ran next to me, his long legs carrying him easily. "He's right, something is very wrong. I'm not sure what, but it's not good."

He said nothing, continuing to run, but the shadows that trailed behind us, growing larger as we went, lifted his dragon-hilted sword from their depths. They offered it to him and he curled his fist around its ginormous grip, swinging it up from the darkness without missing a beat.

"There were dead people, Tali," Wrynn whispered from my shoulder, as the stygian, unlit tunnel appeared before us. "On the upper floors. Descendents and the...others. The ones who should be dead but aren't. Th-they had silver armor on, I thought they were helping, b-but they weren't."

Warped. Kasis's guards.

The ground rocked, a slow build up that grew until the entire mountain shook like a leaf in the wind. I staggered to a stop as the floor swelled under my feet. Wrynn tumbled from my shoulder as the earth quaked with such force I fell to my knees. Kanan grunted, throwing a hand out to stop from crushing me under his weight.

An unholy scream tore through the halls, smashing through the air and scraping against my skin like razors. I gasped, choking on the air in my lungs. My heart raced, faster and faster like it was trying to take flight and flee. I threw a hand to my chest as if that would stop it from escaping, every corner of my soul screeching in terror as the infernal cry died.

Kanan's large palm landed on my back, gripping tightly as an enormous bang erupted from down below. I absorbed that small bit of warmth, holding on like my life depended on it. Every instinct blared with warning, the ancient core inside my body reacting instantly and without thought, spreading throughout until every cell was engorged with power.

The hair along my arms stood on end, the intense feeling of *wrongness* sucking the air from the hall. A bitter cold, like the chill of a thousand winters, spread through the stone; as raw and harsh as the echoing scream.

Minutes passed before I felt like I could breathe again. At some point I had curled in on myself, drawing my knees to my chest. Kanan had crawled over, throwing most of his large body over me. The shallow rise and fall of his chest matched mine, the only reminder that I was in fact breathing.

Kanan shifted atop me, lifting his weight from my back and rolling me over. "Are you alright, love?" he asked, cupping my cheek. Worry shined bright in his bright gaze, scanning over me for signs of injury.

"Yeah," I answered, my voice cracking. "Where's Wrynn?"

"I'm here, Tali." Twisting to the side, Wrynn carefully pushed to his feet. His delicate wings, still lowered from fatigued, appeared unharmed.

Sweeping his thumb over my cheekbone once, Kanan stood to his full height before offering me his hand. I allowed him to pull me up, his arm coming around my waist to steady me until I regained my balance.

"What happened?" I asked, lowering my arm for Wrynn to climb back up.

Kanan leaned over to pick up his dropped sword, twirling it in his hand, the enormous blade singing as it sliced through the air. "I don't know, but it's best if we find out."

We continued the descent, cautious and slower than before. "Go dim, Wrynn," I told the small sprite, whispering as we entered the pitch black hall. His silver glow disappeared completely as he curled closer to my neck.

There was an angry shout followed by yelling, the exact words muffled by distance. Kanan's hand gripped mine, squeezing gently. *I am here. I am with you.* The shadows curled around us protectively, their cool touch becoming more tangible, as if they too were preparing for a fight.

Light filtered into the tunnels, brighter than before. The long crescent shaped corridors took shape, disappearing on either side of us to border the ginormous circular chamber. Stepping through the archways felt different this time, more sinister. The scent of putrid rot, intensifying with every carefully placed step, filled my nose. My stomach roiled, bile rising in my throat at the horrid smell.

"You imbecile!" raged an all too familiar voice. "How could you lose her? Fucking pathetic. Years of planning. Years of preparation down the drain just like that. All because of your incompetence."

Kanan stiffened beside me, going deathly still. If I recognized it there was no way he didn't, the wavering timbre of his adoptive brother probably ingrained into his memory in a way he could never shake.

"Hide upstairs, Wrynn." My voice was as light as a feather as I pointed down the hall. There would be a staircase to the right a few dozen yards away, the opening to the higher levels of the prison cut directly into the ceiling. It was Lilyi who had first told me about it, who had told me to hide within the recesses of the cells, each one having unfettered access to the show below.

Taking flight he hovered directly in front of me, slow and deliberate beats allowing his tired wings to lift him. My tiny, boisterous friend was subdued, the fear around him suffocating with how thick it was, but he still found the strength to smile at me, faith shining through his terror. With one last look he zipped away, no sign of his silver aura as he disappeared around the curve of the hall.

Kasis growled in frustration, his footsteps clapping against the floor aggressively. Those same steps often played in my nightmares, the sickening crack of each one sent trembles through my tense muscles, shivers down my spine. There was a shuffle, clothes rustling, and a scoff of disappointment.

"I'll just have to make adjustments to the plan," he explained calmly, his voice sounding far away making me think he was talking to himself. "Everything will be alright, everything will go according to plan."

"We-we can still—" stammered a weak voice, now quiet and broken from his time down here.

"QUIET!" Kasis roared. Feet shuffled on the floor, Jasco and whoever else had come along jerking from the outburst. Kasis inhaled deeply as he moved around the cavern. "Be quiet. You've already done enough. Did you at least get what I need?"

Jasco cleared his throat. "Ye-ye—"

"Speak you idiot," Kasis commanded, his tone bored.

"Yes sir, we have it," the kinsman finished. Something groaned quietly, a soft mumble followed by the high-pitched ring of metal on metal. There was a thud, a small groan, and then silence.

"Good, give it here," Kasis demanded. "And let this be your one and only warning, maggot. If you fail me again, you will not like the consequences. Do you understand?"

Time stood still, falling away completely as Jasco answered, "Yes, Father."

CHAPTER FIFTY-TWO

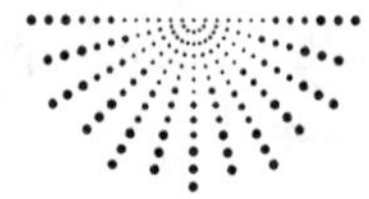

Father?

Jasco was the son of a fallen god, the son of Chaos. Kasis was Jasco's father. Kasis had a son. No matter which way I put it the shock didn't wear off, sticking to the revelation like the dried blood of all the people they had collectively killed, sentenced to a fate worse than death or life combined.

"Kanan?" I reached out, unsure of what to say. What was there to say, was it even possible?

The soft velvet of Kanan's mind brushed against my mind, the startling darkness building along the boundaries, shielding it. *"I heard,"* he said in response, his voice hard as ice and sharp as the crystalline edge of his black blade. *"I didn't know. He can't be much older than a couple decades, maybe a century at most, his mind felt young when I interrogated him. We weren't around when he was born."*

"Or created," I added, giving him a look over my shoulder. Given Kasis's proclivity for messing with the natural order of things, Jasco could have very well been one of his many experiments.

Shifting closer, he reached out and grasped my hip. I longed for a time when I could enjoy the light fluttering feeling his touch created within me, butterflies taking flight in my stomach. Instead, I would have to make do with taking comfort in his presence, his strength, both of us bolstered by the other, stronger together than ever apart. *"I think it's time for a family reunion, love."*

Snaking my fingers through his, I gave it a squeeze. *"Couldn't agree more."*

Stepping into me, his chest against my back, he leaned down and placed a kiss against the side of my neck. I siphoned his warmth, using it to settle my nerves. I could feel his heart beating against his chest, a powerful drum pounding away to the sounds of battle and war. It was in his blood, simmering in his veins. The same buzz of adrenaline that set me aflame during a fight lived in him like an integral piece of his soul.

It was a good thing his soul was the other half of mine. That his fortitude in the face of the unknown could easily become my own. I leaned on our bond, nourished it until it glowed, and felt him do the same. The ethereal bond was crafted in the forges of the universe, and there was no force or magic that could compete with that.

"Together?" he offered, the power of night-kissed death enveloping his voice. He stood in the middle of the bridge, endless black and dazzling gold, a hand outstretched towards me.

"Together," I accepted, the aether of life imbued in my tone. Joining him on the bridge, I accepted his hand and the two halves of our souls were connected again in a place outside the realm of common thought, where empyreal power reigned supreme and we were the center of it all.

As if he too felt our bond strengthen, unfortunately existing on that same plane of power on some level, Kasis's vile green eyes shot over to us as soon as we entered through the archway. Well practiced in hiding his true feelings, a well-crafted mask slid over his features, but not before I saw a flash of surprise, and fear, swell in his gaze.

The first thing I noticed wasn't the dozens of warped guards, a disheveled, unkempt Jasco standing nearby, or even the ginormous hole in the side of the mountain, hundreds of feet of shattered rock piled high near the back of the prison, the dying light from the sun filtering in, backlighting Kasis as he paced in front. It was the glint of a red jeweled hilt at the base of the wreckage, a bloodied dark hand gripping it tightly.

I slapped a hand over my mouth as a cry tore from my throat. Cashim's lifeless body lay beaten and discarded, his ice blue eyes, the same ones his niece had inherited, were without light and no longer held that discerning, calculating spark. Blood seeped from unseen wounds, still steaming, the light refracting off the dark stone and turning it to black smoke as it left his body and soaked through the floor.

"Is-is he dead?" I asked Kanan regardless of the fact I knew the answer in my heart.

"Yes. He's gone," the God of Death replied. His voice had turned brittle and angry, the darkness in my mind vibrating with barely restrained rage. Even though I knew it to be true I still couldn't find it in me to believe it. That a life such as his, full of memories and emotions and greatness, had been extinguished just like that.

"Brother!" Kasis exclaimed, throwing his arms out wide in greeting. "It has been so long."

Even through my grief his words penetrated, and I realized that for the first time in two thousand years, the two brothers, not of blood but of shared existence, were meeting.

Kanan merely spared him a glance, the raging fires within his eyes promising death and retribution. He swung his sword through the air, the black blade consuming all light as he gained his grip on the pommel.

"Aren't you happy to see me?" Kasis continued, taunting the dragon king with a twisted, smug grin.

"I'd be happier if you had stayed dead," Kanan remarked, lifting a dark eyebrow as he looked his brother up and down, unimpressed by what he saw. "Although you were always a bit of a cockroach, so I guess I shouldn't be surprised."

For as hard as he tried to appear unaffected, a muscle in his jaw twitched, those poisonous green eyes glowing neon for a moment before returning to their normal pristine shade. Straightening his suit jacket, an unblemished green that matched his eyes, he brushed away invisible dust. "Oh come now, brother, don't be so foul. It's been a long time since we've caught up, let's not be hostile."

"Why are you here Kasis?" Kanan asked, stepping forward to position himself in front of me. *"Look to your left, love."*

I scanned the shadows gathered along the rounded walls as the two continued to talk. It took several sweeps before I finally saw what he meant. There, unconscious near the base of one of the many pillars, was Xotin. Dust had collected on his robes, grime marring the white fabric. His sapphire locks were tangled around his limp body, some of the pink ends drenched with blood. And then a cold sweat broke out along my hairline, a chill overtaking me, as I saw why.

Dark red drenched his back, more spilling from the two stumps poking from beneath his robes. His dazzling wings, the color of the sea or some nebulous sky, were gone. Excised from his body, ripped away without care for the person they were attached to. Sprites were born to fly. They were masters of the air, beautiful dashes of magic amongst the wind. They gave movement, life, to an invisible force that impacted so much on our planet. Pure spirits, meant to fly free and without restraint.

Magnificence gone without a trace.

First Cashim, my tears of grief still waiting to spill, and now this. The muffled noise of conversation pulled me back from my growing horror. *"I think he's still alive."*

The shallow rise and fall of his slim chest, and the occasional sickening twitch of his amputated wing stems, were the only indicator.

"He is, but his death lingers," Kanan supplied as Kasis remarked on something he said. Kanan kept provoking him, buying time.

"Can you lift him up to the second floor without them noticing? Wrynn can get him out of here and to Moian."

The shadows nearest to the Monarch's fallen body were already encircling him before I could finish, picking up the wounded body of the Flight's leader with care. I held my breath, waiting for Jasco or Kasis to notice, but the dark tendrils slyly carried Xotin over the edge and disappeared from view.

"Still nothing more than a lumbering oaf I see. Playing in the dirt and swinging your blades when you could rule from your throne," Kasis retorted bitterly, his cool, calm demeanor slowly falling away, his gaze shifting to the black heartsglass in Kanan's grip.

"Hmm, I do prefer to get my hands dirty," Kanan purred in amusement, the sound curling over my skin like the slow kiss of death. A grin tugged at the corner of his lips as he glanced down at the massive sword, and when he flicked his gaze up, glowing red irises burning with hellfire, Kasis took a single step back. Even the warped, their minds no longer theirs and instead at the mercy of their master, shifted uncomfortably. Some instinctual part of them recognized what—who—stood before them, and not even corruption could wipe away primal fear.

His grin turned into a full blown smile, fangs bared in predatory satisfaction. A beast enjoying his prey's fear. "Unlike you," he continued, prowling forward, "I find the feel of my enemies' blood on my skin, their terror on my tongue, far more satisfying than any throne." Shadows collected behind him, gathering like an army behind their general, soldiers from a realm of sheer darkness.

Power gathered at Kasis's hands, green streaked through with black, reminding me a lot of the infected wounds I had often cleaned for the workmen of the Outskirts during the planting season.

Kanan, backed by undefeatable darkness, didn't so much as pause. He stalked forward without fear, head held high, only his great-sword in hand. An anger born from pure hatred emanated from every hard line, every unwavering step. This was two thousand years of lost time, an undeniable rage that threatened to crack the stone beneath his feet.

As the mountain trembled before its king, and Kasis truly began to understand what he'd created, I turned my attention to Jasco. Warped surrounded him, dozens, waiting for their master's command. The former Descendents, now creatures of festering flesh, disease crawling through their veins where blood once ran, were cloaked in silver armor. Helms covered their mutated faces, hiding who they once were, and what they had now become under Kasis's foul abuse.

"This has been a long time coming, *brother,*" Kanan snarled as he advanced on Kasis, a black wave of death looming over them both. Swinging his sword, the dragon's jeweled eyes glinting in bloody righteous fury, he brought it down upon the God of Chaos as cosmic havoc blasted from Kasis's hands.

The darkness swelling behind Kanan darted out to meet it, and when the shadows of death smashed into corrupt chaos a thunderous crack tore through the air, the walls of the prison shaking from the force of it. Cracks, splintering from where the two met, spread out and across the stone floor of the caverness room.

Continuing with unwavering ferocity, the muscles in his back tensing and then flexing with every swift movement, he followed through with his swing. Kasis dodged the blow, the blade's long reach threatening to slice him in half. He wasn't fast enough to avoid it completely though, the razor sharp tip scratching his left cheek, and a thin trickle of blood welled to the surface before slowly rolling down his face. His perfect facade fractured, the snarling, horrid monster underneath taking form as the two began to trade blows.

God on god.

Two primordial powers going up against each other, both wielding abilities that could break the foundation of the world. Collectively... one savage blow, a connection of energies never meant to mix, could doom us all.

Avoiding the battling brothers, I made for the distracted warped. Without someone telling them what to do, they became like statues in a garden. Unmoving. Unseeing. They occasionally let out a grunt or gasp, but nothing more than that.

Jasco's green eyes, their familiar vibrant color making sense now, snapped up to mine. I sprinted towards him, slamming into the first row of warped. Slashing my blade across the vulnerable skin of one guard's neck, unprotected by both helm and chest plate, I dashed through their ranks, blasting another with a bolt of gold magic. The warped erupted with confusion, the mindless guards stumbling away from their fallen comrades.

"Remember me?" I goaded Jasco, utilizing the confusion to get to him. Leaner than the last time I saw him, stress echoed throughout his entire demeanor. His features were frozen, the white heartsglass cuffs shackled around his wrists and ankles cut him off from whatever magic he possessed. Dirt and grime coated his skin, and his back was hunched, as if he had spent the past few weeks curled into a ball.

"You bitch," he snarled weakly, taking an aggressive step forward only for his knee to buckle slightly under his weight.

"Oh good, you do remember," I replied enthusiastically. One of the warped, finally piecing together what had happened, suddenly threw a punch. Jumping out of the way, the feeble attempt went wide and dragged the walking set of armor along with it. "I do like to make sure the people I kill know exactly who is stabbing them through their rotten hearts."

The corpse writhed on the ground, unable to get up. I killed the poor creature with a blast of shearing wind, ripping the metal from its withering frame and, to prove my point, finished it off with a blade through the heart.

I forced back a gag as its blood spurted from the wound, the smell of rancid meat fumigating the air.

Jasco laughed maniacally, eyes glinting with malice and something that looked remarkably like sadness, but it was gone in an instant. Slowly standing, he shook his head at me. "Then kill me, you whore. You think he'll care?" He waved towards Kasis, locked in battle with Kanan. The mastermind was losing badly. Every step he took, Kanan forced him back by two more. "Unlike you, my father cares little for his progeny other than how we can serve him."

"Then why serve him?"

A cylindrical silver tube was pulled from his pocket, no bigger than his palm. He smirked, the action forced. "It is an honor to serve the almighty Chaos, to be at his side as he ushers in a new age of greatness. He will reward those who are loyal."

The words sounded rehearsed, a script that he had no doubt repeated a thousand times, but I had no chance to dwell on it. Bringing the metal to his lips, he blew into the whistle and a sharp piercing note cut through the explosive noise of fighting. As one, the disoriented warped straightened, turning towards the source of the sound. Dozens of blank, soulless eyes peered through their helms, waiting.

"And to be honest," he chuckled weakly, glancing up through lowered lashes, "this is much more fun."

He blew into the whistle again, this time a low pitched note that vibrated through my chest, and the neck's of every warped snapped in my direction.

CHAPTER FIFTY-THREE

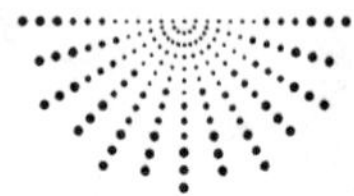

Sweat dripped down my spine, a cool relief for my skin when the molten gold aether swarming underneath flared. Instinct ruled supreme when vicious rotting corpses were rearing to tear into your body, eager to spread their mind-stealing disease.

The ground shook, the walls of the prison taking a beating as Kanan and Kasis attempted to kill each other. It worked to my advantage, the shaking foundation similar to the shifting sands of our sparring ring back in the village. My muscles had been finely tuned for any terrain, Geoff making it his personal mission to ensure any disadvantage was quickly and efficiently cut down.

I wish I could have talked to him. Both of them. The thought drifted in as I crouched in defense, the first warped charging with unexpected speed. I hadn't even thought to speak with them after everything, my anger blinding me past reason. The past few days, weeks, had been so full I couldn't even remember the last time I'd eaten or slept, but right now, facing down what could be our very near future, decaying flesh and all, I wish I had made time to speak with them. Heard their side of the story.

If I survive this, it's the first thing I'm going to do.

"Get moving, cub." That's what Geoff would say to me right now. I

stared down the faceless warped whose contorted fingers, outstretched in my direction, sported jagged claw-like nails. *"It's kill or be killed."*

Kill.

I launched into action, meeting the guard head-on. Diving for its legs, I ducked under its reaching arms, slamming my elbow into the back of its knee, and sending it flying. I winced, my elbow throbbing with the strength of the blow, aftershocks quivering through my bicep.

Surging past I hurled myself at the next warped in view, kicking out with a booted foot. The chest plate crunched underneath, a few cracks following right after. I finished with a blow of power that left nothing but an empty metal shell. I continued clearing my path towards Jasco.

He hid behind a line of warped, the dragon skull emblem on each breastplate eating through my restraint with every mocking flash of its dead metallic eyes. Power pulsed down my arm, my skin radiating light like the sun, and with a single harsh stroke it cut through the air and leveled the warped.

Savage satisfaction rose through the adrenaline pumping in my veins at Jasco's wide eyes taking in the melting armor dripping to the floor, pooling at his feet. He took a step back, then a second one when I followed.

A fist slammed into the side of my head without warning. My neck snapped to the side, the rest of my body following as I lost balance and crashed to the floor. A swift kick to my ribs followed, compounding on the pain stabbing through my head. I coughed as all the air in my lungs was forced from my body.

The clank of metal joints broke through the pounding of blood in my ears, my only warning to throw up a hand as another strike came down. I gripped hard on the smooth metal covering my assailant's leg, yanking back with all my strength. Pulling the warped down, I rolled before the limp weight could crush me. Every movement felt like I swallowed hot coals, the slight crunch when I inhaled only slightly worrying.

I persisted though, surrendering to the pain in order to keep pushing my body forward. Sliding my hand to the gauntlet around my forearm, I gripped one of the minuscule blades Zanaya always insisted I wear and stabbed down into the back of the warped's neck. The body twitched for a couple seconds after, but quickly went still. I left the palm-sized dagger where it was just in case.

I stared down as black blood seeped from under its helmet, spreading across the floor until it touched the sole of my boot. The liquid reflected my image back at me, my eyes alive with gleaming starlight, swirling with unimaginable power that was healing my chosen body by the second.

My chest heaved, an ice cold burn taking up residence alongside the jagged ache of my broken ribs. I slowly glanced at Jasco, all sense of pity I felt for him dissipating with every wheezing breath, and I knew what he saw.

He turned and ran for the gaping hole in the mountain, forgetting the warped he left behind. Gripping my side, urging my magic to heal me faster, I bolted after him.

Warped attacked me as I charged past, attempting to stop me, but I dodged out of the way before any blows landed. I latched on to the whistling wind outside, the chilly currents picked up speed, feeling my presence, and with a simple command it funneled in through the gaping tunnel, lashing Jasco with invisible knives.

He dropped to the floor screaming, a thousand small cuts slicing into his skin. Something skittered across the ground as he fell, the clink of chains along the stone jerking my attention away. The second I saw the white light filtering through the silver chainmail my heart dropped.

Jasco and I shared a look, a feral panic consuming his eyes. We both started sprinting. Even through his weakened and bloodied state Jasco ran like his life depended on it, and I guess if Kasis wanted the Last Breath, it did.

He was closer and reached it first, but knowing what that tiny, otherworldly rock meant to the sprites, I tackled him to the floor without hesitation. Knocking it from his hands again, I pushed off his chest, shoving him hard into the ground, and scrambled after the chain pouch.

I snatched it from where it rolled along the floor. Panting, I turned to find Jasco getting to his feet, eyes locked onto the Last Breath. Before he could think to attack again, I yanked another throwing knife free and sent it hurling through the air with god-like speed. Like an arrow to its mark, it sank into his right shoulder with a gratifying thunk.

"ATALLIA!" Kanan's scream was my only warning before something punched through my back. Muscles tore and ribs cracked under the pressure, but nothing compared to the feeling of a hand gripping my heart.

Blood bubbled up my throat, coating my tongue and the inside of my mouth with its metallic taste. I tried to suck in a breath of air, but only raspy gulps came out of my mouth, blood running down my chin.

The edges of my vision darkened, all of my strength draining from my body and leaving behind a paralyzing weakness. Blood pounded in my ears, the stuttering beat of my own heart thumped loudly. I felt my hand spasm, Xotin's chain bag dropping to the floor with a clink.

All the power humming under my skin sputtered like a dying flame, and then it was dashed away, chains dragging it to the depths of my being until it was nothing but a dim spark in my mind's eye.

"Heartsglass. I don't know how," I informed Kanan, hoping he would hear. The pair bond we had forged became muted, a sluggish force overriding it, but our tether remained strong, thrumming wildly as if it sensed something wrong.

"I'll rip him to pieces," he roared in response seconds later, the words lagging as my mind spun in a million different directions. A haze overtook my thoughts and with every painful breath they were harder to hold on to.

There was nothing left for me to respond with, all of my energy focused on where Kasis's hand dug into my chest, fingers gripping my weak heart. *Gods, that hurts.*

He had to have heartsglass on him somewhere, nothing else had the ability to make godly power this useless. It was like I had thousand pound stones tied to my ankles dragging me beneath some dark ocean where swimming free and breaking through the swell seemed impossible. I didn't even have the ability to shirk away when Kasis stepped closer, my body going limp and leaning up against him as I lost most of the feeling in my legs.

"Ah ah," he warned menacingly when Kanan took a step forward, squeezing his hand around my heart. I whimpered, back arching as I instinctively retreated from the pain. Kanan froze in his tracks, his gaze a raging storm of blood as he watched me struggle. Power unlike any other swirled in those red depths, the glow brushing the tops of his cheeks, and yet I had never seen such defeat in his eyes.

Kasis hummed in satisfaction behind me, the sounds vibrating his chest behind me. "There now, that wasn't so bad. Jasco, take the stone and go, we're expected in the Gravelands."

The worm crept over with wary eyes, his chin bloody from where he must have hit it against the floor. Crouching he picked up the sling, the links of metal scraping over the stone with a resounding defeat. He gave me one last smirk, blood coating his teeth, before scurrying away.

I could hear the scuffle of shoes on rock as he climbed through the massive hole in the mountain, disappearing with the sprites' salvation to do who knows what with.

"Why are you doing this?" I wheezed, coughing up blood.

"Why? WHY?" he repeated incredulously, anger rising in his voice. He chuckled without humor and clenched down on my heart until he ripped a scream from me.

"Kasis, enough!" Kanan roared, his chest heaving and knuckles turning white around his lowered sword.

"I say when it's enough!" the demented fucker screamed back. He jerked his head back in crazed laughter. "Second best for eons. Always the other brother, always the less powerful god, always stuck in your fucking shadows. Do you know what it's like to have everything you want taken from you? Ha," he laughed in mocking self-deprecation. "It wasn't even taken, I was just never even an option. Not even with her."

His hand jerked inside my chest almost without thought, and my lungs felt like they were caving in, all the air slowly leaking out. I didn't need air to survive, but when they collapsed completely and my throat threatened close, I would wish for death.

The irony was not lost on me.

"I was a throw away. The spare. That's what I was, but not anymore." With every word he became more vehement, spitting his venom and insecurities upon us as thousands of years of jealousy shattered any essence of the meticulous, orderly facade he wore. "Now you'll understand what it's like to have everything taken from *you*."

"What do you want, Kasis?" Kanan asked between bared teeth. His fangs were out in full, all four glinting ferociously as if they were waiting for the day they could tear into Kasis's throat.

I could hear the smug smile in Kasis's tone when he replied, "You know what I want."

Kanan smirked, a chuckle shaking his broad shoulders as he hung his head in amused exasperation. He looked back up, his heated gaze meeting mine. Winking he dropped his sword into the darkness around his legs, the blade disappearing to realms unknown.

Never moving his gaze from mine, he slowly lowered himself to his knees, his towering height making him formidable even from the surrendering position. He held his head high, proud and powerful even now.

I knew Kasis was talking, a conceited mumble in my ears, but I couldn't hear a thing. Nothing could have breached the plane Kanan and I existed on, the two of us together against the world. He never once glanced away, his reverent eyes remaining on mine as a crooked smile curled his lips, dimples denting on either side.

And I knew. I knew he did it for me. A dragon bowing, kneeling, not before an enemy, but before his mate, his other half.

My bruised, ruined heart stuttered uselessly. He did everything for me. Always for me.

"I expected a little more from you, if I'm being honest," Kasis goaded. "A snarl, a fight, something. Have to say I'm a little disappointed."

Kanan smiled at me, a lick of heat entering his eyes. "I've never had a problem kneeling before the queen."

"Don't make me laugh," I grumbled inside his head, a pained chuckle making its way out regardless.

Kasis hummed in my ear, his hot breath brushing my cheek, the stench of rot following. "Not your queen for long though."

I jerked my head away in disgust as he brushed his knuckle across my skin, immediately regretting it when a sharp stab had every muscle in my body tensing as the spasm worked its way through.

Kanan's snarl reached my ears. The vicious growl sent a shiver down my spine, a twist of hope looping through my stomach, but even if I told him to, he wouldn't move. Wouldn't risk me even if it meant killing Kasis.

Kasis laughed again, more and more of his madness peeking through. "So docile, Kanan. Had I known it would work so well, I would have taken sweet Atallia sooner."

Kanan said nothing, but with every heaving breath a growl escaped. Onyx black claws curved and flexed on instinct, waiting for the moment where they could rend flesh from bone. He still didn't move though. Not an inch. Not when Kasis's hand disappeared into my back.

"You're forgetting something, Kasis," I purred in derision, though my voice sounded weak even to me. I'd need every last ounce of strength that remained if my crazy idea was going to work.

"Get ready," I told Kanan. A small crease worked its way in between his eyebrows, but he didn't argue.

Kasis shifted, putting a small space between us, his arrogance making him relax. That would be his downfall, here and when we won this fucking war. He approached every situation like he already knew the outcome, foresaw every decision that would be made.

Except the ones he'd least expect.

"Oh and what have I forgotten, darling goddess?" he mocked, hand tightening around my dying heart, each beat weaker than the last.

The pain was horrendous, worse than any physical agony I had ever felt, but it worked to my advantage. Gathering my waning strength, I whispered the words no one would have predicted, "That this body is just a shell."

And with a giant shove against his stomach, I pushed forward, and let him tear my heart from my chest.

I collapsed to the floor, unseeing as my world flashed before my eyes. Power rushed back through me, darting for the gaping wound in my chest, beginning the long, arduous attempt to knit my chosen body back together again.

White hot pain swept over me, every inch of skin, muscle, and bone aching like the fire of a thousand suns burned down from above. The ground shook under my cheek, an explosion somewhere off in the distance, or perhaps close by I couldn't tell.

My reality had shrunk to the chill of the stone beneath me, raw blistering torture accompanying my every twitching movement, and the few thoughts that were able to break through the shroud of agony. All concept of time was lost, seconds seeming like hours, but at some point the explosions and fighting stopped, silence ringing like bells through my ears.

"Atallia," Kanan's voice reached through the fog, hovering over me as he rolled me onto my back. His hellfire eyes stared down at me, burnished rubies filled with anguished concern, shadows curling over his ears and through his midnight locks like a crown of darkness.

So beautiful.

"Atallia," he called again.

Blinking rapidly, I fought through the dreamless oblivion trying to pull me under. *"Kasis?"* I asked through our bond, not trusting my voice to work.

He snarled. "Gone. He went invisible and escaped, ran like a fucking coward."

Dammit. I closed my eyes as both pain and failure ricocheted through me. *So close.*

I cried out as Kanan put his arms under me and lifted me into his lap. "Sorry, love," he whispered, his voice tight.

Swallowing hard, I wet my lips. "Tell me why we decided to take physical forms again? Because this fucking hurts," I wheezed, my lungs faltering, as a wave of pain nearly took me under, blood slipping from the corner of my mouth.

He swallowed, agony contorting his perfect features. Lifting an eyebrow, he attempted a light, suggestive smirk although it fell flat as his bright gaze skimmed over the blood drenching his lap. "Well it has its pluses, don't you think? Worldly pleasures and all that."

I coughed, the taste of iron filling my mouth, but a weak smile pulled at my lips anyway. "I can't believe you're making jokes right now."

"Who said anything about jokes?" He lifted me higher up his chest, thick arms tightening around my limp body. Shadows curled over my legs, crawling into my lap protectively. The skin around his eyes creased, agony reflected in every jagged breath, as if my pain was his. "Just breathe, little goddess, pain is only temporary."

I don't know how long we sat there listening to every broken, gasping breath, my energy solely focused on building a new heart, but at some point I lifted a weak arm, brushing my fingers down the side of his face. His eyes shuttered at my touch and he hugged me closer, enfolding me within his warm embrace, the amber smoke of his scent invading my every sense.

"I love you," I whispered intimately.

"Until the stars are dust in our hands, my love," he answered back and I could have sworn a thrum echoed through my head, a phantom voice repeating something back. It was whisked away as he pressed his lips to mine gently.

His head jerked up as the sounds of hurried footsteps rang through the chamber. I saw Zanaya first, her ice blue eyes, the only of their kind now, scanning over me. The others, all of our friends, our family, the people we loved, filed in behind her. All of them were armed to the teeth, more than ready to fight for us and their city.

Concern fell over Zanaya's face and she rushed to come to my side, but froze halfway when she glanced behind us.

No, no, no.

"Kanan," I whimpered, needing him to do something, anything, as I watched shock and then horror and then irreparable despair crash into her.

"She has a right to know, love. A right to grieve as we grieve."

And so, as my closest friend fell to her knees, an earth shattering scream ripping from her throat that broke the small pieces of my regrowing heart, I let my eyes close and finally allowed my tears to fall.

CHAPTER FIFTY-FOUR

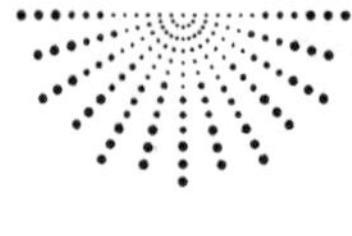

KANAN

The city had lost all sense of time. It flowed around us like a river, and we were the unmovable, immortal stone standing in its path. Except immortal wasn't quite right, because time eroded all things. It tore away little by little until what was left changed completely, and just when you thought you'd accepted this new reality, time hit again. Harder and more fiercely each and every chance it got, until one day, when you least expected it, you would look down and not recognize what was left.

Time stopped for no one. It was an unforgiving fact of the world.

But as ridiculous and impossible as it sounded, time seemed to slow for us. The bruised, battered, and beaten Eskira had been given a small mercy by the universe. Minutes lingered, hours felt like days. In some ways it was a blessing, and in others a curse.

Grief saturated the air, its mark everywhere I looked. On every corner, in every burned house and destroyed shop in the lower city. Not a single soul within our borders could escape its heartless sting.

The number of pyres currently being constructed upon the blackened plinth overlooking the skeleton of a once great forest were too many to count, though I had the number engraved into my mind. Death shrouds, sewn by each of the fallen's family and friends, to later be used in the burning ceremony, hung in surviving windows and doorways, tears staining the delicate black fabric.

Soon dawn would come and I would be expected to descend from the smog still filling our beautiful skies, and light them all aflame. Burn away their tears and sorrows, and carry their loved ones to a place beyond their sight and understanding. A place they only had hope existed, hope in me, in everything they believed in.

"How long have you been out here?" Atallia asked, shuffling out onto the balcony from bed. She'd been sleeping on and off for the past two days, and every time she opened her eyes and smiled at me, she breathed air right back into my lungs. Even a true immortal needed time to regrow a heart.

When we chose these bodies we accepted their limitations with ease, never anticipating they would ever fail us. Thoughts by our younger, more naive selves. Now, when Kasis had proven just how badly they could fail, breaking Atallia's ribs and forcing her to tear out her own heart, I couldn't help but wish we'd never chosen physical forms. Where things like pain could find her.

"Only a few hours," I replied, opening my arm for her to step into my chest. Wrapping it around her, I pulled her close, burying my nose into her hair. Sage and vanilla, warmth and light and all the good things I had come to love about this world. "You fell asleep again, so I figured I'd come keep watch."

She rubbed her cheek against my chest, making my heart race in a way only she could. "Anything new happen while I was out?"

I paused, debating whether to tell her, but my hesitation was all she needed.

"Kanan, what is it?" she questioned, peering up at me, her golden eyes narrowing in suspicion.

I released a heavy sigh, already dreading what would come of this. "The stonemasons found another body buried under the rubble in the dungeons." I glanced down at her, brushing my thumb down her cheek and tucking an errant strand of hair behind her ear. "It was Lilyi."

She gasped, her rosebud lips parting in shock as she took in the news. Her brow furrowed as she asked, "What was she doing down there?"

"No one knows for sure," I said with a shake of my head. The first glimpses of dawn were touching the horizon, the beginnings of a new day rising from the ashes of our destroyed city, illuminating the blackened scars cutting across it near the southern and eastern borders. "Perhaps she overheard Cashim and followed to help a friend, maybe she sensed something was wrong and went to check, but those are only theories."

"Cosmos, how much more can we take?" Gilded lashes fell over her eyes, and she ran a hand down her weary face. "Does she have any family?"

I ran a hand down her back, marveling that I was able to touch her. That she was finally back in my arms. "Mmmm, a sister, I believe. Younger, but not by much. She's an Aether as well, if I remember correctly, so she'll have to take her place on the Council."

"What if she declines?" She glanced out over the city, her eyes stopping on the burnt patch of land to the east, the charred remains of the forest spanning for miles.

"She won't, not when there's a vacuum in the cities' leadership. If she does decline, however unlikely, and there's not another relative in the Jai family who is also an Aether, then she forfeits her family's position on the Council. The Hassere people will designate the next Aether they wish to represent them."

"Seems so…political," she surmised, her eyes never leaving the destroyed woodland just beyond the walls.

I couldn't help but agree, placing a kiss atop her head. "The Council was first created to advise us on matters concerning the people, especially those in the other cities, and give a way for even the least powerful Descendent to have a say in things. At any moment the Council representatives could be removed from their seat if enough people wish it, but after so many years ruling without much oversight, things have slipped. They're often more concerned about fighting and debating with each other than about helping ensure voices are heard."

"Perhaps new blood will offset that then." She pursed her lips in thought. "Simply because something has grown stagnant does not mean it isn't of use, sometimes you just need to get the water flowing again."

I tugged her closer and barely stopped myself from purring when she placed a hand against my heart. Running a finger down her nose, I tilted her chin up until she was looking at me. "How is our new blood doing?"

Her brows furrowed, sorrow overtaking her beautiful features. "About how you'd expect," she answered. She drew patterns across my chest, her gaze unfocused and filled with pain. "They were fighting, and now they won't have the chance to make up. I tried to visit her, but she doesn't want to see anyone right now."

We were both silent, our own grief nestled deep in our hearts. Cashim was a great loss to us all, his intelligence, wisdom, and kindness made him not only a great asset to our Council, but also as a friend. While Atallia may not remember the little boy who used to interrupt his mother's meetings, dark curly hair cut close to his scalp exactly how he liked it two thousand years later, I did remember him, and the man he grew up to be. His was a loss that would be felt long after his passing.

"All this pain, Kanan," she whispered, the breeze carrying her voice into the sky. "All this suffering, for what? Because Kasis is jealous and cruel?"

"Mysteries, love, have confounded many for ages, but none so much as why my brother hates me." The sad truth of it was that Kasis could be doing all of this, causing so much pain throughout our world, simply because he hated me for having what he wanted.

A small kernel hidden deep inside, buried in the fucking pits of my soul and covered by all the horrible shit he's done, hoped it was something else. That all the time we'd spent together before our destinies took shape had meant something to him.

"If only we knew more," I said, smiling down at her. Those unmatched golden depths looked up at me and drove away the convoluted mix of sadness and rage that arose in me anytime I thought of my adoptive brother.

"What if we could?" She gave me a look that I could only describe as cautiously hopeful.

"What do you mean?" I asked out of curiosity.

She stepped away, leaning out over the railing to watch as the remains of our sleeping city began to wake, although I doubted many had slept peacefully. "The Orama said something to me when Zanaya and I visited. She said my memories were shrouded in loving darkness."

I tilted my head at her, not quite sure where she was going with this. The old witch never liked to make things easy, her wording most likely having an unspoken secret hidden within, but what did that have to do with Atallia? "Isn't that how you've always described it?"

She turned towards me. "Yes, but I didn't put it together until recently that the darkness I've sensed," she paused, a weak smile tugging at her lips, "it reminds me of you."

I froze, my spine snapping to attention as fear slithered through my veins. It ate away at my composure until any chance of remaining calm was stripped away, leaving me raw and vulnerable.

I hated it.

But I couldn't lose her again. I wouldn't survive it.

"You can't possibly think I would do that to you, not after all we've been through to get back to each other. I understand if you can't trust me fully, but—"

She put a finger to my lips to stop me, her smile one of amusement, though something far warmer shined through her eyes. "Of course I trust you," she replied sweetly, sweeping away all my fears with one small kiss. "What I'm trying to say is, if my older self was scared, or heartbroken, who would she turn to for help?"

"I see what you're saying, but I'm not sure what you're getting at," I responded, trying to pull the pieces together. Her hidden memories had been a riddle ever since her Awakening. It wasn't something any of us had anticipated when we planned for our eventual return.

"What if old me used our tether to access your power," she explained. "You're a powerful mentalist and you've said it yourself, we're forever entwined, so what if I used your power to shield myself from my past life?"

I pulled her to me when she stepped closer, allowing the slow beat of her new heart to calm the burning fires within me. "You think I can get your memories back?"

"Think about it," she pushed. "How protective your shadows are over me, how they respond to any threat."

She shrugged, that very same darkness she mentioned crawling along the railing to play with the loose curls draped over her shoulders. "If they, if *you,* thought I was in danger, you would do anything to protect me. Even from myself. Even without conscious knowledge of it."

The shadows had always been mine. The darkness was mine to command. I *was* the shadows and darkness, the energy that built me came from the emptiness from which a universe had been born. For it to act without my knowledge was as foreign to me as Atallia's memories were to her. But if they were to do it for anyone, it would be her. Protecting her, even subconsciously, would always be my priority.

"Love," I murmured with a shake of my head, wariness infiltrating my every fiber, "for me to do that without even knowing…"

Whatever had happened to make her reach out and ask the dark abyss that was my soul to protect her…it wasn't anything good.

A crease formed between her brows, but determination turned her eyes to molten metal. "Kasis would have likely spilled something to me during that time, maybe something that could be of use to us. It could be the only way for us to survive this."

I cupped her face, searching for answers within those heart-wrenching eyes. "What if this hurts you more than it helps?"

She swallowed harshly, her hands coming up to grab my wrists as she looked up at me with complete trust, something I thought I'd never see again. "I need to know, Kanan," she whispered, wetting her lips. "I need to be whole again."

I closed my eyes and leaned my forehead against hers. Why did she always know how to get her way? I could understand, however pissed it made me, why she needed this. She'd been missing pieces of herself her whole life, and now there was the possibility of getting them back.

She was already smiling by the time I'd let out another heavy breath. Shaking my head at her, I pressed our lips together. "I love you. Not some idea of you, or some past version. If this works, I need you to know that. Because I'll love you in this life and all the rest regardless."

Her wet eyes gleamed. Biting her lip, she nodded. "I love you."

"Just show me where it is," I whispered reluctantly, wrapping my arms around her as I dove down our bond, heading for the glimmering doorway of her mind.

I felt her reach out, guiding me to the farthest reaches of her mind. It didn't take long to find what we were looking for, the wall of darkness, seemingly impenetrable, rose from the recesses of her memories and hid them away.

Within seconds I realized she was right, that somehow, using our unbreakable bond that could survive the span of time that would separate us, she had weaved my magic around her past memories, secreting them away from herself. The darkness was protection, a shield to keep whatever she didn't want to ever remember from touching her new life.

I hesitated, hand outstretched towards the onyx wall. Ripping away the barrier between old and new, past and present, could open wounds she never knew existed, strengthen the nightmares I knew chased her in her dreams. It went against everything in me to put her at risk, but who was I to deny her?

So I reached out to the ancient magic, a physical remnant from a time long since passed, an embodiment of the lengths I would go for this woman. The things I would do to protect her. The darkness resisted, yanked itself from my grip and returned to its position. It was a sentry, a guardian of death and darkness, protecting her from the depths of her own mind.

But this power was still mine, so I dove deep into its core, straight to the base of the massive wall. It had grown stronger over the years, that much was obvious. The darkness had entrenched itself in the deepest parts of her psyche, like a tree it had tangled the memories of the past within its roots, refusing to allow them to burst free of the shadowy pits.

I placed an outstretched hand against it and was shocked when the darkness flinched away, as if aware of my intentions. My muscles tightened, suspicions rising as an overwhelming sense of alarm shot through me. The magic fought, tooth and nail, against me. Fighting like the world depended on it, and as I loosened the grip it had on her mind, clawing away at the chains around her memories, I knew this would change everything.

I hesitated as the first glimpse of what my shadows had protected hit me in full force. No power could hide the agony underneath, that absolute heartbreak, the shattering of her soul, but it was too late. The shield of darkness had been uprooted, the floodgates opening with the force of two thousand years of pent up energy.

The blast of emotion, of memory, of power, threw me out of her mind on the sweet, broken notes of a lullaby.

And when I came to, the sound of her broken screams echoed across the world.

ACKNOWLEDGMENTS

You know, I never thought I would get to write one of these, let alone two. Yet here I am, contemplating how in the world I'm suppose to get the right words out when my brain feels like mush. I'll give it my best shot though.

This book has taught me so much, both good and bad. Each lesson I learned was just as important as the next, but whether they were easy or not…that's up for discussion. Sleepless nights and mental breakdowns, tears of joy and screams of frustration. All of it was worth it for me to be able to put this story out into the world.

Atallia and Kanan, no matter how many worlds I visit or stories I tell, will always be an integral piece of my heart. Without that one dream, all those years ago, of a golden haired goddess lost in the midst of chaos, a star looking for her beloved darkness, there would be no stories to tell.

I had my moments, don't get me wrong, when I contemplated giving it all up. Growing pains, as I've begun to call them, that were agonizing, but necessary steps to becoming the author I someday hope to be. This was the first time that I didn't have years to dwell on something, no scenes simmering in the back of my mind for months on end, no certainty with where the words were taking me, and no idea how I would ever make it out of all 170,000+ words alive.

It was a struggle, that's for damn sure; but after all the 16oz lattes and chocolate croissants, the screams that have been lost to the void, an obscene number of sticky notes, and those 300 word days, where a single paragraph felt like it took years, I can honestly, and as humbly as possible, say that my writing has improved. It's matured in ways I wasn't expecting for years to come, grown into something I'm truly proud of. All those growing pains now seem worth it.

And I wouldn't have been able to do any of it without the love and support of so many people. Late night calls to my mom, crying over my deadline(it happens, what can you do), my dad reminding me that it's just as important to live in the moment and take care of yourself as it is to get those words down on the page, my amazing street team for being the world's best sounding board, my editor Ciara for being an actual goddess and putting up with my apparent hatred for question marks, and myself…for believing that we could do this even when everything seemed to be falling apart.

And of course, to all of you. Who have decided to go on this journey with me and give me and my characters a shot. To watch them grow and fall, love and lose, to defeat the evils the very tired, probably hallucinating, parts of my brain come up with, and to hopefully fall in love with them as much as I have. Thank you, from the bottom of my heart for taking that chance on us and deciding we were worth.

BOOKS BY ASHLYN B. RUDD

Beginnings and Endings

Of Secrets and Beginnings

Of Memories and Endings

Book Three Coming Soon

ABOUT THE AUTHOR

Ashlyn B. Rudd is living in the States and currently working on her degree in nursing. She spends her day in scrubs going through classes, and at night in between bouts of studying she lives in her head. If she could, she'd spend her entire day living in her fantasy worlds, kicking ass with a sword and casting magic.

When she's not with her friends and family she enjoys stormy days with her animals, a good book, a cozy blanket, and a fireplace. Outside of books, her interests lie in a whole host of things including gardening, horseback riding, cooking, and binging a good show.

If she could, she'd live on a farm in the middle of nowhere, so when she finally takes the dive deep into the woods, don't be surprised if she only comes out for trips to the bookstore and to stock up on snack provisions.

www.ingramcontent.com/pod-product-compliance
Lightning Source LLC
Chambersburg PA
CBHW060542310726
48982CB00009B/1350/J
* 9 7 9 8 9 9 0 6 2 8 1 1 3 *